# ASCENSION

# ASCENSION

## BOOK TWO OF THE BERSERKER CHRONICLES

# KEVIN D. MILLER

BIFROST BOOKS

*To Pepper: our fierce, beautiful bear. Though Odin has called you home. You will furever be in our hearts.*

The dark is generous, and it is patient,
    and it always wins - but in the heart of
    its strength lies its weakness: one lone
    candle is enough to hold it back...

— MATTHEW WOODRING STOVER, STAR WARS
EPISODE III - REVENGE OF THE SITH
NOVELIZATION

# CHAPTER 1

Smoke hung heavy in the air, burning Leif's eyes as he took in his surroundings. Turning in a slow circle, he searched for the source of the noxious fumes. *Where the hell is it coming from? Are we under attack?* Dropping to all fours, he blindly crawled for several minutes, searching for the source. Thankfully, a soft breeze blew in, clearing the smoke from around him. With his eyes stinging, Leif stood and coughed as if he smoked a pack a day. Blinking to clear the tears away, he stared in horror at the ghastly sight before him.

Stretching in all directions, hundreds, if not thousands, of funeral pyres burned around him. Their insidious flames reached high into the sky, belching oily black smoke so thick it blotted out the sun. Goosebumps erupted across his skin as he approached the nearest pyre. Flames scalded his face as he peered into the inferno. Leif somehow knew what he would find, but he needed to look anyway. Chained to their fiery grave, the blackened husk of the poor soul stared unblinking at the heavens. Its mouth was agape in a silent scream. Leif's stomach roiled as he gagged, and his legs went weak at the knees.

"I hope you didn't think hiding here in this backwater realm would keep you or your people safe?" said a gravelly voice from behind him.

Leif turned, his hands flashing to his belt. "Shit!" He cursed when his hands found empty air where his axes should be. Suddenly, he felt the burning edge of Fenrir's blade sliding deep into his stomach. His hands wrapped around the blade. He gasped from the icy pain that radiated from the sword as it cut deeper into his abdomen. The warm, coppery taste of blood filled his mouth, causing him to cough uncontrollably. Grunting through the pain, the razor-sharp edges of Fenrir's straight sword bit deep into Leif's palms. He desperately tried to pull the sword from his gut but was too weak.

Leif's head grew heavy as his vision stretched, then blurred. All the while, his lifeblood poured from his wound. Gritting his teeth, he tried once more to pull himself free of Fenrir's cursed blade. Blood splattered the asphalt as Leif tightened his grip, feeling the blade grind uncomfortably against the bones of his hand, but he was past caring. Taking a firm grip of the sword, he locked eyes with his hated enemy and pushed. It was no use. The wolf god was too strong.

Leif's heart skipped a beat as panic set in. Reaching for the Berserker, he unleashed the demon within him, hoping the fiery power would be enough to save him, but to his surprise, the rage refused to come. *My powers are gone!* As his blood continued to seep from his wound, his hands grew as heavy as anvils. As the last vestiges of his strength drained away, he released the sword, dropping his arms uselessly to his side. The fiery world around him flickered as he struggled to remain conscious. Before the darkness of death took him, Leif's final thought lingered on the disbelief of being killed in such a cowardly manner.

With a vicious yank, Fenrir pulled his sword free of Leif's stomach. Thankfully, he was too far gone to feel anything except an uncomfortable tugging sensation deep in his gut. "Before your soul is consigned to Helheim," Fenrir gloated, "I want you to know that this is just the beginning of our plans for Midgard. Before we are finished here, I will personally see to the extermination of your entire pitiful race. Then once the realm is free of your filth, we shall gift it to the Outsiders."

"No!" Leif screamed as he shot out of bed, bringing his axes up in a defensive position. Fully berserked and breathing heavy, he searched the darkness for Fenrir. Ten seconds passed, then twenty, with no sign of the wolf god. To be safe, he jumped from his bed to peer out his apartment window. *Looks like an ordinary Los Angeles night. No smoke or signs of a fire. There are sirens in the distance, but that's no surprise.* Taking a deep breath, Leif fell back onto his bed with a groan.

With a sigh and grunt of effort, he regained control of the Berserker, relegating its fury to the back of his mind. He reached for his phone but felt nothing except the hard surface of his nightstand. Leif sighed. Setting his axes aside, he rolled out of bed. After a few blind moments of searching in the dark, his hand bumped his phone. The searing light of his home screen flashed on, momentarily blinding him. Once his vision finally cleared, he groaned; it was only four in the morning. Leif knew he wouldn't be able to fall back to sleep, not after a nightmare like that. *Might as well head over to the shop and get the day started.*

Driving to his bookstore, Leif's mind reflected on the past few months. It felt so good to be back. A bed, showers, and anything he wanted to eat was a simple phone call away. However, the euphoria of surviving his fight with Hel hadn't lasted long. *Once Hel and Fenrir learn of his survival, they are sure to hunt for him again.*

He had no idea what the power requirements were to force a bridge open, but if Hel did it once, she can certainly do it again. *How long does it take for a god to recover from a gut wound?* Leif mused. Probably faster than him, and he healed ridiculously fast.

Leif's nightmares began almost immediately after his return. Most of the time, he didn't know why he was waking up in a pool of his own sweat with his sheets twisted in knots, but tonight's dream was different. It was reminiscent of those the Norns used to gift him. *There has to be a reason for these dreams,* he thought as he stared at the red traffic light. If Leif hadn't been at the Well of Urn when Hel attacked the Norns, he would have sworn it was their doing. They were the physical manifestation of fate. They could have set their plans in motion to continue after they were gone.

Before tonight, the dreams had focused on the dead, both those he had killed in battle or lost along the way. Arias and Bargog were regulars, berating him for failing to save them. Those were the hardest to endure. The pain in their glassy, dead eyes haunted not only Leif's dreams, but well into the waking hours of his day. Besides his slain friends, the faces of his dead enemies popped in once in a while to haunt him. He had begun to worry this burden would be with him for the rest of his life. Not even rational explanations for his actions were enough to banish their ghostly faces. *I guess this is what PTSD feels like, huh?*

Before Leif knew it, he was sitting in his car outside the Bragi Books. *Under normal circumstances, I would seek out a therapist, but that's not really in the cards for me. A regular Midgardian wouldn't understand.* So, he did the only thing he could do. He trained harder and smarter. With the Berserker under control, he was determined to protect Midgard. *Gods willing and if I am strong enough, no one else will die on my watch.* With his emotions back under control, Leif grabbed his gym bag and marched into the store.

# CHAPTER 2

Once the nightmares started, Leif knew the only antidote was to push himself past his comfort-zone during his training sessions. His training couldn't focus solely on the physical side of combat, so he split his session in two, mental conditioning and martial arts. Going to any normal gym was out of the question after destroying the last one he went to. He chose to train in the converted storeroom in the back of Bragi books. All the equipment Arias had installed was still there, anyway. The already cramped space housed a human shaped practice dummy, numerous dumbbells, kettlebells, and even a squat rack. Leif had transformed the storeroom into his own little fortress of solitude. Here he was free to push his body past its Midgardian limits without the fear of accidentally hurting any innocent bystanders.

At first, he had used these sessions to reevaluate his past fights by shadowboxing his enemies. Unfortunately, this resulted in several outbursts, causing the unbidden Berserker to raise its angry head. After patching up several holes and twice replacing his practice dummy, Leif was forced to reevaluate his control over his power. In the short time he had been back on Midgard, Leif realized he had let his mental hold on the Berserker slip, allowing the rage to subvert his control when he least expected it. Thor's warning when they had last spoke rang true. "The life of a Berserker, even when not at war, is perilous. The Berserker is always there, lurking in the back of your mind, waiting to be released." Because of this danger, Berserkers must maintain complete control over their thoughts and emotions.

Not only did Leif's relapse in control frustrate him, but it caused him to fall into episodes of depression. It emphasized how alone he was. Before, that damn Ljosalfar was always there to step in when he lost control. Leif had grown annoyed with getting knocked out by Arias. But funny enough, he missed it now. Arias had been his mentor and a friend. Under his tutelage, he had learned not only to reign in his power, but to bend the burning rage to his will. But he was all alone now. Even amongst his fellow Midgardians, Leif stood apart. Being the last known Berserker is a lonely road to be on. Alone, Leif knew he could only push himself so far. He needed to figure out how he was going to grow strong enough to challenge a god, and fast. Hel had made her first move; it was only a matter of time before Ragnarok spilled into Midgard.

Settling into a lotus position, Leif breathed deep before exhaling all the thoughts and fears that plagued him. With his mind clear, he slowly brought forth the Berserker. He reveled in the power of the Berserker as it emerged from the depths of his mind. His skin flushed red from the rising furnace of rage. Then, just as the fire grew too hot to handle, his veins would turn to ice as he was suffused with the Berserker's energy. It was an intoxicating feeling, especially on Midgard where he would be hailed as a superhero if he showed off his power.

While berserked, Leif's power urged him to move, to hunt, and to kill. Even now, in his meditative state, he could feel his power shouting at him, warning him he had been idle for too long. It urged him to strike before his enemies did. Leif was struck with a strong compulsion to take up the bridge stone and hunt Hel and Fenrir down. It was a seductive prospect, but his rational side was stronger. He knew he wasn't ready. He survived by the skin of his teeth last time.

The Norns had hinted there was more to the Berserker. They said with proper training, he could push past his current level, becoming something that could even challenge the gods. A Berserker literally held a sliver of Thor's power within their veins. If Leif was to defeat Hel and her ilk, he would need to harness the mysterious power for his own. The only problem was he didn't know how.

After meditating, Leif stood, stretching out his stiff muscles and took up his twin axes. With practiced ease, he moved through the katas Arias had taught him. Each kata served a specific purpose: offensive, defense, or a mixture of both. For the first few rounds, he would move with excruciating slowness, warming up his muscles. With his enhanced healing, Leif wasn't sure if he could pull a muscle, but it was better to be safe than sorry. Once the beads of sweat appeared on his forehead, he would increase the pace, seamlessly moving like a well-trained dancer. When finished, he gasped for breath. With each completed kata, he would momentarily beam with pride. Leif had endured hours of scrutiny and name calling by Arias when he first learned the forms. He only wished Arias could see him now, moving through each kata perfectly. *Of course, Arias would have found some small misstep to berate me with,* Leif thought with a smile.

Leif let out an explosive breath as he finished his final set of squats, re-racking the barbel with a loud crash. Toweling off, he sat down next to his weight set, looking around at the odd assortment of old books, weapons, and weights that filled his storeroom. He still found it hard to believe Bragi Books was his now. He remembered finding the letter postmarked the day they had left for Alfheim. He had torn open the letter, recognizing Arias's flowing script.

Leif,

My friend, soon we will depart on our quest to find the Norns. With any adventure, especially one where the gods are involved, there is an inherent danger. The possibility that one of us will fall in the attempt is high. Alas, I remain hopeful. If we are victorious in our travels, I have come to a decision, though it saddens me. The time for me to return to Alfheim has finally arrived. I have lived on Midgard for decades. Though I have enjoyed my time, I find myself missing the lush forest of my home realm.

With a heavy heart, I will not be returning to Midgard with you upon completing our journey. Do not despair, my friend. Though I may be a realm away, I would be happy to explore the mysteries of the nine realms once again with you, just as I once did with Alexander. Since I won't be returning to Midgard, I will be transferring all my assets to you, declaring you a long lost relative. Though I hope to personally continue your education, I would recommend you raid my collection of books, maps, and journals I have accumulated during my many travels. You never know what useful information you may find. I'll be seeing you.

Arias

When Leif had first discovered the keys and letter, his vision had blurred with thick tears. It was as if the band-aid over his heart had torn open. His knees had turned to putty as he sank to his apartment's mailroom floor. Survivor's guilt had all but incapacitated him. He stayed that way for some time, wallowing in grief over his lost friend. Once he was all cried out, he had stood up, sniffled once, then drove over to inspect his new store.

*With Hel and Fenrir still out there, I better get started combing through those books. Hopefully, somewhere within them is an answer to my problems, be it an ally or some powerful artifact,* Leif remembered thinking as hope rose within him.

Upon his return to Midgard, everything had worked out well for Leif. Over the past two months, he had gotten into a routine. Since he wasn't sleeping very much, nightmares and all, he spent most of his morning training. Then the rest of the day, he read through Arias's old books and managed the front counter at Bragi Books. Not surprisingly, the indie store didn't have much of a customer base, which was fine with him. With little foot traffic, Leif was free to spend hours on end combing through the treasure trove of Arias's hidden collection.

In the beginning, Leif scoured the tomes, taking in as much information as his brain could handle about the various beings, creatures, and realms he saw during his hunt for the Norns. He spent hours reading through old books until his eyes hurt. He aimlessly bounced between topics, just as one may do on Wikipedia, jumping down the rabbit hole. That was until he came across a curious journal entry from a Dokkalfar smuggler. Leif couldn't be sure, but he believed he pieced out the smuggler's name, Pjofur.

Pjofur's journey quickly became Leif's favorite thing to read. The dark elf was meticulous in his note taking regarding his exploits. This Dokkalfar's journal, unlike many of the others, was written in a form of pidgin English. It wasn't a perfect translation of modern day English, but it was close enough. The smuggler took extra care to note the names, dates, and locations of many of his black-market dealings. How Arias got a hold of the book was another point of interest, but sadly it was one he would never learn.

While reading one of Pjofur's entries, Leif learned about the smuggler's need to have a crate of precious stones covertly transported from Myrkheim to Vanaheimr. To do this, the smuggler contacted a group of beings Leif likened to an underground criminal organization. The thought of a supernatural black market spanning the nine realms was fascinating, but that wasn't the information that had his heart racing. During the meeting with the underground group, Pjofur mentions a Midgardian man with glowing eyes and a short temper. Leif's skin tingled at the familiar description.

"Another Berserker!" he shouted to the empty bookstore. *How has this bloodline stayed hidden for so long? I wonder if this guy's descendants are still out there hiding in the shadows.* Suddenly, Leif had a mission. Any Berserker that could survive this long amongst the realms must be powerful. They may know the secret to the Berserker's hidden strengths the Norns had mentioned.

Leif spent his days scouring Arias's trove of books for any mention of the Berserker or his underground organization. Unfortunately, after months of reading, he had found nothing. Leif sighed as he blinked his bleary eyes at the sea of books before him, waiting to be read.

"Yay! Another day of hunting. Gods, I know I'm going to need glasses after staring at all these books for days on end," Leif grumbled as he lifted the still steaming cup of tea to his lips.

Before meeting Arias, he had been a coffee person, but since his return, he had opted for brewing a cup of tea each day in Arias's honor. Today, Leif selected an aromatic rose black tea. Inhaling the flowery aroma, he was temporarily transported to the rose garden at the Huntington Gardens. Once the moment passed, he grabbed the first book from the stack and cracked open the hefty volume.

At a glance, the book appeared to focus on Aesir governance. After some time perusing the pages, Leif snapped the book shut, causing a dust cloud to explode into his face. He sneezed. "Point to you, old book," he wheezed, looking down at his attacker. "You got your revenge; I won't treat you or your kin so rudely in the future." *Did I just talk to a book? How long has it been since I had a conversation with an actual person?* Leif thought. He had been so focused on his training that he stopped going out or talking to his friends.

He had tried a few times after his return from Asgard. Choosing to grab a drink with his friends James and Will, but he just couldn't engage. He couldn't talk about his adventure or what happened to him; they'd have thought he'd lost his marbles. Leif didn't care about current Midgardian politics or who tweeted about what, not with Hel still out there. He knew the moment she recovered, she, or her attack dog of a brother, would show up. It was hard to enjoy a mai tai with the knowledge that two gods could show up at any moment. After that night, much like the Aesir, Leif withdrew from his social life, choosing instead to focus on getting stronger.

# CHAPTER 3

After reading for hours about the politics of the realms and their exclusion of Midgard, Leif decided he had enough for the day. The front door to the bookstore dinged as he stepped outside. Locking the door behind him, he turned with a smile. Happy to be free of the dusty confines of the store, he closed his eyes and reached high overhead, stretching his cramped muscles. Taking a deep breath, he felt the light breeze waft across his face. *Ah, I already feel better. Maybe I just needed a little vitamin D,* Leif thought.

BAAMMM! He suddenly flew backwards with an "ooof," escaping his lips as he crashed through the front door to Bragi books, only to come to a bone jarring stop against one of the book stacks. Several of the heavy bound books rained down on and around his crumpled form. Blinking to clear the stars from his vision, Leif struggled to process what had just happened. *Did I accidentally step into the street and get hit by a car?* He coughed, producing a red flecked mist. "Wha–, what happened?" he slurred as blood spilled over his lips.

Crunch, crunch, crunch.

The sound of footfalls on glass drew Leif's attention. Blinking the blood from his eyes, he saw two blurry figures step through his ruined door.

"You didn't think I would forget about you, did you now, little Berserker?" said a familiar gruff voice that sent chills down his spine.

"How did you find me?" Leif asked, head still reeling from being slammed through his storefront. Thankfully, he could feel the odd, prickly sensation of his enhanced healing kick into overdrive as several broken bones began to mend along with, he surmised from the splitting pain in his forehead, a cracked skull.

"This pitiful creature is the one that gave you and your sister so much trouble, Fenrir?" asked a voice in a condescending baritone. "Tut, tut. I am disappointed in you. Now kill this sad excuse for a realm's guardian. I wish to begin subjugating his people as soon as possible." Leif didn't know the newcomer, but he already hated him.

The arrogant asshole was tall, at least six foot five inches, but Leif was crumbled in a heap on the ground, so everyone looked tall to him at that moment. The newcomer's skin was the color of smooth caramel, and he had the build of an Olympic sprinter. His silky black hair was pulled back into a tight ponytail that fell to his shoulders. His eyes, like the other gods, contained no pupil or iris, but instead, the sockets housed two glowing orbs. However, unlike the Aesir, whose eyes were like an electrical storm, this god's eyes glowed orange like a jack-o'-lantern on Halloween. Leif noticed the god had a tattoo inked over his right eye. The tattoo looked vaguely familiar to him, but he couldn't place where he had seen it. It rimmed the god's eye like eyeliner, coming to a point at the far-right side, then went straight a few inches along the side of his face, just below his temple. A thick line forked out one side and another line went straight down from the left corner ending an inch below the eye, while the other ran down at an angle from the left corner of his right eye ending in a tight curl directly below the first line. The man wore black trousers with no shirt. A strange sickle-like sword hung from a gold-lined leather belt around his waist.

Painfully turning his head, Leif eyed Fenrir as the damned wolf god approached. Fenrir was a sharp contrast to the bare-chested figure who stood beside him. The wild god was clad in dark leather pants, a black shirt, topped off with a heavy fur cloak draped over his wide shoulders. His tear drop face and lightening blue eyes stared daggers at Leif. Raw, animalistic power radiated from the imposing god. With a sound more akin to a growl, Fenrir boasted, "Ragnarok is nigh. Hel has gifted us with making the opening play. We will burn your world to cinders as we sacrifice your precious Midgardians to the mighty Ra," Fenrir said as he gestured toward his companion. Fenrir's other hand firmly clasped the handle of his short sword, which hung from his belt.

At that moment, the wolf god released his grip on his sword. Leif lashed out and with an arsenal of blunt objects at his disposal, he released his hold on the Berserker. With supernatural speed, he grabbed two thick hardcover books and flung them with all his might. Knowing the projectiles wouldn't be anything more than an annoyance to the gods, he rolled onto his stomach and bear-crawled toward the back storeroom where his axes were. As he crawled, he heard the double impact of his missiles slamming home, causing him to smile mischievously.

Feeling he was mere seconds from death, Leif lowered his shoulder and plowed through the wooden door that led to the backroom, causing a shower of kindling. The red haze of the Berserker swirled in his vision as he blurred across the room. With no space to maneuver, Leif slammed into the table where he left his axes, pulverizing the white plastic table upon impact.

Grasping his twin axes, he pivoted and readied himself for combat. Thanks to the Berserker's power coursing through his veins, any trace of fear, doubt, or thoughts of fleeing evaporated into the fire burning in his chest. Leif was sure the two gods could feel his rage from the other room. Seconds ticked by, but no attack came. Unable to contain his eagerness any longer, Leif bellowed, "FIGHT ME!" Clanging his axes together in a challenge.

An answering snarl, like the revving of a Harley Davidson, reverberated through the building. A moment later, Fenrir boldly stepped through the shattered doorway with his naked blade in hand. Seeing his opportunity, Leif rushed forward, his axes swinging high and low. With Fenrir caught in the doorway, he hoped his opponent would be unable to dodge, but the wolf god was a millennia-old combat veteran. In the blink of an eye, Fenrir blocked the ax aimed for his chest and with his free hand, he caught Leif's left wrist. Using Leif's momentum, Fenrir pivoted, slamming him through the wall and back into his showroom.

Plaster and wood exploded in all directions as Leif was once again sent sailing through the air. Ra, who had yet to move, took one step to the side as Leif's body temporarily occupied the space he had been standing in, only to crash back into his partially destroyed front door. Pain exploded across his body as hundreds of tiny glass shards bit into his exposed skin. Leif inhaled to scream his pain away, but his breath hitched as he felt a sharp pain burn across his ribs. Thankfully, just as quickly as it started, it subsided with the icy burn of the Berserker. It drowned out the pain, allowing him to take a shuddering breath. Leif stood, giving himself a quick once over. He watched as dozens of small cuts closed before his eyes. Unfortunately, just as many deeper wounds continued to seep blood. A small part of his subconscious mind worried he was taking too much damage. He worried that his healing wouldn't be able to keep up with any more injuries, but a snarl of anger drowned out the caution.

Knowing he needed to change the game, Leif stepped backward through his ruined door onto the sidewalk. *No more walls or doors to throw me through now, asshole,* the berserked Leif growled into his mind. Wind whipped at Leif's ragged and torn clothing as he backed up onto the street; his eyes never left his ruined storefront. Only minutes ago, a sunny late afternoon sky had shone down on

Los Angeles, but now thunder rumbled across the darkened sky, and forks of lightning flickered deep within the bank of clouds. Any thoughts of the strange weather quickly evaporated as Fenrir and Ra stepped through the crumbling storefront. Fenrir's eyes were alight at the prospect of coming violence. Ra waited with his hands in his pockets, a look of utter boredom plastered on his chiseled face.

As the gods stepped out onto the street to meet Leif, Ra turned to Fenrir. "Kill the Midgardian now, or I will. We have pressing matters to attend to. I promised Hel that I would permit you to be the one to kill the Midgardian, but I am growing tired of this game," Ra said with a clear note of annoyance in his voice.

"Silence!" Fenrir snarled. "You may lead the Outsiders, but don't forget who you are speaking to!"

Ra raised an eyebrow at Fenrir's challenge; then he looked back at Leif. The bored expression never leaving his face.

This enraged Leif more. *Who the hell do they think I am? I am a Berserker. I am not some weakling who can be so easily written off.* Before Leif could voice his challenge, the hairs on his arms stood on end as the storm that had gone unnoticed reached a crescendo. Lightning burst from the clouds, and thick beams of electricity rained down around them.

# CHAPTER 4

The electrical storm crashed around Leif in a terrifying staccato, burning his retinas in the process. A wave of static energy washed over him, tingling his skin as the earth shook from the cascade of lightning bolts that slammed into the ground terrifyingly close. Then, as quickly as the storm appeared, it was gone. Bright yellow sunlight spilled over Leif as his nose was filled with the thick smell of ozone. He blinked to clear the flashing spots from his vision; he nearly jumped out of his skin at the sight of Thor standing not two feet away from him. The mountain of a god was dressed for war. His body was encased shoulders to boots in gleaming silver-plated armor. His trusty war hammer, Mjolnir, was held firm in his right hand. Glancing at Leif, the thunder god gave him a quick smile before returning his focus to Fenrir and Ra. Following his gaze, Leif was shocked to see, unlike him, the two dark gods had not come out of the storm unscathed.

A look of pure hatred wafted from Ra; the ancient god seethed in anger so palpable Leif thought he could taste it. The god's simmering orange eyes flared like the fires of Duat, causing the berserked Leif to take an involuntary step backward. Ra's shirtless torso was covered in forked electrical burns, and his leather pants had been ripped to shreds from repeated lightning strikes.

Likewise, Fenrir appeared to have fared no better. His fur cloak was gone, probably disintegrated in the attack while his shirt and pants were in tatters. He too had a look of outrage on his face, but hiding behind that façade, Leif saw true fear. With Ra at his side, Leif knew the damned wolf couldn't back down, not when he talked such a big game moments ago.

Bolstered by Thor's presence, Leif let out a war cry, swinging his axes in a complex pattern, warming up for the fight. He prepared himself to charge the battered gods, but a gauntleted hand clamped down on Leif's shoulder, giving him pause.

"No, my friend," Thor said in his thundering baritone. "You are in no condition to fight. I know your blood boils, but you must know you are outclassed. Let me deal with them," Thor said, taking a meaningful step forward. As if to accentuate his point, lightning burst from the Aesir's armor, momentarily encasing the god before flickering out.

Leif desperately wished to join the fight, but a tiny part of him knew he wasn't strong enough. If he were to fight, he would just get in Thor's way, or, gods forbid, get himself killed. Gritting his teeth, Leif remembered his vow to not let his weakness be the cause of his comrades' deaths. So, he held himself back. The sheer rationality of his control surprised him. When he had first awakened to his powers, the only thought he could muster while berserked was who to fight next. Now, he was capable of at least a modicum of rational thought while maintaining his berserked state. If he survived Ragnarok, he will be a much more deadly warrior.

Leif stepped back to give Thor some space, while Ra and Fenrir looked at each other for a silent second. Ra unsheathed his strange sickle-shaped sword, and it glowed with the same amber orange of a sunrise perfectly matching his smoldering eyes. Fenrir bared his teeth in a snarl as he soundlessly unsheathed his blade.

The atmosphere grew still, as if the very weather was holding its breath. Then the trio moved. It was then that Leif fully understood why Thor had restrained him. As the gods moved back and forth on the street, minor sonic booms rang out as all three warriors cut loose. Even berserked, Leif could barely follow their movements, let alone comprehend what they were doing. The air and ground around them shook with their fearsome power.

Leif briefly feared for his friend. Thor was one of the most powerful gods of the Aesir pantheon, second only to Odin the Alfather, but he was up against, Fenrir The Godkiller and Ra, who was a complete mystery to him outside of being the chief god amongst the Egyptian pantheons. From what Leif could see, Thor had equipped himself well. He held the two dark gods at bay. He figured Fenrir must have been a bit rusty after being imprisoned for a millennium or more.

As the fight continued, Fenrir made the first misstep. The mistake resulted in the wolf taking a hammer blow to the face, knocking him to the ground, stunned. While Fenrir recovered, Thor brought his full attention to Ra. Attacks flashed between the two as they danced around each other. All the while, Leif was transfixed on Ra's strange sword; it flashed back and forth, clashing with legendary Mjolnir.

Shaking himself, Fenrir recovered, smoothly jumping to his feet to charge headlong at Thor's unguarded back. Leif tried to shout a warning, but by the time the thought registered, and his neurons fired to sound the warning, Fenrir had already closed the distance. His sword point led the charge.

Just before the point of Fenrir's sword pierced the thunder god's back, a flash of blue-white electricity covered the length of Thor's body. Thor wore a suit of armor made of lightning. The moment Fenrir's blade came into contact with the protective current, a booming crash sounded as lightning arced up Fenrir's blade, slamming into the surprised god. Fenrir screamed as a bolt of lightning the size of Leif's thigh struck the unsuspecting god in the chest, throwing him backward.

The smell of burnt flesh filled the street. Leif rapidly blinked to clear his vision. The wall Fenrir smashed into collapsed, half burying the wolf god in a shower of broken concrete. A large electrical burn spanned the entirety of Fenrir's upper body. Neither Thor nor Ra paid Fenrir a second glance as they continued their duel.

To Leif, the combatants moved so fluidly it was as if they stood still. Both Thor's hammer and Ra's sickle flashed in an ever-evolving dance. Leif knew that if he were to come within range of the dueling gods, he would be cut to shreds. The pair moved as one, as if they had practiced together every hour, every day, for the past year. There was no wasted movement between the two. Thor aimed for vital and vulnerable spots on Ra's body, but the god's curved blade was always there, meeting Mjolnir. Wherever those mighty weapons met, sparks bloomed to life.

Thor pushed the sun god toward a small pothole in the street that had been caused by the electrical storm. Ra, unaware of the uneven ground, took a single step backwards into the small divot, causing his balance to shift unexpectedly. If he had been fighting anyone else, the misstep wouldn't have been a problem, but he wasn't.

Off balance, Ra thrust his sword forward, but he missed its mark. The blade sailed past Thor's right ear, scoring a thin line of blood along his cheek. The thunder god rushed forward, kicking Ra in the off-balanced leg, causing it to buckle. He followed up with a swing of the mighty Mjolnir, striking Ra in the chest with a shower of forked lightning. Ra flew backward, crashing into a brick wall a few feet from Fenrir.

"If you two end this foolish rebellion and swear fealty to the Aesir here and now, I will spare your lives," Thor's deep voice boomed.

Coughing, Ra spit a glob of blood on the street, locking gazes with Thor. "I will die before I submit to the Aesir. Look at him," Ra said, gesturing towards the stunned Leif. "We should rule these weaklings. Their lives are a speck of dust in the universe. We may have failed today, but it was only due to your coming to protect your pet project." Ra sneered. "It only means the other realms we attacked are less defended. This was merely the opening act," Ra said with mock laughter. "Why would we ever submit when the Aesir are on the cusp of defeat?" Ra reached for the unconscious Fenrir, as his free hand pulled a small black ball the size of a marble from a tattered-looking pouch on his belt. Pulling Fenrir close, Ra smashed the strange object into his chest. The resulting flare of magic was so strong it felt like a hot knife had jabbed into Leif's brain. "I look forward to our rematch," Ra said as both gods were engulfed in a black inky substance reminiscent of the bridge the Jontar had used when Leif was ambushed in the snowy Icelandic forest. Then they were gone, leaving a gaping hole in the masonry of the boutique they had destroyed.

# CHAPTER 5

Neither Berserker nor Thor let their guard down. Leif scanned the smoldering ruins of the street, looking for any sign that the retreat may have been a ruse. After all, Fenrir is the son of Loki, the trickster. As seconds turned to minutes and there was no sign of their enemies, the two warriors visibly relaxed.

Suddenly, another thought stabbed its way into Leif's mind. "Shit! The cops!" He shouted like a teenager caught with a forty of beer. "There's no way that fight didn't go unnoticed." He had become accustomed to these surprise attacks, but that was on other realms where it was no big deal. On the mundane realm of Midgard, where there is a codified legal system, a no-holds-bar brawl in the middle of the street would be frowned upon. Leif knew no one would believe him if he said all the damage to the street and surrounding buildings was caused by a fight between gods. As if summoned by his thoughts, the telltale woompp, wooomp, of police sirens could be heard in the distance and were getting closer, fast.

"Thor! We need to go, now!" Leif yelled as he ran to the Aesir, who looked confused by the sudden change in him. What frightened Leif more was how tired the thunder god looked. He hadn't come out of the fight unscathed. Blood dripped from the cut across his cheek and between the seams in his armor. "Why? So soon? What has you so afraid? That noise? Isn't that merely your law keepers? We have nothing to fear from them," Thor said. He did not understand the seriousness of the situation.

"No! We can't involve them. They won't understand. We need to go now. Can you do the lightning trick to take us to Asgard?" Leif asked as he grabbed the confused god and pulled him back through the ruined door frame of his bookstore.

"No, not both of us. I used up too much of my strength in the fight," Thor said, sounding a little more like himself. "Asgard is too far away, but I could probably manage to get us to Alfheim. Though I must warn you. It isn't like traveling through the Bifrost. It won't be a pleasant trip for you, but for the power we share, you wouldn't be able to survive the journey at all," Thor cautioned.

"Shit!" Leif's mind kicked into overdrive. "Do you think they will come back?" He asked as he rummaged through the rubble of the destroyed store.

"Not immediately," Thor said. "They will return to report to Hel, recover their strength, and join the fight for the other realms. You were the only being strong enough to pose a threat to them on this realm. They will most likely hold off until they dominate the other realms before returning, especially now that their first attempt failed so spectacularly."

"If it's me they really want, maybe I should cross to another realm. Maybe they will leave Midgard alone for a time." Leif speculated as he pulled his go bag free from the rubble. "What did Ra mean by opening act?"

"That the final battle of this age has begun. Hel has begun her assault on the nine realms."

"What?" Leif nearly shouted.

"Yes, it is entirely possible there is an Outsider army crossing into several of Aesir protected spaces as we speak. Hel chose to only send Ra and Fenrir to Midgard because Fenrir wanted his revenge, and your people are viewed in such low regard. The Outsiders didn't believe any more would be needed," Thor commented.

"Holy shit! We need to get a move on then. I assume you are going to fight them?" Leif asked.

"Of course. Once I take you to Alfheim, I will report back to Odin and see to the disposition of our forces." Thor said.

"Thor," Leif said as he ran over to him. "Screw Alfheim. Take me with you. I want to fight. I went toe-to-toe with Hel before, and I can do it again."

A twinkle appeared in Thor's eyes as he placed a powerful hand on Leif's shoulder. "You certainly have grown strong, Berserker, but you got very, very lucky when you last fought Hel. If she had not exhausted herself from a fight with the Norns and opening two bridges, you wouldn't have stood a chance. Hel is no fighter, but she is still of Aesir blood. I will be fighting beings that are just as strong or stronger than her. You just aren't ready for a fight like that."

Leif felt the hackles on the back of his neck rise as the Berserker responded to the challenge. "But–"

"Go to Alfheim." Thor interrupted. "I know the Ljosalfar. It won't be easy for Hel to strike at you there."

Before Leif could respond, Thor lifted Mjolnir in his other hand. A flash of magic enveloped them in a bright white light, blinding Leif. His entire body was suddenly wracked with pain. It was suffering like he had never experienced before. He felt paralyzed as fire pulsed in lazy waves, bouncing from the crown of his head to the tips of his toes for what felt like an eternity.

A few years ago, before gods, Berserkers, and the realms, Leif had agreed to a dare when drinking with friends at his apartment. He allowed himself to get zapped by a taser that his friend, Linh, carried for self-defense. The pain he now felt reminded him of that drunken night, dialed up to an eleven.

After a few seconds or years, it was all the same to him. The blinding light and pain mercifully stopped. His feet abruptly hit solid ground, and he collapsed into a twitching heap. Every fiber of his being screamed in agony. His muscles painfully spasmed as if he had run to the top of the Empire State Building wearing a weighted vest.

Once he was free of Thor's lightning, the pain slowly receded. Leif slowly wiggled his toes and fingers, then his arms and legs, and finally moved his head from side to side. Reassured that he wasn't dead or paralyzed, Leif finally opened his eyes to a very confusing sight.

Thor had transported them into the middle of a large wood paneled chamber. Gloomy gray light spilled through long rectangular windows that were evenly spaced around the circular space. Between the windows, Ljsoalfar warriors in colorful plate armor stood still as statues. Looks of shocked outrage were etched on each of their tear-drop faces. Each armored warrior carried a long, steel-tipped spear that was pointed at Leif and Thor.

Pulling his eyes away from their weapons, Leif cast his gaze towards the regal looking Ljosalfar men and women of the room. Many sat in expertly carved wooden chairs positioned around the room. Each Ljosalfar wore brightly colored silken garments of various cuts and styles. They all wore expressions of shock, and many stared open-mouthed at Thor in his battered armor.

Turning his head, Leif spotted a raised platform on one side of the room. Several black clad knights stood in a diamond formation around a woman garbed in a flowing dark purple dress. Her regal features were exaggerated due to the spectacle playing out before her. Her brightly glowing eyes had gone wide as they bounced between Leif and Thor as her mouth fell open. Then She blinked as recognition flashed across her Elvin face. Her yellow eyes zeroed in on Thor and her beautiful face flushed with relief, and her shoulders sagged ever so slightly before she straightened to her full height again. The woman was breathtaking. Her silvery hair shimmered in the low light that spilled into the chamber. Her sleeveless gown hugged her shoulders, showing off toned shoulders and arms. It was hard to tell in the light of the room, but he could have sworn she glowed with a soft inner light.

Leif pressed his palms into the polished floor, moving to get up, but he was stopped by a shout from the guard directly in front of him. The floor beneath his hands rumbled as the spear wielding guard charged. Leif was forced to duck to the side, avoiding the spear that was angling towards his face. To his relief, a loud command in Ljosa stopped the guard in his tracks.

"Rise, companion of Thor. You need not fear us. We were merely startled by your sudden appearance." The Ljosalfar in purple spoke in a soft voice. "We are honored by your presence. And to you, mighty Thor, the Ljosalfar are grateful that one as powerful as yourself has chosen to appear before us in our time of need."

At the mention of his name, gasps and whispered conversations erupted around the room. As Leif finally got to his feet, he stretched a little as he took stock of his battered body. Many of the seated Ljosalfar wore looks of awe, while others displayed disbelief at the silver haired Ljosalfar's revelation. More surprising, Leif watched as all the spear wielding guards set their weapons down and kneeled, bowing their heads in reverence.

Thor wore an expression of pleased amusement on his face. He smiled at the Ljosalfar, who had addressed him. "Rise, my friends," Thor said to the kneeling guards. He then turned to the woman. "Well met, your highness. It gladdens my heart to know the Aesir have not been forgotten in our long absence from this realm. Though it saddens me to bring dark tidings then depart, but the safety of the nine realms demands it. For Ragnarok has begun; the realms are in danger," Thor said as he swept his gaze around the room, meeting the eyes of all in attendance.

"We know," the queen replied.

"You know?" Thor asked, shifting his weight.

"See for yourself," the queen said, pointing a delicate hand to the window.

Following her directions, the pair moved to the nearest window. The chamber they were in must have been in the skyscraper sized tree that Arias had called the Monarch because they towered hundreds of feet over Karcoa. The lush green canopies of the city spread in all directions, except for one area at the outer boundary of the tree city.

Thick plumes of smoke belched high into the air, blotting out the sky over one section of the city. Below the caustic fumes, large flames writhed, slowly engulfing the massive elktre trees the Ljosalfar use as homes, shops, and restaurants. For now, the forest fire appeared to be contained to that single quarter, but Karcoa was a city of trees, and a fire of that magnitude could become a real problem if it wasn't dealt with quickly.

"What happened?" Thor asked as he walked back to the center of the chamber.

The four black knights, who surrounded the queen, shifted out of their defensive position at a gesture from the queen, gliding back to a menacing line directly behind the throne. A knight with a crossed sword and horn embossed over his right chest plate stepped forward and said something to the queen in Ljosa. The knight's muffled voice sang out in their lyrical cadence through his slitted visor. Unfortunately, Leif didn't understand a lick of Ljosa, so whatever the warrior said was lost on him. Thankfully, Thor picked up on Leif's confusion, stopping the warrior.

"I apologize, Kafteinn, but my friend here doesn't understand your language. He will need to hear this. I believe he will be of tremendous help in the battles to come."

A snort from the Ljosalfar in red robes seated to Leif's right momentarily drew all eyes to him. But when the elf said no more, Thor continued. "If you don't mind, could you speak in English so he may understand the situation as well?"

"Of course, mighty Thor," the kafteinn said, switching to heavily accented English.

*I know that voice.* Leif realized. *That guy and his friends saved Arias and me from the Orc assassins. What did Arias call them? Skogur something.*

"Yesterday, in the dead of night," the kafteinn began. "The Outsider, Ares, accompanied by a contingent of Dokkalfar and Jontar shock troops, emerged from the forest demanding the surrender of Karcoa and the abdication of Ljsoalfar rule on Alfheim. When we refused, they attacked. Unfortunately, at that time, a majority of our Skogur Borg squads were out in the field. Even so, the battle was fierce. We did what we could to slow their advance, but we paid the price in blood. To make matters worse, during the fight, Ares had his minions light several fires, which, as you can see, continue to burn, endangering the city."

"Where are the invaders now?" Thor asked.

"They retreated to the edge of the forest," the warrior responded immediately.

"What have they been doing since their initial incursion?" Thor asked, returning to the window.

"Our scouts report Ares has set up their encampment. It appears they are content to let the fire do their work for them," the kafteinn reported.

"Hmmm," Thor vocalized. "Anything else?

"Yes, mighty Thor. Small bands of Dokkalfar have been spotted, slinking through the city. We've dispatched teams of Skogur Borg, but by the time they get there, the enemy is gone," the kafteinn said.

"Why make such small moves?" Thor asked. "What is Hel's plan?"

"I can't claim to know the enemy's mind. But our patrols have discovered several hidden caches of weapons and gear dispersed amongst Karoca's elktre."

"What of the occupants of the trees?" Thor asked.

"Slaughtered," the knight said, anger seeping into his voice.

"Mighty Thor," the queen said, demanding everyone's attention. "What of the other realms? Have there been other attacks?"

"Yes," the god said, turning away from the window. "Ra and Fenrir invaded Midgard earlier today. They targeted Leif here." The mention prompted everyone to look at Leif.

"Why would the leader of the Outsiders and The godkiller travel to a backwater realm like Midgard just to kill this lowly Midgardian?" the red robed Ljosalfar asked in a mocking tone.

*Lowly Midgardian?* Leif growled within his mind. As the insult stirred the Berserker, his hand went involuntarily to his axes as he pictured slamming them into the smarmy Ljosalfar. Thor eyed Leif, shaking his head ever so slightly. Gritting his teeth, Leif clamped down on his spiraling rage.

Unfortunately, the red-robed noble continued. "Who cares about Midgard? The Alfather closed their realm for a reason. Let the Outsiders have that pitiful excuse of a world. It makes me sick to think Thor was forced to come to their aid when you could have been here defending a realm that matters, like ours. This weakling..." the Ljosalfar said, pointing at Leif, "shouldn't even be in our presence, let alone in Queen Thyra's or yours, mighty one."

A deep growl escaped Leif's lips as the icy fire of the Berserker suffused his body. The council chamber grew still as Leif took a menacing step towards the haughty elf. The guards stationed along the wall glanced at each other, unsure how to respond. To their evident relief, Thor's gauntleted hand shot out, clamping down on Leif's shoulder, stopping him from moving closer.

"Skarde!" Queen Thyra shouted, half rising from her throne. A look of disgust marred her regal features. Whatever the queen was about to say was quickly cut off by a wave of Thor's hand. The atmosphere in the chamber grew uncomfortably heavy as thunder rumbled above.

"I have heard enough." Thor intoned. The words crashed over everyone in attendance as if they had been punched in the gut. "I grow tired of your mulling voice, Skarde of the house Knarr. You would think one who has risen to such high esteem within your clan would know when to keep his mouth shut. If there wasn't an invasion force at Karcoa's doorstep, I would demand a *Holmgang* for daring to insult one in my company."

At the mention of *Holmgang*, everyone in attendance gasped, and Skarde cringed in abject fear. Leif wanted to ask what the word meant, but he figured now wasn't the time.

"The one you so freely disparaged is none other than a savior of the realms. He alone stood against Hel in the bowels of an Asgardian prison. This so-called lowly Midgardian fought my traitorous niece to a stalemate on his own, managing to foil a coup d'état that would have seen the Aesir dead and you under Hel's dark dominion. Only a fool presumes to know the strength of a stranger. Your asinine outburst is proof you are nothing more than an armchair commander. Count yourself lucky this day, Skarde of the house Knarr. Matters greater than your idiocy demand my time, and I do not wish to deprive Alfheim of one of its clan elders in a time of chaos, even if he is as witless as you."

During Thor's dress down, Skarde's pale face grew red with anger or embarrassment, Leif wasn't sure. Though it did appear the arrogant clan elder had learned to keep his mouth shut, even if his eyes were filled with defiance.

"As rightful ruler of Alfheim, named Eternal Queen by my subjects," Queen Thrya said as she knelt on one knee, "I humbly beg your forgiveness on behalf of my foolish vassal. During these dark times, I have encouraged the members of this war council to speak their minds, but it seems one amongst us has decided to take that too far." The queen stood, shooting a glare at the red-robed Ljosalfar. "There will be no need of *Holmgang*, for I shall see to it that the House Knarr is punished accordingly. You have my word as Eternal Queen."

"I shall leave the matter in your hands, your highness. Due to this ridiculous tangent, I fear I have idled for too long on this realm and must return to Asgard so I may inform the Alfather of my findings, so he may best decide how the Aesir shall respond," Thor remarked.

"I beg your forgiveness, mighty Thor, but will you not stay to aid Alfheim in repelling Ares?" Queen Thyra pled, her voice cracking with fear.

"Alas, I cannot. If Hel has chosen to send such a small contingent to Alfheim, I fear she is using the bulk of her Outsider led armies to attack in force somewhere else." Thor shook his head. "Quite possibly, Asgard itself. If Asgard were to fall, the other realms will not stand a chance."

"How will we repel Ares, then?" Skarde angrily asked.

If looks could kill, the one Thor shot the disgraced Ljosalfar would have seen him dead on the spot.

"By force," Thor said, as if the answer was obvious. "It is a small force, is it not? The Outsiders are formidable, but so are the Ljosalfar. Your Skogur Borg…" Thor said, giving a nod towards the black armored knights, "are known throughout the nine realms for their warrior prowess. Remember, you need not kill the treacherous Outsider, but merely force him to retreat. You only need to hold out until Odin has devised our counterattack. The Aesir will not allow this or any realm to fall. Not while we still draw breath. You have my promise. Hold strong. Once I have been given leave, I shall return with a host of Asgardian troops, and together we shall root out the evils that befall your lands.

"As a token of my confidence, I shall lend you Leif. He is one of my chosen, a Berserker, who is of a small number to have fought and survived a fight with the gods. Use him in the coming battles. He knows how the enemy fights, and he will be instrumental in the defense of Karcoa."

"What?" Leif shouted.

Thor smiled. "I bid you all good luck in the coming battles. I, or one of my kin, shall return once we know more of Hel's plan."

Leif beamed with pride as Thor touted his accomplishment, but doubt gnawed at his insides like some undiscovered tapeworm. *Am*

*I strong enough to earn his praise? Sure, I survived a fight with Hel, but she also pinned me to the floor with a freaking sword so wraiths could devour my soul. Fenrir practically used me as a sledgehammer to perform an impromptu renovation on Bragi Books' interior.* Before Leif fell too far into the well of self-doubt, Thor caught his eye.

Thor placed two meaty hands on Leif's shoulders. "I know what you are going to say. When you have lived as long as I, you learn a thing or two about reading people. Do not fear; you are strong, stronger than you know. Both here…" he said, tapping Leif on the chest, "and here." Thor tapped him on the temple. "Do not forget. Unlike your previous fights against the gods, you are not alone here. Use your time here wisely. There is much you can learn from the Skogur Borg. They are among the elite warriors of the realms. Use their knowledge to grow stronger."

"I will. I am just worried," Leif said under his breath, shifting from foot to foot. "You talked me up so much. I don't want to fail them in the field."

"This is war, Leif. Good people will die; that is inevitable. There is no guarantee you, or anyone for that matter, will survive the fights to come. We are warriors. The only thing you need to concern yourself with is ensuring those who die don't die in vain. Keep your head, follow orders, and don't over commit. You will be fine." Thor said, smiling down at Leif like a doting teacher. "I have no doubt I will be seeing you soon, whether it's on the battlefield or within the halls of Valhalla. Fight hard and fight smart, Berserker." Thor gave Leif one final nod. He lifted his hammer high overhead, and Leif felt a tingle of static electricity crackle across his skin. A bright flash accompanied by the boom of thunder shook the chamber. Blinking the spots away from his eyes, Leif was left with the smell of ozone in the god's wake.

"Wait, in the halls of Valhalla?" he shouted, but Thor was already gone.

# CHAPTER 6

In the wake of Thor's departure, the war council descended into chaos. Many of the members of the Elvin council rose to their feet. Some were shouting in Ljosa, others in English. Many pointed at Leif or out the window toward the burning fires beyond.

"Silence!" Queen Thrya shouted, but her voice was drowned in the commotion.

Leif saw she tried again, only in Ljosa. Again, she was either ignored or unheard. Having enough of being ignored, the queen gestured to the Skogur Borg. A knight saluted and rushed forward, snatching up a spear from one of the bodyguards against the wall. Striding to the center of the chamber, mere feet from Leif, the warrior raised the spear high overhead and slammed the butt of the weapon down in quick succession.

BOOM, BOOM, BOOM.

The impacts reverberated throughout the room. By the third impact, all in attendance had gone silent. "Thank you, Kafteinn," said the queen, pulling everyone's attention back to her. "In a show of respect to Leif, who I assume doesn't speak our language, the rest of this meeting shall be conducted in the trade tongue. Does anyone object? I would remind you all, Thor himself chose to address us this way as well," the queen finished, daring anyone to challenge her decree.

Leif could tell there were a few who wanted to, but they were the minority and kept their mouths shut. Nodding her head, the queen continued, "We all heard Thor's warning. The goddess Hel has freed the godkiller, Fenrir, and they have aligned themselves with the Outsiders, declaring war on the nine realms. It was my hope, with the blessing of the council, that we send word to our representatives in Vanaheimr to request aid, but if the other realms are as besieged as ours, I doubt they can send reinforcements." Thyra paused for dramatic effect. "We must cease operations throughout Alfheim and recall any Skogur Borg units still in the field. I also believe it is time to rally the noble houses' bannerman for the defense of Karcoa." A chorus of murmurs burst from the chamber, but the queen paid them no mind. "Not since the end of the Ljosa-Dokka war has Alfheim faced such a grave threat. Now is the time for us to band together in defense of our great realm."

"But, my queen," a Ljosalfar in a teal toga interjected. "How can we be expected to challenge one so powerful as Ares?"

"Fear not, Havlor," Queen Thyra soothed. "The enemy took us by surprise, attacking in the night. Yes, they wounded us, but we are not dead. We are at our most dangerous when wounded and cornered. After discussing the matter with the Skogur Borg kafteinns, we believe a calculated counterattack in the heart of Ares's camp should be sufficient to stall their advance. Hopefully, it will be long enough for Aesir reinforcements to come to our aid.

"Council members, return to your houses and rally your guards. I give you leave to seek out any of Ares's troops who have taken up residence in your quarters. While you drive out those who have taken root in the city, I have tasked the Skogur Borg with directly attacking Ares. But I warn you. If I learn any of your houses are withholding troops or using the chaos to invade a rival clan, I will not be merciful. You are dismissed."

Grumbles wafted around the chamber as the council members shuffled out of the room, though Leif noted none were brave enough to voice their discontent. Once the clan leaders and their bodyguards were gone, Queen Thrya glided back to the throne, motioning the Skogur Borg warriors to step forward.

All four Skogur Borg knights reacted immediately, moving on silent feet from behind the queen. *I've got to figure out how they move so silently in a full suit of armor,* Leif thought.

"My kafteinns, we cannot allow the enemy to take root within our city. The longer we wait, the harder it will be to uproot the scourge. Send word to squads deployed outside Karcoa to return immediately. If what our scouts say is true, then the enemy is fortifying their position as we speak. We must act before the fire grows too large and Ares's fortification becomes too well defended. I want a battle plan by sunset today. We attack tomorrow under the cover of darkness. That will give the units that are away from the city time to return, to recover, and to be fresh for battle," the queen commanded.

Leif, not knowing what his role would be, mentally debated whether he should interrupt the queen's directives. He didn't want to be cast aside or placed in the reserves, so he figured he should be assertive. Taking a deep breath, he mustered his courage and stepped forward. "Queen Thrya, what will my role be, if you don't mind me asking?" An awkward silence ensued that did little to comfort him. *Shit! Maybe I made a mistake,* he thought.

"He can join my squad," said a kneeling knight. The kafteinn rose smoothly to his feet, unclasping his helmet. "I have seen how the young Berserker fights, and I believe I am best suited to integrate him into my team.

Unsurprising, it was the leader of the group who had saved him. *What is his name again?* Leif thought, racking his brain. He had features that were cut from stone as he regarded Leif briefly before turning his attention back to his queen. Leif shivered slightly as the kafteinn's cold yellow eyes regarded him.

"Very well, Kafteinn Jaeger," Queen Thrya said with a smile.

*Jaeger! That's right, I remember now,* Leif thought.

"The Berserker shall join your squad. While he stays with us, he will be part of your unit. See that he lodges within your unit's barracks. Also, take him to the quartermaster. I do not wish to send a companion of Thor's into battle unprotected," Queen Thrya said to Jaeger. She leaned back on her throne to address all her kafteinns. "Rise and attend to your troops. Inform the squad leaders of their assigned posts and prepare our battle plan. Now go, and may the Aesir bless you."

The three knights who had remained kneeling stood as one. All four saluted, pounding a clenched fist over their chest. The three kaftienns, who Leif didn't know, quickly turned with silent feet and exited the chamber.

Jaeger turned to Leif. "Well met, Berserker." He held out a gauntleted hand. Leif was momentarily caught off guard, but recovered, taking the Ljosalfar's hand.

"You can call me Leif," he responded.

"Of course," Jaeger responded with a nod. "Where is your friend? Arias, if my memory serves me right."

The mention of Arias's name was like a hammer blow to his gut. Outside of his thoughts, Leif hadn't heard Arias's name spoken since his death. "Arias. Uh, he died not long after we met you. Hel sent a group of Jontar to ambush us at a Svartalfar village. They cornered us, and he was gravely injured. We escaped, but his injuries were too severe. He died not long after," Leif said with grief tinging his voice.

"Ah, then he died a true warrior! None could ask for a more fitting end to one's journey than to die fighting for what one believes in. Hopefully, I will meet him again within the halls of Valhalla. Come, you look as if you were on the wrong side of a beating. Let's get you back to my squad's quarters. We can patch you up and let you rest while I meet with the rest of the kafteinns and plan our counterattack. Follow me," Jaeger said, ushering Leif out the door.

In the corridor, Leif fell into step besides the kafteinn, but he had to keep dodging out of the way as frantic Ljosalfar sprinted past him in the opposite direction. "Jaeger," Leif started, "Do you know where Ares and his warriors came from? Ra and Fenrir used a strange black ball that ripped open a bridge in midair. But I can't imagine those are easy to use or else they would have popped up right in the center of Karcoa or even in the queen's throne room."

"We do," Jaeger said. "Two days ago, we received word from a Skogur Borg scouting unit stationed at a common bridge location. The missive stated the warrior assigned to bridge watch saw the early signs of a connection, which is a common occurrence at that location. It is the very reason we assigned a unit to keep watch over it. It is one of the peculiar spots on Alfheim that has a high number of random bridge connections."

"The Skogur Borg monitor bridge connections?" Leif asked.

"Yes," he responded matter-of-factly. "All realms are to keep watch for any newly formed bridges."

"But how do you know where a bridge is going to emerge? I know that there are certain hard points where there are permanent bridges. Just like the one Arias and I used to cross over to Myrkheim. Those would be easy to monitor, but how do you watch for and guard a randomly occurring bridge?" Leif asked.

"We don't catch them all. The bridges connect on the whim of Yggdrasil. But over the millennia, Ljosalfar explorers have been mapping any bridge sightings they come across. Long ago, Queen Tove initiated a reward-based system for any confirmed bridge locations. After that, we've kept extensive records on all discovered bridges, where they lead, duration and frequency of emergence in a specific location. Even with this information, little was learned about bridge connections, so Queen Tove dispatched several Ljosalfar high mages to investigate those areas that appeared to have an abnormally high number of random connections. During their study, the mages learned that for a bridge to form and connect to another realm, several criteria must be met beforehand. I'm no expert in bridge mechanics, but I know the basics. Location is important, as is the season and magical index of the location. Using this information, my people-built cities in many areas to help furnish commerce. Small fortifications were built in locations too hostile for cities or too hard to travel to and from. In those areas with below average connections, we built scout outposts."

"Gotcha," Leif said, trying to process the information. Jaeger furrowed his brow and turned to Leif as they continued to walk. "What does 'gotcha' mean?" Jaeger asked, with a perplexed look on his Elvin face.

"Oh, sorry. It means I understand." Leif answered. *I will have to choose my words more carefully.* Leif thought. Arias had been living on Midgard for a decade or two, so he understood Midgardian English well, but the elves didn't have an urban dictionary for the trade language. "So, you had guards stationed at a bridge site and something happened?" Leif asked, getting back on topic.

"Yes," Jaeger said as they headed down a wooden stairway. "Before any two bridges connect, there is a flash of magic that ripples out from the epicenter. If one is attuned to it, it can be felt. Depending on the type of bridge and connection, the effect can be felt minutes or seconds before it opens."

"Ok," Leif said as they exited the stairwell. The previous floors were packed with Ljosalfar in fine colorful clothing, scurrying from door to door with looks of panic plastered across their teardrop faces. Now there were only black clad knights calmly chatting or going about their duties with determined steps.

"The one and only letter we received from the scouting unit stated the preliminary signs of a bridge connection had been felt with more information to follow once it opened. But none ever came. All attempts, both magical and physical, to contact the scouts were met with silence. Then last night, Ares and his warriors stepped out of the forest and began their assault. Lucky for us, they chose a shock and awe approach. Rushing in to cause as much death and destruction in a short period before pulling back to set up their base camp. To tell you the truth, the enemy's actions have me worried. Ares is an outsider. He's no idiot. He wouldn't attack Karcoa with such a small force without a plan." Jaeger said, a hint of worry creeping into his voice.

"What do you think he is planning?" Leif asked.

"With the new information Thor provided us today, I've got two theories. Either Hel is so confident in Ares's abilities as a military commander that she felt his small band would be enough to conquer Alfheim. Or, and I think this is the more likely result, Ares was sent in advance of a much larger invading force. Hel is probably focusing her troops elsewhere, and only sent Ares to the heart of Alfheim in hopes of putting us on our heels, maybe even force the queen to abdicate the throne to Hel. That way, she avoids decimating her troops here and can use them elsewhere. I wouldn't be surprised if we receive word from Ares today or tomorrow, demanding our surrender. Most likely before hostilities begin again."

"I'm no military commander," Leif said. "Hell, I barely consider myself a warrior, but what you say rings true to me. Especially if this is THE Ares we are talking about."

"You know of him?" Jaeger said as he whipped around to face Leif.

"Only from mythology," Leif said, backtracking a little. "Ares is one of the gods from an ancient culture on Midgard. Ares was believed to be the god of war. So, I doubt a being literally worshiped for his warrior prowess would do anything that didn't advance Hel's tactical advantage during Ragnarok."

"Troubling indeed. For Hel to send Ares cannot bode well for my people or this realm. This is something I will discuss with the other kafteinns as we determine our battle plans." Jaeger pushed open the wooden door they had stopped in front of.

Following Jaeger inside the room, Leif was met with three hard looking Ljosalfar knights. Three sets of yellow cats' eyes locked onto him, sizing him up. He felt the icy sensation of the Berserker stir as the knights glared at him. Leif slammed down on his mental control lest he do something stupid.

Before the tension escalated into something more dangerous, Jaeger addressed his squad in English. "The war council has decided upon a course of action. Though I must say…" he paused to nod in Leif's direction, "it was a very unusual meeting, to say the least. I will not bore you with the details. The important facts are, the mighty Thor, with his companion Leif, visited us, informing the council that not just Karcoa, but many of the nine realms are under siege. Queen Thrya requested Thor's help in fighting against our attackers, but she was denied. In his stead, Thor left Leif here to assist in our counterattack. Having seen Leif in battle once before, I volunteered to have him join our squad. We all briefly met some time ago, but that was under different circumstances. So let me formally introduce you to your new squad mates, Jol, Selga, and Foste." Jaeger gestured to each Skogur Borg warrior in turn. "Jol is my second in command, Foste is our scout, and Selga is our weapons expert. There isn't a weapon on Alfheim she hasn't mastered."

Jol was tall, towering over Leif's six-foot one inch frame, and muscled like a Crossfitter on steroids. His tear drop face and sharp nose could have cut diamonds. Next to him stood the shorter blonde-haired warrior named Foste. Shorter and thinner than her companions, Foste was lean like a cheetah. The final warrior was the most memorable to Leif. Selga sported a tribal tattoo with sharp dark angles crisscrossing the right side of her face, giving her an Amazonian appearance.

None of the elite warriors looked happy about Leif joining the squad. But while Foste and Selga were able to mask their frustration with looks of quiet indifference, a look of frustration flashed across Jol's stern features, giving Leif a vexed once over. Before Jol could voice his suspicion, Jaeger continued, putting an edge of steel in his voice. "Thor himself vouched for Leif's warrior prowess, so any grumbling will not be tolerated," Jaeger said, eyeing Jol.

Jol slightly straightened at the chastisement. "Of course, Kafteinn. What of our counterattack?"

"The eternal queen wishes for our assault to begin at sunset tomorrow." None of them shouted or broke military decorum, but they shifted from foot to foot while clinching their fists. Leif could easily see these knights were eager for a fight, and he couldn't blame them. Jaeger continued, "Already, a call has been sent to all Skogur Borg units in the field to return to the city. In a moment, I will be leaving to meet with the other kafteinns to plan our battle strategy." Jaeger said. "You three, prepare your gear and get some rest while I am gone."

Jaeger turned to Leif, ushering him to a corner of the room where an empty bunk was laid out. "Leif, I must leave you for the moment. As Thor said, you need to rest and recover to be up for the battle ahead, so please take my bunk. I will have an aid send you food and gear later this evening. Get some rest and heal up..." Jaeger said, holding out his gauntleted hand, "for tomorrow we go to war." Leif responded in kind, grasping Jaeger's armored hand. Jaeger then turned and left the room, leaving him alone with his three new squad mates.

# CHAPTER 7

Leif's new squad mates approached him like a pack of wolves encircling their prey. The three warriors wore tight black tunics with black baggy pants, like sweatpants. The Skogur Borg's white insignia of a crossed sword and horn was stitched over their left breast.

Leif stood in uncomfortable silence as the three warriors conversed in Ljosa and eyed him with open mistrust. Foste stepped forward, getting within a foot of him before snapping something out in their sing-song language, which he, of course, didn't understand. When he didn't respond, Jol joined in, again speaking in Ljosa. Once it was clear Leif didn't understand, Selga sneered, saying in a heavy clipped accent, "It appears the Midgardian doesn't know our speech." It was clear that she spoke English proficiently but didn't have the occasion to use it, putting emphasis on odd syllables. The other two snorted with derision.

"You are the Midgardian we saved in the forest, isn't that right?" Foste asked.

Jol's eyes scrunched up slightly as he searched Leif's face. "Your right, Foste," Jol said. "You and that Ljosalfar were attacked by a group of Orc, right? And we saved you two. How are we supposed to trust you to have our backs when you and your friend couldn't even handle a single band of Orcs?" Jol scoffed.

"We were ambushed!" Leif defended. His hackles raised as the feeling of being penned in grew.

"Jol has got a point," Selga said, joining in. "We are on the eve of battle and suddenly the kafteinn expects us to trust that a Midgardian will be able to keep up, to fight alongside the finest warriors on Alfheim? Unlikely. All this will do is get you killed, taking one or all of us with you."

"The kafteinn won't be back for a few hours," Foste noted. "Why don't you run back to Midgard where you belong? We won't say a word about it to Jaeger. We'll just say you went out and never came back. Seems fair."

By now, the three Ljosalfar had spread out, cornering Leif against the vacant bunk. He could feel the stirring of the Berserker in the back of his mind, but he held it in check; it wasn't time to let it out just yet. He was getting tired of the Ljosalfar looking down on him, but he needed to play this cool. Thor believed in him, and Jaeger must have seen something in him as well, or he wouldn't have let him join his squad. Then something Arias had said to him from the early days of their training flashed across his mind.

*"Since you are a Midgardian, the other races will look down on you as a weakling. Use that to your advantage."*

Leif's annoyance vanished, quickly replaced with an excited energy. *Alright, assholes,* he thought. *It's about time I teach you all a little lesson.*

The three warriors must have picked up on the change in Leif's demeanor, because all three changed their stance, shifting their balance, with feet slightly apart and knees bent. It was a sure sign that he went from prey to something unknown and to a predator; the unknown is dangerous.

*Good,* he thought. *Looks like they know, even if subconsciously, that I'm no pushover.* "Alright," Leif said, "Why don't you put your money where your mouth is? I'll spar with one of you. If I win, I fight with your squad. If I lose, I will pack up and you will never see me again. How does that sound?" Leif asked.

The three looked at each other, speaking in rushed Ljosa. A few seconds later, Selga asked, "What does 'put your money where your mouth is' mean? Why would putting money in our mouths determine if you are worthy to fight alongside the greatest Skogur Borg unit in Karcoan history?"

*Damnit,* Leif thought with a sigh. *I've really got to stay away from Midgardian idioms.* "It's a Midgardian saying." Leif tried to explain. "It means if you are so confident, then let's make a wager of some sort."

"Ah!" Selga said, her eyes lighting up. "I get it, but why not just say so in the first place?" she asked, still confused.

"Forget what I said," he said, growling in frustration. "What do you say? Do we have a bet? A friendly fight: the first person to cry mercy loses?" He held out his hand.

"Deal," Selga said, taking Leif's hand. They shook on it, and he couldn't help but notice how calloused and strong her hand was.

"What!" Both Foste and Jol protested at once. "Why should you be the one to fight the Midgardian?" Jol complained.

"Aye!" Foste said a second later.

"He shook my hand! It means I accepted the challenge. You two will just have to settle for being spectators today. Besides, this will be over in an instant. Then we can get back to preparing for tomorrow," Selga said as she rolled her shoulders and cracked her neck.

"Fine," Foste said with annoyance creeping into her melodic voice.

"Good, it's settled then, but where will we spar?" Leif asked.

"Why not here?" Selga asked, spreading her arms out wide. Looking around, Leif didn't doubt the room was perfect to spend their downtime in. It was a large squarish room; four cots were evenly spaced out at each corner, with a small wooden cabinet set to the right of each bed. In the center of the room, a round wooden table with four chairs sat oblivious to its probable destruction. Two dancing flame lanterns hung on opposite sides of the room. "Don't get me wrong," Leif said. "This room is more than fine to sleep and eat in, but there just isn't enough space to properly fight. I don't want to risk destroying your furniture or accidentally injuring you by knocking you into something."

Surprisingly, Selga agreed. "Come on, there is a training room just down the hall. It is for Skogur Borg members only, and since we are supposed to battle tomorrow, I doubt anyone will be there." The Ljosalfar said as she turned and headed for the door.

Selga was right. The training room was completely empty. There were no traditional style weights, no floor-to-ceiling mirrors, nor were there any punching bags. Leif half expected he would see a gym like back on Midgard. The room was large, close to fifty feet across and thirty feet wide. Like every other room, hallway, and stairway he had been in since Thor dropped him off, the walls, ceiling, and floor were entirely made of wood. Large rectangle windows dominated one side of the room. Except for the massive smoke clouds wafting lazily across the forest cityscape, the view from the room provided a breathtaking view of Karcoa and the surrounding forest. Along the opposite wall, several weapon racks were filled with all manner of wooden weapons of war. Leif noticed traditional swords and spears along with several he didn't have a name for. At one end of the training room, he spotted several large round rocks of varying sizes. He guessed the Skogur Borg used them for strength training, like those in Strongman competitions back on Midgard. The rest of the gym was separated into three sparring circles. Interestingly, the ground within each circle was different. One had sand, another loose gravel, and the final was made of finely cut grass.

Turning to Jol, Leif asked, "What's with the circles?"

Snorting in derision, "You think your enemies will let you choose the terrain to fight on? No. One must be prepared to fight, no matter the arena the gods have chosen for you. And so, we make it a point to spar on different terrain, to ensure our footing is always sound."

*Damn, the arrogant elf has a point,* Leif thought.

"So, Midgardian, which arena do you wish to fight in?" Selga asked, pulling Leif away from his thoughts.

Looking between the circles, "I choose sand. Hopefully, it will be enough to cushion your fall after I knock you on your ass," Leif boasted, even though he felt the stirring of nervous butterflies take flight in his stomach. *Gods, I hope I don't lose. I'm still healing from the beating I took from Fenrir. I really can't go back to Midgard now. Besides, the Skogur Borg are my best hope of becoming stronger. I'm no use in the fight to stop Ragnarok as I am now. No, I got this,* Leif thought, psyching himself up.

"Sand it is," Selga said with a smile. "Even though you are the challenger, you are still new to our ways, so I will be gracious enough to let you choose the weapon, wooden of course. I wouldn't want to have to explain to Jaeger how I accidentally killed his new pet Midgardian."

"I'm no one's pet," Leif growled, feeling the Berserker stir at the challenge. But he held it back. He knew from his many sparring sessions with Arias that the Ljosalfar are a deadly race. They were far stronger and faster than regular Midgardians, but Leif was no mere Midgardian. He was the Berserker who challenged a god and survived... barely. So, Leif's plan of attack was to play this fight slow and feel out Selga. Then, if he was truly outmatched and things got desperate, which he knew was a definite possibility, he would let the Berserker out. Then the real fun would begin. This would also be a good test of his control of the Berserker. He didn't want to gain their trust to only berserk on the battlefield and end up attacking one of his squad mates. *Boy, would that look bad,* Leif chuckled to himself. "I choose hand-to-hand combat. What better way to test my mettle" Leif growled, releasing a flash of the Berserker.

"Good," Selga said, giving him a feral grin. "Show me that fire,

Berserker," she said before approaching the ring and taking her boots off. With the sound of sand crunching beneath bare feet, Selga gestured for Leif to follow. The sand felt cool as it shifted between his toes. Squaring up to Selga, Leif asked. "So, what happens now?"

On cue, Jol sidled up to the edge of the ring while Foste took a seat along one of the many wood benches against the back wall. A mischievous grin was pasted on her face.

"The rules are simple," Jol intoned. This is a hand-to-hand challenge between Selga and Leif. "Knocking an opponent unconscious, stepping out of the ring, or a call of mercy are your avenues to victory," Jol said, looking between Leif and Selga. "Anything but a killing strike shall be permitted. The attempted use of a killing blow will cause you to forfeit the match and be taken to the queen for punishment. Understood?" Jol said seriously.

"Aye," Selga said, sliding into a guard position.

A second passed before Leif realized it was his turn. He quickly responded, "Yes." Then, in an abundance of caution, he took two steps back, giving Selga some distance before shifting to the balls of his feet.

Both combatants stared silent daggers at each other. Jol bellowed, "FIGHT!"

In a blink of an eye, Selga crossed the distance between them. Her right fist whipped forward to smash into Leif's right cheek. Selga was going for the quick and brutal way to end this fight, knocking Leif out in one swift overpowered punch, most likely breaking his jaw in the process.

Without Leif's enhanced speed, he would have been demolished. Jerking backwards, Selga's fist streaked past his face, grazing his ear. The abrupt dodge by Leif caused his back foot to land awkwardly on the uneven sand. Knowing he was off balance, Leif cursed himself for being unprepared as he searched for Selga's follow up attack, but the punch never came. Instead, Selga stopped, arm extended, eyeing Leif.

"Well..." Selga chuckled, "you're fast. I'll give you that, but don't think I didn't notice you stepping off balance. If I had pressed the attack, you would have been finished. I won't be extending the same courtesy a second time."

"Enough chatter," Jol chided. "This is supposed to be a duel, remember?"

"Yes," Selga said, dismissing Jol with a flick of her hand. "Looks like this will be more fun than I imagined." She said as she slid back into a fighting stance.

*Alright, no more screw-ups,* Leif thought. *This is my only chance.* Just then, a thought occurred to him. Each ring was set up a little differently, forcing people to think on their feet and adapt to their surroundings to best their opponent. *So why not use the very arena against them?*

Leif moved back into a fighting position. His eyes were glued to Selga as she circled him like a shark getting ready for the kill. Leif wasn't going to give her the chance. Timing it perfectly as Selga lifted her foot to charge. Leif kicked out, but instead of kicking at Selga, he flung his foot forward, pelting Selga in a cloud of sand, momentarily blinding her.

Selga let out a cry of frustration. "UGGGH!" Sand slammed into her open eyes and mouth. Capitalizing on her distraction, Leif sprang to his left, not wanting to attack her head on. By luck or experience, Selga dodged Leif's first punch, but she was too slow to dodge his follow up. His right fist connected solidly with Selga's left flank, causing her to grunt in pain. Still blinded by the sand, but now knowing where Leif was, Selga's hands flashed forward, grabbing Leif's outstretched arm. In one sinuous movement, she turned, letting out a grunt of effort, flinging Leif up and over her back. He was momentarily airborne before coming down hard on the sand with an "Oof!"

Coughing, Leif fought to recover from having the air knocked out of him. He rolled to his feet while Selga furiously spit and rubbed her eyes. Back on his feet, he rushed forward, but by then,

Selga had cleared the sand from her vision and met him head on. Selga's eyes blazed with anger as she went on the offensive. She was fast, much faster than Arias, though not as strong. That was little comfort to Leif. Every move had purpose, allowing her to flow from attack to attack seamlessly, and Leif was paying dearly for it. All he could do was bob and weave, hoping she would present an opening.

The two combatants moved around the ring, sand flying as they fought. In between his dodges, Leif would lash out, sending punches and kicks at any opening he could find, but sadly none did any damage. Each time, Selga would pivot, twist, or guide his fist or foot to less vulnerable spots on her body.

As Selga extended a right hook, she dropped her guard ever so slightly. Not wanting to miss the opportunity, Leif side-stepped the punch and counter attacked, hoping to sneak past the dropped guard, but it was a ruse. As Leif's fist flew forward, Selga's left hand batted his punch away, leaving one side of his body unprotected.

"FINISH HIM!" Foste yelled, coming to her feet as she sensed the fight was coming to an end.

Seizing on the opportunity, Selga slammed her fist into Leif's unprotected flank. His body was violently jerked to the side by the force of Selga's powerful punch. The Skogur Borg warrior followed up with a feint to Leif's uninjured side, and he fell for it again. As he shifted his defense for a punch that never came, Selga sent a vicious haymaker that connected perfectly with Leif's left temple. He careened into the sand as stars streaked across his vision. The cool sand was a welcome comfort to his battered and bruised body. A small cloud of sand puffed out as Leif snarled, "Enough." He released the awesome power of the Berserker. Immediately, the ice-cold rush of power coursed through his veins. Suffused with power, Leif's aches and pains instantly vanished.

"Wooh!" Foste called out from somewhere to Leif's left.

"The Midgardian has got heart, but that can only take you so far," Jol commented.

The soft crunch of sand alerted Leif of Selga's approach, but he held still, not wanting to give himself away.

"It ain't over yet," Leif shouted as he sprang to his feet. Selga's yellow cat eyes went wide in shock a split second before his supernaturally enhanced fist connected with a THWACK across her tattooed cheek. The strength behind Leif's berserked fist sent Selga stumbling backward and falling to the sandy floor mere inches from the boundary line.

*Damn!* Leif thought. *So close.*

"AHHHHH!" Screaming a war cry, Leif sprinted toward the downed Selga. Sand exploded backward as he went. Leif kicked with all his might, hoping to launch Selga out of the ring. But at the last second, she rolled to her left, causing him to miss. Without using her hands, Selga swung her legs up then down, flinging onto her feet, like a martial arts expert.

Fully berserked, Leif had a much easier time contending with the Skogur Borg. She was still incredibly fast and strong, but nowhere close to Hel's or Fenrir's level. Leaning into his finely honed instincts, Leif countered and dodged Selga's endless punches and kicks, but just barely. Sweat poured down Leif's neck and face, but he couldn't say the same for Selga. The warrior had hardly broken a sweat. Exacerbating his predicament, Leif's ribs and legs pulsed with pain from injuries sustained during Fenrir's beating, but he couldn't quit now. The Berserker howled from within that victory was within reach; he just needed to push further. However, Leif's rational side pushed through the rage. *We are both taking too much damage here. We are supposed to fight as a team tomorrow. If we continue our duel any longer, one or both of us are likely to get injured.* The Berserker railed against this train of thought. A few months earlier, his thunderous bloodlust would have won out, but he was different now. He was stronger in both body and mind. He knew the fight needed to end now.

Seeing his opportunity, Leif punched, holding back some of his power. Selga fell for his ruse, and her hand caught Leif's fist in his halfhearted attack, just as he hoped. Selga yanked Leif's trapped fist to unbalance him. Moving with the tug, Selga did exactly what he had expected. She lashed out with a punch of her own. A resounding thwack echoed through the training hall as Leif caught Selga's punch. Not wanting his quarry to get away, he clamped down on her fist, trapping her in place. Berserker and Skogur Borg knight struggled for control. Seconds ticked by, with neither gaining an advantage over the other. Leif could tell she was stronger than him, but she was not strong enough to overpower him.

Panting with exertion, Leif wheezed, "We could do this all day. Beat on each other until one of us yields or is knocked unconscious. All that will get us is more bruises going into tomorrow's fight. Or…" Leif emphasized. "We can call this match a draw. You tried to knock me down, but I've shown that isn't so easy. I've proven to you I'm no ordinary Midgardian and though I'm not a master, I can at least hold my own in a fight. So, what do you say?"

Leif hoped his little speech would be enough to stop Selga, but he was wrong. As he spoke, Leif saw the warrior's pride prevented her from relenting. *If they are as badass as they think they are, there is no way she would risk tarnishing her reputation or that of her order.* Seeing the predicament too late, Leif sighed, knowing he was going to have to finish the fight.

Suddenly, Jol surprised the combatants. Stepping into the ring, the imposing warrior approached the still struggling combatants intoning, "I declare this duel a draw. Selga, you have exemplified the speed and lethality of a Ljosalfar of your rank. No one can question that, but what the Berserker says is true. At the beginning of this challenge, I had expected it to be over in an instant, with the very real possibility that we would need a healer or we would have a dead body on our hands. However, Leif has distinguished himself as a worthy warrior. I have never had the honor of seeing one of your kind in battle, but you truly live up to the title of Berserker. I

would be honored to fight by your side in the defense of my realm."
Jol placed his hands on each of their shoulders.

That was the final straw. Selga, to Leif's relief, released her
death grip on his fist. He followed her lead and released his hold a
second later. Selga let out a yell of annoyance as she kicked the
ground, birthing a cloud of sand that pelted Leif and the spectators.
She turned her rage filled eyes on Jol, "Why did you interfere? This
was a fight until mercy! I nearly had him! How dare you call a draw!
A Midgardian fought a member of the Skogur Borg to a draw?" She
bellowed as Foste placed a restraining hand on Selga's shoulder.
Leif doubted she would attack, but he sympathized with her
frustration; he was familiar with the battle lust that calls to
warriors. Luckily for him, due to his training, he had a lot of
practice suppressing those feelings.

"If this were to get out, the reputation of the kafteinn, our unit,
and the Skogur Borg will be tarnished. A Midgardian!" Selga
screamed. This time, it was Foste's turn to placate Selga. Foste
placed both her hands on Selga's shoulders, but Selga violently
shook them off.

"Selga, it's ok. No one will question your abilities," Foste
soothed. "In fact, no one needs to even know this duel took place.
Look around," Foste said, sweeping her arms out wide. "No one is
here. Besides, Leif isn't a simple Midgardian. The fight and his eyes
demonstrate he is god touched." Selga's blood was still boiling from
the fight and wasn't listening to reason. With a shout of frustration,
she turned away from Foste and stormed out of the room. Her bare
feet stomped with an audible thump as she slammed the training
room door behind her.

"You will have to forgive Selga. She is the newest member of our
squad and feels it is her duty to protect Jaeger's honor and that of
all the Skogur Borg." Foste said as she picked up Selga's boots and
hurried to follow her friend.

"Well, that was certainly enlightening," Jol said. "Let's get you
cleaned up. The sun has set, and we have a big day ahead of us."

# CHAPTER 8

Leif woke to the sound of people bustling around the room. After opening his eyes, he sat up expecting to feel every ache and pain he had suffered from the past day, but to his surprise, he only felt achy and a little stiff. It had been a fitful sleep, tossing and turning as the usual characters haunted his dreams. His body was still covered in a multitude of cuts and bruises, but that was it. With a smile, he stood up, catching the attention of the other occupants in the room.

"Ah! You're up," Jol commented. He set the dagger he was sharpening down and approached Leif. "How do you feel? Did the salve help with your injuries?"

"Yes, thank you," Leif said, testing his healed body by stretching his arms above his head. There was a slight twinge of pain in his back and ribs, but it was nothing that would prevent him from fighting. *The combination of my enhanced healing and the salve really worked. I will have to ask for a bottle or two if I survive the fight to come*, he thought. "I feel great. After, you know, I got over the horrible smell, I finally fell asleep," Leif joked.

"The salve smells foul, but it has saved our lives on many occasions," Foste said, joining the conversation. "All the Skogur

Borg units receive a few bottles before getting sent into the field. It helps sustain us on prolonged assignments or when we are expected to be on the hunt for multiple days. It numbs the pain as it stimulates the healing process, but be warned. As amazing as the potions are, it won't save you from any life-threatening injuries," Foste said nonchalantly.

"That's amazing!" Leif said. "You wouldn't happen to know where I can buy a few bottles while I am on Alfheim, would you?" Leif asked

"No. The salve is extremely difficult to brew. It's an alchemical compound that requires rare herbs and a blood moon in the sky as it is brewed. We've even been sent out on occasion to procure the ingredients. Rarity aside, with the kafteinn adding you to the squad, you are now eligible to receive a bottle from the quartermaster before we depart," Foste said, pulling out the familiar glass vile filled with a green mucus colored liquid.

"Awesome," Leif said. "So, when do I get to see the quartermaster?"

"Soon," said a voice from behind him.

Jaeger had silently entered the room. *What is he, part ninja?* Leif thought to himself.

"Gather around," Jaeger said, surveying the room. "Where's Selga?"

"She just stepped out, sir." Jol moved next to Jaeger. "She said she would be right back."

Shrugging, Jaeger continued. "I met with the other kafteinns last night, and this is what we came up with." Moving over to the table in the center of the room, Jaeger un-tied the small cord wrapped around a scroll, unfurled then flattened it on the table. Leif recognized it as a map of Karcoa. The map showed the city divided into several sections, with the Monarch in the center. Each section of the map contained small trees with lines running between them. Leif assumed those were roads. Black runes ran along the outer edge of the map with one large glyph in red in the center. Near the runes, it looked like someone took a black crayon and started shading in several areas. Before Leif could ask what it all meant, Jaeger started talking.

"First, I know it will take a little getting used to, but while Leif is with our squad, to prevent a breakdown in communication, we will speak in the common tongue."

"Aye," Foste and Jol responded.

"Reports from our scouts in the field state these areas here..." Jaeger said, pointing to the black glyphs, "are where our enemies have fortified themselves. They took over several of the larger elktre. The red rune at the edge of Karcoa is their encampment, and it is believed that is where we will find Ares.

"Sir," Jol interjected.

Jaeger nodded once, giving Jol permission to speak.

"Has there been any word from the enemy's camp?" He asked.

"Yes, one of Kafteinn Ragnar's scouts came across the body of Clan Elder Ubba." The warriors froze at the mention of the dead elder.

"A sword had been rammed through Jarl Ubba's chest, pinning him to the ground. There was a note addressed to the eternal queen clutched in Ubba's bloody fingers."

"What did it say?" Foste said in a deadly whisper that caused a shiver to run down Leif's spine.

"It demanded the immediate abdication of Queen Thyra and the surrender of the Alfheimian realm to Ares," Jaeger said with a growl.

"To war then," Jol said.

"Aye," Jaeger answered. "Each Skogur Borg unit has been assigned an enemy fortification to attack, and I volunteered our squad to assault their main base, hopefully forcing Ares to retreat, or, if the stars align, killing him in the ensuing chaos."

"They will burn for what they've done to our city!" Foste said, slamming her fist into the table. Jaeger lifted one perfectly manicured eyebrow at the outburst, quieting Foste. He then reviewed the Skogur Borg's attack plan. Leif had expected some elaborate scheme, but it was straightforward. He liked it. *No plan lasts longer than meeting the enemy anyway,* he mused philosophically.

"Alright," Jaeger said into the silence that followed his explanation. "You two familiarize yourself with the route we are taking. Then double and triple check your gear. When Selga returns brief her. In the meantime, I will take Leif to the quartermaster. With luck, we can piece together some unenchanted armor for him." Jaeger clapped Leif on the back.

IT TURNS out the quartermaster's storeroom and workspace were situated far underground between the roots of the Monarch. Leif had asked what the floor was called, but it proved to be too complicated of a word for him to pronounce, so he just stuck with calling it the basement. After leaving the peace and quiet of the Skogur Borg quarters, Leif and Jaeger waded through frantic Ljosalfar administrators and guards, frantically carrying out their duties.

While entering another cramped stairwell, Leif asked, "When was the last time Alfheim saw combat on such a scale?"

"Blood and destruction of this magnitude haven't sullied our great realm for hundreds of years, especially here in Karcoa, not since the Ljsoa-Dokka civil war. With the formation of the *Rao* on Vanaheimr, the realms entered a new age of relative peace. Small raids still take place from time to time, and no matter the realm, cutthroats and underground criminal organizations still plagued our civilized worlds. But with the threat of the Aesir watching, few were foolish enough to openly break the peace.

"The Aesir are the supreme authority throughout the nine realms. After defeating the Outsiders and laying claim to the nine realms. The Aesir, with their Asgardian agents, took an active role in policing the realms. As peace reigned across the realms, Odin slowly recalled his forces to Asgard, choosing to interfere only if a threat to multiple realms loomed. Once it became clear the Aesir and their warriors were gone, there was a power vacuum left at the realm level. Factions clashed across the realms, vying for control. It wasn't long before war broke out across the realms. After many bloody years, a conclave was called amongst the races on the mountainous peaks of Vanaheimr. It was during that decade-long meeting that the Rao was born. The Rao was tasked with maintaining peaceful relations and open commerce amongst the realms. Each realm would send an ambassador to Vanaheimr to sit on the council, acting as their respected voice on the Rao."

"What about Midgard?" Leif asked.

"The Rao specifically chose to not include Midgard on the council. Due to the relative weak nature of Midgardians and their short life span, it was believed Midgardians couldn't appreciate the long-term effects of the Rao's decrees."

Leif gave a little snort, and Jaeger smirked but continued.

"Even with the threat of Thor or, gods forbid, Odin descending from the heavens to dispatch those wrongdoers, each realm founded their own internal law keepers, such as the Skogur Borg. Generally, we are only dispatched to hunt down truly dangerous individuals or groups, leaving clan guards to handle the less serious infractions within their respective territories."

"Why is that?" He asked.

"The realms are a dangerous place. Many of the races can live for hundreds, if not thousands, of years. None of those beings wish to have their long life cut short. That is why so many of the realms' beings carry weapons. They know the gods aren't going to protect them from a cut purse or random attacker. However, if there are a string of attacks or an unsanctioned killing, my order will be sent on the hunt. This makes the city centers of most realms quite safe. No one wants to risk attacking someone, lest they bite off more than the attacker can chew."

"I guess that makes sense," Leif responded. "There's been

something else I have been wondering about." They reached the bottom of the staircase, entering another long corridor. Unlike the previous hallways they had walked through, the Ljosalfar that ghosted through the hall wore the dark armor of the Skogur Borg. None of them ran or appeared nervous as they went about their business. As Leif passed the stoic warriors, he noticed much of their armor was scratched or dented. He assumed they were the warriors who were out on assignment and were just called back in for the assault. "I beg your pardon for my ignorance on the matter, but from the very first day that I awoke as a Berserker, it seems like Hel and the Outsiders have mainly used Dokkalfar and Jontar to act out their dark desires. Here and there I've crossed blades with other beings of the realms, hell I was almost gutted by a pair of nymphs, but for the most part it's been Dokkalfar or Jontar. Why is that?" Leif asked.

"That is an astute observation, Leif. For the Dokkalfar, that's easy. Since their banishment from Alfheim in the aftermath of their failed civil war, the Dokkalfar leadership has sought revenge against the Ljosalfar. Specifically, they wish to retake their lost lands in the southern hemisphere of Alfheim, but with the Aesir in power, they don't have the strength to openly challenge us. Thus, an alliance between the Midnight King and Hel makes perfect sense," Jaeger said matter-of-factly.

"That brings up another question," Leif said as the pair stopped outside a reinforced steel door with the seal of the Skogur Borg embossed in the center. The door appeared to be out of place to Leif. It caused him to lose his train of thought and he stopped asking his questions.

"Welcome to the armory. Now I must warn you, Gungnir is a bit protective of her creations. Principally by virtue that she cloistered herself behind this monstrosity of a door she built." Jaeger placed a hand on the vault door. "She is different from most Ljosalfar, albeit the most gifted magical metallurgist outside of the Savartalfar," Jaeger said with a shrug.

"Oh! I remember," Leif blurted as Jaeger knocked on the vault door. "I keep hearing about the Dokkalfar being banished from Alfheim, but I've encountered several on my previous visit to Karcoa. On one occasion, it didn't even end in bloodshed, so I can't believe that they are all bad. What exactly do you mean when you say they are banished?"

"Ah, another good question. You are the first Midgardian I have met, but the stories of your kind, being dim-witted, seem to be untrue."

"Thanks," Leif said, unsure if he should be offended or not.

"Immediately after the civil war, the eternal queen banished all Dokkalfar from Alfheim. Over the millennia, those restrictions have been relaxed. Before Ares's invasion, there hadn't been any open conflicts between our cousins and us for a very long time. A Dokkalfar here or there walking the streets or acting as a bounty hunter, a chief profession for them, isn't cause for too much alarm. Don't get me wrong, many Ljosalfar are old enough to remember the war, and they still harbor a sense of hatred towards the Dokkalfar, but they don't feel it necessary to get involved if they see a Dokkalfar or two walking the cobbled streets. However, if there was a group of them seen within the city, that's another story. Skogur Borg squads often get called to investigate sightings of large numbers of Dokkalfar roaming the cities or causing trouble in Karcoa. They are immediately dealt with." Jaeger said with more than a little scorn in his voice.

Leif knew there was a story there, but he chose to ignore it. "Okay, makes sense, but what about the Jontar?" Leif asked, getting back to his original question.

"The Jontar's mindset is a little harder to decipher. Unlike most of the other races of the nine realms, the Jontar society consists of large roaming bands. There are a few large settlements, but overall, they roam the ice flats of Jontaheim, following the migration of their livestock. Much of their society is concentrated on feats of strength and martial aptitude. They don't have a central government like the other realms. Though there have been incidents, usually where there is some threat to Jontaheim or its people as a whole. When a calamity of that size occurs, Jontar chieftains will call for a conclave of clans so they can present a united front. However, from what I've heard, those meetings will often end in bloodshed between rival tribes, accomplishing nothing but blood feuds. The Jontar were even granted a seat on the *Rao*, though they rarely send a representative." Jaeger brought his thumb and forefinger to his chin in a very humanlike gesture. "I guess, given their warrior-centric mentality, Hel or the Outsiders offered them the chance to fight, to win glory for themselves and their tribe," Jaeger finished.

"Yeah, you're probably right. So then what about–" Leif began.

Before Leif could finish asking another question, Jaeger reached out and turned the handle on the heavy door, pushing it open on silent hinges.

"Leif, as much as I would like to sit down and discuss inter-realm politics with you, we have a battle to prepare for," Jaeger said, letting a hint of exasperation ooze from his voice.

"Oh, right. Sorry. It's just, the only person I had to talk about this stuff with was Arias, and he's gone." Leif said, letting the sentence drop.

"Of course. If we survive the battle, I would be glad to discuss whatever topic you would like. And, if we don't, you and Arias will have all the time in the world to talk." Jaeger said with a feral grin and a slap on the shoulder as he stepped through the hulking door.

*Well, that's a fun notion to think about,* Leif thought as he followed Jaeger into the quartermaster's chamber.

The quartermaster's space was one massive chamber, reminiscent of a factory floor. Large dancing-flame lanterns dotted the ceiling, spanning the warehouse. Depending on the whim of the living flames, dark shadowy pools filled many of the alcoves and cramped alleyways of the storeroom. Roots from the Monarch jutted from the ceiling through the floor or crisscrossed through the space, bisecting the area in several places. The smell of wet dirt and metal filled permeated the space.

Leif's eyes adjusted to the low light and noticed that several of the invasive roots acted as walls or shelves. Wooden boxes sat in neat rows on large racks, taking up much of the free space in the chamber. Along one wall, several wooden crates were stacked on each other. Ljosa runes were burned into them.

It certainly wasn't what Leif expected. For some reason, he imagined a small bare waiting room with bland white walls, uncomfortable chairs, and a plexiglass window with a small slot to pass papers through. He thought they would be greeted by a balding, overweight bureaucrat asking if the necessary documents were filed to check out items. *Hmm, maybe I've been watching too much Archer*, Leif thought. A call in Ljosa pulled Leif from his thoughts and he looked around for the source.

A slender hand appeared behind a small set of roots that ran parallel to the ground. A moment later, a shadowy figure vaulted the root and approached them. Leif immediately noticed the glowing eyes of the approaching quartermaster that marked her as a Ljsoalfar. Jaeger acknowledged the approaching figure with a raised hand. The light of the lantern found its way to a petite female Ljsoalfar with long silver hair that fell loosely below her shoulders. She wore a tattered, stained gray apron over a skintight black tunic and baggy pants. She glided forward like an Olympic figure skater, making little to no sound as she moved, a trait Leif was beginning to think all Ljosalfar possessed. Vibrant calculating eyes sized him up as she closed the distance between them. Jaeger snapped a quick salute, a closed fist over his right chest. She smirked, waving her hand in a noncommittal gesture. Confused, Leif looked to Jaeger, but the warrior remained stoic as he released the salute.

The quartermaster addressed Jaeger with an unexpectedly low and raspy voice.

Jaeger shook his head, asking, "Gungnir, how's your common tongue?"

The quartermaster raised her pale, scarred hand, waving it side to side as she said, "Not best."

"I will translate then," Jaeger said.

"Works for me," Leif responded.

What followed was a long interview between Gungnir and Leif about the limits of his abilities, his weapon preferences, magical abilities, and whether he had ever fought with armor before. Much of the conversation went smoothly, Jaeger only jumping in to clarify a point or two that was lost in translation. Leif found the quartermaster extremely hard to read. Out of all the Ljosalfar he had met, Arias was the most jovial, essentially wearing his emotions on his sleeve. Leif chalked it up to his living amongst Midgardians for so long. Jaeger and his Skogur Borg squad mates acted more militaristic, but here and there Leif caught a hint of their individual personalities. Gungnir was something different. Her face and body language conveyed nothing to him. In fact, outside of the movement of her eyes as she looked between Leif and Jaeger, she remained still as a stone. She moved so little it was hard to tell if she was even breathing; it was disconcerting. Then, abruptly, she turned and disappeared down an aisle to their left.

Leif looked at Jaeger, but the kafteinn merely gave him a don't ask me look before following the quartermaster through the warehouse. They hopped over, ducked under, and in one instance, walked through an opening cut in one particularly large root. The trio eventually stopped in a dark corner at the back end of the massive chamber. Leif desperately wanted to know what secrets were contained in the boxes they passed, but he kept his questions to himself.

This area of the chamber was cut off from the rest of the warehouse by highly decorated wooden walls and a heavy steel door. As a pool of light from a lantern above flickered over the walled off area, Leif admired the image of black armored knights locked in combat with all manner of creatures. Gungnir placed one hand on the metal door, briefly turning to look at Leif and Jaeger.

She mumbled a few words as she turned the knob to open the door. Leif felt a brief flare of magic from what he reasoned was Gungnir disarming the wards before ushering them inside.

In this new room, the inner wall held a floor-to-ceiling honeycomb of shadowed cubbies. At the very center of the room, there was a raised square dais. Three lit candles stood as watchful guardians before a partially crushed Skogur Borg helmet and broken sword. A fresh floral scent fought against the dank earthy odor that permeated the rest of the quartermaster's storeroom.

Gungnir drifted away from the pair. Stepping up to the dais, and to Leif's surprise, she performed a perfect salute, mirroring Jaeger's earlier greeting. She then turned and walked along the wall, peering into several dark alcoves as she went.

"What is this place?" Leif asked in a whisper. Speaking in his normal voice felt disrespectful, though he didn't know why.

Responding in kind, Jaeger said, "Each piece of Skogur Borg armor is specially crafted for the individual warrior that wears it. When a warrior dies in combat, so do the enchantments, returning the armor to merely hardened steel. But even so, our brothers and sisters fought and died in their armor, thus we bring the pieces we can back from the battlefield to lay them to rest here."

"Woah," Leif intoned, overcome with emotion. "But why would you grant me such a privilege?"

"It is not uncommon for squad mates or kin to incorporate one or two pieces of our fallen brethren's armor into our own. Typically, it's a smaller piece since they are unenchanted, but it is a way to honor them." Jaeger commented. His eyes were affixed to the altar at the center of the room. Leif thought he saw a glimpse of something behind the kafteinn's luminescent eyes, but then the warrior blinked and it was gone. "The queen has granted you the right to don the armor of a dauoi for two reasons: one, you have been temporarily inducted into the ranks of the Skogur Borg by volunteering to fight with us against Ares."

"Makes sense," Leif shrugged. "And the second?"

"Gungnir doesn't have time to forge a full set for you, nor are we sure you would have the magical capacity to trigger the enchantments imbued into the armor. With the battle close at hand, we lack the time to test the theory. Thus, we believe the dauoi won't have any objections to their armor being used once again in defense of the realm they gave their life to protect."

"Whats a dawy?" Leif whispered to Jaeger,

"*Dauoi,*" Jaeger said, slowly pronouncing the word. "They are the recovered armor of Skogur Borg warriors that died in combat."

"Berserker," the graveling voice of Gungnir interrupted in a harsh whisper.

The pair approached the quartermaster. As Jaeger passed by the dais, he paused. Turning quickly, he gave a crisp salute to the broken helmet and sword, paying his respects to the slain warriors of his order. Meanwhile, Leif observed that the quartermaster had pieced together a complete set of black Skogur Borg armor.

The sleek armor, even unenchanted, was a glorious sight to behold. The black metal drank in the minimal light of the room, causing Leif's vision to fuzz when he focused too long on any specific piece. Giddy with excitement, Leif kneeled to get a better look at the ensemble.

Gungnir caught Leif's eye as she mirrored his movement. She squatted to eye level with him. Locking eyes with Leif, Gungnir said, "You respect," then she stood, speaking a phrase to Jaeger.

"Try it on," Jaeger translated.

After thirty minutes and lots of translated questions, Leif finally closed the slotted visor over his head. He immediately sympathized with Anakin Skywalker in the final scene of *The Revenge of the Sith* when the iconic black armored helmet slowly lowered into place over the Sith lord's mangled visage. Anakin's eyes widened in momentary fear. Unlike Darth Vader, who depended on his armored suit to live, Leif had no such limitations.

His vision was cut by nearly fifty percent. His movements felt sluggish and ungainly. He knew if given enough time, he would adjust to the additional weight and tunnel vision, but on the eve of battle, it was suicide. Pulling the nearly fifty-pound helmet off, he took two stumbling steps as the weight of the armor momentarily pulled him off balance. "I can't wear this. I would literally be dead weight."

Letting out a hiss of frustration, Jaeger said, "I was afraid of this."

"How do you guys make this look so easy?" Leif asked, lifting a gauntleted hand.

"We have been fighting in our armor for over a century. It's magically tied to its user, so it is as light as a tunic to us." Jaeger flatly said.

"Well, that's cheating," Leif huffed. Then an idea occurred to him. During the relatively few fights he had been in, he remembered seeing some warriors wearing only a small piece or two over vital areas. So, after much experimentation, Leif found a configuration that provided him a measure of protection in his vital areas. He ended up with cuisses over his thighs, a single pauldron over his left shoulder, and two vambraces over his forearms. That was his limit. He held his arm up to admire his vambrace and said, "Thank you, these will do perfectly."

# CHAPTER 9

Leif proudly set down his newly acquired gear just as Jaeger called a meeting at the small table at the center of their squad's room.

"Tonight, we take back our city," Jaeger said with certainty. Jol, Selga, and Foste simultaneously slapped the table. "We are going to drive Ares and his ilk from our realm once and for all." Again, they slapped the table. "We are the best Skogur Borg warriors Alfheim has seen in millennia. We will be the tip of the spear that pierces Ares's black heart." Another slap of the table. "Tonight, we will battle the enemy of the nine realms, a being that believes he has the right to take whatever he wishes, merely because he is strong. But they made a grave mistake in attacking Alfheim." Another slap. "With all of you by my side, I know we will be victorious." A double slap this time. "The horn has been blown; the hunt has been called. We of the Skogur Borg will return victorious or not at all." Two slaps again. "Gear up. We move to the staging area in ten." Jaeger finished and this time, he slapped the table three times.

Leif watched as Jaeger, Jol, and Foste moved to their bunks. However, Selga stayed behind, locking eyes with him. "I wanted to apologize for my actions in the ring. You and Jol spoke the truth, but I was too deep into the battle madness to see it. I let my anger get the better of me," Selga said.

Leif chuckled, "There is no need to apologize, especially about anger issues."

Selga smiled, and it lit up her face. She was achingly beautiful. "Either way, that is no way to treat a comrade. Especially when they have shown nothing but respect. Foste mentioned you were given permission to wear our armor. Is this true?" Selga asked with a raised eyebrow.

"Yes. Though, unlike you, I was never trained to fight in armor, so I decided against sporting an entire suit. And besides, I am nowhere near as strong as the Ljosalfar. It would slow me down, then I would be nothing but a burden to your unit," he commented.

"Smart, but remember, Leif." When Selga used his name for the first time, it sent chills down his spine. He found himself briefly wondering what it would be like to date a Ljosalfar. "Strength isn't everything. You taught me that during our fight. The warrior who thinks on his feet is far more dangerous than the one who merely bashes their way through a fight. I have a feeling we will need this," Selga said as she tapped lightly on Leif's temple. "As much as this." She flexed her well-toned biceps.

*Wait,* Leif thought. *Is she flirting with me?*

"Ah, I got side-tracked," she said with another heart-stopping smile. "Since you will be fighting with us and wearing our armor, I got you these." Selga held up the same black under armor-esk garments the other Skogur Borg warriors wore under their armor.

Selga's cat eyes bore into Leif as she handed the clothes to him. Blushing slightly, Leif accepted them and thanked her. Selga smiled and excused herself to get ready. The black, long-sleeve shirt had the Skogur Borg logo sewn over the left breast. The stretchy material reminded him of the tightfitting workout shirts people wore to the gym. The pants were thicker and heavier, closer to sweatpants. Pulling off his Midgardian hiking boots, Leif put on his new combat shoes. They fit perfectly and were light as a feather, with nice cushioning and arch support.

As Leif was inspecting his new clothes, Foste ghosted next to him, causing his heart to leap into his throat. Foste wore the same form fitting outfit that Selga had just handed him. Jol pulled his shirt down over a well-muscled chest and stomach while Selga pulled out a fresh shirt and pants from a bin under her bunk. Turning his attention back to Foste, Leif couldn't help but note the Skogur Borg's outfit emphasized Foste's fitness model physique. *Damn Ljosalfar! Not only do they live for centuries, and can wield magic, but of course they are all effortlessly gorgeous as well,* Leif thought.

"That was nice of Selga," Foste said with a smile. "She is the newest member of our squad. Younger members often feel like they have something to prove and can be very, um, how do I say it in the common tongue." Foste pursed her lips and scrunched up her forehead as she searched for the word she was thinking of. "Ah! Protective of their units. The younger members never think anyone is good enough to join their squads, Selga especially. Several Skogur Borg warriors have petitioned to join our unit, but Selga has said no to all of them. You must have really made an impression on her during your fight yesterday," Foste said with a wink.

Shocked, Leif eloquently said, "Uh…"

Foste waved his response away. "We can talk about that later," she said with a smile. Foste was also strikingly beautiful, but her smile didn't send Leif's heart a flutter like Selga's did. "The shirt and pants that Selga graciously grabbed for you were specifically made to wear underneath our armor. See." Foste lifted her forearm and pointed at her wrist. Leif noticed several small metal rings sewn into the shirt. "There are small hooks on the bottom side of the armored plates. You hook them into place before locking the armored straps into place. It is an added measure to prevent the armor from sliding out of place and to keep your clothes from bunching up. On prolonged assignments, it really helps."

"Thanks," Leif said as he inspected his new shirt, only now noticing the small metal rings strategically stitched into the shirt.

"Hey, you two. That's enough idle chatter. We need to be at the staging grounds in thirty minutes. Get your armor on and let's move!" Jaeger ordered.

Foste's cat eyes dilated in excitement as she grinned and slapped Leif on the shoulder. "The hunt is about to begin," she said before turning and running to her bunk.

Leif moved his armor from the table to his temporary bunk. Fifteen minutes and more than a couple of mistakes later, Leif finished dressing in his armor. He finished by clipping his twin axes to his belt. His limbs felt slightly heavy, but not enough that he felt it would slow him down in any significant way. Ignoring the confusion from the rest of his new squad, Leif performed a few stretches, double checking that his armored frame didn't obstruct his range of motion.

Jaeger, Jol, Foste and Selga, fully armored with their straight swords sheathed over their backs, stared at him near the exit. "Time to go, Leif," Jaeger said, with an odd expression on his face. Leif wondered if Jaeger was second guessing his choice to let him join his squad.

"Yes, right. Let's do this." Leif said, feeling some heat in his cheeks.

Leif followed Jaeger and the rest of the squad through the now vacant hallways of the Monarch. It was a little eerie that just a few hours ago, the place was filled with Ljosalfar warriors, guards, and council members going about their daily duties, and now it was deathly still. He wanted to ask where everyone went, but the intense looks of concentration on his teammates' faces silenced his curiosity. He didn't want to break their pre-combat focus.

After traversing more empty halls and stairways, they exited the Monarch, stepping onto the smoke clogged streets of Karcoa. Inside the Monarch, everything was calm, but it was another story on the ground. The roar of the forest fire could be heard all the way from the outskirts. Smoke hung heavy in the air, causing Leif to cough every time he inhaled. The smoky veil only allowed him to see twenty to thirty feet in front of him. All around him were the frightened citizens of Karcoa, seeking sanctuary.

Surveying the crowd, Leif observed that many were injured, either from the initial attack or the chaos afterward. Everyone was coated in soot that rained from the out-of-control fire. The squad moved along the ornately cobblestoned streets through the huddled mass of civilians. The citizens watched the warriors, and expressions of hope transformed their grim-encrusted faces. Through it all, no one spoke. At the very edge of the square, spear wielding sentries were posted in a loose formation every twenty feet, ready to protect the scared Karcoans should Ares attempt to strike the Monarch.

Leif's throat burned from the smoke inhalation. As they passed the relative safety of the inner city, the landscape took on a nightmarish atmosphere. The squad hurried to the staging area. The massive fires raged, carpeting the city in smoke and blocking out the sunlight that attempted to pierce the canopy above. The smoke combined with the falling ash, emitting a post-apocalyptic vibe. Leif wouldn't have been surprised if a horde of zombies shambled from around a shadowed corner. *Wait a minute. ARE ZOMBIES REAL!* He mentally shouted. He had fought along and against Draugr, long-dead warriors, whose bodies were so decomposed only bones remained... *If they are real, why wouldn't flesh eating Zombies exist too?* He desperately wanted to ask one of his squad mates about it, but one look at their determined faces warned him not to.

As the band of warriors traveled further from the royal district, Ljosalfar clan guards in green armor were posted in key intersections. Leif remembered seeing a female Ljosalfar in green robes in the war council. It was reminiscent of a Sori in cut and style. The armor they wore was well made, but still paled in comparison to the work of art Gunginr forged. Each time Leif and the squad crossed paths with the clan guards, they saluted and offered words of encouragement in Ljosa; at least, that is what Leif assumed.

After walking another ten minutes, Leif heard the din of conversation over the ever-present roar of the fire. A few moments later, the group rounded a large tree and stepped into a clearing half the size of a football field. Even with the absence of the gigantic elktre, large car sized branches crisscrossed the canopy, blotting out any fading light from the Alfheim sunset that could break through the smoke. Hundreds of colorful lanterns hung from the mammoth sized branches. Leif remembered this was the spot Arias had told him about during their first trip to Karcoa. He was mesmerized by the phenomenon before him. Acorn shaped lanterns hung in brightly colored sections, creating a rainbow of light. Each section shone brightly in its designated color. If it had been under different circumstances, he would have pulled up a chair with a pint of Savartalfar ale and enjoyed staring at the cascading colors. Sadly, this was not the time. *Once the realms are safe, I will come back and toast those I've lost along the way,* he vowed.

At each checkpoint, younger looking Skogur Borg warriors looked at Leif with a mixture of shock, confusion, and in a few cases outright hostility. None were brave enough to call him out, especially while he was in the company of Kafteinn Jaeger and his squad.

While passing into the innermost section, Leif observed several clusters of Skogur Borg warriors, checking their gear and huddling in hushed conversations. At the center of the area, three Ljosalfar kafteinns in their signature gleaming black armor were in a deep discussion at a round table. From Leif's guess, there must have been close to fifty Skogur Borg warriors assembled.

Jaeger instructed the squad to recheck their gear and for Jol to double check Leif's armor as he jogged to the kafteinns' table, joining the discussion. Turning to Selga, Leif asked, "How does the command structure work in the Skogur Borg? Because, so far, I've only seen those four kafteinns, but looking around, there are clearly more squads than kafteinns. So, who oversees those units? And the guards along the perimeter? Are there other kafteinns that aren't present? If not, who leads all the other units?"

"Ah, observant, as well as a good fighter," Selga said with a crooked smile. "If you had been born Ljosalfar, you would have made a great Skogur Borg warrior."

Leif's stomach fluttered as he straightened his back and smiled.

Selga cleared her throat and looked down at her feet. "The eternal queen is the head of our order. She has many duties as this realm's monarch, so she has authorized the kafteinns to work as her chief commanders." Jerking her head toward the table, she continued, "Those four are the highest ranked members of the Skogur Borg. They oversee the disposition of squad members, training, admissions, and hand out missions. On top of their administrative duties, each Kafteinn commands their own squads made up of huskral and lagr."

"Made up of what?" Leif asked, interrupting Selga.

Chuckling, Selga pointed to herself, Foste, Jol, and then at the rest of the warriors arrayed in the clearing. "We are all huskral. That is the designated rank just below kafteinn. We are essentially squad leaders, but before we can be given our own squad of lagr, all the huskral must train with a kafteinn squad for a period of five years, or when our kafteinns deem us ready to lead a squad of lagr."

"Oh, so you guys are all extra badass then?" Leif said with a smile.

"Badass?" Selga asked with a raised eyebrow.

"Never mind," Leif said, shrugging. He looked into Selga's eyes and felt his heartbeat increase. He pointed to the guards manning the checkpoints. "What rank are they?"

"Lagr," Selga said with a smile. "They are the newest members of the Skogur Borg. They are still in training or haven't been picked up by a squad yet." She gestured to the milling crowd of black clad knights. "Outside of the four squads lead by the kafteinns, all the other units are made up of one huskral and three to four lagr."

Just then, someone called out in Ljosa behind Leif. Everyone in the clearing stopped what they were doing, looking toward the voice. A nervous energy suffused the area. Selga shifted from foot to foot. Foste cracked her neck and then her knuckles, while Jol opened and closed his gauntleted fists. Leif watched the other warriors display similar acts of fitfulness as everyone closed in on the four kafteinns.

A tall blond kafteinn spoke in a loud, confident baritone. He had a scar that ran from his left eyebrow to his chin, disappearing beneath his armor. Leif, unfortunately, didn't understand a thing he was saying. Looking at Jol, he raised a questioning eyebrow. At first, Jol didn't understand, but then Leif pointed to his ear and shrugged his shoulders. Comprehension lit Jol's eyes, and he leaned in to translate for him.

"Who is he?" Leif asked

"That's Rollo. He is a fellow kafteinn, same as Jaeger."

Leif noticed a few of the Ljosalfar standing near them turned their heads to glare at him, but no one said anything.

Rollo kept speaking, and Jol translated. "He says 'The hour is upon us. Not since the Ljosa-Dokka war has an enemy such as this set foot within our borders. Nor have they had the audacity to set fire to our sacred elktre. At the conclusion of the civil war, our blessed queen founded the Skogur Borg order. It is our duty to act as both the sword and shield for the citizens of Alfheim. The very life of our realm is under attack, and we will ride out to meet that threat. The horn has been blown; our prey is within sight. We shall go forth to hunt those who would do harm to our people. We will wash over the enemy as a great dark tide. We must make an example of these invaders. Our victory must be swift, brutal, and leave no doubt of what the fate will be for any who dare repeat such a heinous crime against our realm.'"

Leif watched as Jaeger turned away from Rollo, lifting an old wooden chest with red carvings inscribed along the seams. He placed it on the table. Then, as gingerly as possible, Jaeger unlatched two gold buckles on each side of the chest and slowly opened the top. The kafteinn's eyes lit up with awe as he pulled out a three-foot-long horn carved from the antler of some large beast. Jaeger lifted the horn to his lips and paused.

Leif pulled his attention back to Jol's translation of Rollo's speech. "Go! Reclaim our great city! When it is all done, we shall toast to our victory, whether it be here or in the great halls of Valhalla!" Then Jaeger blew the horn.

Leif was ashamed to admit it, but he alone slammed his hands over his ears when Jaeger sounded the call. It was like someone walked up beside him and blew a foghorn in his ear. He had no doubt the entire city heard the resounding call.

After a long minute, Jaeger lowered the horn, and as if that was the cue, everyone in the crowd fastened their helmets over their head, formed up with their squads, and sprinted away, disappearing on silent feet into the gloom.

The echo of the damnable horn continued to reverberate inside of his skull, and Leif felt the pre-battle jitters disperse. They were replaced with the thrill of the upcoming fight. He turned to follow his new comrades, swearing to himself he would not be the cause of their deaths, like Bargog or Arias. As if in response to his vow, he felt the brief flare of the Berserker within affirming his oath.

# CHAPTER 10

The multi-pronged counterattack began at moonrise. An errant thought pierced Leif's consciousness. During none of his adventures, had he come across a clock or time keeping device. On Alfheim, they seemed to rely on the position of the sun and the moon. But what about the Savartalfars and their underground cities? *Surely, they would have developed some alternative version,* Leif mused.

Once all Skogur Borg squads moved away from the staging area, the black clad knights silently melted into the shadows, disappearing without uttering a single word. It took every ounce of concentration for Leif, who was making up the rear of his squad's battle formation, to keep pace with the others. Confusing matters further were the complicated hand signs the squad used to communicate.

A flair of annoyance washed through Leif as the group huddled against the trunk of an abandoned elktre. Their hands flashed in the light from dozens of small fires dotting the area. *Keep your cool, Leif,* he said to himself as he took a deep breath. He hoped to banish the frustration that was building. He wasn't here to gain intelligence on Ares or even to retake Karcoa like the rest of the Skogur Borg. He was there to get stronger and ask about possible Berserker sightings. So, he remained silent.

Once the squad left the protected portion of Karcoa, the scenery drastically changed. What was once a lush, tranquil and bustling city had been transformed into the aftermath of a Michael Bay movie. The heat was oppressive and grew hotter the further they traveled. The energetic shops that he had gawked at were now a smoking ruin. An ever-thicker film of ash coated the Karcoan floor while smoke poured from the upper tiers and walkways that lined the city. Occasionally, a gust of wind would blow across the street, scalding Leif's throat with flame-tinged air. Under the wall of toxic fumes, Leif caught ghastly sights of Karcoan civilians cut down during the initial attacks. In the past, he would have looked away, wanting to curl up in a ball with despair in his heart, but not now. He knew he was partly responsible for all this carnage. If he had only stopped Hel and prevented Fenrir's release, the Outsiders may have never attacked. He used the rage at these gruesome sights to bolster his resolve. Just like Bargog and Arias, he had been too weak to protect these innocent souls. But that would change. He would prove he was strong enough to stand by Thor's side and make these monsters pay. He was no longer just a Midgardian with a Berserker locked away. Instead, he was Leif the Berserker. Soon the Outsiders would know his wrath. With his resolve solidified, he turned from those that had been lost to silently catch up with Jaeger's squad.

Jaeger held up a balled fist, stopping the squad. Everyone ducked, crouching low. Leif crouched a second later. He watched as Jaeger pointed with his left hand into the trees, then made a walking gesture with his left hand on his right palm, followed by holding up two fingers. Leif was no expert in military hand signals, but he felt the meaning was clear as he peered into the trees. At first, he didn't see anything, but as the wind shifted, clearing the excessive smoke from the area, he could see two Dokkalfar warriors hiding in the shadows like watchful gargoyles.

Neither sentry had sounded the alarm; his party hadn't been spotted. Jol and Foste made simultaneous, curt slicing motions with their right hands before moving to the front of the group. Meanwhile, Selga looked down. Her hands roved over the forest floor in search of some unknown object. A moment later she stood, hefting a softball sized rock in her hand. She tossed it and caught it, testing the weight. Then she signaled she was ready. The three other Skogur Borg nodded. Jol and Foste both held up a gauntleted forearm and pulled a thin blade the same color as their obsidian armor from hidden sheaths. Leif watched as Selga whip-cracked her arm forward, hurtling the rock like a meteor into the tree to the left of the Dokkalfar sentries. The thwack caused both Dokkalfar to rise, draw, and loose arrows from their recurved bows. Their movements were silent and sudden. The two arrows streaked through the air, glowing an odd purplish light, striking precisely where the rock had landed. If someone had been there, they would have sprouted extra holes and suffered from whatever that purplish light did. The moment the Dokkalfar had stepped from cover to attack, Foste and Jol launched their counterattack, flinging their knives with such force that Leif, even with his enhanced senses, couldn't follow their trajectory. A fraction of a second later, a muffled gurgling sound met their ears. Leif watched a dying Dokkalfar stumble forward to slip off the edge of the branch, plummeting to the forest floor with a sickening crunch. He expected to hear a second impact a moment later, but when it didn't come, he grew alarmed. But a quick check by Jeager confirmed the second Dokkalfar lay dead, slumped against the trunk of the tree.

Before anyone moved, Jaeger held up a balled fist, signaling them to remain still. Seconds turned to minutes, but no one came to investigate the unnatural sounds of the Dokkalfar's deaths. Once Jaeger was satisfied that no one was coming, he released his fist, motioning the squad forward. On silent feet, they crept along the cobblestones toward the dead sentry. The Dokkalfar was covered in black cloth from head to toe, looking a lot like a ninja on Midgard. The dead warrior was armed with a short blade slung over one shoulder and a small quiver of arrows tied to his belt. Selga pulled an arrow from the quiver to inspect it. She pointed to the arrowhead. "There are runes etched into the arrowhead on each side. They must be the source of the magical flare."

"What exactly do the etchings do?" Leif asked, eyeing the trees nervously.

"I don't know," Selga said with a shrug. "I've never seen magic like this before. It's entirely possible this is a new form of advanced Dokkalfar battle magic, but I honestly don't know."

"How is magic different between your people and the Dokkalfar?" Leif asked.

"SSSHHH," Jaeger hissed. "This isn't the time for a magic lesson! It is most likely of Outsider design. As you should know, Leif, the Aesir and Outsiders can wield power, magic, whatever you want to call it, on a scale we can't even comprehend. Selga, hide the bodies. We can investigate the arrows *after* we've reclaimed our city."

Selga returned the arrow to the quiver while Jol retrieved his knife. Together they dumped the two corpses in a burned-out husk of an elktre, throwing them in a shadowed corner filled with debris. With the dirty work done, they melted back into the shadows, continuing toward their target. The squad came across two more hidden sentries, and the squad dispatched them with the same quiet efficiency as professional killers as before. It was only after slitting the throat of a lone Dokkalfar, who had stepped into the shadows to relieve herself, that the squad set their sights on their objective.

Peering around the tree, Leif had a direct view of Ares's encampment. In the short time the Outsider had been there, Ares had built a crude defensive wall, using materials from the surrounding forest. Due to the numerous irregular sized objects used in the barrier, there were several gaps that permitted Leif to see directly into the area. At one side of the camp, several pillaged wooden tables were positioned with all manner of junk arrayed upon them. A large bonfire encased what looked like a large piece of meat on a spit. The roast filled the air with a mouthwatering aroma that was a welcome change from burned wood and ash. Nestled against the back wall of the compound, Ares's blood red pavilion was aglow from within by what had to be several lanterns.

Four Jontar warriors could be seen within Ares's command center. One stood guard at a little opening in the fence. One walked the parameter of the fence, while the final two stood just outside Ares's tent. For now, all eyes were glued to the two sentries at the tent.

Two gagged and bound Ljosalfar lay at the foot of the pavilion's open flap. One Ljosalfar wore fine sky-blue robes that reminded Leif of the war council meeting he had inadvertently attended. The other prisoner appeared to be a clan guard. The bound warrior's armor was dented in several places, showing he didn't go down without a fight. Leif couldn't be sure because of how far he was, but he thought he could see dried blood plastered all over both prisoners.

Each Jontar looked to be eight to nine feet tall. Their cobalt skin was filled with muscles that would make the mountain from *The Game of Thrones* jealous. None of them wore armor; instead, they were clad in a leather loincloth. Animal bones, leather pouches, and belt knives hung from the ice giants' leather belts and bandoliers. Each Jontar had a single tattoo inked over their right breast of a large crimson circle with a spear piercing through the bloody circle.

This was the first time Leif had laid eyes on a Jontar since Arias's murder. The mere sight of the blue giants brought back fiery flashes of the burned Savartalfar village. Without realizing it, he had drawn both his axes, squeezing the grips so tight his knuckles popped. He felt a feral growl rip through his chest as he subconsciously pulled on the Berserker to aid him in a suicidal charge. The mission, Hel, and finding more of his kind, dissolved as his desire to avenge Arias took hold.

Some preternatural warning must have alerted his companions, because four sets of glowing eyes locked onto Leif's. He acknowledged their stares but was slowly passing the point of caring what they thought. Only killing each of the Jontar in front of him would sate the bloodlust that was calling to him. He continued to draw on the Berserker, feeling the cool fire of its power lending him the strength he would need to vanquish his foes.

Suddenly, a gauntleted hand sailed out of the darkness to smack him across the face. It was the combined might of Leif's iron will and shock that stopped him from attacking his assailant. "Control yourself, Berserker," Jaeger hissed at him. *How the hell had he snuck up on me?* Leif thought as he rubbed his throbbing cheek.

"Sorry," he said, feeling chastised. "Jontar killed Arias. I haven't forgiven myself for letting him die. When I saw them, my vision went red, and all I could think about was getting revenge." Leif said in a gruff tone, gritting his teeth.

"Death on the battlefield is expected of a warrior. Don't sully your friend's death by dying on some foolhardy attack. All you will accomplish is getting yourself and most likely my squad killed in the process," Jaeger said. Leif gingerly touched his cheek where Jaeger slapped him, working his jaw as he flinched at the warrior's words.

*He's right,* Leif thought. *I swore I wouldn't be the cause of my comrade's death, and here I was about to get them all killed by my selfishness. I must be smart and work as a unit with Jaeger's team.* His face hot with embarrassment, Leif closed his eyes and took a deep breath before exhaling. Resolve took hold as he looked at Jaeger, signaling he was back in control.

Nodding in acknowledgment, Jaeger returned to his place in the lead. Everyone resumed studying the enemy's encampment.

A shadow moved within the command tents, drawing Leif's attention away from the Jontar. A moment later, a figure in bronze armor stepped from the tent, casually stepping over to the bound prisoners. The newcomer's armor reminded him of Brad Pitt's character, Achilles, in the movie *Troy*, but with a few differences. The breastplate was designed to look like a well-muscled man's torso. Underneath, he wore a dark red, skintight, long-sleeve shirt that contrasted with the bronze armor. His thick forearms were protected by large bronze gauntlets. He wore tan pants with bronze plated armor over his thighs and shins. A naked gladius hung from his waist. The armored figure had a full black mustache and beard that jutted down from his chin, ending in a well-oiled point. Curly black hair hung in ringlets to the god's shoulders. Thick, prominent eyebrows shaded his brightly glowing orange eyes that mirrored Ra's.

*I wonder if their different eye color has something to do with being away from the Nine Realms,* Leif thought. *The Aesir and Outsiders are all brothers and sisters. But why the different eye color? One of life's great mysteries,* he thought with a mental sigh.

Stopping in front of his two hostages, Ares's deep voice rang out like the revving of a Harley Davidson. Leif had to give the robed Ljosalfar credit. He neither cowered nor flinched from the imposing god. With calm determination, he stared the war god directly into his unnerving eyes.

Leif shuffled closer to Foste and whispered, "What are they talking about?"

"It's a little hard to hear from this distance, but it sounds like Ares wants to know why the queen hasn't surrendered the city yet."

Apparently displeased with what he heard, the Outsider unlimbered his sword and with one mighty swing; he decapitated both captives. Their bodies briefly fountained blood before collapsing to the ground. Ares gave the dead a contemptuous snort before disappearing into his tent. All four Skogur Borg went ridged as they witnessed the casual execution of their comrades. The hairs on the back of Leif's neck stood on end. Seconds passed before Jaeger held up a fist, with a single finger raised, drawing everyone's attention to him. The Kafteinn made a circular gesture with his index finger. Leif, not knowing what the signals meant, waited for the others to respond and he followed suit.

Stepping away from their vantage point, the group retraced their steps back a hundred feet from the enemy's stronghold. Believing they were far enough away not to be overheard, the squad huddled and lifted their visors. "We have four Jontar and Ares to deal with. Easy. We can be done with them and back to the Monarch by morning for a hardy breakfast and a good ale." Jol joked.

"Any ideas on how we should proceed?" Jaeger asked.

"If it was just the Jontar or Ares, we could overwhelm them, but right now, the numbers are too even. We need some way to trim their numbers down," Jol said, emphasizing his point by smacking his gauntleted fist into his palm.

"I think I've got a plan that might give us an edge," Selga said, eyeing the group then the surrounding elktre.

# CHAPTER 11

The squad took their time dissecting the proposal, running several scenarios, and playing the 'what if' game with each one. Leif was fascinated as he watched these battle-hardened warriors' war game the upcoming attack. It was only after discussing several potential outcomes that the group felt they had a plan of attack. The plan was simple; each warrior added their unique skill set to the scheme.

Once each of Leif's companions had their role in the ambush ironed out, Jaeger clapped each of his team members, Leif included, on the shoulder. He then dismissed them with a quick nod. All but Leif slid their visors back in place on silent hinges and disappeared into the shadows that flickered in the firelight. With the rest of his team moving into position, Leif slinked back to the bend in the road that led to the Outsider's encampment. Using the calm before the storm, he scanned the area, double checking that all their targets were still in view.

The problem with fighting against Jontar, and especially Outsiders, is their immense strength. None of the others had ever fought an Outsider, but they knew the danger of going up against a being of such power. Adding the Jontar into the mix could potentially be disastrous. The giants' ability to soak up damage and keep going makes each giant the equal of two armored warriors at a minimum. If Ares had chosen to surround himself with Dokkalfar, Leif would have been confident the squad could bull their way into the camp and dispatch their wayward cousins before Ares even exited his tent. But that's not the case with Jontar. Each member of the Skogur Borg is a weapons master, but that still doesn't guarantee they will prevail in a one-on-one duel with those blue tanks. Then there's Ares.

"Hopefully, with his Jontar honor guard dead, the odds will shift in our favor, causing Ares to retreat," Selga said as she detailed her plan to the squad.

Leif's simmering hatred toward his enemy burned anew. *Hold strong Leif. Just a little longer, and the fury I hold will be unleashed upon my enemies, like Mount St. Helens erupting all over again.* Leif used his rage to prepare himself for the upcoming battle.

Four quick bird calls chirped from the canopy, causing Leif to smile as he unhooked his axes and slowly released the mental hold on the Berserker. The slow burn of its power coursed through his veins. With the help of meditation, he learned to control his change and slowly release the power, letting him retain more control of his impulses.

Seconds trickled by as Leif continued to mentally visualize himself slowly turning a waterspout, increasing the flow of power until he was filled to the brim. The typical red haze colored his vision as the dam he had built to restrain the Berserker cracked. A supernova of fury flowed through him, screaming to be released upon his enemies. He held the impulse at bay, crouching in the shadows. He watched his quarry like a stalking jungle cat. Fortunately, the signal echoed through the area. Leif burst into motion.

Bellowing his war cry, Leif erupted from cover. The world blurred around him as he sprinted toward his target. Zeroing in on Leif, the arrogant Jontar snorted in derision as he raised his oversized war ax into a guard position. Leif was unperturbed. Once he came within ten feet of the brute, three black blades streaked out from the branches like hungry hawks diving for prey. Two of the knives found their target, slicing deep into the Jontar's chest, with the last sailing past the Jontar's bald head, scoring a thin line across the giant's temple and lodging itself into the cobblestones in a shower of sparks.

The plan was set up for contingencies such as this. Leaping toward the Jontar, Leif smashed his twin axes into his foe's corded neck. With two knives in his chest and axes in his neck, the giant still refused to fall, but Leif wasn't done. Pulling his axes free in a spray of purple blood, Leif head butted the Jontar, then brought his axe down on the crown of the giant's head with as much force as he could muster, splitting his enemy's skull open like a ripe cantaloupe. Only then did the Jontar falter, taking a single step backward before toppling to the forest floor in a pool of its own blood.

The clearing went deathly silent as three sets of blood-red eyes zeroed in on Leif. Cracking a manic grin, Leif watched four dark figures swoop from the large, branched walkways like the Caped Crusader himself. Their midnight blades drank in the firelight. Judging by their slender armor, Leif guessed Foste and Selga targeted the same Jontar, while Jol and Jaeger each had their own.

Foste and Selga slammed feet first into the back of their unsuspecting target. All three went down in a tumble of black armor and blue flesh. Alerted to the threat of attack, the two remaining Jontar raised their mammoth swords at the last second. Sparks bloomed in the firelight as steel met steel.

With Leif's target dead, his role was to act as support, moving in for killing or distracting blows while the more skilled Skogur Borg dueled their opponents. They had hoped to dispatch one or two in the surprise attack, shifting the odds in their favor early, but sadly, no plan survives meeting the enemy.

Unaccustomed to fighting in a team, Leif froze, unsure who to help. He looked at Jaeger and Jol. The two Skogur Borg warriors dueled their respective Jontar to what he felt was a standstill. He wanted to help, but the combatants were unleashing a flurry of strikes relatively close to each other, and Leif feared if he moved to help, he may accidentally obstruct one of their attacks or, gods forbid, get hit by an errant slash. Looking to Selga and Foste, the three combatants remained on the floor, grappling for control. He wanted to scream in frustration, but then the decision was made for him. While he watched Selga and Foste maneuvering for a submission hold, the giant momentarily freed his right arm from the press of attack, and with a mighty thrust of his palm, he launched the Skogur Borg, straddling his chest five feet into the air.

Now the Jontar had only one opponent to contend with. The Ljosalfar knight pulled the giant's right arm out in a textbook arm bar. But in a show of incredible strength, the Jontar bellowed his defiance as he lifted the knight up off the ground and brutally slammed her back down. There was a loud crunch as enchanted metal gave way under the power of the giant. A muted scream of pain escaped from the armored figure before she went limp, releasing her hold of the Jontar's arm.

"NO!" Leif screamed. *Not again,* he cried. Blurring forward, Leif was beside the Jontar in an instant, bringing down his axes even before he was in position. The Jontar was clearly a veteran. His red eyes displayed contempt as he snatched up his double-bladed axe from where it had fallen, bringing it up to block. The echo of metal on metal clanged through the clearing, causing Leif's hands to go numb.

Leif struggled to regain the feeling in his hands. The Jontar kicked out, hitting him square in the chest, laughing. The combination of a boot to the chest and his breakneck impact with the cobblestone street deflated his lungs in a painful OOAF! Gasping for breath, Leif used his axes to regain his footing, but the Jontar had moved in to loom over the crumbled body of the downed knight. His axe descended for a killing blow. Time slowed as Leif's vision telescoped, knowing he would be too late. He ran anyway.

A bright burst of sparks caused Leif to cry out, assuming he was too late. He was wrong. A thin Ljosa blade had materialized above the unconscious warrior, stopping the Jontar's ax in its tracks. The warrior who had been thrown earlier had recovered and was back in the fight. Reorienting himself, Leif moved in to attack the Jontar from his unprotected side.

Just as Leif engaged, a cry from behind him drew him up short. "LEIF!" a breathless voice called out. The command in Jaeger's voice was clear. Turning toward the call, he spotted Jaeger and Jol, still in heated combat with their respective opponents. Though it had been less than five minutes since the assault began, the fenced in area of Ares's camp looked like it had been hit by a hurricane.

The tables set out near Ares's command tent were shattered. Ares's pavilion had collapsed, temporarily trapping Ares. In moments, the war god would be free, once again changing the dynamics of the fight. Again, Leif found Jol and Jaeger, and he was momentarily mesmerized by the skill on display. One hardly gets a chance to watch a master in their prime. It was like seeing Monet paint *The Water Lily Pond*. Each stroke was neither fast nor slow, but perfectly timed. There was no wasted movement as they flowed between attack and defense. Leif theorized the only reason his friends had yet to cut their opponents to shreds was due to the Jontar's unrelenting determination. Jaeger and Jol were battered in numerous spots, but Leif couldn't see any blood coming from them. Meanwhile, the Jontar was bleeding from several sword wounds, but the blue giant showed no signs of slowing.

If Leif had a bucket of popcorn, he would have sat and watched the duels, but a crash behind him pulled him from his stupor. The Jontar he had briefly fought was now engaged with either Selga or Foste. The Skogur Borg warrior was limping and favoring her right leg. Shaking himself out of his daze, Leif moved into aid his wounded squad mate.

"No!" Selga shouted between grunts of pain. "You have to hold off Ares, or all will be lost!"

"But you're injured; I can help!" Leif shouted in frustration.

"Go! I am not someone to be coddled. I am a huskral of the Skogur Borg. This isn't the first time I've been injured in battle. If you don't hold off Ares until we defeat our opponents, then this will all have been for naught," Selga hissed as she dodged away from an axe swing meant to sweep her legs out from under her.

"AHHH!" Leif screamed in frustration. He knew Selga was right, but his mind protested, turning his back on an injured companion. Just then, a shout of triumph came from Ares as he cut the final tent piece away from his body. He watched Ares, the god of war on Midgard, survey the battlefield and carnage in front of him. The manic grin of a man who relishes combat spread across the god's face. He targeted Jaeger's unguarded back. Leif realized Ares's strategy for winning the battle was to cut down the enemy's commanding officer.

To Leif's surprise, Ares didn't rush forward or throw his sword to impale Jaeger. He merely stood there, smiling, eyes drunk with battle lust. The flames surrounding the encampment matched the burning orange eyes of the god as he slowly stalked Jaeger's unprotected back.

*Time to slay a god,* Leif thought, and he rushed forward.

# CHAPTER 12

D rawing on the Berserker, Leif charged across the clearing. Casually, Ares raised his gladius overhead. Even with the enchanted armor Jaeger wore, he knew the god's sword would cut through it like paper mâché. When Ares's blade reached its zenith, his eyes widened with excitement at the coming bloodshed. Watching the short sword descend towards his friend's back, Leif leaped. Like a human battering ram, he collided into Ares's torso.

Pain blossomed across Leif's head and neck upon impact.

Leif had hoped to bowl the god over, but all he did was push Ares off balance a smidgeon. Luckily for Jaeger, Leif's foolhardy plan paid off. Ares stumbled enough that his attack was thrown off course, causing his sword to veer off target. Instead of hitting Jaeger, it sliced the outstretched arm of the Jontar Jaeger was dueling. With ears ringing, Leif crashed down just as a well-muscled blue forearm, sword still in hand, made a wet thwacking sound next to him. The severed limb coated Leif in dark purplish gore for the second time that night.

Leif's vision was laced with stars as he lay on the ground. Shaking his head did not clear his vision. Instead, it fuzzed his surroundings and made his stomach roil. *Ugh, that asshole is built like a brick wall. I think he gave me a concussion.* Thankfully, his vision slowly cleared as his accelerated healing released the pressure in his jumbled brain. With the concussion dealt with, the high-pitched whine in his ears changed into a rhythmic clang, clang, clang of steel on steel from somewhere close.

"LEIF!" someone called from far away.

CLANG, CLANG, CLANG

"LEIF! SNAP OUT OF IT! I NEED YOUR HELP!" The voice was a little closer now.

CLANG. CLANG. OOAHFF. CLANG. CLANG.

"LEIF! GET YOUR MIDGARDIAN ASS IN THE FIGHT!"

This time, Leif registered the screaming voice as Jaeger's, and he wasn't miles away, but right behind him, fending off Ares. Leif knew from just a glance that the god was merely toying with him. It was like a kitten excitedly batting around a mouse; he was having too much fun to kill his prey just yet.

Leif knew he needed to do something quick, but he feared even berserked the two of them wouldn't be enough to best the warrior god. Jol was still locked in combat and was no use to them. Then his eyes fell on the fallen sword still clutched in the Jontar's severed hand, and an idea occurred to him. Snatching up the fallen blade, he painfully turned away from Ares and Jaeger. He would have to trust Jaeger was skilled enough to hold out for just a little longer.

Leif left nothing to chance as he picked up speed, running with the stolen sword held out. The weapon was so long in his Midgardian hands that if he had been riding a horse, it would have looked like he was jousting. Channeling Heath Ledger in a *Knights Tale*, Leif kept his eye on the target, slamming the point of his blade square into the Jontar's back, severing his spine. He didn't stop there. He kept running, pushing the five-foot-long bar of steel through the Jontar's back and out his chest to the hilt. The impaled Jontar eerily made no sound as it died. In an instant, he was on the floor, dead. Jol, who hadn't seen Leif coming, shouted in surprise, jumping backwards when the blade suddenly burst forth from the Jontar's chest, like the Xenomorph in Alien.

Without missing a beat, Jol scanned the battlefield, sizing up their next move. Slapping Leif on his unarmored shoulder, he said, "Go help Jaeger. I will aid Selga."

As Leif engaged the next target, he looked upon his fallen foe. A feeling of pure animalistic joy welled up inside of him. The wound of Arias's death will never heal, but the death of two Jontars at his hand sent a savage pride coursing through his veins. The sound of battle then a cry of pain pulled Leif back to the present, and he cursed himself for losing focus. Breathing deep, he attacked.

Leif appreciated the foresight of the Skogur Borg's sparring rings. The area that Ares and Jaeger battled in was a muddled mess of debris. A shredded tent, gallons of purplish Jontar blood, and jagged table pieces lay everywhere. Getting to the fight was a perilous journey. Leif lost his footing on more than one occasion, nearly stabbing himself with a sharp table shard as his foot slipped in blood.

Once clear of the wreckage, Leif flanked Ares, looking for his opportunity to join the fray. Jaeger seamlessly adjusted to Leif's arrival. Diving out of the way, Jaeger attacked Ares's flank, making room for Leif. Sparks spewed from their weapons as Ares met Leif head on. An arrogant smile was on his face as he effortlessly blocked his onslaught. Leif was a hurricane of rage as he attacked, sending a complex series of axe slices at the god of war. But no matter what he tried, Ares's blade was there, blocking or diverting his axes off course. Suddenly, Ares changed tactics, stepping closer to Leif, and he punched him hard across the face. The force of the godly strike rocked Leif backward, causing his vision to momentarily blacken when his head smacked into the cobblestone street. Groaning, Leif pushed himself back up, shaking his head. *What the hell just happened?*

Ares's face split in a psychotic-grin, and he chuckled, "The pet Midgardian." He sounded like a pack-a-day smoker. "Hel told me about you. I guess this means Ra and Fenrir failed. From that childish display just now, I can't believe you bested those two," Ares queried. "No, not possible. Which means you had help. No doubt my brother lent you aid. So odd of Odin. What is his interest in you, mortal?" Ares's eyes narrowed at him. "No matter. I shall present your skull as a parting gift to him. If whoever saved you also managed to kill Ra or Fenrir in the process, they may have presented me with a wonderful opportunity to ascend the ranks." While Ares spoke, he gently tapped the flat of his blade against his head. The god of war acted as if he didn't have a care in the world. The Outsiders were a millennium old. He probably viewed Leif and the Skogur Borg as if they were ants to be crushed under his boot. A notion Leif hoped to rob him of.

Thankfully, as Ares taunted, reinforcements finally arrived. The armored figures of Jaeger, Jol, and Selga stepped to either side of him. *Where's Foste?* Risking a glance over his shoulder, Leif spied her prone, unmoving form at the edge of the battlefield. The body of her attacker lay a few feet from her. A thick pool of blood slowly spread from underneath the fallen giant.

Ares was positively vibrating with excitement. He slowly met the eyes of each of the warriors. "Ah, it's about time." Ares brought his blade down into a low guard. "I had hoped that one over there..." pointing with his sword to Foste's still form, "would have recovered enough to join the fight. Alas, it wasn't meant to be. It has been ages since I had a proper duel. Please don't disappoint. It would be a shame to burn the entire realm without at least one memorable fight."

Leif was dumbfounded. *Ares in some cultures was the god of war, but he can't seriously think he is strong enough to fight all four of us at once, right? I mean, I fought Hel, and she wasn't THAT good. If Arias had been with me, we could have taken her. This guy's crazy,* Leif thought.

Moving on an unspoken cue, Jaeger, Jol, and Selga boxed in Ares. Ares merely watched, letting himself be surrounded. *Ok, this dude has either gone crazy with old age... OR he really is that strong and we are all dead.*

"Time for some fun," Ares whispered as he became a blur of bronzed armor and hardened steel.

Leif braced himself, thinking he would be the focus of Ares's first attack, but he was wrong. The canny god juked right, causing Leif and Selga to shift to a defense, raising their weapons to block. But it was for nothing. Jol was Ares's target. The grizzled warrior brought his blade up just in time to block the first slash, but as if by magic, the moment their blades met it vanished. It reappeared for a second, then a third slash. It was as if Ares's blade was everywhere at once. The speed and ferocity of Ares's opening salvo caught everyone but Jol flat footed. The sparks of Jol's desperate blocks pulled everyone back into the fight. As Ares's blade blurred back in for its fourth impossibly fast attack, Jaeger lunged with the black blade gleaming in the firelight. Selga followed suit, aiming low. With little area left to choose from, Leif aimed a cut for Ares mid-section.

With no possible way to successfully block all four blades careening toward him, Ares jumped, summersaulting over the wall of blades. He smashed his right boot into Selga's helmeted head as he came down. Jaeger recovered first. Blocking, Ares quickly ducked out of the way as the point of Jol's sword stabbed at the god. Leif was the slowest to recover, but he lashed out with his left hand, sending his ax in a diagonal cut. Without missing a beat, the god dove forward, rolling away from the four attackers. Leif marveled at the spectacle he had just witnessed. Ares had just successfully blocked, dodged, and counter attacked all of them nearly at once.

Leif and his Skogur Borg companions flowed around Ares, reengaging the war god. Blades flashed while Ares danced about, ducking and dodging. He moved like water, flowing seamlessly around their blades. To an outside observer, Leif imagined the scene resembled a Jet Li or Jackie Chan movie. The ones where Li or Chan battled multiple bad guys at once, swords and fists flashing as they miraculously blocked multiple attacks. As much as Leif loved those fight scenes, he always knew that no one was that good. He was wrong. Ares lived up to his title. A jolt of excitement coursed through Leif. He could feel a savage joy emanating from the Berserker as he faced a worthy opponent. *The thrill of killing a god,* he thought as he grinned.

The fight spanned several long minutes, but to Leif's horror, Ares showed no signs of fatigue. The god of war tirelessly danced amongst their blades. With the numbers on their side, Leif and his comrades controlled the flow of the battle, hoping eventually the god would slip up, and then he would be finished.

Just as the fight took on a monotonous feel, Ares changed his strategy. He moved faster, changing the rhythm of his movements. Between his impossible blocks and dodges, he perfectly timed his attacks. He was never too fast to get past Leif or the Skogur Borg's defense, but it was close. His maneuvers slowed the assault enough that Leif finally felt he could take control. Ares barred his teeth; his eyes burned like the fires of Hades.

The real battle had begun. Leif pulled hungrily on the Berserker. He risked losing his mind, but to not give in would be risking death. Rage coursed through his veins as his vision took on a red tinge. Even so, Leif struggled to keep pace with Ares. Moving on instinct, he redirected the more dangerous cuts and slashes from hitting his vital organs.

Once Ares switched from a playful defense to an attack, the encampment became awash in sparks as the Outsider tested the Skogur Borg for weaknesses. For the less armored Leif, this posed a problem. Not only were there bright flashes as steel met enchanted armor, but blood as well. Small cuts appeared along Leif's unarmored ribs with accompanying dents and gouges in his armor.

Moving too fast to follow, Ares stepped forward, far too close for bladed weapons. If Leif attacked, he would hit one of his squad mates. Within everyone's personal space, Ares used his shorter gladius to its advantage. He thrust the thin blade between two armored sections in Jol's torso. Leif winced. It was a surgical strike, in and out in one sinuous move. Everything happened so fast. Blood sprayed, Jol collapsed, and there was nothing any of them could do but keep fighting.

Leif felt his mind growing sluggish with fatigue. This was the longest he had stayed in control while Berserked and it was wearing on him. The pressure in his head felt like a migraine forming as the full might of the Berserker howled to be released. The pull to throw caution to the wind and just launch himself at the frustrating god was sounding more and more reasonable. But Leif held firm. He knew it was a false hope. It would most assuredly lead to his and, quite possibly, the squad's death. Preserving his hold, Leif used the rage to sharpen his focus.

Then, defying the adage that lightning never strikes twice, Ares darted forward, quicker than a striking cobra. This time Jaeger went down, blood spurting from the wound to his abdomen. Seeing a third friend go down caused Leif's knees to go weak. He stumbled, throwing Ares's timing off for his next attack. As Ares reacted to Leif's unexpected movement, the Outsider's sword thrust at Selga, missing the weak point in her armor. The sword point glanced off her armor, sending her spinning away.

Leif recovered. A supernova of hate burned in his chest. He knew it was up to him to finish the fight. He had come too far and risked too much to be killed now. Not only Midgard, but all the realms, depended on him. With Selga momentarily out of the fight, Ares stalked forward toward Leif, smiling like he had already won. Needing time to think and to let Selga recover, Leif took several quick steps backward, giving himself some space. Unfortunately, his foot came down in a pool of blood, causing him to slip. Without lifting his foot to prevent slipping even more, Leif shuffled backwards. Ares pushed forward, his battle lust forming a sneer.

As he sidestepped through the warm, viscous blood, an idea popped into Leif's head. Not wanting to give his plan away, he was careful to stay close to the edge of the spreading pool. Ares twirled his sword in an impressive but pointless display of skill as he stalked forward. Hoping to use his unnatural speed to his advantage, Leif planned to attack the moment Ares came within range. He did his best to defend against the tidal wave of sword cuts the god sent his way. Finally, with arms and legs growing heavy with exhaustion, his patience paid off.

Leif had discovered Ares's weakness. The god was addicted to the fight. He reveled in it. He was the god of war. The thrill of the battle was his drug. During the god's attack against Selga, a light flicked on in Leif's brain. He noticed a tell that no one had survived long enough to discover. Before Ares killed an opponent, he spent the time memorizing their fighting style, soaking up all their tricks, timing, and idiosyncrasies. Only then, when he felt the fight had gone on long enough to master their technique, would he kill his opponent. He did it with Jol, Jaeger, and he would have against Selga, but Leif had figured it out. When Ares gave the slight, almost imperceptible pause before switching from learning to killing, Leif was ready.

Pushing off his back foot, Ares lunged at Leif. His sword point blurring forward, but Leif was ready. Pivoting backwards, Leif pulled his body out of Ares's deadly attack while simultaneously striking with the ax in his right hand. Drawing on all the speed the Berserker could provide, Leif hooked his axe over Ares's blade and pulled with all his might, shouting his defiance. With Ares's balance compromised by the slick blood, the sudden yank from Leif pulled the god right off his feet.

Ares tumbled sideways as if in slow motion. His orange eyes flared wide like a sunburst as he processed what had happened. Locking eyes with Leif as he fell, the god he shouted, "I am the god of war. I will not be defeated."

Leif knew Ares was finished. All the god's speed and power meant nothing as he fell. Knowing this was his only chance, Leif threw himself after Ares, landing on top of the god, axes descending.

Ares shrugged off his first two attacks, deflecting them with his gauntlets, but Leif wasn't done yet. With victory at hand, Leif rampaged. His twin axes flashed in the firelight as they rained down into Ares. Batting the unarmed god's hands to the side, Leif committed all his berserked strength to ending the fight in a death blow, aimed for Ares's jugular.

The god kept his cool, bucking his hips upward. The action threw Leif's aim off target as his axes crashed down, missing Ares's throat, and burying in the cobblestones, but not without sheering off several locks of Ares's dark curls in the process.

Seizing the opportunity, the god's hands clamped down on Leif's gauntleted wrists, preventing his escape. Even berserked, Leif could only mount the briefest of resistance as Ares pulled his hands away from his axes. Furious at being out muscled, Leif screamed in frustration, redoubling his effort, but to no avail. Leif was strong, stronger than any human and possibly some Ljosalfar, but Ares was on a whole other level. However, Leif refused to give up, futilely fighting for every inch. The Outsider slowly rose, lifting his back off the ground. Leif knew if Ares pushed him away, he was finished.

Suddenly, a shadow passed over the two combatants a moment before a black blade descended into view. The crushing pressure pinning Leif's arms in place vanished as the tip of Selga's blade pierced Ares's left eye seconds before bursting out the back of his skull, pinning the god of war to the cobblestone street.

Exhaustion washed over Leif as he toppled over, careful to avoid the razor-sharp edge of the sword still imbedded in Ares's head. Panting, Leif looked into the black visor of his savior. The armored knight was doubled over in pain, taking deep, ragged breaths. Lifting her visor, a pained but smiling Selga beamed at him. Leif's eyes fell on a golf-ball-sized dent where Ares had tried to gut her.

"Even a master..." she wheezed, "can lose to overconfidence and bad footing." She wheezed again. "Can you stand? We must help the others."

"I, I think so." He said breathlessly. "Can you help me up?"

With a gauntleted hand, Selga pulled him up, wincing in pain. Together, they limped over to their downed comrades. Jaeger had managed to roll onto his side, pulling off his helmet in the process. The kafteinn was sickly pale; his black hair was pasted to his forehead. His lips were ruby red with blood. He was in the process of unclipping his chest plate when Selga and Leif approached.

"Go. Help Jol and Foste. I will be fine," Jaeger said as he weakly waved them away.

"Are you sure?" Leif asked.

"Yes, this isn't the first time I've been stabbed through the gut, and by the Aesir, it won't be my last. See to Jol and Foste," he ordered.

As Leif made his way to Jol and Foste, pain exploded across his body, causing his knees to buckle. He was not only exhausted, hurt, and bleeding, but he was mentally and emotionally drained. The fight with the Jontar and Ares had pushed his connection with the Berserker to its breaking point. With Ares's death, Leif could weakly feel the Berserker's desire to shout their triumph. The rational part of his brain recoiled, fighting to suppress the battle lust that called Leif to hunt down the other Jontar camps and slaughter them all. It was a challenge, but having the other members of his squad nearby gave him something else to focus on, which helped suppress the Berserker.

Limping and bleeding from more cuts than he wanted to count, Leif followed Selga. With practiced ease, she stripped off Jol's armor one piece at a time. Next, Selga took a firm hold of the skintight undershirt and ripped it apart to expose Jol's torso. Leif gasped at the motley patchwork of bruises that canvased the unconscious warrior's torso. Besides the ragged and leaking wound, Leif did not detect any other open injuries, which was a testament to Gungnir's skill as a blacksmith. Whether Jol's internal organs and bones withstood Ares's onslaught was a different story.

"Put pressure on the wound, and do not remove your hands until I tell you to," Selga said as she rose to leave.

"Wait! Where are you going?" Leif exhaled.

"To get our packs," she said over her shoulder. "We have first aid equipment in them."

Less than five minutes later, Selga's armored form sprinted into view, with numerous black bags slung over her shoulder. Sliding to a stop on the bloody ground, she unbuckled a pack and pulled out three long, thin green leaves.

"Ok, take your hand off the wound," she instructed. Leif watched as Selga took one leaf in her hands and delicately folded it like Origami. She then pressed the leaf deep into Jol's open gash.

Jol's body violently twitched as he let out a weak moan of pain. Ignoring the reactions, Selga methodically shred the second leaf. With her hands full of what looked like grass clippings, Selga balled the contents into her tight fist, crushing it. She then opened her hand, showing Leif that the torn pieces had turned into a foul-smelling mush. The sharp acidic odor reminded him of a hospital room. Selga dipped a finger into the paste and smeared it around the wound. Then, with the final leaf, she gingerly placed the flat of it over the wound like a bandage. Taking hold of one end of Jol's torn shirt, Selga used her belt knife to cut a long thin strip from the shirt and tied the cloth around Jol's waist, binding his wound closed.

"Did you see what I did with the *laeknir* leaves?" Selga asked him.

"Uh, yeah. You put one in the wound, crushed, then smeared the second one, and the third you put over the wound before binding it."

"Good," Selga said, reaching into the bag by her feet to retrieve three more of the smelly leaves before handing them to Leif. "Go help the kafteinn. I need to check on Foste." She picked up a bag and ran toward her unmoving friend. Leif's body painfully protested his standing, but he hobbled back to Jaeger's side, who by then had already stripped off most of his upper body armor and was inspecting the outer edges of his wound.

Looking up at the sound of Leif's labored approach, Jaeger nodded at the green bundle in Leif's hands and sighed in relief.

"Give me one while you crush the other." Jaeger said weakly. Leif numbly did as he was told, pushing the memory of Arias's mortal wounds from his mind. "Snap out of it," Jaeger commanded. "Neither I nor Jol will pass into the void now. The *laeknir* will stop the bleeding and prevent infection from forming. Both of us got lucky. If we had taken these types of injuries deep in the forest, away from Karcoa's healers, it would have been a different story. You need to get used to comrades getting injured in battle. Your hesitation and self-loathing will kill more friends than your enemies ever will."

Though Jaeger's words stung, Leif knew them to be true. Redoubling his efforts, the two of them had Jaeger's wound bound in no time. The kafteinn sighed in relief and leaned back, using his dented breastplate as a backrest. "Thank you, Leif," Jaeger said, closing his eyes. "You performed well today. You are worthy of the Berserker mantle, but it's clear you are still haunted by the death of your friend. I see it in your eyes. If a comrade goes down, you have to keep moving. We got lucky today. You must rid yourself of those mental demons or one day your indecision could get you or your sword brother killed."

Leif hung his head in shame. Jaeger, who has known him for a short time, easily saw his shortcomings. It stung, but he knew Jaeger was right. Until Leif could overcome his fear of losing a friend on the battlefield, he was a liability.

"Leif, we are warriors; we chose this life. The Valkyries are always a hair's breadth away. Death is our fifth squad mate, always accompanying us when we get sent out on a mission. That is just a fact of life. If one or all of us must forfeit our lives to defend the weak and protect what we cherish, not one of the Skogur Borg would hesitate. That is an outcome all warriors must come to terms with."

Leif stared down at his hands.

Jaeger said a little more gently, "But don't misunderstand my words as a rebuke. You are young, even by Midgardian standards. Choosing the mission over aiding an injured comrade is a struggle all warriors must face. In time, if you survive long enough, you will know when and how to act." Jaeger's face and body suddenly sagged, as if the last vestiges of strength had left him.

For a panicked second, Leif thought he had died, but the grizzled warrior cracked one bloodshot eye open, locking gazes with him. "I'm still here. Just resting. Go help Selga attend to Foste. With luck, she hasn't stepped through the vaunted doors of Valhalla. Tell Selga, once she can stabilize Foste, to return to command and report to Kafteinn Rollo of our victory and of our need for immediate aid.

"Ok," Leif said, rising to his feet.

"And if Foste is a lost cause…" Jaeger said, holding Leif's gaze, "Selga is to leave immediately. Now go."

With Leif no longer drawing on the Berserker, his body drooped with a savage adrenaline crash. His limbs pulsed with pain as he shuffled toward Selga and Foste. He knew most of the minor wounds he suffered during the fight would be predominantly healed or scabbed over by tomorrow, leaving much of his body black and blue. He would take that over being bedridden for the next week or so, recovering like a normal Midgardian.

By the time Leif reached Selga, she had already unclasped much of Foste's upper body armor and was working on her legs. There were no visible injuries on Foste's exposed upper body. However, Leif did see a small trickle of blood leaking out of her pointed ears, but she was breathing. Her breath was short and shallow, but she was breathing. Free of the armor, Selga unsheathed her belt knife, cutting a long line from Foste's ankle to mid-thigh on both legs, pulling the torn clothing aside. A rainbow of bruises covered her torso and legs. Throughout Selga's examination, she maintained a stoic mask, displaying only a tightening around her eyes.

Selga stopped her examination, rolling back onto her heels.

"Jaeger said if–" Leif began.

"I heard him," Selga interrupted quietly.

Selga let out a huff of frustration before handing Leif her pack. She unhooked her helmet, dropping it to the street. "Guard them while I'm gone. We don't know if any of the other squads accomplished their missions. If there are any surviving Jontar or Dokkalfar, they will return here to their commander for new orders. Be on your guard, I will be back with help as soon as I can." Selga rose and ran into the smoky landscape, disappearing on silent feet into the burning forest.

# CHAPTER 13

Luckily for Leif, no enemies returned to the base. In his battered and bleeding state, it wouldn't have been much of a fight. For the better part of an hour, he guarded the three unconscious Skogur Borg warriors. With each snap from a nearby fire or groan of wood from a swaying tree, he would jerk from a silent stupor to defend his squad from the unseen enemy. Thankfully, his rescue was much like his first encounter with the Skogur Borg. One moment he was alone, and the next, ten black armored figures materialized from the gloom. Moving with silent determination, the reinforcements surrounded his downed squad mates, administering aid before loading them onto stretchers and carrying them away.

While he watched the rescue efforts, a gauntleted hand pressed down on Leif's shoulder, causing him to jump as he fumbled for his axes. He was exhausted and missed the grips. "Peace, Leif," the battered figure said from behind him. The warrior crouched in front of him, and Selga's tattooed face smiled weakly at him to relax. Realizing his watch had ended, his reserve of energy finally fizzled out. He felt a wave of fatigue start from the top of his head and course through his body to the tips of his toes. He attempted to stand, wobbled once, then collapsed backwards.

"Thank the gods you guys are here. If you don't mind, I'm just going to rest my eyes for a bit." Leif said, slurring his words.

"Rest well, Leif. You proved yourself well today. We will take it from here," Selga said, pulling a twig from Leif's hair and brushing a strand of hair from his closed eyes.

"HOW COULD YOU BE SO WEAK!" Arias screamed from his bed. "If it wasn't for you, I wouldn't even be here! I thought you were something great, a Berserker to outshine them all! But now this. I was killed because you wouldn't control yourself!"

"I'm sorry!" Leif shouted as he shot bolt upright. A confused haze settled over him as he took in his surroundings. He was no longer under the dreaded Savartalfar village, nor was he on the burning streets of Karcoa. A heavily bandaged Selga and Jaeger stood in the entrance to their barracks; confused looks lit their bruised faces. Cheeks burning with embarrassment, Leif dropped his gaze, mumbling an apology for startling them.

"Nightmares?" Jaeger asked.

Leif nodded sheepishly.

The two knights shared a knowing look before the kafteinn jerked his head in Leif's direction. "Be quick about it," Jaeger said as he turned to leave. "We can't be too late."

"Be late for what?" Leif asked, moving to a seated position. A thousand aches and pains flared to life across his thighs and back.

"Queen Thyra is holding a banquet to honor the Skogur Borg's victory over Ares," Selga said as she seated herself next to him on his bed. Her thigh brushed against Leif's, causing the pain in his body to momentarily wane.

"A banquet? So soon? Wasn't the fight just last night?" Leif inquired.

"You've been unconscious for nearly three days," Selga said, giving Leif a once over.

"WHAT?" he shouted.

"Truthfully, we were beginning to worry. It appears you heal like a Ljosalfar, but the process takes a heavier toll on your body, requiring more energy to knit the wounds together. After hearing your exploits, the queen visited you herself. Our healers cautioned us not to wake you, lest we do more damage. So, we let you sleep. Jaeger and I decided to check on you one last time before heading to the dinner. Now that you are awake, if you are up to it, you should join us. My people will be happy to see you."

Leif took a mental inventory of his body, wiggling his toes, shifting his legs, and rolling his shoulders. Nothing screamed at him. His body ached, but the soreness was like the post pain of a punishing workout and not a life-or-death struggle. Pushing himself off the bed, he took a few practice steps. Again, his muscles protested, burning across his legs and torso, but it was manageable.

It was then that Leif noticed he was in nothing but his boxer-briefs. He felt his face grow warm. *What the hell am I embarrassed about?* he chided himself. Holding his chin up high, Leif turned to her. "I'm in."

"Great," Selga said, pointing to a set of folded clothes on the table. "The queen had those commissioned for you."

"What are they?" Leif asked, picking up the silk garments sitting on the table.

"They are our formal uniforms," Selga said, standing and pointing to herself. She wore black slippers with flowing silk pants tied with a red corded rope that ended in two tassels. She wore a sleeveless vest with red lining and a low neckline, but it was not enough to be considered indecent. The Skogur Borg insignia was prominently displayed over her heart.

His clothes were identical to Selga's, all the way down to the cut and black slippers.

"While you dress," Selga said, nodding toward the clothes in his hands, "If you don't mind me asking, could you tell me what your nightmare was about?"

Letting out a heavy sigh, he pulled on the pants. Leif started to protest, not really wanting to talk about it, but Selga stopped him with a raised hand.

"We all get them, Leif," she said gently. "You would have to be an emotionless monster not to have the dead haunt you." She placed a gentle, calloused hand on his shoulder. He flinched, not from the touch, but the sudden sting of pain that sprung from the contact. It was the exact spot he had used foolishly to tackle Ares. Selga lifted her hand, giving him an apologetic smile of understanding.

"It was of Arias, the Ljosalfar I was with when you saved us from the Orcs," Leif whispered. "Not long after we parted ways, we were ambushed by Jontar. Outnumbered and boxed in, I let go of the Berserker. When an avenue of escape opened, it was too late. I continued to fight instead of running. I was eventually knocked out. Arias stood his ground going toe-to-toe with a Jontar. The Jontar fatally wounded him. We only escaped due to the intervention of the Savartalfar hiding underneath the village. Arias died not long after from a sword wound."

"Did this Arias blame you for his fate?" Selga asked.

"No, but if I had just been stronger, more in control, he wouldn't have died." He said, releasing a restrained sob.

Selga placed her arm around his shoulders. "Many feel as you do. You cannot play the 'what if' game, especially looking back over past battles. I have seen regret destroy good warriors. You said Arias did not blame you. So why do you?"

Leif opened his mouth to respond, but Selga placed her finger on his lips, forestalling him. He sharply inhaled, allowing her sweet earthly aroma to fill his lungs. He felt his lips slightly pucker, and Selga gently dragged her finger down his lips. She smiled and said, "You need not answer me. I do not need to know. This is a mental battle only you can fight. You must, in your own way, come to terms with the fact that friends, comrades, and squad mates will die in battle. You cannot let their sacrifice cripple you. You must come to terms with their choices and not let them hobble you in the fights to come."

LEIF PUT his hands on his knees as he gasped for air from the climb to the top of the Monarch. "Sweet baby Jesus! Would it kill you guys to put an elevator in or something?" He wheezed, looking at Selga. "What the hell? Are you even winded?"

A mischievous grin crossed her face.

"Oh, come on, that's not even fair." After a few more seconds of labored breathing, Leif pushed past the nausea, finally taking notice of his surroundings.

His fatigue was all but forgotten while he drank in the otherworldly vista spread out before him. The Ljosalfar had transformed the crown of the Monarch into an elegant open air banquet hall. The monstrous crisscrossing branches of the tree's canopy created a majestic ceiling. Thousands of luminous ribbons were strung amongst the interlocking branches. Hanging from those ribbons, an army of dancing-flame lanterns lit the hall. At the very center of the room, an undulating free-floating ring of water encircled an immense purple-flame lantern. Fat drops of water cascaded from the floating ring, only to be caught in a large depression at the center of the floor. A gigantic luminescent waterlily floated in the center of the pool. Beautiful long petals flowed out in all directions, shifting amongst the colors of the rainbow. The iridescent green stem of the lily jutted from the center. The tip of the stem ended in a bulb that pulsed with a white incandescent light. *Hmm, what the hell was the bulb at the end of the flower called again? Stigma! Thank you, college biology,* Leif thought with a mental high-five for remembering the anatomy of a flower.

Selga followed Leif's gaze and turned back to him. "Ah, the *Bjartr Hrrt*. Magnificent, isn't it?" Selga asked.

"It sure is. Why is it so shiny? I've never seen a flower like that. Nothing came close to looking like that in the forest we traversed," Leif commented, looking into Selga's eyes.

"The *Bjartr Hrrt* is the shining jewel of the Ljosalfar society," Jaeger said, causing Leif to jump as the kafteinn materialized from the crowd of milling Ljosalfar dignitaries. The flower's color shifted from bright red to green and was now a vibrant yellow. "As far as we know," the kafteinn continued, "it is one of a kind. It is said that the flower has remained in bloom for the entirety of Queen Thyra's reign."

"It's beautiful." Leif could almost hear Arias chiding him for his eloquence, but he didn't care. He was mesmerized.

"Let us find a table. I am sure many in attendance will want to speak with you. Moreover, Kafteinn Rollo mentioned he wanted to speak with you tonight," Jaeger spoke while wading through the crowd to the tables beyond. As Leif followed, many Ljosalfar paused in their conversation to give him a polite nod or pat on the shoulder. Clearing the crowd, Jaeger had commandeered an empty table at the back of the hall.

Taking the proffered seat, Leif surveyed the banquet hall from this new post. The area was full of Ljosalfar in brightly colored robes, eating, drinking, and generally having a good time. It was a stark contrast from the war council meeting he had barged into days ago. Leif found it a bit unnerving to be surrounded by so many Ljosalfar. They all moved with a fluid grace that no human could match. It made him self-conscious, knowing he must stick out like a sore thumb.

As Leif people watched, he had no trouble pointing out the Skogur Borg warriors mingling amongst the crowd. It wasn't just because of their matching garments or how they clustered in groups of three or four, but it came down to a primal extra-sensory feeling. All Ljosalfar move with the grace of a gold metal figure-skater, but as Leif observed the warriors move through the crowd, he thought about a panther prowling amongst house cats. There was a deadly elegance to their movements; they could be reaching for a drink or impaling an enemy. Each gesture comprised of the same energy. It was unsettling, but it also gave him a sense of pride. There's no way he would have noticed before, which made him believe he was growing into his Berserker senses.

The edge of the gathered Ljosalfar suddenly parted, revealing Queen Thyra and her retinue. To Leif's astonishment, the Queen's gown mirrored the luminescence of the *Bjartr Hrrt* in both style and color. As she floated forward, he watched as both the mystifying flower and Queen Thrya's gown shifted from sea foam green to teal, to blue, and so on. She was the very depiction of regal beauty. Everyone stood at the queen's approach. Jaeger, Selga, and Jol, who had recently joined them, started to kneel, but they were stopped by the queen with one elegant hand gesture.

"There will be none of that today," she said in a commanding voice so all in attendance could hear. "This evening, we honor you and all the brave members of the Skogur Borg who fought in defense of our great realm." The queen paused, holding out one porcelain hand. An attendant placed a drink in it. "Friends, clan elders, Skogur Borg warriors, and Leif the Berserker, on this most welcome of evenings we have gathered to pay tribute to those who conquered our enemies, the vile Ares and his warriors who laid siege to our beautiful city. Though we lost many in the campaign, Kafteinn Ragnar amongst them, Kafteinn Jaeger and his squad, with the aid of the Berserker Leif, engaged the enemy commander, the Outsider Ares, killing the vile monster in the process. Tonight, we raise our glasses in celebration of our brave knights!" She paused, raising her crystal flute, and everyone followed suit. "Tomorrow, we rebuild what was so cruelly taken from us. Honor to Alfheim." The queen then brought her drink to her ruby lips and took one quick sip. The room erupted in unison, "Honor to Alfheim!" The gathered crowd of Ljosalfar downed the contents of their drinks and then cheered the Skogur Borg interspersed among them.

It was a humbling experience for Leif. He was a lowly Midgardian from a realm that he was sure most Ljosalfar looked upon with disdain, yet they were clapping for him. Well, his team, but he was a part of that team. Jaeger briefly clapped Leif, Selga, and Jol on the shoulder as the crowd returned to their previous conversations and festivities.

"We did well," Jaeger said, beaming with pride. "Enjoy the night because tomorrow we go back to work. Well, we do," he said, nodding to his compatriots. "You, my friend, are free to remain if you wish, though I have a sense you are searching for something," the kafteinn cryptically said.

"What do you mean?" Leif prompted.

Before Jaeger could respond, the queen glided to Leif and his companions. She opened her arms out wide, as if to embrace them all. "I cannot begin to tell you how proud I am of you all, my knights. Your squad exemplifies the ideals that your order was founded upon so long ago. And Leif, our most honored guest, you cannot begin to understand the number of objections I received from the clan elders over you." Queen Thrya's eyes twinkled.

"I'm sorry, your highness. I didn't mean to cause you any trouble," Leif said.

Cracking a wide grin, the queen continued, "It was no trouble. The elders like to challenge me every few hundred years. It's a game of sorts. A game I won when you two..." pointing to Leif and Selga, "killed Ares." Turning her full attention on Leif, she said, "You have earned my people's eternal gratitude for your action. You will always be welcome on Alfheim." The queen placed her delicate hand on Leif's wrist. "And if you shall ever need our assistance, you have but to ask." She addressed the table as a whole. "Sit, relax and enjoy yourselves. You have earned it." She then floated away and disappeared within the throng of mingling Ljosalfar delegates.

Not long after the queen departed, a finely dressed Ljosalfar served the guests plates heaped with food and drinks. They began to eat just as a tanned, dark-haired Ljosalfar in a silk emerald robe approached their table. With a wide smile, the newcomer took the empty seat to Jol's left. With a respectful nod, the Ljosalfar greeted Jaeger in Ljosa. "I beg your pardon, elder. Our friend here..." Jol gestured to Leif, "doesn't speak our language. In deference to him, we ask you to speak in the common.tongue," Jaeger said.

The elder paused for a moment, narrowing his eyes as he minutely shook his head, then nodded. "How is Foste's condition?" he asked in a clipped tone. "I hear she was gravely injured in the final assault."

"She is stable," Jaeger said, shifting in his seat. "She is still unconscious, but the healers are confident she shall wake soon."

"I hope she makes a quick recovery. Kafteinn, if you don't mind, can you please tell me of the final duel with Ares?"

"Ares was a battle hungry adversary," Jaeger said. "There were several times when the Outsider could have killed us. It was clear the god loved to fight and yearned for the battle, which led to his downfall, but I cannot claim credit for his death. The god felled Jol and me with two terrible strokes of his blade. Events after that are murky. It was these two true heroes that won the battle, Leif and Selga," Jaeger said with a gracious smile.

"I can't take much credit either, Clan Elder," Selga commented. "It was Leif. His keen mind and swift action are the reasons we won. He is the true hero." Selga said, flashing him a smile that sent blood rushing through his body. WAMP! The Ljosalfar slammed his fist down, causing Leif to jump. His face reddened and the elder spoke in Ljosa at rapid fire speed. It sounded like rhyming death metal. Every few lilting syllables, the angry elf pointed at Leif. The commotion drew the attention of the queen from across the room. Her face revealed a frozen fury that chilled Leif. Scanning the room, he watched the Skogur Borg warriors in attendance zero in on the speaker. The warriors silently encircled their table. The elder, oblivious to the danger closing in, continued his angry tirade, now pointing at Jaeger, who sat in stunned silence.

When the Ljosalfar rant finally came to an end, there were close to thirty Skogur Borg warriors surrounding them. Breaking the pregnant silence, Jaeger spoke in a cold and detached voice, "Clan Elder Ivar, though Leif may be what you refer to as a backwater Midgardian, that same lowly Midgardian, donned the black and bled for Alfheim. Did you? Or your clan guards? Did they duel a god and win?" Jaeger leaned in close to Ivar, nearly touching his nose with his own. His voice quivered in restraint. "I will say this just once. If you ever demean a member of my squad or the Skogur Borg again, I will cut your mortal coil." Jaeger allowed the gravity of his words to sink in before continuing. "Look around you." Jaeger leaned back, allowing Ivar to get a better view. His eyes widened when he noticed he was surrounded by black-robed killers. Leif had to give it to Ivar. He didn't flinch. "I don't need you to believe what Leif did because your opinion doesn't matter. We were there. We saw him fight, and that's all that matters. So, If I were you, I would keep your opinions to yourself. It would be a tragedy if you were to have an unfortunate accident." Ivar gave one final glance at the scowling faces around him, stood up, and quietly left the banquet, disappearing from the celebration.

The normal sounds of the party resumed. People chatted, laughed, and the dings of silverware and the clings of glass filled the room. When the crowd thinned from around Leif's table, he spotted Queen Thrya speaking with Kafteinn Rollo. She met his eyes as she stood before his table.

"I would like to personally apologize for the actions of Clan Elder Ivar," The queen said in a formal voice. "He was warned to keep his more extremist views about Midgardians to himself. It appears he has gone against my decree. Royal guards were dispatched to his clan's elktre, and I shall be speaking with him about his disobedience." Her tone grew frosty with each word that escaped her lips.

"Your highness," Leif said, feeling the need to speak. "There is no need for such drastic action. I don't even speak Ljosa, so I could not take offense to what I did not understand."

"You are an honorable warrior, Berserker Leif," Rollo said, speaking for the first time. "Whether you took offense or not, Ivar not only disobeyed the queen's word, but by insulting you, he insulted the integrity of the Skogur Borg during the very event that we honor the members who died in the battle against Ares. And that…" Rollo tightened his eyes, causing the glow in his eyes to smolder, "we will not allow."

"Well-spoken, Kafteinn," the queen said. "I will not allow such an insult to go unpunished, especially during a celebration for those that he just insulted. But do not worry yourself with such trivialities, Leif. This is a night of merriment." She smiled, but anger wafted out from Queen Thrya in tight waves. It was so palpable that the Berserker perked up. Closing his eyes, Leif took a deep breath and willed the Berserker into his subconscious. It took a few seconds, but he felt the cool power recede. He opened his eyes to everyone staring at him; after seeing Leif was in control, they resumed as if nothing happened.

"Leif," Rollo began. "During Jaeger's after-action report to the war council, he described the changes you exhibit, both mentally and physically, when you berserk."

"Ok," Leif drawled, not knowing where the barrel-chested warrior was going with this.

"Not two moons ago, I came across a female Midgardian Berserker in a tavern while acting as a varangian for the Eternal Queen during a diplomatic trip to Vanaheimr."

"What!" Leif shouted, getting to his feet. "How do you know?"

"The woman was obviously a Midgardian, but her eyes glowed the same electric blue as the Aesir. When she fought, she was like a demon, attacking with a speed and ferocity that no one of your kind should possess."

"This could be the lost Berserker clan I was researching!" Leif said to himself. Then to Rollo, he asked, "Please tell me everything that you remember about her?"

"May I sit with you?" Rollo asked, pointing out an empty chair.

"Of course," Jaeger said, pulling out the chair for him.

Smiling, Rollo took the proffered seat. He pulled out a small metal flask and unscrewed the lid, saluting to the group. "Before anything, I would like to honor all those who fell in glorious battle against our hated foe. May they be welcomed within the halls of Valhalla!" Rollo took a deep pull then handed the flask to Jaeger. Jaeger raised the flask in thanks and took a sip. All at the table followed suit, including Leif. A hint of honey and strawberry touched his tongue before the burn kicked in.

"Now my friend," Rollo said, turning to face Leif. "One evening, after being relieved of the day's duties, I decided to visit a familiar Savartalfar ale house named The Hammer and Anvil. As I enjoyed my drink and listened to their bard, a fight broke out between a hooded figure and a drunk Ljosalfar. At first, I had no interest in the squabble. Ale house brawls are not uncommon. But something caught my attention. The room had suddenly gone as silent as a tomb. The Ljosalfar had pulled the cloak from his opponent, revealing a Midgardian with red-blond hair tied in a thick war braid. Her eyes glowed, just as yours do when you berserk. The gathered crowd froze, confused at what they were seeing. The drunk Ljosalfar laughed, slurring that if he killed her in a fight, no one would even report her death to the authorities. The Ljosalfar demanded an apology from the strange woman, but she refused, which only enraged the drunkard more. The crowd sensed violence was moments away and wisely spread out.

"The Ljosalfar attacked with a fist. He was so much larger and stronger looking than the Midgardian that the crowd assumed the fight would be over with that single punch. I suspected otherwise. There was something off about the woman, a stillness that set me on edge. I watched as she knocked the Ljosalfar's punch off course and simultaneously lashed out with a punch of her own. The woman's fist connected cleanly with her attacker's jaw, sending him tumbling backward. Murmurs broke out amongst the crowd. The Ljosalfar barely got to his feet. I watched as the fool unsheathed a small belt knife, waving it in his opponent's direction. Moving with speed beyond that of your people, she snatched the knife out of the surprised drunkard's grip, reversed the blade, and slammed it into the Ljosalfar's thigh. He screamed and fell over, clutching his wounded leg.

"Afterward, the Midgardian addressed the crowd, speaking in perfect Ljosa, 'If anyone else wants to take a swipe at me, I'll be here all night.' She then sat down and ordered another pint. No one came close to her for the rest of the evening. When Jaeger spoke of you, he described the exact same kind of, um, how do you say in your tongue? Pressure, presence, or maybe killing intent. From his description, I have no doubt this Midgardian was a Berserker, just like you."

A chill ran down Leif's spine when Rollo described the woman. This was it, proof that another Berserker was out there and not just a story written in a random journal. And she was powerful. As strong or stronger than a Ljosalfar. *I must find her and learn how she attained it,* he thought ecstatically. "You said two moons? What is that, like two months?"

"Possible, though I am not familiar with your time," he shrugged.

"Can you take me there, to the ale house you saw her in?" Leif asked emphatically.

"Fortunately, the queen is sending me to Vanaheimr tomorrow to report to the *Rao* and hear of the fate of the other realms. You are welcome to accompany me through the bridge. Due to the time variance between realms, I will have time to escort you to the ale house. Who knows, maybe the Berserker is a regular there. If not, the brawl was noteworthy. It's possible someone may know of her whereabouts," Rollo said.

"Really?" Leif asked.

"Oh yes. Midgardians are rare anywhere in the realms. But she fought and won against a Ljosalfar; that event would not be taken lightly." Rollo commented. "Someone will know something."

"Thank you so much," Leif said, smiling.

"Great," Rollo said, clapping Leif on the shoulder. "The bridge is located here in the Monarch, so we will leave tomorrow after breakfast." Standing, Rollo added, "Enjoy the rest of the evening. I'll see you tomorrow." The kafteinn disappeared into the mass of revelers.

The rest of the celebration flew by in an intoxicated blur. Many of the Skogur Borg from other units visited Leif's table, wishing to hear tales of the final fight with Ares. Many of them brought Leif a drink. He had thought he had a high tolerance; he was a bartender after all, *but damn the Ljosalfar can drink*. As the night turned to morning, the party wound down. *Work waits for no man, and no one enjoys getting up early with a hangover.*

More than a little tipsy, the group called it a night and joined the procession of party goers down the Monarch's steep staircase. While Leif stumbled down the stairs, he noted none of the Ljosalfar were unsteady on their feet as they ghosted their descent. Hell, they were all moving as graceful as ever with only a slight sway to their step. He thought they looked as if they were dancing. Meanwhile, a heavy-footed Leif clomped his way noisily down the stairs. *The bastards,* he slurred through his mind.

Mercifully stepping onto their barrack's floor, Leif followed his squad down the wooden hallway and into their communal quarters. Foste's bunk was still empty. She was still in and out of surgery. Leif sloshed his way to Foste's empty bed, since Jaeger was back and pulled off his vest. With his back to the room, he nearly jumped out of his skin when a warm hand pressed into his shoulder. After catching his breath, he turned to face Selga, who was inches from his face. Her pale, porcelain face and striking tribal tattoo were slightly flushed, while her glowing eyes blazed intently. Leif's eyes traced a line from her chin down her neck all the way to her naval.

She too had removed her vest, revealing a physic to make Aphrodite jealous. Three long scars ran down her toned abdomen, looking like she had got into a fight with Wolverine. Her strong lean arms pulled Leif against her, crushing him into her plump chest. She kissed him with her full lips. Leif's eyes widened with both surprise and pleasure. Pulling away briefly, he whispered as he scanned the room, "What about the others?" His eyes darted around the room.

With a feline smile, Selga purred, "Gone," into his ear before smashing her lips against Leif's once more as she pulled him onto the bunk.

# CHAPTER 14

Leif woke the next morning sore, achy, and hungover, but he couldn't keep a smile off his face. The bunks the Skogur Borg slept in couldn't be bigger than a twin bed, so he was confused why he couldn't feel the warm, lithe form of Selga curled next to him. Rolling over, he saw she wasn't there. His smile faltered. Leif figured since he was up, he should get ready to leave with Rollo. Swinging his legs off the bed, he realized his mistake. His head swam and his stomach turned sour. He grumbled, "Damn, I haven't been this hung over since the day after my twenty-first birthday."

As Leif cinched up his backpack, he heard the door open behind him. He turned just as Selga walked in, slightly out of breath. She was even more beautiful with sweat glistening on her forehead. A small, knowing smile crept across her lips.

Rubbing the back of his neck, he asked, "Do Ljosalfar not get hungover?"

A confused look crossed Selga's face. "What is hungover?"

"Beauty, grace, close to immortal, and no hangovers. Life really is unfair," he bemoaned.

Selga shrugged and glided next to him, giving him a gentle kiss.

"I sparred with Rollo this morning. He said to meet him in the mess hall. From there, he will take you through the bridge."

"Where is that?" Leif asked

"I'll show you the way. It's on the way to the washroom." Selga said, gathering her things.

"Awesome," Leif said, before awkwardly clearing his throat. "Um, so."

Selga smiled, giving him another brief kiss. "There is nothing to say, Leif. Last night was…" Her gaze settled on his lips. "Very enjoyable. But we are both warriors with callings that pull us in different directions. Nothing needs to be said. However, if your quest ever brings you back to Karcoa, don't hesitate to stop by." She winked and leaned in for a final deep kiss.

LEIF FOUND Rollo surrounded by his squad, eating something akin to porridge. When Rollo saw him approach, he smiled and bid him to sit down. The Kafteinn had an attendant bring Leif a plate of food. Using their version of silverware, an odd cross between a spork and a knife, Leif dug in, already feeling the hangover subsiding. Most of the conversation bounced around the table in Ljosa, but Leif didn't mind. He was content to eat.

Once they were done, Rollo bid farewell to his friends and gestured for Leif to follow. The kafteinn led them through numerous corridors and stairways filled with Ljosalfar moving through the Monarch like blood through veins and arteries. Rollo peppered Leif with questions about life on Midgard. The Ljosalfar kafteinn was particularly interested in television and movies. When Leif promised to take Rollo to a movie, the kafteinn smiled with joy.

After a time, the pair passed through the hustle and bustle of the bureaucratic wing into a more secure portion of the Monarch. The hallways were empty, save for Ljosalfar in bark-like armor. The sentries stood guard at several heavy wooden doors or were positioned at intersections.

"Hey Rollo, who are the guards in the bark armor? They aren't dressed like the Skogur Borg or clan guards I've seen," Leif whispered as they passed another pair of the stoic warriors.

With a chuckle, Rollo said, "They are the *Konungr*. Like the Skogur Borg, they have to relinquish all clan responsibilities. But unlike our order that is sent out to hunt the enemies of Alfheim, they swear absolute fealty to the Monarch. They protect the Monarch and the numerous bridges of the great tree houses. They are a secretive group, even more so than the Skogur Borg."

The hallway branched into a large ornate antechamber. Two Konungr guards held leaf headed spears and stood at each side of a large set of double doors. The doors were carved with several columned buildings set on a mountain. Upon their approach, the Konungr menacingly brandished their spears. Without missing a beat, Rollo reached into his satchel and presented a rolled-up scroll with a wax seal. Speaking in Ljosa, Rollo gestured to the scroll. The guard standing directly in front of the Kafteinn stepped forward, taking the proffered scroll. He briefly inspected the seal before cracking it open to read its contents. The guard quickly reviewed the parchment before rolling it back up and pocketing it. The Konungr nodded and then pulled the doors open.

Passing through the heavy doors, the pair was stopped by another set of guards. The heavy boom of the closing door caused Leif to jump. He turned around and was surprised to see the backside of the doors were carved in an intricate portrait of Karcoa. The Monarch was split down the middle of both doors, taking up a large portion of each. Turning away from the door, Leif looked at the gaping abyss of a permanent bridge. However, unlike the bridge he crossed to Savartlfheim, which was made of stone, this bridge was cut straight into the trunk of the great tree itself. Along the outer edge of the bridge, several glyphs had been burned into the heartwood, reminding him of *Stargate*.

"Rollo, what are those glyphs for?" Leif asked, pointing to the edge of the bridge.

"Ah, you are an observant one. I can see why Jaeger likes you. Legend says, long before Karcoa was anything but a dense forest, the great tree, Yggdrasil, chose this very tree to become the Monarch, affixing the first bridge to its trunk. As time went on, with the bridge permanently present, my people and the Dokkalfar took up residence within the surrounding forest. During those early years of Karcoa's settlement, my people noticed the Monarch was growing at an exponential rate. It wasn't only the Monarch. All the trees in the surrounding forest. The mage council of the time was tasked with investigating the abnormality. Through much experimentation, the wizards learned it was the cosmic energy Yggdrasil used to maintain the bridge connection. This energy fed the Monarch, strengthening it to support the bridge. However, so much energy was being poured into the bridge that some was bleeding into the forest. The surrounding trees siphoned the excess energy at an alarming rate. Those early settlers took advantage of the situation, turning the trees into the elktre you see today. The continual flow of cosmic energy from Yggdrasil keeps the trees strong and healthy, even with several floors cut into them. Worrying the elktre at some point would eventually collapse under their immense size, possibly destroying Karcoa, the mage council added the power limiters." Rollo pointed to the etchings along the mouth of the bridge. "They stemmed the overflow of the energy, causing only a trickle to bleed into Karcoa. With the limiters in place, just enough energy is siphoned into the surrounding forest to maintain the strength and durability of the elktre that makes up our city."

"But what happens to all the excess energy?" Leif asked.

"It is redistributed out into the arcanosphere," Rollo said.

"The what?" Leif asked.

"The arcanosphere," Rollo repeated. "It is the naturally occurring energy that permeates Alfheim. The mages redirected the excess energy away from the Monarch and surrounding forest, spreading the energy out. With all the extra power coursing through the very air, Alfheim now has a much higher rate of evolution with regards to magical plants and creatures."

"Wow, that's pretty cool," Leif commented. "I wonder if I were to stay on Alfheim for an extended period, would I gain magical powers?" Leif mused.

"That is an interesting thought," Rollo said. "For you, I would think not, but if you were to sire children here, it's possible they would be magically inclined."

That caught Leif's attention. *Hmm, I could create a Berserker-mage bloodline. Now that would be a force to reckon with.* He thought about Selga and wondered if there were rules about Ljosa-Midgardian relations. *I don't know if we can even reproduce. Something to think about if I survive,* Leif thought.

"Enough history for the day. Let's get going," Rollo stated. "Don't misunderstand me, I too find the mystic arts a fascinating subject, but I never enjoy being selected to act as the queen's Varangian. With the recent losses within the ranks of the Skogur Borg and Kafteinn Jaeger not fully recovered, the queen chose me for this mission. I am happy to be of service to the eternal queen, it's just that I am not a fan of politics. I detest intra-realm politics even more. The *Rao* and their incessant fighting and political backstabbing drive me crazy. That's why I love the Skogur Borg. We are given a target, then we hunt them down. Simple and clear cut."

"I hear ya," Leif said. "I have never been a fan of Midgardian politics either. Politicians never do what they promise. It's just one big fraud."

The pair made their way through the yawning mouth of the bridge. Once inside, Leif inspected the walls and ceiling. Just like the other permanent bridge he had walked through, the glyphs in the traitorous Kaldrec called the Kravoc hummed with power. Within the bridge, he didn't even need to concentrate to feel the magical pressure pressing against his skull.

Turning from the ancient, enchanted script, Leif noticed Rollo had gotten a few yards in front of him. So he jogged to catch up. Not much further, he could see a literal light at the end of the tunnel. The pair came within a few yards of the opening and a guttural voice called out in a challenge. What surprised Leif was their challenger wasn't Ljosalfar, but Savartalfar. Rollo, nonplussed, responded by reaching into his side satchel, pulling out another scroll like the one he had given the guard on Alfheim.

"Wait here," Rollo whispered as he stepped forward, keeping the scroll in view while his other hand stayed far from the handle of his sword. The light emitting from the end of the bridge was a blinding contrast to the dank darkness of the bridge. The contrast obscured Leif's vision. So, the further Rollo got, the harder it was to see him, until eventually the kafteinn was nothing but a fuzzy blur. A moment later, Leif heard a faint rustle of paper, a cracking of a wax seal, followed by several weighty seconds. Finally, Rollo called out for Leif to approach.

Moving forward, Leif shaded his eyes as they adjusted to the blinding light. Blurry figures coalesced as he found himself in a circular room made of cream-colored marble. He did a double take when the source of the blinding white light came into view. Unlike the dancing flame lanterns used by the other realms, the light from the chandelier wasn't a flame at all. Instead, several small motes of pure white light brilliantly lit the chamber. It was as if he was staring at a lightbulb without the glass covering. Leif wanted to ask Rollo about it, but the kafteinn was tapping his foot impatiently, staring down at the Savartalfar guard, who was taking extra time to read the contents of the scroll. Two other guards in polished armor stood at either side of a set of double doors. A large tree was engraved into the center of the door. Nine colored circles of gold, green, ice blue, dark blue, red, brown, gray, black and yellow surrounded the tree. The same symbol was embossed over the right breastplate of the Savartalfar guards.

While reading, the guard's eyes occasionally flicked up, scanning them up and down. There were a few more clipped questions before the guard finally seemed satisfied. Rolling up the scroll, the Savartalfar walked to the double doors, slamming his gauntleted fist against it. BOOM, BOOM, BOOM. It was only then that Leif noticed the doors leading out of the chamber didn't have handles. A loud CLICK reverberated throughout the room just as the two bridge guards stepped away from the door. As if on cue, the heavy doors swung outward, revealing three heavy steel bars that had been retracted from within the doors, unlocking them.

Leif followed Rollo into the next room, which was an even bigger bare chamber. There was another set of heavy oaken doors at the end of the space. This room housed four armored bridge guards, two on each side of the doors with weapons in hand. Two guards stood on a balcony about twenty feet to the right of the exit; bows with arrowheads that burned an angry red were drawn and aimed at Leif and Rollo.

"Oh shit," Leif gasped. Taking a single involuntary step backward, sliding into a defensive position while his hand simultaneously dropped to his twin axes. Preparing for a fight, Leif released the dam holding the Berserker at bay. Rollo watched Leif with a mixture of shock, surprise, then horror as he took in the situation. Suddenly, the Skogur Borg warrior took three quick steps forward and stood in front of Leif, screaming a flurry of Ljosa words.

"STAND DOWN!" Rollo shouted with his arms wide in a placating manner. "This is just the second guard station; we are not under attack. With Fenrir on the loose and the realms being invaded, the *Rao* has added extra security measures for any intra-realm travel to Vanaheimr."

While Rollo tried to soothe Leif's rage addled mind, the Berserker roared to cut down the arrogant fools who challenged him. But Leif wasn't the same weak-minded Berserker he once was. So even with the Berserker raging, his conscious mind heard Rollo's plea. Leif turned his attention to the warriors in front of him. He eyed each guard in turn. The archers still hadn't loosed their arrows, nor had any of them moved. Leif bit down, pulling the Berserker back into his subconscious. Rollo breathed a sigh of relief.

A wide smile spread across the rugged kafteinn's face at seeing Leif return to normal. "By the Aesir, that was exhilarating to see. You really were going to fling yourself at the guards, weren't you? From the power I felt coming off you, I would have given you even odds on who would win. I can now confirm without a doubt that the woman I saw at the Hammer and Anvil was a Berserker. You both exude the same aura of wild, uncontainable power. It's truly amazing that your kind has this well of strength hidden within. It is an amazing gift. Fascinating. No wonder Jaeger wanted you on the squad for the attack on Ares's camp. Once you accomplish your quest, you will always have a place with the Skogur Borg!" Rollo excitedly said.

Leif took a deep breath, and Rollo beckoned for Leif to stand next to him. Rollo called out in Ljosa. He was answered a second later, and the two conversed in Ljosa. While they talked, Leif looked around the room. It was almost identical to the bridge room, but for its larger size and the balcony. The door was much larger than the first, but it contained the same symbol carved into the oak frame. However, unlike the bridge room, the guards here were a mixture of the races. Besides the obvious short stature of the two Savartalfar, the other guards' races were a mystery. Leif assumed some were Ljosalfar, but with their visors down, he couldn't tell.

A few moments later, the guard signaled for the door to be opened. Again, a guard pounded on the large double doors, "BOOM, BOOM, BOOM." There was the loud click of metal bars being retracted, and the doors swung open without a sound. Bright sunlight streamed in, bringing with it a current of fresh, crisp mountain air. Leif took a deep, cleansing breath, not realizing how stuffy the air was in the guardroom.

The pair walked out of the oppressive guardroom and into a

bustling courtyard. Large marble columns ran the length of the open-air courtyard, giving off a distinct ancient Greek vibe. Everything was made of white granite or marble. Robed figures of all races moved among the shaded pathway between pillars. It reminded Leif of the first time he saw Karcoa. Outside the columned walkway, a perfectly mowed lawn with a loose rock walkway led to a circle of stone benches in the center.

"Everyone looks so tense?" Leif commented.

"Whenever the Rao council meets, the whole city goes into a frenzy. Hel's invasion and a couple of failed assassination attempts have put everyone on edge. The general hastiness of the aides you see here stems from everyone wanting to get their jobs done as quick as possible so they can return to their home realms."

"I have fought two separate Outsiders and a fallen Aesir in the past two weeks; I can understand their general fright," Leif commented.

"True enough," Rollo said, clapping Leif on his back. "Now come on. Let's head to the *Hammer and Anvil*. We can grab a pint before I have to leave for official duties."

## CHAPTER 15

White fluffy clouds lazily drifted by as Leif and Rollo stepped away from the archway, revealing a panoramic view of Vanaheimr's capital city and its surroundings. The city itself was carved into the peak of an enormous mountain. A very crowded cobblestoned street zig zagged its way down the mountainside.

The marbled columns and imposing architecture of the city were a breathtaking sight, but it all paled in comparison to the physics defying sight that hovered before him. One hundred feet from the edge of the mountainside city were three gravity defying islands. Each island varied in size, ranging from the smallest being roughly one hundred by one hundred feet to the largest being bigger than a football field. Thick corded ropes anchored the floating anomalies to the mountainside, which Leif assumed kept the islands from floating away. Large wooden walkways were strung between each island and the city, allowing people to move freely between them. White marbled buildings with large columns and domed roofs sat atop of all but the smallest islands. Leif watched beings move along the islands and open-air walkways.

"*Mikill Stoar* is a beautiful city, isn't it?" Rollo asked as he took a deep breath, enjoying the crisp mountain air. "The city founders wanted it to be difficult for any invading army to attack by land, so they built it into the cliff face of the tallest mountains they could find. Whether it was the will of the Aesir or some cosmic luck, multiple bridge points formed once construction began."

Peering over the ledge of the cliff, Leif spied a white stone road twist its way down into the cloud layer below. Along the winding road, a multitude of squat square buildings sat on several tiers cut into the mountainside. Turning to look back the way they had come, three towering buildings with thick columns and domed roofs loomed above the gated courtyard they had just exited from. Stairs stretched the length of the three buildings, leading to their separate entrances. Guards in polished armor similar to the gate guards could be seen methodically checking anyone who wished to enter the governmental buildings.

Once Leif was done admiring the Acropolis, he nodded at Rollo and the pair descended to the lower levels of the mountain city. The city designers cut deep into the mountainside, creating massive terraces. The back quarter of each level was enclosed within large man-made caverns. The first level they passed housed a large market filled with wooden carts and stalls. Just behind that, a large cavern contained row upon row of uniform square buildings. Leif moved through pockets of smells ranging from spicy curry to the warm smell of baking breads. If he had the time, he would have sampled every food vendor he came across. Interspersed between the milling food carts, several stalls offered all sorts of curios from across the realms.

After descending two more levels, Rollo turned off the crowded cobblestoned path, moving into the interior of the terrace. Leif openly gawked at the layout of *Mikill Stoar*. They passed more venders, living quarters, and a gated section with two scowling Savartalfar guardsmen. Finally, they reached a section filled with raucous laughter, slurred singing, and several scantily clad Ljsoalfar, Savartalfar, and Orcs. Leif had no doubt they reached the seedy underbelly of *Mikill Stoar*. Runic graffiti ran along many of the buildings' outer walls. A large group of disheveled beings played dice games or slept off the excess ale. Upon Leif and Rollo's approach, some of the more alert vagrants reached for concealed weapons, but a sharp look from Rollo quelled any ideas of attacking.

The pair moved into the artificial cave. Large flickering torches illuminated the space in a dim glow reminiscent of Myerkheim. Leif suspected that wasn't a coincidence based on the large number of Savartalfar that stumbled past, singing and gulping down large tankards of beer. Turning down a small side street at the back of the large cavern, Rollo gestured towards an unassuming squat building with a wooden sign of a hammer resting atop an anvil.

"Let me guess," Leif said, pointing to the building. "This is the place."

"Observant as ever," Rollo said with a smile. "Now come on. Let's have a pint before I have to give my report to the Rao." He opened the door for Leif.

The cramped bar room was filled with the typical sights and sounds. Unlike the last Savartalfar pub Leif had visited, which was occupied solely by Savartalfar, this bar was a veritable melting pot of the races. Savartalfar drank with Ljosalfar, Orcs, and Dokkalfar. The oddest pair of patrons was a green scaled humanoid with molten golden eyes sitting with a golem. The strange duo was deep in hushed conversation as they shared a large tankard.

Leif felt his shoulders slump at not seeing the female Berserker. He had secretly hoped she would be there. Rollo tapped on Leif's shoulder, pointing to an open table near the bar. Jockeying their way to the table, Leif smiled to himself. He thought that no matter what realm he was on, all bars were the same. Stuffy, slightly sticky floors, and a general background noise making it hard to hold a conversation. *Gods, I miss working at the Slumbering Lion,* he thought just as a red faced Dokkalfar bumped into his shoulder.

Rollo cut a path toward the overwhelmed Savartalfar barkeep, while Leif claimed the table for themselves. Taking in his surroundings, he noticed the establishment really went the extra mile to maintain the theme. Along the walls, various types of blacksmithing tools hung on the wall, ranging from hammers, tongs, and accordion looking bellows. Though in Leif's opinion, the shining star of the tavern was the lighting. A very determined artisan hollowed out several iron anvils, stuffing a dancing red flame into the hole and covering it with clear glass. The unique flaming anvils hung in a square pattern from the rafters.

Not long after sitting down, Rollo appeared carrying two of the biggest tankards of beer Leif had ever laid eyes on. It reminded him of the first and last time he bought a Yard drink on the Vegas strip. Lifting the weighty mug, he thanked Rollo for his generosity and took a deep pull of the amber liquid. It was delicious. The ice-cold draft washed over his taste buds, refreshing him as it went down. He let out a contented sigh as he felt the tension of the past few days wash away.

"Good, right?" Rollo asked, wiping away a foam mustache. "It's a nice hidden gem that I try to visit whenever I am here and have a small amount of time to myself."

"It really is. After the insanity of the past week, it feels good to be back in a bar, surrounded by people trying to enjoy a drink with their friends." Leif said.

"True enough," Rollo said as he hefted his drink and downed the contents in three mammoth gulps. "AHHH!" Rollo set the now empty mug down. "I do wish I could stay; I have a number of questions I would like to ask you, but I must meet with the Rao. I spoke with the barkeep about our mysterious Berserker friend. Sadly, he has not seen her for several weeks."

Leif felt his shoulders slump at the prospect of a wasted trip.

"But..." Rollo continued, "he mentioned her associates have become regulars at the pub. They typically show up around sunset. He wasn't completely confident, but he thought they were part of a mercenary group that uses the Hammer and Anvil as a meeting place. So, if you hung around for a day or two, he said he would point them out to you the next time he saw them. I'm sorry, Leif. I had hoped to have more."

"No," Leif said, waving off the kafteinn's apology. "You have done more for me than you know. Before now, I thought I was the last Berserker. The only other hint that another survived was from an old book. You've given me hope."

"That is encouraging." The kafteinn scratched the back of his neck. "Happy hunting, Leif. Remember, if you choose, there will always be a spot available for you within the Skogur Borg."

"Thank you," Leif replied, holding out his hand to shake Rollo's farewell. With a twinkle in his eye, Rollo instead plunged his hand into his traveling satchel. There was a loud clicking sound as he pulled out a full coin purse, slapping it into Leif's waiting hand.

Eyeing the cloth bag, he asked, "What's that for?"

"That is a small thank you from Queen Thyra. She foresaw a situation just as this. You can use the coin for food and lodging here in *Mikill Stoar*. There are thirty pieces of Alfheimian stamped gold in there. It is a pittance for what you've done for my people, but it should be enough for now. If used prudently, the gold should last you at least a month." Pointing toward the bar, Rollo continued, "The Savartalfar barkeep has a basic understanding of the common tongue. He can help you with lodging. He knows you are a friend of mine, so he shouldn't try to take advantage of you."

Gratitude welled up in Leif. "Wow, thank you. I figured I would camp out on a bench or something for a few days, but this." Leif held up the bag of coins. "It's amazing. I don't know how to thank you."

"No thanks are necessary, Leif. You defeated an Outsider that was threatening my people. For that, you have earned my respect and the Skogur Borg's eternal gratitude."

Leif knew it would be rude to refuse such a gift, so he pocketed the purse and held out his fist. Rollo raised an eyebrow. Leif thought it was a very human gesture.

Shaking his hand slightly, he said, "This is a sign of respect among Midgardians. I know you have an interest in my people. Make a fist."

Rollo's eyes lit up. "Oh!" Rollo made a fist.

"Cool," Leif said as he bumped his fist against Rollo's.

"Thank you, Leif," Rollo said. He turned on his heel and made his way through the crowded bar, waving farewell as he disappeared out the door.

Sitting back down, Leif nursed his drink. A hint of fear spider-webbed through his gut. He was alone on a strange realm; his only ally was gone and the only information he had on the female Midgardian was the word of some random bartender. *What the hell have I gotten myself into?* he thought. Before he spiraled too far, he reminded himself that his grandfather had explored the realms on his own, too. Leif shook his head to clear away any doubt. He leaned back in his chair, enjoying his drink in peace.

Leif stayed at the pub for a few more hours, people watching. Mythical creatures were literally feet away from him. It was a mind-blowing experience watching a Ljsoalfar toast with an Orc, or to see a chugging contest between a pair of Savartalfar. After his second tankard, the world began to tilt around him, blurring at odd angles. He felt the sudden craving for fresh mountain air on his flushed face, so Leif drunkenly got to his feet and swayed through the crowd toward the exit. If he had been sober, he may have noticed a table in the back corner occupied by a Ljosalfar, Dokkalfar, and Savartalfar who had been eyeing him for quite some time. They followed him out. Suddenly struck with the urge to pee, Leif stumbled down the first alley he could find and peed against the wall.

Once relieved, Leif went back out to the main road, walking back to the massive cave mouth. He bought a few random sticks of something he hoped was meat and found a table near a host of food carts. Feeling the light breeze waft by, Leif marveled at the darkening sky. The bright yellow sun had turned an amber orange as it lazily crossed the cloud filled horizon. The sky, which was a dark blue when he arrived, had darkened to a vibrant purple. Leif took in the bright colors of the veil snapping across the sky. He hadn't had the chance to admire the veil for some time, but it had always been there since he first inherited the Berserker. The sight was so majestic that words temporarily failed him. Drunkenly staring out over the fading sunset, he was completely caught off guard when strong hands clamped down on his shoulder. The sky abruptly shifted from lavender to the midnight black when a cloth bag was forced over his head. Before he could utter a cry of alarm, something hard smacked into the back of his head, knocking him unconscious.

# CHAPTER 16

L eif woke to a sharp slap and total darkness. A few seconds later, the hood was painfully ripped away. He tried to shield his eyes from the sudden brightness, but his hands were bound behind his back. Closing his eyes, Leif felt a moment of panic as his mind struggled to pull itself out of the dark well of unconsciousness. A shout from deep within his subconscious drained away the onset of panic that had been building up inside. *Calm down! I am a Berserker. Simple bonds can't hold me.* The thought caused Leif to smile. Taking two calming breaths, he opened his eyes, exuding a nonchalant demeanor, as if getting kidnapped was just a stroll in the park.

After his eyes adjusted to the onslaught of light, he saw he was inside a canvas tent with two mundane oil lamps hanging at both ends. Two elves, a Dokkalfar and a Ljosalfar, stood over him with looks of contempt painted on their flawless faces. Leif let his eyes roam over the entirety of his flimsy holding cell. *They must have taken me for an ordinary Midgardian if this is all the precautions they took*, he thought. Putting on a predatory grin, Leif finally looked at his captors. *They are underestimating me. Time to give them the surprise of their semi-immortal lives.* Flexing with all his might, Leif pulled at his bonds, but they didn't budge.

"Shit," Leif breathed as the ropes failed to break. The Dokkalfar and Ljosalfar smirked. The Dokkalfar stepped forward to slug him across the face, knocking him unconscious.

"Ahhh," Leif involuntarily yelled when he was yanked from unconsciousness by an ice-water bucket bath. Blinking and sputtering cold water out of his mouth, nose, and eyes, he yelled, "Shit! You never realize how important your hands are until you get something in your eyes." He surmised his kidnappers wanted something from him or they would have just killed him. Being the defiant millennial he was, Leif chose to screw with the Dokkalfar and Ljosalfar a little.

"Listen, Beavis and Butthead, I've seen enough movies with interrogation scenes in them to know if you wanted to kill me, you would have done it already. You clearly took me for a reason, so why don't we dispense with the painful parts and just ask me questions?"

Beavis, the Dokkalfar, said something in Ljosa to Butthead, the Ljosalfar, causing them both to laugh. Beavis then faced Leif and asked him a question in Ljosa.

"Hey, asshole, I don't speak your language," he said. He had hoped to sound brave when he spoke, but being soaked to the bone in freezing cold water had him uncontrollably shivering, causing his voice to crack. Butthead was clearly not impressed with his bravado, backhanding Leif across the face. It hurt, but not badly. The pain of the slap muted the shivering in his limbs for a few moments.

"Why were you and that Skogur Borg dog looking for Lagertha?" Beavis asked in a jumbled sing-song rush of English.

"Who or what is Lagertha?" Leif asked.

SMACK. This time he was hit so hard his chair rocked backwards.

"What business does the hunt have with Lagertha?" Beavis asked again.

The second hit was considerably harder than the first; it rocked Leif's head to the side, and it set his ears to ringing. If his body hadn't been enhanced through the Berserker, it probably would have broken his neck. Leif felt the stirrings of the Berserker in the back of his mind, but he kept a hold on it. *They clearly don't work for Hel or The Outsiders or he would be dead by now. So, who the hell were they?* Leif held the Berserker at bay. Sometimes inaction is the best action.

"Seriously guys, who is Lagertha?" Leif asked again.

SMACK. Again, the force rocked his chair to the side.

"DAMN, that hurt!" Leif yelled into the silent tent. *All right. I'm done with this,* he decided.

Leif mentally sighed as he slowly released the Berserker. His pounding headache vanished as icy fire flooded his veins. He noted with a smile he was no longer cold. *How dare they bind me, question me? It's time to put the shoe on the other foot,* Leif growled into his mind.

Shock and confusion flashed across Beavis's and Butthead's faces a moment before Leif, still bound to the chair, lunged forward. Just before he tackled Beavis, he twisted so that as the two fell. The legs of the chair slammed into Butthead's stomach. Butthead "OOFED" as the wind was knocked from him. The chair shattered into several pieces as all three went down in a heap of tangled limbs.

Though free from the chair, his hands were still bound tightly behind his back, which made it surprisingly hard to get to his feet. After a few seconds of flailing limbs, angry shouts, and what Leif suspected was a whole lot of cursing in Ljosa, he got to his feet at the same time as Beavis and Butthead. With his strength augmented by the Berserker, Leif smiled as he strained against his bonds. This time, the rope held for a fraction of a second before ripping apart with a loud snap. Leif had one hell of a rope burn, but he hardly registered the pain as he balled his fist and charged his captors.

The two elves were caught off guard by Leif's sudden escape and ferocity. He slugged Beavis in the face, sending him stumbling backwards where he tripped over the broken chair, falling down. He followed up by drop-kicking Butthead in the chest before the stunned Ljosalfar could react. Butthead flew backwards, crashing into the tent posts. The sudden sound of wood splintering filled the air as one of the posts holding the tent up shattered into kindling. Leif's world once again went dark as the canvas collapsed over him. It was surprisingly heavy and coarse against his skin. Feeling with his hands, he searched for the edge of the tent, but he was unexpectedly shoved from behind. Leif rolled to his stomach as his unknown assailant lashed out, kicking him in the side, knocking the wind from his lungs. The Berserker filled Leif with enough rage to blot out the noonday sun. Gasping, he crawled forward, still searching for the exit. While his attacker continued to kick him.

Suddenly, the heavy weight of the tent was ripped away. Not wasting time, Leif rolled to his right, away from his attacker, and then he sprang to his feet. He quickly appraised the large, misty encampment. Giant flame torches stood as beacons, marking the outskirts of the settlement. Just beyond the firelight, the tall shadowy outlines of trees overshadowed the camp. South of the site, a large bonfire lit a huge semi-circle of boulders. A second crackling fire blazed in the center of the settlement, pushing back at the heavy mist that wafted all around him. Laid out in military precision, the central fire was encircled by several large, tan canvas tents like the one he had just escaped from. Several mist-shrouded beings poked their heads out of their respective tents, staring in his direction.

Beavis and Butthead stood in front of Leif, but now they were armed with two short, curved swords with no cross guards. He readied himself for the fight. He strategized that he would kill one of them quickly and take their sword. Once armed, he could fight his way to the edge of the camp, then use the mist to disguise his retreat into the surrounding forest.

Shifting his feet to attack, Leif was completely blindsided. His head rocked to the side and his body followed. The force of the unseen strike sent him careening to the ground, where he rolled once before coming to a stop. His vision swam painfully in darkness for several seconds before he was able to refocus on his new attacker. She was tall, about five feet ten inches. She wore thick dark brown leather boots and baggy tan pants that were tucked into the tops of her boots. Her white homespun button-up shirt was covered by a vest made from the pelt of some black furred beast. A silver chain belt with several small leather pouches attached to the chain was wrapped around her waist. A double-bladed ax with a grip at least three feet long was horizontally strapped to her lower back. Leif had never seen someone sheath their weapon like that before, but he guessed it made for an easy draw. Her red-gold hair was tightly braided around her head, forming a crown. She had a tanned oval face with eyes that glowed electric blue.

The moment Leif locked eyes with his attacker, a jolt of electricity thrummed through his body. He knew without a shadow of a doubt this woman was a Berserker. With that realization, he felt an odd twisting sensation in his gut. It was a strange mix of wishing to reach out and embrace his fellow Berserker combined with the primal urge to attack. He was both drawn to the woman and felt the desire to challenge her to single combat, *Mortal Kombat* style. He noted from the complex flurry of emotions crossing the female Berserker's face she felt the same way about him. After several tense seconds, his attacker mastered herself. A mask of emotionless mistrust settled over her face, and her right hand slipped to the haft of her ax, but she didn't draw it.

"Who are you?" The female Berserker demanded in a harsh whisper.

"You, you are a Berserker like me," Leif said in wide eyed astonishment. Then it clicked. "You're Lagertha."

Her eyes narrowed, and the female Berserker drew her ax, pointing the razor-sharp edge at Leif. "How do you know my name?" She hissed.

Lifting his hands, palms out, Leif very slowly pointed with his left hand towards Beavis and Butthead, who stood transfixed. Their eyes bounced between the pair of Berserkers. "In between punches, those two kept saying your name. I didn't understand at the time!" Leif said, raising his voice as he eyed the two elves, then turned back to Lagertha. "But now it makes sense. Before I was so rudely kidnapped, I was at the *Hammer and Anvil* with a friend looking for clues to a recent Berserker sighting. After I found myself blindfolded and beaten, it appears that I am speaking with the exact person I was looking for."

Lagertha pursed her lips. Leif could tell she was confused and mistrustful of his words, but there was no denying the strange chorus of emotions roiling inside them both.

"Another Berserker?" Lagertha asked. "How is that possible? The other Berserker clans died on Midgard ages ago? Where are you from?"

"Midgard, where I was believed to be the last living Berserker. My ancestors were able to maintain some amount of control over the Berserker within, which allowed my line to survive. Much like your ancestors, if I were to guess." Leif put his hands down and pulled the Berserker back, but he wasn't able to fully extinguish the fire within.

"Ha, control your gifts," she boasted with an arrogant smile. "It's true, you are a Berserker. I can feel it in my bones, but you are nothing like me. I can see it in your eyes. You still battle for control."

Something Lagertha said tickled the back of his mind, a memory from his brief time with the Norns. They were going to teach Leif how to harness the Berserker. They said he had only scratched the surface of its power, then Hel killed them, cutting off his chances of ever learning their secrets. "You're right," Leif placated, "There is much I still don't know about being a Berserker. It is the very reason I searched you out, to learn from a fellow Berserker about the power living within us."

"Me?" Lagertha asked with a raised eyebrow.

"Yes, you," Leif said. "It's clear from your continued survival that you have unlocked the secrets to our gift. And that's why I searched you out, to learn to become more powerful. I'm not here to fight, at least not anymore," Leif said with a sharp look towards Beavis and Butthead.

Lagertha held his gaze for a moment longer before nodding. With the threat of continued violence quelled for the moment, Leif took several slow, controlled breaths as he reigned in the burning rage of the Berserker. To his surprise, it was harder than it should have been. He mused it had something to do with the strange energy of being so close to another of his kind.

Once the last vestiges of his power were safely in the depths of his subconscious, Lagertha commented, "You lack control. You are dangerous. Unascended Berserkers such as yourself are the reason our kind died out. They ran around as if our powers were a new toy, letting it control them and not the other way around. You must assimilate with the Berserker. To truly call yourself a Berserker, you and the power must become one, body and soul."

"Can you teach me?" Leif asked.

"Maybe. Your existence has given me much to consider," Lagertha said as she abruptly turned and walked away. Over her shoulder, she ordered, "Give him a tent for the night." Addressing Leif, she said, "Tomorrow we shall see if you are worth the effort."

# CHAPTER 17

Brushing the dirt from his pants, Leif stepped up to the two scowling elves. Not being able to help himself from getting one final dig in, he hooked a thumb in Lagertha's direction, saying in a haughty voice, "The boss says I get to stay." He winked, but then he realized they probably didn't have the same social context for a wink. "So, which one of these fine-looking tents shall be my abode for the night?"

Yellow and black eyes crinkled in annoyance, and then Beavis said something in Ljosa, causing Butthead to bark a quick laugh.

"Come on, guys. That's not fair, I don't speak Ljosa?" Leif sighed, annoyed.

"Then you should learn," Butthead said, with a heavy accent that made him sound Russian. Leif didn't know why, but it made him seem that much more imposing.

"You know, you're right, I would love to learn Ljosa, but right now isn't the time. So, if you don't mind, I'm tired, cold, and in pain. I would really love to lay my aching head down for a little." Leif said, softening his voice in hopes of a parley.

His two tormentors shared a knowing grin before Butthead said, "Of course, of course. Your tent is right there." Leif let out a groan of exacerbation. His new tent was the very same one he had helped destroy in his fight with Beavis and Butthead.

"That's karma for ya," he sighed as he assessed the tangled mess of his sleeping quarters. "Whatever. I got this. In Scout camp one year, I had to build a lean-to out of scraps from the surrounding forest. So, this should be a piece of cake," he told Beavis and Butthead. The elves either didn't understand or didn't care because they merely shrugged his comment away before disappearing into the gloom.

Leif didn't have it. Over an hour later, he was still struggling to untangle the tarp. Apparently, breaking the support pole while fighting off several assailants underneath said tarp makes for one giant knot. For much of his time, he cursed, kicked, and pulled the canvas apart, but it was no good. If he was going to unclutter the mess, he was going to need help.

During his struggles, darkness fell over the misty camp, further frustrating his efforts. The large bonfires and torches lining the camp served to banish just enough of the swirling mist to alert Leif to the numerous figures ghosting through the camp. Sadly, none of them chose to aid him in his struggles. Adding the cherry on top of the disappointment cake, the mouthwatering aroma of roasting meat and general chatter assaulted Leif's senses, signifying it was dinnertime.

Thankfully, a short time later, a Midgardian male in his late teens to early twenties stepped out of the shadows, carrying a small wooden plate piled with meat and vegetables.

"Sorry to bother, friend, but would you like something to eat?" the Midgardian asked.

The newcomer had short strawberry blond hair and a red five o'clock shadow over a strong jaw. He also had bright emerald eyes. The man wore black pants with a white homespun long sleeve shirt with the sleeves rolled up to his elbow, revealing a small circular tattoo with an angular rune within. The tattoo shimmered in the low light, as if it was made of reflective ink.

"Oh, thank the gods," Leif said, throwing the cursed canvas to the ground. The young man silently handed over the steaming plate before turning away and disappearing into the hazy darkness. If it wasn't for the bonfires and torch fires, Leif would be blind to his surroundings. The fog was so thick that even the veil was a pale shadow of its former glory. Only the barest hint of its light could be seen flickering above.

Plate in hand, Leif looked around for a chair or stump to sit on, only to realize the sole chair he had seen was destroyed in his botched escape attempt. Just as he was about to sit on the moist forest floor, the young Midgardian materialized again out of the haze, rolling two stubby tree stumps. The moment Leif's seat was in place, he plopped down, stuffing his face with spiced meats and vegetables. The meat tasted like pork that had been lightly dusted with spiced curry powder. The vegetable dish was some type of boiled potatoes and what he thought was blue carrots. The veggies were a bit bland for his taste, but in his current state, he couldn't care less.

"The rumor around the camp is that you are a Berserker from Midgard," the Midgardian asked. The excitement was clear in his voice. "Is that true?"

With his mouth stuffed full of food, Leif raised a finger until he was able to scarf down enough food to banish his hunger pains. The Midgardian untied a small water-skin from his belt and silently passed it over. Smiling in gratitude, he took the proffered skin and drank deeply, savoring the ice-cold liquid.

"Ahhhh! Thank you, friend. Yes, I am from Midgard. And what's crazy is that up until I took on the Berserker mantle, I had no idea any other realm but Midgard existed." Leif said, taking another bite of the meat.

With a confused look on the youth's face, "What do you mean? How could you not know of the other realms? Everyone knows about the realms."

"Not on Midgard. My home world is very different from the rest of the realms. To us, the other worlds are nothing but fictitious places from our ancient myths." Leif commented.

"But that makes no sense. How do you explain bridges or the Ljosalfar or Savartalfar? They clearly aren't from Midgard, so they must come from somewhere. Tribe warriors travel the realms all the time when they are out on missions."

"Have you ever been to Midgard or heard of someone from your tribe going there?" Leif asked.

"No," he said with a hint of sadness in his voice. "The few Midgardians in the tribe are descendants of those clan members who chose to follow my ancestor, one of the first warriors gifted with the Berserker mantle. As far as I know, no one of the tribe has ever gone back. The tribe is my home, but even so, I would love to see Midgard for my own one day."

"You should!" Leif encouraged. "Though I have only visited a few of the other realms, I feel it is safe to say that Midgard is like no other."

"How so?" the young man asked eagerly.

"Midgard is a world devoid of magic." Leif sighed. "In the absence of Ljosalfar magic, Savartalfar craftsmanship or Aesir influence, my realm became one of technological advancement. Concrete jungles have replaced much of the natural world. It is honestly hard to describe since many words I would use have no context here. I sure would have loved to see how Midgard would have progressed if the Aesir hadn't burned most of the bridges connecting my world to the others. I have no doubt earth would have become the shining jewel of the realms. A society equal parts magic and technology woven together." Leif took another swallow of food and drink. "I'm Leif, by the way," he said, holding out his hand.

"Bjorn," the young man responded with a smile as he grasped Leif's forearm.

At first, Leif was a little taken aback by the greeting. Then memories of similar greeting styles from movies and TV shows about the Viking and Crusade era flashed through his mind.

"You have no idea how crazy it is that you are here, a Midgardian from our home realm and a Berserker at that," Bjorn chirped excitedly. "In all the long years of the tribe, not one of our people has come across another. Sure, we heard stories here and there about other battle-crazy Midgardians with strange glowing eyes off fighting in odd battles, but nothing was ever confirmed. Throughout the years, Mom and the rest of my Berserker elders just assumed they were tall tales. We had come to believe our bloodline was the last one left. If you don't mind, could you tell me about your clan?"

"That is a long story," Leif chuckled as he set down his empty plate. Now with a full belly, his shoulders slumped heavily as a wave of exhaustion swept over him. He looked at the knotted mess of his sleeping quarters. "I am exhausted, and I still need to pitch my tent."

"I can help with that!" Bjorn said with a smile.

The pair made quick work of the tangled mess. However, during Leif's fight with Beavis and Butthead, one of the wooden support posts had been broken. He tried and failed to *Macgyver* the mangled pole, but it was a no go. Disheartened, he was about to call it quits and just roll the canvas up into a makeshift sleeping bag. *It won't be too bad*, he told himself, resigning to the idea. But then, Leif saw Bjorn's eyes widen as an idea took hold of the young warrior's mind. Bjorn quickly left the tent, jogging into the misty camp.

Five minutes later, the soft crunch of grass alerted Leif to Bjorn's hurried return. He came into view, holding a metal tipped spear in one hand. With a hint of pride in his voice, Bjorn said, "If you drive the spear deep enough into the ground, we can use the shaft as a replacement post."

"Well done," Leif said, taking the weapon from his outstretched hand. It was heavy, but the wood was smooth to the touch. He had no illusions of the lethality of this simple but deadly weapon.

Making sure he was level with the other pole, Leif lifted the spear high over his head, then he slammed the metal tip into the ground at his feet. There was a loud THUMP as the spear sunk several inches into the soft grass.

Holding his breath, Leif released the shaft, half expecting it to fall over. But a few tense seconds later, the spear remained firmly in place. Two quick minutes later, Leif had himself a slightly lopsided tent. "Thank you, Bjorn. I couldn't have done it without you. Stop by anytime and I will tell you of my home realm."

"Will do," Bjorn said with a smile as he disappeared back into the gloomy night.

# CHAPTER 18

The barest whisper of canvas parting woke Leif from his nightmare addled sleep. As he struggled to free himself from sleep's embrace, he was momentarily confused as to why the door to the Skogur Borg's sleeping quarters had been replaced by a tent flap. Then the events of the past few days slammed home. Fearing his unannounced guest may be an assassin, Leif curled his hand around the axe he tucked beneath the balled-up cloak he was using as a pillow.

Knowing he may be seconds away from getting his throat cut, Leif worked hard to keep his breathing even, as if still asleep. When he sensed his intruder was close enough, Leif kicked out, flinging the light sheet toward his unknown assailant. Jumping to his feet, Leif sprang forward but stopped when he spotted the lightening blue eyes of Lagertha staring at him through the gloom of his tent. She had an amused smile on her face.

Leif glared at his fellow Berserker as he once again felt his stomach twist into knots at the nearness of Lagertha. He felt so drawn to her. Yet interwoven into the allure was a desire for violence. He felt the compulsion of the Berserker to fight and to prove he was the superior warrior. It was very confusing. With axe in hand, he felt the Berserker pushing to bury his blade deep into her chest, but he held back. Not only would that defeat the very purpose of finding her, but she was an enigma to him. From her glowing eyes, she was clearly berserked, but she was also in complete control. One doesn't attack a foe he doesn't understand. That is a quick way to end up six feet under.

"So are we going to fight it out, or would you mind putting those away," Lagertha said into the tension filled silence.

To Leif's chagrin, it took more effort than he would have liked to stand down. "Sorry about that," Leif said.

"No offense taken. You are a warrior in an unfamiliar camp. I would expect no less of a fellow Berserker," Lagertha said with a wave of her hand. "Now come. We shall eat a quick breakfast before I test you." She exited his tent. Snatching up his rumpled shirt, Leif followed.

Cold morning dew sparkled on the green forest floor. Leif pulled on his shirt and hurried after Lagertha. Though the mist was swirling through the air, obscuring much of his view of the camp, he could hear the familiar chorus of sounds he associated with a large group of people getting ready for the day. Much of the camp seemed engaged in their morning chores.

Next to the large rock outcropping that acted as a natural barrier for one side of the camp, an army of cook fires and boiling stewpots waited to feed the hungry camp. To the right of the cooking area, Leif saw the large bonfire from last night. Dozens of occupied tree stumps dotted the area. Tribe men and women chatted while eating their morning meal. At the end of the cooking area, a squat Savartalfar ladled food into the waiting people's proffered bowls. With bowls of their own, Leif and Lagertha sat down on empty stumps near the fire.

"Bjorn thinks I can trust you," Lagertha said as she took her first bite.

Leif froze. There was an awkward silence before he spoke up. "You sent him to spy on me, didn't you?" he asked accusingly.

"Of course. Only a fool lets a stranger, a Berserker at that, into their camp without keeping an eye on them. People are much more forthcoming to a friendly face baring food," Lagertha said with a shrug. "From what I gather, I do not believe you are a threat to the tribe. But if my assessment of you is true, then with your lack of full control of the Berserker, you can become a danger to my people at the slightest misunderstanding."

"Lack control? For being a Berserker for less than two years, I feel like I'm doing pretty damn good. I stopped myself during our fight yesterday, and that was after you sucker punched me. There's no way I could have managed that when I first gained this power," Leif said defensively.

A knowing smile spread across Lagertha's face. "True, I can see you maintain a good hold over your power. But you are far from mastering it. Keeping yourself restrained is an easy way to get yourself killed. My ancestor, Jarl, discovered the key to unlocking the true potential of our Berserker, making us far stronger and faster."

"For real?" Leif asked with childlike excitement. "Is it possible for me to gain this power?"

"That remains to be seen. The path to unlocking the true potential of our power has been a closely guarded secret within my clan. My ancestors chose to leave Midgard and escape the needless bloodshed being sown by the first-generation of Berserkers with their short-sided world view. So, even if you prove to be ready mentally and physically for the trial, I must get to know you. I do not wish to have you ascend to my level only to one day find our blades locked in combat. Though I make no promises at this point, I must also warn you. The path to unlocking our powers isn't an easy feat. Many who have devoted themselves to it have failed in the undertaking."

"I am up to the task," Leif said, feeling a rush of adrenaline flood his veins.

"We shall see. I am interested to see what kind of warrior Midgard has trained you to be." She put down her empty bowl and gestured for Leif to follow.

Silently pumping his fist in excitement, he said, "Midgard had nothing to do with my training. I owe everything I am to a Ljosalfar who trained me."

"You continue to be an enigma, Berserker," Lagertha commented. "I do hope you prove worthy. I believe there is much we could learn from each other."

MANY WITHIN THE camp watched the pair of Berserkers walk through their midst. It was an uncomfortable feeling. It made the back of Leif's neck itch. Though he didn't like all the attention, it did provide him with an excellent chance to observe the camp and its inhabitants. From what he could tell, the tribe wasn't selective in its members. Nor did there appear to be a division among races. Dokkalfar and Ljosalfar worked side by side, repairing tents. In the cooking area, beings of each race known to Leif answered to a squat Savartalfar that looked like she carried the weight of the nine realms on her small shoulders. He also noticed that everyone, save for the young, was armed in one fashion or another.

Following Lagertha, the pair passed the outer ring of torches marking the camp boundaries. Once in a small clearing, Leif determined that the mist on Vanaheimr was a permanent fixture in their location. It mercifully wasn't so thick as to obscure the clearing that Lagertha had led him to. Even before the haze thinned, he could hear the familiar sounds of wooden weapons and yelps of pain. Leif inwardly winced at the phantom pains those sounds evoked.

The small clearing was set aside for training. It contained four rows of three sparring rings. Stern faced instructors walked up and down the rows with eyes glued to their charges, shouting words of encouragement or criticism. Most of the combatants looked to be in their late teens or early twenties. Leif had a sudden thought. *If the other races live for hundreds of years, do they age at a slower rate? Like they may look twenty but are, in fact, fifty.* Just then, he spotted Bjorn in one sparring ring. He was dueling a young Dokkalfar female with a pixie cut. He was a skilled fighter, but clearly no match for the sword wielding dark elf.

"So, what's up with the mini militia you've got here?" Leif asked with a raised eyebrow.

"Living on the fringes of society doesn't lead to an easy life. Though the fog obscures our camp from prying eyes, we still get raided from time to time," Lagertha responded unabashedly.

"Makes sense," Leif said.

"By necessity, we are a nomadic people. We move throughout the realms whenever we feel we have overstayed our welcome. We hunt and grow a small number of staple crops, but we try to keep a low profile. In order to do that we must have coin. Many of the adult members of the tribe, myself included, hire ourselves out to sell swords.

"All tribe members are taught to fight from a young age. Once they reach the age of maturity for their race, they are added to the guard rotation. When they grow older, they are given the opportunity to take mercenary work for the tribe. Our training process has the dual benefit of making every member of our tribe capable warriors, which discourages any rival groups from attacking us. Although, it still happens more often than not."

"If it is so dangerous, why do you all live in the wilds? Why not settle down in a more civilized area?" Leif asked, perplexed.

Lagertha's features tightened as she pressed her lips together in a hard line. "The beings who govern the realms are not as accepting as you have been led to believe. Every member of the tribe has been cast out or hunted by the ruling bodies of the realms. The people of the tribe long ago grew tired of constantly being hounded for our differences or past mistakes. They have chosen to forsake the corrupt governments of the realms for the tribe," Lagertha said, opening her hands out wide in a welcoming gesture. "We find there is safety in numbers."

Leif's mind recoiled at what his host was saying. *Sure, I had a few bad run-ins. Most recently, that asshole council member, but overall, most people have been nice to me.* Leif was about to respond, but Lagertha interrupted his thoughts.

"I can see you wish to continue this conversation, but that topic will have to wait for another day. We have dawdled enough. It is time to see if you are worthy of carrying the Berserker mantle." She gestured toward the empty sparring ring.

Leif stepped into the ring, rolled his shoulders a few times, before turning to face his fellow Berserker. "Alright, so what are the rules of engagement?" he asked.

"You attack me. We fight, and at the end, if you are in control and worthy, I will let you stay," Lagertha said nonchalantly as she stepped into the ring.

"Ok, but what are the rules? How are we going to determine who the winner is?"

A burst of arrogant laughter escaped Lagertha's lips before she said, "There is no doubt to how the fight will end, young Berserker. You cannot hope to defeat me as you are."

Leif felt his hackles rise, and the Berserker responded to Lagertha's casual dismissal. "Fine then," he growled, letting a bit of the Berserker out. "Show me where your practice weapons are, and then I will make you regret underestimating me."

"Wooden weapons?" Lagertha said disbelieving. "Those are for whelps. What use are wooden or blunted weapons to warriors? If you do not fear getting cut, then your mind will not react like it's a true battle. For those of us who have seen real combat, we must train as if every fight is to the death. There is no greater teacher than pain. Now, enough talk. I grow bored of this."

Shrugging his shoulders, Leif unhooked his axes and charged.

Snorting in derision, Lagertha blurred forward, meeting Leif head on. Stunned by her speed, Leif was helpless to react as Lagertha's hand flashed out, swatting the flat half of his leading axe with the back of her hand. Simultaneously, she stiff armed him in the chest with her other hand. The force of Lagertha's simple attack was like hitting a brick wall. He was slammed backward, knocking the back of his head painfully against the packed forest floor, causing stars to streak across his vision. Blinking to clear the twinkling lights, Leif tried to get up, but the weight of Lagertha's boot pressed firmly against his neck, stopping him.

Careful to not press harder than necessary, Lagertha leaned down. Her bright glowing eyes narrowed, and with a forced smile she asked, "What use are your powers if you don't use them in a fight? Never, EVER underestimate an opponent. Now attack me for real or get the hell out of my camp." Releasing her foot, Legertha moved to the center of the ring, letting Leif get to his feet. She still had not drawn her weapon.

*You want me to take the gloves off? Fine then,* Leif thought as he rushed her, releasing the Berserker. He relished the power that accompanied the burning rage. It gave him focus. He barreled forward, homing in on the arrogant female Berserker like a lion after an injured gazelle. Just as he came within the outer range for his axes, he swung, aiming the axe in his right hand at his opponent's collar bone. In hopes of catching Lagertha off guard, Leif struck out with his left hand, sending his axe in a horizontal slash across her hip.

Lagertha pivoted backward, taking her out of range of Leif's first attack, but the axe in his left hand remained on target. There was a flash of silver as Lagertha unsheathed a concealed dagger from her thigh, deflecting his second axe in a shower of sparks. Berserked, the strange compulsion he felt toward Lagertha was amplified tenfold. His blood ran so hot he thought it might actually boil. All of his hard-fought control was shunted to the side, and his

Berserker asserted control. A single thought vanquished all his reason: to utterly destroy the Berserker in front of him.

Leif's axes were a flurry of razor-sharp steel as he used every technique and combo his muddled mind could think of. The training grounds quickly filled with the staccato CLANG, CLANG, CLANG of battle as the two god-blessed warriors applied their deadly craft. Somewhere in the melee, Lagertha produced a second dagger, matching Leif's flurry of blows with ease.

Leif drew more and more on the Berserker to fuel his attack, and his perception of the world condensed to a single target, Lagertha. His rage was like the sun, fueling every action he took. The small voice at the back of his mind called out for him to slow down, to reassert control, but a snarl from his primitive Berserker silenced his rational self. With each failed attack, he pulled harder on the burning reservoir of power. The rage filled voice of the Berserker grew louder, while his conscious mind quieted. The only coherent thought that remained was, *there can be only one.*

Though Leif attacked with blinding speed, Lagertha's daggers were always a step ahead, blocking or redirecting his blades. It infuriated him. His fellow Berserker was unlike any opponent he had ever crossed blades with. She moved with determination, flowing between attack and defense with brutal efficiency. Leif had fought more powerful foes, but unlike those deadly beings, Lagertha fought with no arrogance in her swift brutal attacks. Hel had drained herself when he fought her in the depths of Asgard. When he faced Ra and Fenrir on the streets of L.A., he got the distinct feeling they were just toying with him, like a cat swatting around a mouse. And then there was Ares, who treated battle like a game. Lagertha was unlike all of them, but no less deadly. She fought with no emotion, nor pride, which for a Berserker was a crazy notion.

Seconds turned to minutes as the two Berserkers clashed. Lagertha was like the wind, flowing between attack and defense with effortless ease. Throughout their prolonged duel, Lagertha snuck in small cuts and slashes, just deep enough to draw blood, but not to hurt or maim. After what felt like hours, Lagertha decided she had seen enough. With effortless speed, Lagertha slipped past Leif's guard, slamming him to the ground.

Growling his annoyance at so easily being downed, Leif got to his feet.

"ENOUGH," she commanded. "Show me your control by suppressing the Berserker."

The authority in her voice was impossible to ignore. The tone and force of it pierced Leif's murderous rage, going straight to the rational part of his mind. Under normal circumstances, with the hard-fought control he had painstakingly worked to gain, Leif knew he would have been able to pull back, reasserting control. However, this was far from normal. Neither Leif nor Arias had ever anticipated he would come across another Berserker. Nor had they envisioned the effect it would have on him. Everything about Lagertha incensed the berserked Leif. He was annoyed with her clear superiority in power, martial skill and the way she dared command him to stop. He was a Berserker chosen by Thor to fight in Ragnarok. No one had the right to tell him what to do. Or so the rage fueled monster had him thinking.

"Stand down, Leif," Lagertha demanded once more. "I know what you are feeling. I feel it too. Our blood sings for battle. Even ascended, my power calls for it, but we must resist. If you can't regain control, then we are done here. Do you understand me?"

Though he didn't vocalize his answer, he shifted back into a bladed stance, his axes at the ready. Leif made his intentions clear to his fellow Berserker.

Though Lagertha sighed in resignation, he could see from the gleam in her eye that she was enjoying the fight just as much as he was. Her eyes never left his as she sheathed her daggers and called out, "Kandor! Sword now!"

Any mental fight for control within Leif went out the window when the glint of a short sword sailed from the gathered crowd and into Lagertha's waiting hand. The berserked Leif immediately recognized the threat Lagertha posed as she mirrored his stance. Her sword was held over her head with the blade pointed directly at his chest.

"So be it," Lagertha whispered. She blurred forward, appearing before Leif in a blink of an eye. Her sword slashed down with incredible speed. Leif got an axe up just in time to block. Their weapons clanged as the two opposing forces met. It had been a ruse. As Leif focused on blocking the blade, he completely missed Lagertha's balled fist as it careened towards his face.

A moment later, there was a meaty THUMP and Leif was knocked unconscious.

HE WOKE TO A LIGHT SLAP. Confused, he sat up, blinking a few times. "Where am, OW," Leif moaned. His hands shot to the pain on the side of his face.

"We are back in your tent," Lagertha said from the log she was sitting on.

Turning his head in her direction, a hot bar of pain seared down the muscles of his neck. "Jesus Christ! Did you have to hit me so hard?" he mumbled as he rubbed his bruised jaw.

"You are a Berserker," she said, leaning back. "It is better to be safe than sorry. I wanted to make sure you stayed down. It is safer for everyone." Lagertha gave him a pointed look.

"So, what happens now?" Leif asked somberly.

"You are not ready," she responded without hesitation. "Your control is lacking. If you were to attempt to ascend, there is a strong likelihood you would lose your mind in the process. You would become nothing more than a mindless beast that would have to be put down. It is possible the slip was due to the compulsion we both feel. An unexpected complication, but one that would need to be overcome if you stayed. Take a day to recover. Come find the tribe once your will is absolute. Then you may try again. I will be leaving to meet a Savartalfar about a job. When I return the next day, I will lead you to the cloud layer." Standing up, Lagertha gave him a quick nod and left him in silence.

"Shit," he moaned as he laid back on his bed roll.

# CHAPTER 19

Sometime later, Leif mustered the strength to get out of bed and face the world. He felt like the wind had been knocked out of him. So much was riding on this meeting, and he blew it. Leif went to the front of his tent, taking a seat on one of the stumps. He looked out the front of his tent into the dense fog. Where he could only see the ghostly outlines of tribesmen as they moved about the tent city.

Not really knowing what else to do, Leif gathered several stray branches around his tent. Pulling on his time as an Eagle Scout, he spent several long minutes trying to light a fire. It was not as easy as he remembered. He shouted like Tom Hanks in *Castaway* once some embers finally took to the flame. Sitting back, he stared into the tiny flickering flame, willing the fire to tell him what to do, like it had all his answers.

His mind was numb with defeat. He felt his life shrink into a tiny bit of oblivion. He imagined it floating away on a bit of ash that was taken by the soft breeze. The swirling fog slowly dimmed, denoting the oncoming night. Suddenly, a shadow detached itself from the gloom, resolving into Bjorn. His long sleeves were rolled up, revealing the strange reflective tattoo. The young Midgardian warrior nodded at Leif before taking a cross-legged seat next to him.

"I heard about your fight with Lagertha. Do not lament. My mother said she would give you another chance in time. Any lesson you can live to correct is a boon when one lives as a warrior, my friend."

"You don't understand," Leif commented soberly. "The realms are at war, but I am too weak to do anything about it. I cannot afford to wait. By the time Lagertha thinks I'm ready, it will be too late. I must get stronger now, or my enemies will catch up to me and I won't be equipped to beat them."

"That's a heavy burden you carry." Bjorn shifted in his seat. His words revealed wisdom far beyond his years. "But also, it is good motivation. Do you know where you will go?" Bjorn asked.

"I have an idea," Leif commented, staring back into the snapping fire.

"Tomorrow morning, my training group is assigned to gather firewood. You should join us as we scour the surrounding forest. It would be good to meet the group. You never know when you may need an ally. Besides, my mother won't return until tomorrow afternoon. So, you won't have anything to do anyway. You could tell us tales from Midgard and the battles you have fought," Bjorn pressed with a smile.

Leif wanted to say no, but he knew that was just disappointment talking. Besides, Bjorn had a point. He really didn't have anything better to do than wallow in his own misery. "Deal." Leif sighed, resigned.

"Good," Bjorn said, getting to his feet. "Be at the cook fire at dawn. Hesvik will have breakfast ready for us before we head out.

LEIF HAD a fitful sleep that was plagued by dreams of friends and foes condemning him for his failings. When he wasn't gasping awake in a panicked sweat, he tossed and turned. As the dark swirls of mist brightened, Leif groggily got to his feet, dressing quickly before belting on his axes. "Gods! I really miss electronics sometimes. I could have really used an alarm clock. Who the hell sets an arbitrary time like sunrise without a way to tell time?" He grumbled as he stomped out of his tent, heading toward the bright orange glow of the bonfire.

He was the last to arrive, of course. Bjorn and five other young tribe warriors waited, including two Ljosalfar, a Savartalfar, Dokkalfar, and surprisingly, a female Midgardian. They laughed and joked with each other as they gulped down the oatmeal-like gruel the army of cooks prepared.

When Leif stepped from the mist, Bjorn excused himself from the group, trotting over to him with the youthful exuberance of someone who has never needed coffee to get going in the morning. After a quick round of pleasantries that Leif mumbled through, he was quickly rushed to the chow line, which was steadily growing despite the early hour. Moving on autopilot, Leif shuffled through the line. Once he reached the end of the line, he was given a wooden bowl filled with the gray-brown slop by a Savartalfar male that was glaring daggers at him. Leif risked lifting his eyes and saw similar looks of anger and mistrust plastered on other supernatural faces around him. Knowing there wasn't anything he could do to soothe their animosity, Leif gave them his best smile and walked to Bjorn's group.

As he approached the raucous group, the laughter died away. The shift in the mood made Bjorn jump to his feet. "Come on, you guys," he moaned. "Don't be like that. Leif is a warrior, just like all of us. He deserves our respect."

"True, but we don't go on rampages when we lose our tempers," said a Dokkalfar female with cheekbones so sharp she could have cut glass.

"Berserkers are not new to the tribe. Nor is one losing control. We have all sat around this very fire as the elder recounted story upon story about my mother and my Berserker ancestors. Leif's actions should not come as a surprise to any. And it is also a precursor to when I take up the mantle. I say it was good for us to see the strange ferocity of an unascended Berserker. We all, Leif included, came out smarter from the incident." Adopting a haughty tone, Bjorn continued. "I say anyone too afraid to have Leif accompany us on the dangerous mission of gathering firewood is a coward."

All five young warriors jumped to their feet, shouting in different languages. Bjorn smiled to himself as he gestured for Leif to take the proffered seat. Sitting down, Leif quickly slurped down his breakfast while his new companions wearily eyed him. Wanting to get the show on the road, Leif took three mighty sips from the bowl before the silence grew more awkward.

Seeing that he was done, Bjorn signaled everyone to get ready as he jogged toward the cook fire. A moment later, Bjorn came back with a matronly looking Savartalfar. She wore a food-stained apron tied around her waist. Any illusions of the plump women with rosy cheeks being a sweet, motherly figure was swept out the door the moment she spoke.

"All right, you whelps," the Savartalfar began, rolling up her homespun maroon sweater's sleeves to reveal the same reflective tattoo that Bjorn had. "Today you are mine. Just because Galen won't be around to babysit you beyond the camp doesn't mean you all can slack off. Last time you lot were assigned to me for a morning, I spent too much time hand holding you brainless airbags, causing both lunch and dinner to be delayed." That elicited a few snickers from the group, earning a sharp glare from the diminutive dwarf. "So, I figured I would kill two birds with one arrow today. You all will gather as much firewood as you can carry and bring it back here. I want so much wood that I won't need to ask for help for several days. Do you hear me? Now, off with you. And if you disappoint me, you can bet your asses none of you will be getting dinner tonight. Am I understood?"

"Yes Hesvik." The group intoned as one.

# CHAPTER 20

The group moved through the foggy woods with eyes glued to the forest floor. The mist was so thick that when Leif looked left or right, he could only make out the ghostly outlines of the other young tribesmen and woman moving through the shrouded forest. After passing the torches that marked the boundary of the camp, they fanned out in a wide line, slowly gathering any stray twigs they could find.

"The tribe has been in this location for a long time," Bjorn said, as his eyes scanned the forest floor. "We have already scavenged much of the useful resources in the surrounding area. Up until a short time ago, we purchased much of our lumber at one of the peak city markets. But with word of war breaking out across the realms, many have begun to hoard their supplies. We will most likely have to forage far and wide for lumber today."

"So, what's the deal with all of you having to pick up wood?" Leif asked. "Aren't you all warriors in training? Shouldn't you be more focused on your martial training than this random chore?"

Chuckling, he answered, "That is a sentiment all trainees share, and not just my group. Whenever any of us brings it up, we are given the same answer. If you don't wish to help with the upkeep of the tribe, you are free to leave."

"Makes sense," Leif said, scanning the area. "The tribe is large. It can't be easy keeping it running, let alone fed. Then why not just cut down the trees that surround the camp? I'm sure these tall behemoths..." Leif slapped the trunk of a massive tree, "could keep the tribe's fires going for weeks on end."

A somber look crossed Bjorn's face, and his eyes shot around and up the trees.

"What?" Leif asked. Hands dropping to his axes reflexively.

"When we first came to this gloomy forest, we did just that. The clearing we settled in couldn't be more perfect. A small area free of trees pushed up against the side of all those fallen boulders. It is perpetually hidden in the mist and protected on one side by massive rocks. The tribe scouts were ecstatic. In the beginning, the forest floor provided more than enough fuel to keep our fires going, but once the surrounding area was picked clean, a couple of enterprising Savartalfar took it upon themselves to fell a few trees for Hesvik.

"The pair didn't go far past the encampment's boundaries when they cut down a swath of trees. Everyone felt it when the large pines came crashing down to the misty forest floor. The duo had informed many in the tribe of their intentions, so no one was surprised when they felt the ground tremble as the ancient trees came crashing down. But after the third tree came down, a blood-curdling scream pierced the silent forest."

"Oh shit," Leif commented, eyes flicking to his surroundings.

"Galen, the tribe's weapons master, my mother, and a troop of our warriors went to investigate," Bjorn continued. "I wasn't with them, but from what my mother recounted, it was a grizzly scene. The Savartalfar couple had been lashed with ivy to the trunk of one of the trees they cut down. Then all their limbs were lopped off."

"Jesus!" Leif exclaimed. "Your leaders still felt it was safe to stay in the location?"

"Galen, an old grizzled Ljosalfar, spotted the hazy outline of a forest nymph watching the group as they inspected the bodies. He took the nymphs' presence and the manner of the Savatalfars' deaths as a warning. We are welcome to stay within the forest, so long as we don't take more than we need. Since that day, no one has been allowed to walk the forest alone. We don't cut down trees anymore either. We just harvest their fallen branches or when times are tough, we will cut off low-hanging branches, but never from the same tree."

"And have there been any attacks since then?" Leif inquired, still not sure if he should draw his axes or not.

"From the Nymphs? No," the youth said. "But we aren't the only beings who roam Vanaheimr's misty surface. Many of those who live in this realm choose to live in the mountain peak cities, high above the fog layer. But there are still outlaws, trolls, Gakin, and many other beasts that can be found in the misty shadows. Groups have been attacked in the past, but now that we move in numbers, we are usually successful in repelling any attack with minimal injuries or death."

"Why does the tribe choose to stay down here if it's so dangerous?" Leif asked, perplexed.

"That's a question for the tribe council," Bjorn commented. "I am still young, nor am I a full-fledged warrior yet, so I am not privy to those decisions. Though I would guess from what I have heard from other members, it is because we are considered rogues and outlaws. Our group doesn't fit within the social construct of the realms. Many who have joined the tribe were driven out for one reason or another."

*Hmmm.* Leif thought. *Rogues and outlaws, huh?* Leif wondered for the first time about the odd lifestyle the tribe lived. *There is a big difference between Robin Hood and the Mafia.* Not knowing how to respond, Leif channeled his inner millennial, giving a non-committal, "Got'cha."

Holding out his hand in a stop gesture, Bjorn scanned the area.

"Ok," the youth said. "Looks like we have gone far enough," he yelled to the shadowed forms of the rest of the group. "Fan out, but stay within shouting range. Let's start a pile here," he pointed to a flat area. "Once we have as much as we can carry, we'll head back."

A chorus of responses came in English, Ljosa, and Savata. Though Leif had come with Bjorn and the others to gather wood, he was more interested in exploring the strange forest they were in than doing grunt work for the group that was kicking him out.

As he walked away from the group, he casually collected any fallen branches that crossed his path. Unexpectedly, he felt a tug at the back of his mind. He was immediately on edge. Leif recognized the feeling as someone or something using magic nearby. In a flash, he had his twin axes out. Stilling his breathing, he listened for any hint of attack, but nothing came. Seconds turned to minutes, but still no attack came. The magic was still there, pulsing softly. Deciding to investigate, Leif silently moved through the gloomy woods, using the magical pulse to guide him.

He tiptoed through his murky surroundings, attempting to channel his Skogur Borg friends' natural stealthiness. That's when Leif spotted something he hadn't seen in days, sunlight. Wary of a trap, but too intrigued not to investigate, he crept towards the golden light. The pulse of magic grew stronger with each step. Stopping along the edge of mist and sunlight, confusion and awe battled to make sense of what he saw. He rubbed his eyes in disbelief as he stared out over a circular swath of forest sparkling in the bright sunshine. Within the radiant circle, a grove of trees unlike any he had seen before were positioned in a sacred-like arrangement. Their leaves glowed with arcane power, pulsing to an unknown beat. He felt the source of the magic somewhere in the heart of the hidden grove. He stepped onto the swath of grass that marked the barrier between fog and sunlight, feeling a soft pressure sweep across his body as he crossed the threshold. The hidden area was made up of four concentric circles of trees, each growing smaller the closer they were to the center. At the center, there was a large stone plinth with a silver bar of some kind sticking out of it.

Lifting his face to the sky, Leif basked in the warm glow of sunlight. *Damn, this feels good! I never thought I would miss the sun so much,* he thought. Not sensing any danger, he pressed on. He felt like a toddler in Disneyland for the first time. Reds and blues bounced off the sparkling leaves. If it wasn't for the pain signifying the start of what Leif knew to be a horrific headache, he could have stayed in the grove all day. With each step he took, the magical force grew stronger. Leif stopped to consider whether this was the best idea. After a few moments of introspection, he decided it wasn't a trap and approached the stone at the center of the magical circle.

"No way. This must be some joke," Leif exclaimed as he stared at an object straight out of Midgardian legend. Plunged into the center of a large stone was a broadsword. The length of the sword not encased in stone had runic carvings running up the blade. *Excalibur?* The mythical sword gleamed in the golden light. *So, what do I do? Do I pick it up? What if it comes free of the stone?* His mind made up, he took a deep breath as he reached for the hilt of the sword.

Inches from the handle, Leif's mind fuzzed as a massive amount of arcane energy slammed against his senses. His knees went weak like wet noodles, and for a moment the magic threatened to overwhelm him. Leif felt a warm liquid trickle down his nose. He dabbed at it and looked at his fingertips. They were red with blood. "That can't be good," he whispered. He ignored the throbbing, and reached out, wrapping his right hand around the polished handle of the sword.

An electric current thrummed through his body as an alien presence shot up from the sword and into Leif's mind. The foreign intelligence whipped through his psyche, inspecting every aspect of him. Memories from his earliest childhood until a few minutes ago flashed across his mind's eye in rapid succession. It was too fast for him to follow. Then, as quickly as it had started, it stopped. The presence retreated from his mind, down his arm, and back into the sword.

It was then that Leif was assaulted with the knowledge that he could pull the sword free of the stone. With the sword in his hand, he would become a warrior with no equal. One that hasn't been seen in the realms for thousands of years. His enemies would cower before him. But he also knew this power would come at a price. He knew without a shadow of a doubt that he could free the weapon from its prison, but also that he wasn't the intended recipient of the mythical artifact. If he were to release the sword before the realms needed its power, a great calamity would befall them all. He felt that a corruption would spread across the worlds, snuffing out the light wherever it stood against the unknown foe. Leif recoiled from the knowledge the sword imprinted upon him, then pushed back. He summoned images of Hel, his fight with Fenrir, and Karcoa burning. He tried to convey to the sword that a darkness was already here, and it was spreading. However, the sword or whatever protected it remained firm, showing Leif an image of what looked like Midgard, but not like he remembered. It was different somehow. He watched the strange city with cars and pedestrians going about their daily business suddenly become shrouded in a large shadow that spread across the landscape. Then the image fuzzed, and Leif was shown another vision of shadowed beings, wielding strange weapons and fighting a familiar figure in gleaming armor. The figure raised his arm, weapon in hand (it could have been a hammer or even an ax), calling down large swaths of forked lightning. The massive beams of chaotic electricity vaporized the shadow creatures in large swaths, but there were thousands more to take their place. A second figure appeared, cutting a way through the nightmare creatures, swinging a great glowing sword in mighty arcs. The sword wielding knight rushed to the other being's side, and as the two warriors fought back-to-back, the vision slowly faded. A moment later, the last remnants of the vision left Leif's mind, leaving him with way more questions than answers.

However, one thing was certain. The sword must remain in the stone so its true owner may find it.

Opening his eyes, Leif noted he still held the handle of the great sword in a white knuckled grip. At first, his fingers wouldn't respond to his urging, refusing to release his hold on the sacred weapon. Closing his eyes, he willed his body to respond, feeling his fingers slowly release their grip. As his body gave voice to his mental command, he felt the sword offer a silent thanks before the presence retreated into the weapon.

Leif stepped away from the sword with a gasp. He knew its name: Dainslief. *That's odd,* he thought. *How did I know the true name of the sword?*

Once he broke contact with the blade, the crashing waves of magical energies resumed their mental barrage, alerting him that he needed to leave. Jogging out of the ring of trees, Leif sighed when the pain lessoned. Thankfully, the migraine inducing pulse receded back to being just an annoyance once he was back in the fog. He wiped the blood from his nose. "I could really use a couple Excedrin right about now," he moaned as he hurried to put some distance between himself and the sword.

After a few minutes of blindly stumbling through the mist, Leif found himself in front of a large pile of wood. "Where have you been?" Bjorn accused. The others stopped what they were doing to stare daggers at him. "And why don't you have any wood with you?"

"Uh," Leif eloquently muttered. He had been so focused on getting away from the grove, he failed to have an excuse. His mind was still reeling from everything Dainslief had showed him. "Sorry, guys," he said, making eye contact with the annoyed mob. "I was gathering wood when I heard something large crashing through the underbrush. That was when I realized I had wandered off from the group. I am new to this mysterious forest and thinking about what Bjorn told me on the way out here, I cut and run." He lied smoothly.

A Dokkalfar said something in Ljosa, and the group snickered. Leif guessed from her tone it was something snarky. Bjorn decided to move the group along. "Just to be safe, let's head back. If there really is something out there, we don't want to get caught unaware. Everyone, grab what you can, and let's go." There were a few grumbles, but everyone stacked as much wood as they could in their arms while simultaneously keeping one eye on the surrounding forest.

A few splinters later, Leif and the group started back to the tribe's encampment. Unlike last time, where they all walked in a loose line, the group now huddled together, everyone chatting amicably. At some time during their return, Bjorn asked Leif to tell the group about Midgard. As he was in the middle of describing cars, planes, and other common modes of transportation, he heard a crashing sound in the distance. A moment later, several throaty roars echoed through the forest. Leif felt the hairs at the back of his neck stand on end as the unknown creatures belted out a mighty challenge. The group quickly looked at each other before dropping their loads to sprinting back to the encampment and the source of the roar.

# CHAPTER 21

Leif was fast, but not as fast as the Dokkalfar and Ljosalfar that ran ahead of him. Running blind through the mist, it took everything he had to merely keep the speeding elves within sight. During the mad dash, he felt the Berserker prowling his mental hold, howling to be released. But he held fast, knowing he needed to see what they faced before he berserked.

Just as the sounds of combat reached Leif, he spied the orange glow of the tribes' torches, signaling they were close. He unclipped his axes just as the shadowy outlines of the three elves from his group stopped underneath one of the large torches with their weapons drawn.

Stopping next to the elves, Leif caught his breath as he assessed the situation. Huffing from their exertion, they all peered into the gloomy camp, searching for the enemy.

The ground trembled with surface impacts as something large and heavy moved toward them. A moment later, a hulking shadow appeared within the mist, swinging a large object. A soft breeze pushed past Leif, clearing the fog. The brief glimpse revealed a towering figure carrying a tree trunk with a stone larger than Leif's head tied to the end.

"A mountain troll," Bjorn cursed, as he caught up to the group.

"Can it be killed?" Leif asked as he studied the massive creature. It was easily fifteen feet tall, with gray, pockmarked skin. Eyeing the monster, he zeroed in on the troll's green, blubbery shoulders and stomach.

"With steel," the Dokkalfar scoffed as he nodded at his Ljosalfar companion. The two elves, both wielding dual short swords, dashed forward directly for the lumbering troll.

"No, wait!" Bjorn shouted, but it was too late. The troll saw them coming. It swung its mighty club as the elves closed in. The Ljosalfar was quick on his feet, managing to dodge as the troll swung its massive club at him, getting away with nothing but a glancing blow to his right leg. The Dokkalfar wasn't so lucky. His feet got tangled in debris concealed by the swirling fog. The stone club impacted with a sickening crunch.

Lifting the blood-soaked club, the troll searched for its next victim.

"Mountain trolls aren't very smart, but they have thick hides. The fatter they are, the harder it is to hit anything vital. Our best bet is to keep it distracted while one or two of us aim for soft spots at the back of his knees or underneath his arms. If we can bring him to his knees, go for the eyes."

"So, you've fought one before?" Leif asked.

"No," Bjorn replied. "I've only heard stories from other tribe warriors." Thunderous booms reverberated through the forest floor as the troll charged their party, cutting their conversation short.

The troll roared, sounding like a cross between the trumpet of an elephant and the roar of a lion. Moving too fast for something so large, the beast was on their group within seconds, sweeping the club in a horizontal arc. Leif and the remaining female Ljosalfar reacted immediately, jumping out of the way as the stone head sailed by. Bjorn and the Midgardian weren't so lucky. Bjorn rolled forward, reacting incredibly fast for an ordinary human, but still not fast enough. The troll's club clipped his lower back, sending him sprawling to the ground with a thud where he lay unmoved. The female Midgardian was caught flatfooted. There was a meaty SMACK as the club impacted the girl square in the chest. One second, the tired warrior was standing next to them, and the next she was sent flying backwards, disappearing into the misty forest beyond.

Seeing that his assault was only partially effective, the troll roared as its verdant green eyes zeroed in on the unmoving Bjorn. The monster surged forward, punching out with a moss covered fist the size of a tree trunk. Leif reacted on instinct, releasing the Berserker to help him. Closing the distance, he knew his axes would be of little help, so he did the only thing his berserked mind could think of. He slammed his body painfully against the descending mass of the troll's outstretched arm with enough force to push the attack off target. The troll's fist contacted the forest floor next to the unconscious Bjorn with a dull thud that Leif felt through the soles of his shoes. Hoping to pull the troll's attention away from his downed comrade, he shouted his defiance at the lumbering creature, retreating to where the last remaining member of his party stood.

Any fear or hesitation he felt at facing the towering beast evaporated as the Berserker boiled through his veins. Leif kept a tight rein on his power, knowing he needed to play this battle smart. Keeping one eye on the troll, he addressed the last standing member of his party, the female Ljsoalfar.

"I don't know you and you don't know me," he said, addressing the blond elf. "And I have no idea if reinforcements are coming, so we need to work together." The Ljosalfar shakily shifted from foot to foot, but the determined elf nodded in agreement. "Good. As much as the Berserker within is howling for me to refute it, you are far faster than me. Which means I'm going to need you to act as the rabbit while I hit it from behind in its weak spots, got it?" With a nod, The Ljosalfar and Leif moved in opposite directions, hoping to flank the troll just as the heavy club crashed down, dimpling the soft ground where the two had been standing.

Seeing the green eyes of the creature follow him, he feared their plan had already gone awry. Its gaze never left Leif's as the creature hefted its club and prepared to charge. Only to be frustrated, a rock the size of a softball smashed into the right side of the troll's face. The monster roared in pain. It swung its conical bald head in the direction of the thrown rock, spotting his Ljosalfar companion. Seeing she had gained the monster's attention, she smiled as she unsheathed her twin short swords. Leif watched in fascination as the warrior banged her swords together once, issuing a loud clang and a shower of sparks in hopes of keeping the dim creature focused on her.

Knowing it was now or never, Leif bolted forward, drawing on the power of the Berserker to cross the short twenty feet in the blink of an eye. As the lumbering creature prepared to charge the lone Ljosalfar, Leif swung his twin axes, biting into the soft flesh at the back of the troll's unprotected knee. The axes did little more than slice two thin lines along the creature's hide. Thick red brown blood welled up in the cuts, but that was all. Though the cuts were superficial, they surprised their enemy, causing the behemoth to stumble, then go down to one knee.

The Ljosalfar warrior, not content with sitting back while the Berserker stole all the glory. She seized the moment, closing the distance between herself and the mountain troll. She leaped onto the troll's knee before burying both her swords deep into the troll's eye sockets.

The monster's reaction was immediate. Two enormous wart covered hands wrapped around the Ljosalfar before she could jump away. Thick bloody tears streamed down the troll's face as it raised the trapped elf to its face. Opening its mouth, it revealed a series of crooked yellow teeth. The Ljosalfar desperately struggled to free herself from the troll's grip, to no avail.When she came within reach of one of her swords, she ceased struggling, seeing she would only have one chance to make her attack count. At the last possible moment, she reached out, taking a firm hold of a hilt. In one smooth movement, she pulled the blade free with a wet sucking sound, only to immediately thrust the sword into the troll's open mouth and into the soft gray matter of its brain, killing it instantly.

With a loud thud, the troll fell to the ground, releasing the elf, who dropped gracefully to the ground.

## CHAPTER 22

With the biggest threat in the vicinity dealt with, Leif felt the Berserker's urge to seek out the next enemy in line. His eyes fell on the Ljosalfar. She was clearly a skilled warrior. A surge of red flashed across his vision as the power responded to the perceived threat the elf presented.

Leif knew now was the time for iron control, lest he accidentally attack the next person to approach him. Closing his eyes briefly, he bore down on the Berserker, letting it know who was in control. For a moment, his mind went blank as an uncontrollable rage surged through him. But he was no noob. Leif rode the wave of rage until it burned itself out. Opening his eyes, he smiled as he reasserted control over his power.

Still Berserked but with his mind in the driver's seat, Leif scanned the misty surroundings, looking for the other mountain trolls. But he neither saw nor heard anything. The bellows of challenge and the cries of the injured from just moments ago had gone completely silent, which was either a good or a bad thing. Hoping for the good but expecting the bad, Leif trotted over to the female Ljosalfar.

He knew from the elf's posture she was pleased with herself for felling the beast. "We should help the others," she said as Leif approached, but he shook his head.

"Not until we know if there are more of these things in the area," Leif kicked the dead troll in the arm. "We don't want to get caught off guard."

The Ljosalfar nodded a moment later saying, "You're right," with her melodic accent. "We should search the area."

Leif nodded, and the two slowly crept deeper into the camp. The crushed bodies of those unlucky enough to get caught in the initial attack littered the ground in all directions. Both young and old victims made up the gruesome scene; it made him sick. Images of the burning dwarf village felt fresh in his mind. Leif looked for his companion and saw her cheeks glisten with tears as she passed the lifeless bodies. After passing next to a particularly mangled corpse, she heaved and threw up her breakfast.

Leif tried to be respectful of her sorrow, but he was on edge. Every sound she made had the potential to alert an enemy of their location. It wasn't long before several blood-soaked tribe warriors, led by Lagertha, sprinted out of the mist. Several tense seconds followed as Leif felt the strange instinct the Berserker emitted when Lagertha was near. The two berserkers stared each other down. It didn't help that Leif was surrounded by warriors wielding weapons.

He felt his power smolder with the belief that Lagertha meant to cut him down, but he held himself back. He had lost control in front of her before, and it had cost him. Doing it again would cement her decision to send him away. So, with all the strength Leif could muster, he scrunched up his eyes, willing his Berserker to recede. The mental battle lasted longer than he would have liked, but in the end, Leif proved he was the master of his mind.

With the rage abated, he breathed a sigh of relief. When he opened his eyes, Lagertha gave him an approving nod. With a flick of her wrist, she sent her warriors away. "Go, search for survivors, and bring the injured to Hippocrates in the caves," Lagertha commanded.

"I'll go with you," Leif's Ljosalfar companion chimed in. "Several in our party were injured at the camp's edge. But Krystal and Dalec..." she trailed off. Her voice cracked with emotion. "Are dead. I can lead you to them." The warriors looked at Lagertha, and she nodded her assent.

"Bjorn?" Lagertha asked once they were alone.

"He got clipped in the back by the troll's club. It looked like a glancing blow. Unless something happened after we left, he should be alive. Nothing fatal from what I saw," Leif replied honestly.

Lagertha's face contorted into a mask of rage at his words as she hissed, "You left an injured companion behind."

Leif wasn't cowed in the slightest by Lagertha's outburst. In fact, it had the opposite effect. He felt the Berserker respond, raising his hackles to the challenge. "It would have been foolish to stop to give aid while there was still a risk. We couldn't risk getting caught flat-footed by other trolls! With this damn mist messing with my vision, stopping to help a downed comrade could spell the end, not just for the wounded warrior, but for me as well. So, glare at me all you want, but I stand by my decision."

Lagertha's grip on her axe tightened. The power flooded through Leif's veins as he found himself not only anticipating Lagertha's attack but hoping for it. He had no doubt this was the Berserker's influence on his perceptions, but he desperately wanted to fight her again, to show her that he wasn't some mulling pup to command. He was a Berserker, beholden to no one but the Aesir.

To his surprise, Lagertha blew out a weary breath, sheathing her double-bladed ax behind her back. "You are right," she sighed. "I am normally in complete control. Once a Berserker ascends, much of the pressure from our power to attack is dampened. But the strange compulsion we feel when we are close, the mountain troll raid, combined with hearing that Bjorn was injured, has weakened my self-restraint. You have done the tribe a great service today," she said with a small smile. "Maybe I was too quick to judge you."

Leif perked up at the praise, thinking she may reconsider her decision.

"Come, let's make a final sweep through the camp before I give the all clear."

# CHAPTER 23

The pair of Berserkers moved on silent feet as they surveyed the damage, alert for any trolls in the vicinity. They crossed three dead mountain trolls. If there were any others, they had either fled or were killed in the raid. With no threat in the immediate area, Leif saw no reason to remain berserked, so he took a few moments to completely suppress the power.

Breathing a sigh of relief at his show of control, he said, "I had no idea how big the tribe was. The fog does an amazing job concealing the camp, but it sure makes finding people hard."

"It's a pain in the ass, but it serves its purpose. We like to keep our whereabouts a secret. What better place to hide than in a forest shrouded in a perpetual mist? Law keepers have sought out our location for years on this realm, but the fog and fear of what lurks within keeps them at bay. The mist, combined with our concealing wards, keeps us well protected."

"Concealing wards?" Leif asked, raising an eyebrow.

Lagertha went rigid. The female Berserker was quiet for several seconds before rolling up the sleeve of her home spun shirt. She pointed to the reflective tattoo he had seen on Bjorn and others of the tribe. "These are concealing wards."

"What does it do?" Leif asked.

"It hides the bearer from far sight," Lagertha said.

"What's far sight?" he asked, staring intently at the metallic tattoo.

Lagertha gave him a confused look. "You really are from Midgard, huh?"

"Why would I lie about that?" Leif asked defensively, feeling the Berserker rumbling in the back of his mind.

He wasn't sure how, but Lagertha seemed to pick up on his Berserker's annoyance, giving him a sharp look as she shifted her stance. "Because you are an enigma. My bloodline has been wandering the realms with the tribe for hundreds of years, and we have only heard tales of our kind. But here you are, a young Berserker, appearing out of nowhere with a kafteinn of the Skogur Borg. Which leads me to think you are a spy. But then you say something like 'what's far sight.'"

Leif opened his mouth to respond, but Lagertha held up her hand to forestall any response.

"I do not mean to insult you. It is just an observation I have made. You do not move and act like someone from our realm. You have a childlike curiosity. When you look around the tribe, you act as if you are seeing things for the first time. Ljosalfar, Dokkalfar, Savartalfar, Orcs, even me as an ascended Berserker. Your eyes widen and you subconsciously follow these beings with your eyes. These are not the actions of a trained Skogur Borg spy. Yet you somehow are connected to the wild hunt. You really are an enigma, but that is a topic for another time. Far-sight..." she said, getting back on topic, "is the ability to locate someone or something from a great distance."

"Even across realms?" Leif asked, thinking about all the times he was ambushed.

"Technically, yes. But a cross realm far-sight would require an immense amount of power. Aesir level power," Lagertha said as she eyed him.

Leif still wasn't sure whether he should reveal his involvement with Hel's coup. He decided to heed Arias's warning. "You never know who's listening." Lagertha may not have any connection to Hel or the Outsiders, but who's to say what or who is concealed in the mists? So, Leif worked hard at keeping a neutral expression. "And it…" Leif pointed at the tattoo, "blocks the spell?"

"Yes, it grounds out the spell, making the wearer effectively invisible," Lagertha explained.

"That's amazing. How do I get one?" he asked.

"That is no easy feat for one not of the tribe," Lagertha said with a chuckle. "You would need to travel to the Dokkalfar town of Myrkarl, deep underneath Myrkheim."

*Damn!*

Out of the blue, several tribe warriors strode out of the mist. "We've canvased the encampment and the surrounding forest. There is no sign of any reinforcements," the dark-skinned Ljosalfar said as he raised a hand in greeting.

Lagertha mirrored the weapon master's greeting, asking, "Thank you, Galen. Any wounded?"

Galen looked at his diminutive companion, who shrugged. "Our people are still sweeping the area, but we have at least forty wounded. We expect that number to grow as we look through the destruction of the sleeping area. One of those moss-covered bastards ran straight through it, sweeping its great club back and forth, destroying a score of tents in its wake."

"Hesvik, how many are dead?" Lagertha asked with a cold fire in her voice.

"At least a hundred of our people were killed. We killed all five of the trolls that attacked. My men took down four, while Leif and Strijder got the last one," Galen said with an appreciated nod toward Leif. "Should we send a scout to hunt for their lair?" The weapons master asked.

"No!" Hesvik shouted angrily. "We can't risk losing anyone else. We have lost enough of our people this day. I see no point risking any more of the tribe." Hesvik said with finality.

"As much as my blood howls for vengeance, I agree with Hesvik. Especially because this forces us to reconsider the decision we made last night. I believe we now have no choice but to attack the royal Savartalfar prison convoy," Lagertha added. "Our plan to free our captured brethren must be advanced. We will need our best warriors if we are to accomplish the task in such a short time."

"Nonsense," Hesvik said in shocked horror. "It's bad enough the Skalny Rycerz are looking for us, but you want to risk angering the Myrkheim royal house as well, and during a time of war!"

"We lost many during the mountain troll raid," Lagertha said, anger creeping into her voice. "We are down a hundred people, you say? That means we need to replenish our ranks before we are attacked again. There is no better chance than now. With the realms focused on defending themselves from Outsider invasion, the prison convoy will be lightly guarded. The Savartalfar royal house has way bigger problems than a prison break at the moment."

"Hmmm." Galen tapped the pommel of his scimitar with his index finger. "Lagertha's right; things have changed. I advised against the raid when it was first proposed, but times are desperate. I agree with freeing our warriors."

"But with what force?" Hesvik asked. "Many were injured in the battle. We will be vulnerable with you taking more."

"Do not worry, Hesvik. Galen and his remaining warriors will be more than enough to protect the tribe. Especially if you remain in the caves until we return. It will afford you the best defense while we are away. Besides, aren't you anxious to get your son Henan back?"

"Bah!" The Savartalfar said with a wave. "It does the dumbass good to be locked up for a time. It will teach him not to be so hot headed. If he had heeded the retreat when you called it, he and his friends wouldn't have gotten caught. Fine, fine. You have my blessing as well, but I better not hear any grumblings about smoke from the cook fires."

"Good," Lagertha said. "Galen, please select ten of your best raiders. Preferably those who won't be worried about any injured family members. We can't have their focus divided during this one."

"Will ten be enough?" Galen asked, doubt lacing his voice.

"Aye," Lagertha said with a knowing smile. "Because two Berserkers will be accompanying them."

"Wait what?" Leif exclaimed.

## CHAPTER 24

H ours later, Leif found himself moving in formation with a band of dangerous looking warriors. The lot of them prowled with predatory grace, moving as a pack on the hunt. Leif's Berserker howled to attack the formidable-looking warriors, but he held the power in reserve. The group consisted of seven Dokkalfar, twin Ljosalfars, and an unusually tall Savartalfar. The two Berserkers covered the back of the formation.

"Are we allowed to talk?" Leif asked in a whisper.

"Why wouldn't we?" Lagertha responded in her normal voice.

"Oh," Leif said, embarrassed. "I just assumed since we are on out in the field on a secret prison raid, we had to remain silent, lest someone is spying on us."

Lagertha scrunched up her face in the universal way women do when they are considering whether you're an idiot or not.

"Got it," Leif said, forestalling any response. "It got hectic this afternoon after the attack. I didn't get a chance to ask you why you changed your mind?"

"You, an outsider, came to the tribe's aid. You could have easily turned your back to our plight, and no one would have held it against you, especially after I said no to your request to train you."

Lagertha looked him straight in the eye. "I spoke with Bjorn and Strijder. They said you were able to think tactically while berserked, even when facing an unknown enemy. Strijder told me how you sacrificed your body to stop the troll from killing Bjorn. Words alone can't convey my gratitude for that. Our powers push us to think that everyone is a threat, but you, in a group of strangers, were able to focus on the mountain trolls while working in tandem with Strijder. That was proof I was wrong. I made a snap decision after a single fight. That is unlike me. I think it has something to do with the compulsion we feel towards each other. Even ascended, it has an effect on me."

A shout from ahead pulled them from their conversation. Leif peered through the fog, and he could just make out a yawning darkness, signifying a break in the jagged rock wall of the mountain base.

"Good work, Biknre," Lagertha shouted. "We've made excellent time. If we push now, we will make it through the bridges with time to spare. Lead on."

Leif stepped forward to follow as the group pressed on toward the cave, but Lagertha placed a restraining hand on his shoulder.

"Hold," Lagertha commanded.

Confused, Leif raised an eyebrow in question.

"Now is the perfect time to begin your training," Lagertha said.

"Here?" he asked, looking around the area.

She smiled and said, "We aren't going to fight. The next step will take place up here." She poked Leif in the temple. "You are to remain berserked for the remainder of our time together."

"But what if I slip and attack one of you?" he asked.

"I would advise against that," she said, nodding toward the group. "They won't hesitate to kill you. This is a critical time in your training. Leaving yourself open to the Berserker will better attune your mind and body. The more in sync you are, the easier it will be to ascend. It won't be easy. Especially being around me, but you need to show me you are in full control."

"Are you sure about this?" he asked.

"Trust me. We are perfectly safe," Lagertha said confidently.

Shrugging, Leif took two quick breaths before slowly releasing his power. The fire coursed through his veins before turning to ice. As the power took hold, he felt the rage zero in on Lagertha. The strange feeling they felt around each other intensified, pushing him to strike. His hand jerked towards his axe, but he pulled it back just as quickly, asserting control.

"Good," Lagertha said. "Now come on, let's catch up to the others."

The two Berserkers once again took up position in the rear of the raiding party. Peering through the low light, Leif made out the rocky tips of stalactites poking out from the gloom. The soft drip of water echoed off the walls as a dank, musty smell wafted through the area.

Leif followed their Savartalfar guide as he expertly navigated their party through a series of twisting tunnels. Several times, he was forced to squeeze himself through waist high crevices or passageways so tight he was pressed flat against the wall. He worried he might get stuck. Mercifully, he managed to squeeze through. After hiking for another twenty minutes, Biknre finally signaled the group to stop. At that point, Lagertha left Leif's side, jogging up to their guide. The two spoke briefly before the dwarf pointed to a shadowed corner darker than the surrounding cavern they had stopped in.

"All right, it looks like we made it," Lagertha said, addressing the group. "Bjartr, you go first. Scout the other side. Make sure there aren't any surprises for the rest of us. Everyone else, follow in thirty-second increments. If there are hostels on the other side, call back through the bridge."

"Aye," the group said in unison as Bjartr, the female of the Ljosalfar twins, calmly stepped into the shadowed alcove. Bjartr vanished, disappearing from Leif's sight entirely. He watched as, one by one, the raiders stepped into the shadow and disappeared.

"What the hell am I seeing?" Leif asked, turning to his fellow Berserker.

She chuckled. "It is the only bridge I have ever seen that opens in the floor." Lagertha gestured for him to follow as she moved into the darkness. "This bridge can always be found within one of the caverns that snake through the mountain range. Each time Biknre seeks out the bridge to his home realm, it is in a new spot. But no matter the location, it always opens in the floor." Standing just outside the dark pool, Leif peered into the murky abyss but could only see an empty darkness. Just as he leaned over, a strong hand slammed into Leif's back, flinging him into empty space. Twisting as he fell, he looked back to see Lagertha laughing a moment before he fell below the edge.

Leif screamed into the whipping wind as his stomach rose into his throat. His mind reeled at the growing realization that he was about to die.

Plunging headfirst through the bridge, a flicker of torchlight rushed into view from ahead of him. Thoughts of a painful death flashed through his mind as he flew headfirst through the room. Gravity suddenly shifted toward what was now the floor, causing Leif to crash headfirst into the hard packed floor with a bone jarring THWACK in the torch lit room on Myrkheim.

A chorus of "OOHHs" echoed through the chamber as Leif went down in a heap, cartwheeled once, and coming to a painful stop against the chamber wall.

*I'm not dead?* He thought in amazement a moment before the pain set in, making him wish he was dead. He lay there breathing heavily as his enhanced healing went to work. What surprised him was the small amount of damage he had taken from the fall. He had fully expected to go splat, but now that he wasn't a pile of mush, the adrenaline of not dying surged through him, making him smile.

Leif looked up just in time to see Lagertha fly out of the mouth of the bridge on the opposite wall. Falling feet first, he watched as the gravity of Myrkheim took hold of her. It was clear from the smooth way Lagertha rolled forward when her feet touched the floor. She had done this before.

The supernova of anger burst to life within his chest upon seeing Lagertha. Before he knew it, Leif was on his feet, bringing his axes down in an overhead cut. There was a flash of metal in the torchlight as his axes crashed into the flat of Lagertha's waiting blade. Shouts of alarm sounded from around the room from the tribe warriors, who stared in confusion at the two Berserkers.

"How was your trip? Lagertha mocked over their blades.

"What the hell's your problem?" Leif growled. "I thought I was going to die!"

"Just a little joke," she said with a smile. "We play it on everyone's first trip through this strange bridge."

"I could have died!" He challenged, bearing down on his axes.

"Ha!" Lagertha laughed in his face. "You're no frail Midgardian. Besides, once the gravity shifts, the fall only amounts to a few feet. You were perfectly fine. The fall also served another purpose. I wanted to see how you reacted."

"This was a test?" Leif asked incredulously.

"Everything is a test. Either you pass and survive, or you fail and die. Everyone who gets pushed freaks out once they get through. But I knew it would send you over the edge. No matter how strong your control, a near death experience would set any unascended Berserker off," Lagertha explained.

"So, you wanted me to attack you?" he asked, confused.

"I did," she responded with a smile. "I wanted to enrage you, then see how you reacted after I explained it was just me hazing you. That this joke was played on each member of this party before. Isn't that right, Floki?"

"Aye," said a hawkish Dokkalfar with a smile. "I even took a swing at Lagertha as she and the group laughed at my fright."

The Berserker surged through Leif, egging him to press his attack against Lagertha for the indignity she showed him. But he bit back, seeing the test for what it was. Gritting his teeth, it took him longer than he would have liked to disengage from Lagertha. He yearned to banish the Berserker back to his subconscious, giving his tired mind a break from holding his power's violent urges at bay, but that would mean admitting defeat, so he held strong. He turned away from Lagertha, closing his eyes as he sheathed his axes.

Sensing he was in control, Lagertha shouted, "Alright, we made great time. This chamber is as good as any to set up camp for the night. Kira, assign who's on watch then post guards at the exits. Everyone, get a quick bite to eat, then get some rest. We have a long trek through the lower caves tomorrow. If we make good time, we should be at the ambush site by mid-morning on our second day. If time is on our side, we should be back by the time this bridge reopens." As if on cue, the bridge behind Lagertha silently snapped shut.

# CHAPTER 25

The following morning, the group set out through the tunnels.

"So, what's the story with the prison break?" Leif asked Lagertha.

With a resigned sigh, Lagertha looked around the large subterranean tunnel. The light from their torches was enough to light their way, but it did little to illuminate their surroundings. The plethora of bioluminescent fungi took care of the rest. Large man-sized mushrooms dotted the long walkway, giving off a bright green glow. Besides the massive mushroom caps, large patches of glowing lichen ran along the walls and ceiling, giving off just enough light to impress upon Leif how large the tunnels were.

"A couple months ago, one of our scouts got word of the Outsider invasion. Fearing a protracted battle across the realms, we took a chance, attacking Viscount Baindus's wagon train. Word was the convoy would be chock-full of provisions. The only problem was there were more guards than we anticipated. When we attacked, members of the Skala Rycerz jumped out from hidden compartments in the wagons, supplementing the viscount's personal guard. Outnumbered, we were forced to retreat. In the ensuing chaos, a small group got cut off, and they were taken prisoner."

"All who are taken prisoner here on Myrkheim," Lagertha explained as she flicked a glowing mushroom cap. "No matter the sentence, are sent to the mines. One of our sources learned those of the tribe would be in the next convoy and provided us with the route they would be taking. When I brought this intel to our best tracker, Biknre, he believed we could intercept the prison train at a tunnel intersection. So we will ambush the convoy as it passes by. Hopefully recruiting a few of the freed prisoners along the way."

"Who or what are the Skala Rycerz?" Leif asked.

"Bastards, that's for sure," she said with hate plain in her voice. "They are the secret police of the Savartalfar crown. Best described as a combination of the Skogur Borg and Konungr of Alfheim. I will grudgingly admit the members of those two Ljosalfar organizations maintain a sense of honor as they relentlessly pursue their directives, but the Skala Rycerz are completely opposite. There hasn't been a single knight or officer that I have met that wasn't corrupt. Like all members of their race, they are obsessed with gold, precious stones, and finely crafted metal, which makes it easy to bribe your way into or out of bad situations."

"If they are so easily swayed..." Leif said as he stepped around a small forest of long-stemmed luminescing fungi, "why are we about to raid a convoy? Couldn't you just pay off the guards?"

"We tried that already," she said with a frustrated sigh. "But because Viscount Baindus and his family were also present during our original raid, the Savartalfar royal court has taken a personal interest in seeing our people condemned to the mines. Not one of the Skala Rycerz is willing to risk their position or their lives on this one."

"But won't it be obvious who hit the prison convoy?" Leif asked. "I would think the Savartalfar court would take more direct action against the tribe once they are made aware of the raid."

"Aye," Lagertha conceded. "Which is why the council voted against the raid when I first proposed it several weeks ago. But things have changed now. Myrkheim has been slammed by the Outsiders. Much of their military has been sent to fight the invaders. Our scouts say the wagon train is only minimally guarded. Besides, the royal court has a bigger problem. They won't have the resources to hunt us down, especially across realms. The Rao would hardly entertain such a request with a multi-realm war on their hands."

"If the court is so pressed for warriors, why send the convoy at all? Seems like the Skala Rycerz are needed at the front," Leif said.

"When the invasion began, the king ordered that all jails should be emptied, sending all to the mines. The court feared if there were a jail break, they wouldn't be able to split their defenses, fighting an enemy within their walls as well as one without," Lagertha stated.

"Harsh, but makes sense."

"Nah," she said with a wave of her hand. "I would have just killed all the prisoners. It frees up your warriors and sends a message to the criminal underground that now is not the time to act out."

*Woah,* Leif thought. *I definitely don't want to get on her bad side.*

When he didn't respond, Lagertha eyed him briefly before giving him a feral smile. "There is no questioning your warrior prowess, but you still carry the frailties of your home realm. There will be a time when you need to make a choice, Leif. When that time comes, I pray you do not flinch." There was a brief, awkward pause in the conversation, then she raised her voice. "Biknre! We have been walking for some time now. You know the tunnels better than anyone. When should we stop to rest and eat?" Lagertha asked.

Leif could just make out the Savartalfar through the gloom. The Savartalfar looked around the large tunnel before placing his small hand to the dirt packed floor. Murmuring softly to himself, the dwarf waited for several seconds. Apparently finding whatever he was looking for, he pulled his hand away from the ground, saying,

"There is a large tunnel junction ahead. We should stop there. It will take me some time to determine the proper route from there. Making it the perfect spot to stop."

"You heard him," Lagertha intoned. "Just a little longer till we can have a hot meal and a rest."

# CHAPTER 26

"A little longer" turned out to be an hour long trek through the underground tunnel. During that time, no one spoke. Leif realized outside of the few times he and Lagertha spoke, no one else uttered a single word. The others of the raiding party only responded when prompted. This got Leif wondering if it was his presence that caused the silence or if it was the eerie tunnel they moved through.

Thankfully, they came upon the junction just as Leif's stomach grumbled. He already felt like an outsider, and he didn't need his stomach's echoing growls to further set him apart from the stoic war party as well. The junction was a cavernous half dome where seven separate tunnels converged. Biknre brought them to the center of the intersection. The Savartalfar slowly turned, carefully eyeing each darkened tunnel. Everyone warily watched the dwarf as he completed his circuit. Whatever the Savartalfar saw during his survey must have satisfied him because he plopped down at the very center of the junction, signaling that it was all clear and for everyone to do the same.

"Y'all might as well make yourself comfortable," Biknre said, getting into a comfortably seated position. "This next *leita* will take some time. I need to seek out the proper path that intersects with the prison convoy. With this many tunnels crisscrossing between cities, it will take me a while." Biknre then placed his flat palm on the dusty floor as he murmured softly to himself.

"Alright, you heard the man," Lagertha said. "Floki and Connor, you two prepare some food. Depending on how far Biknre says we must trek to get to the ambush point, we may have to hustle, so it will be good to get some food in us now. Everyone else, hydrate and check your weapons. I don't care if you checked them this morning. I won't have any screw-ups here because of poorly maintained equipment."

Sidling up to his fellow Berserker, Leif asked, "Is there anything you want me to do?"

Lagertha gave him a crafty smile as she shouted, "Kira, Bjartr, mark out a sparring ring. Leif here has just volunteered to fight you both."

"I what?" he asked, eyeing the two tribe warriors that immediately began drawing a large circle in the hard packed dirt. One would think the sight of two physically fit warriors who moved with deadly grace would cause him to break out in nerves, but it had the opposite effect. The Berserker pulsed within, sending an icy fire down his arms into his fingertips in anticipation of the carnage to come.

Kira was a female Dokkalfar with midnight black hair tied in a single war braid that fell to her waist. She had obsidian eyes with a sharp nose and full lips. She wore black leather pants with a homespun cotton shirt under a hardened leather jacket. A thin Elvin blade, like a rapier, hung from her waist along with a series of pouches and throwing knives. Bjartr had radiant blond hair cut into a bob. Her vibrant yellow cat eyes and hooked nose complimented her heart-shaped face. She wore a long white sleeve shirt trimmed in gold with brown pants. She had a long silver chain wound several times around her waist with a long dagger sheathed at her belt.

Once the ring was complete, the duo stepped into the ring. Leif followed a second later. "What are the rules?" he asked, eyeing his opponents.

"To first blood or exiting the ring," Lagertha said simply. She then spoke to Kira and Bjartr in Ljosa. The subterfuge caused the fire in his chest to burn hotter. Both Dokkalfar and Ljosalfar nodded their assent. The pair immediately separated, moving far enough apart that Leif had to continually turn his head side to side to keep a constant watch on both women."

The clearing, save for the soft muttering coming from Biknre, grew silent. A soft breeze blew in from the tunnel to Leif's right, temporarily cooling the stuffy intersection. His eyes flicked between his opponents as he watched for the slightest hint of motion. No one had drawn their weapons upon entering the sparring circle, so Leif kept his attention firmly on their hands.

In the blink of an eye, Kira dashed forward, drawing her blade. She crossed the distance between them in two powerful strides. Leif had just enough time to bring his axes up in an overhead block. Sparks flew as steel met steel. Kira's blade flicked out in a series of thrusts, forcing Leif back with each successive attack. With his back against the boundary, Kira's right foot lashed out, aiming to drop kick him square in the chest. Channeling his inner Daniel LaRusso, Leif ducked under Kira's booted foot, sweeping her leg out from under her.

Smiling triumphantly, Leif moved in, knowing with Kira out of the match, the odds would shift in his favor. Before his axe could draw blood, there was the brief clink of metal before a ball attached to a metal chain wrapped itself around Leif's descending arm. He was firmly pulled to the side as the chain links went taut. Leif barely managed to stay on his feet. Bjartr gripped the chain with both hands. She smiled, showing off way too many teeth, before she flicked her wrist, sending a ripple through the chain.

The chain around his wrist unwound itself, freeing his arm. The Ljosalfar twitched once more, and the heavy metal ball went flying back into her outstretched hand. Then, in quick practiced movements, her eyes never leaving Leif's, she unsheathed the dagger and attached it to the other end of her chain. *Awesome*, he groaned to himself as Bjartr, dagger in one hand, twirled the chain in her other hand, setting the weighted ball whistling around her in tight arches.

The soft thud of footsteps alerted Leif to Kira's approach, prompting him to dive to the side, narrowly missing her thin sword as she swiped at him. Coming to his feet, he was forced to dodge Bjartr's weighted ball as it careened through the space he had just been standing a second before. Thinking the Ljosalfar was a ranged fighter, Leif attacked Bjartr, hoping to catch her off guard. Kira reacted immediately, moving so fast she had a literal afterimage following her.

Kira once again was on the attack, slashing with the ease of a sword master. He quickly grew frustrated as he was forced back onto his heels. The Dokkalfar's thin blade was everywhere, forcing him to block with both axes lest one of her quick thrusts found its mark. The red haze swirled in his vision, growing thicker as the Berserker urged him to abandon his control and attack.

Twice his control slipped, letting the Berserker's recklessness bubble to the surface, but he quickly recovered. Leif knew if he was to win this match, he would need to be smart and use the Dokkalfar's assumptions to work to his advantage. There was a flash of gold to his right, alerting him that Bjartr had moved into position.

Pain blossomed in his right shoulder as the weighted ball smacked into the meat of his shoulder. If his opponents thought pain would be enough to throw him off, they would have been wrong. Within seconds, the pain was gone, buried underneath his fury.

Knowing he needed to do something drastic to win, he abandoned the traditional notions of a fair fight. Lowering his shoulder, he dodged the horizontal sweep of Kira's blade a moment before he gut checked the Dokkalfar. She may be supernaturally fast and strong, but Leif easily had fifty pounds on the dark elf. Kira was sent flying backward. She landed on her back with an audible "Oaf!"

With Kira temporarily out of the fight, Leif faced Bjartr. The golden haired Ljosalfar whipped her wrist forward, sending the weighted ball in his direction, but he was ready for it. With perfect timing, there was a loud CLANG as Leif swatted the weighted ball out of the air with the flat of his axe head. In a pulse of eagerness, the Berserker's battle lust surged. Blurring forward with all the speed he could muster, Leif closed in on Bjartr.

All of a sudden, Biknre shot to his feet screaming, "OH SHIT!"

# CHAPTER 27

Leif was not one to fall for a ruse or distraction. He stayed on target and brought down his blade. Suddenly Leif spotted a flicker of movement, and Lagertha took a position between himself and Bjartr. Her hand caught his descending axe at the handle. A tremor ran up his arm as Lagertha effortlessly stopped his attack. He shouted in frustration as he bore down, pressing with all his might against her.

"WE NEED TO MOVE NOW!" Biknre shouted.

Lagthera's head snapped in the Savartalfar's direction. "What's coming?" she asked while holding Leif back.

"I don't know what's coming, but there's A LOT of them, marching in formation," Biknre said.

"Leif, back down. I know I just had Kira and Bjartr spend time riling you up, but I need you to snap back, like now!" Lagertha demanded. She looked at Biknre, "Ways out?"

"Uh, they are only a few yards from turning the bend in that tunnel," the dwarf said, pointing to a passage to their left. "We won't be able to pack up in time," he said.

"Can we hide?" She queried.

"Yes, but we have to hurry," Biknre shouted.

"Lead the way," she responded. Turning back to Leif, she looked at him in his berserked eyes. "If you don't back down now, you risk our capture. I can't allow that. I will kill you if need be. Are you with us?"

"Ahhh!" Leif shouted as he fought with the Berserker. The threat from Lagertha had the opposite effect than she intended. The Berserker pulsed with rage at her casual threat, but he knew something was wrong. Biknre's reaction was evidence of that. So, he pushed the urge to fight to the back of his mind. Through clenched teeth, he said, "Yes, I'm with you. Just give me some space to cool down."

Releasing her hold on his axe, Lagertha nodded once before turning to the group. "You heard the dwarf. Something's coming. Leave your stuff. Weapons, and emergency kits only. Now move." Everyone reacted as one, dropping what they were doing to unsheathe weapons as they followed the Savartalfar into a side tunnel.

Lagertha took two steps and turned to Leif. "You coming?"

Still worked up from the fight, he growled, "Yeah." He followed at a distance.

The group left their torches behind, so the only light they had was the soft neon light emanating from the fungi. Biknre took a sharp turn twenty feet into the passageway, directing the group to squeeze into a small alcove. Pressed up against the wall, the party held their breath as they waited to see if they had been spotted.

A couple of minutes later, Leif detected a soft tremor through his boots. A moment later, the soft scrape of booted feet echoed throughout the tunnel. He watched as Lagertha detached herself from the wall and crept to the edge to peer around. He heard several people speaking in Ljosa. Followed by a strange hissing noise. Lagertha turned back to the group, whispering, "It's a company of Outsider's shock troops. There are at least thirty Thrall being led by three Dokkalfar."

"Did they see us?" Kira whispered.

"I don't think so," Lagertha said, looking back around the corner. "They found our stuff and are discussing what they should do." A few minutes passed before she spoke again. "They are dividing into groups. I think they are going to inspect all the tunnels. Prepare for combat."

"No wait!" Biknre hissed, going pale in the low light.

"What is it?" Lagertha asked. Her sword was already halfway out of the sheath.

Biknre's face grew shiny with sweat as he whispered, "A skalv is heading this way."

Lagertha froze.

"If we hold still, I can smooth out our vibrations. With luck combined with the racket they are making..." the dwarf said with a jerk of his head, "it might slide past us."

"What's a skalv?" Leif whispered.

Biknre shushed him as he once again squatted down to resume his murmuring.

Thankfully, Bjartr, who was pressed next to him, whispered in his ear, "Skalv are blind, deep dwelling carnivores, who hunt by feeling the vibrations in the ground. They come up from beneath their prey, pulling them under to devour them at their leisure."

Eyeing the ground nervously, "I've been to Myrkheim before, and no one warned me I might get sucked into the ground."

"They prefer to stay close to the heat from the core, so they only haunt the lower tunnels and cities of Myrkheim," she responded.

As if summoned by their thoughts, the packed dirt of their tunnel rumbled, and a mound of dirt lifted out of the ground not five feet from their hiding spot. Leif heard Biknre's whispers grow frantic as he worked to conceal them. He tensed as the mound rumbled closer, stopping not far from Floki's foot. No one moved, nor could Leif hear them breathing as the beast paused, searching for prey. Mercifully, the skalv descended beneath the surface, causing Biknre to sag in relief.

"You all are going to want to see this," he whispered, joy plain in his voice. "If you move slowly enough, you should be fine."

No one moved. Thoughts of getting sucked underground kept everyone from breathing. Not surprisingly, Lagertha was the first to move. With exaggerated slowness, she stepped next to Biknre. Confident in her decision, everyone followed, pressing together at the corner. The group peered around the corner.

Leif crouched to see around the crowd. Placing a single hand on the ground for balance, he tensed. He felt he was moments away from being pulled under. An explosion of rock, followed by a blood-curdling scream, caused him to flinch. Looking to their abandoned camp, he stared open-mouthed as dirt and rock flew through the tunnels. A nightmare-inducing creature with a maw filled with row upon row of jagged teeth clamped down on a black robed Dokkalfar. Blood sprayed as the skalv tore a chunk the size of a watermelon from the dark elf's shoulder.

The ground boomed as the skalv crashed down, burrowing its horned head into the earth. The armored worm momentarily disappeared, sending the surviving Dokkalfar and Thrall into a panic. The beast resurfaced immediately, pulling a running Thrall, which was a gray-scaled lizard humanoid, beneath the surface with hissing screams. The Thrall, who Leif had never seen in person before, were tall powerfully built creatures that walked on flat clawed feet. No matter how fast they ran though, they were no match for the swift deadly attacks from the skalv.

It was like watching a terrifying real-life version of *Shark Week*. Once the dust had settled, only pieces remained of the Outsider army. The blood-soaked mound that denoted the skalv's location slowly slumped below the floor, disappearing from view. No one moved or uttered a breath as they processed the swift brutality of the attack.

Finally, Biknre breathed a sigh of relief as his muttering ceased. "And that, my friends, is why you never travel the under tunnels without a Savartalfar," he said as he brazenly walked out from their hiding place toward the carnage of the junction. The group was quick to follow.

Stepping out from the tunnel, Leif was astonished to see the amount of destruction a single worm creature could do to an unshielded group. Even with Biknre close, he moved much more deliberately, not wanting to risk another encounter with the skalv. What Leif found more terrifying than the plethora of severed limbs was the half-submerged bodies. Several unfortunate Thrall and at least one Dokkalfar had been dragged beneath the surface, leaving only the top half of their torso free from the clinging depths. All had died in the same manner, mouth open in an eternal scream of pain as their terrified eyes desperately searched for someone to save them.

Thankfully, Lagertha didn't have the squad remain in the area for long. The group collected what gear they could from their hasty retreat. They pilfered anything of use from the dead. Leif had never been comfortable looting the dead, so he stayed back, happy to act as a lookout while the others performed the dirty deed.

After a few minutes, Lagertha called off the cleanup. "That's enough team," she said. "The wagon train will be passing the ambush point by mid-morning tomorrow. We've lost a lot of time with this unfortunate distraction. We will have to double time it to the fork. Let's head out. Biknre! You're in the lead."

# CHAPTER 28

Leif leaned back against the tunnel wall with an exhausted sigh. Lagertha had been anxious about getting to their destination with enough time to rest and fully recover before the attack tomorrow. So, she had the raiding party run the remaining distance, with Biknre setting the pace. Leif was in good shape from his rigorous training schedule on Midgard, but he had not prepared for sprinting with his gear strapped to his back for six hours straight. Since he had no real means of telling time in the perpetual dusk of the tunnels, he was only guessing it was six hours. It felt like an eternity. Even while berserked, the trip was taking a toll on his body. *Hell, I am not fully recovered from the beating Fenrir gave me.* So, when Biknre finally slowed to a fast walk, it took all Leif had not to collapse on the spot. More disturbing was he was the only one who appeared to be winded from the wild flight across Myrkheim.

Thankfully, Lagertha must have picked up on his exhaustion because she left his name out when she named the first watch and dinner duty. With her official duties over, she sat next to Leif, asking, "May I join you?"

"Go ahead," he tiredly mumbled.

"I realized during our run that we haven't had much time to talk. I know who you are, but I don't know what drives you. After initially denying your request, everything seemed to spiral out of control, leading us here with you joining our raid to free our people. It is quite a spectacular turn of events, wouldn't you say?"

"You have no idea," Leif said with a smile. "Not long ago, I thought I was the last Berserker in existence. I am shocked to not only find another Berserker, but one who has ascended. What are the odds of that?" he asked. *What are the odds? It almost feels like fate, but the Norns are dead, aren't they?*

"The Norns must favor you," Lagertha said, meeting Leif's gaze. He waved it off as just a figure of speech and decided to not tell her that the Norns died at the hands of Hel. "So, Leif," she said, fixing him with an electric blue stare. "What is driving you so hard to ascend?" she asked.

"Revenge," he said, surprised by the amount of venom in his voice.

"Ah," she responded. "That is a motivation I know well. Who has wronged you?"

Leif considered what he should reveal. Arias's warning to not reveal too much rang through his head. He probably would have trusted Lagertha with the true story before all this, but after Kaldrec's betrayal at the Well of Urn, he was much more guarded about his true intentions. Deciding it was probably best to keep his real aim a secret, he wove a tale about his grandfather. "A Jontar Chieftain named Ijskoud believed my grandfather used trickery to defeat him in a duel. The Jontar tracked him down to Midgard, killing him and my mother to sate his anger." Leif let out a weary sigh.

Lagertha chimed in. "A truly worthy goal," patting Leif on the shoulder. "And one fit for a Berserker. Jontar are formidable. That is one reason why the tribe goes out of the way to avoid Jotenheim at all costs. But fear not," she said with a sly smile. "Once you have ascended, it would take more than a mere Jontar chieftain to stop you."

Looking around, Lagertha considered those who were on watch. She stood and said, "Get some rest. I know this was a taxing day for you. To be sure you are fresh for the fight to come, I will take your shift on watch."

"Thank you," he said, feeling the weight of sleep pressing in on him.

Lagertha waved his gratitude away, saying, "Think nothing of it." She turned away from Leif and left him in the bioluminescent gloom.

LEIF AWOKE to someone prodding him in the stomach. He shot to his feet, hand on his axes as the surfaced Berserker raged awake. The problem he had realized with maintaining his Berserker state, is that for the first few moments after waking, his defenses were down. While sleeping, he was more susceptible to the Berserker's darker suggestions. The nightmare only compounded the issue.

He raised his axe as the Jontar he and Arias had been fighting stood in front of him. Shouting, he brought his axe down, but the Jontar was gone. Only To be replaced by Kira's confused scowl. Gathering his will, he retook control of his mind, stopping his axe a hair's breadth from the Dokkalfar's pale nose. To Leif's astonishment, the dark elf didn't flinch. Arching a dark eyebrow, she said, "Battling the nightmares of our past is a curse we all must bear. Time to wake. Lagertha says it's almost time. Get some food and gear up," said Kira before she stalked off.

Lagertha ordered everyone to get ready as the heavy prison wagons rumbled past their hiding spot. Leif was in his usual spot at the back of the party. The plan was simple: Disable the guards, free the prisoners, and get out before reinforcements overwhelmed them. He took a deep breath, relishing the pre-battle rush that thrummed through his veins.

Several tense seconds later, Lagertha raised her sword over her head, shouting "ATTACK!" The party rushed forward, engaging their assigned targets. Leif swept his gaze left to right. Prison wagons stretched out before him in a long line, each wagon was stuffed full of beings. The carriages were pulled by a set of three-toed lizards the size of an ox. Their lumbering stride easily pulled the heavy-laden convoy.

Leif spied strange rock-looking creatures perched at the head of each prison carriage. They suddenly stood up, revealing Savartalfar warriors in rock armor. One of the knights dropped the reigns to the lizard-thing and lifted a boulder sized mace. Leif's mouth fell open as the warrior easily wielded the massive weapon. Similar action took place up and down the convoy as the Skala Rycerz moved to defend their wagons.

The ground shook when the knight from the nearest wagon dismounted directly in front of Leif. The warrior was completely encased in stylized stone armor. The helmeted head swiveled in his direction. The deep-set brown eyes narrowed as they locked onto Leif. The Skala Rycerz hefted the mace, taking it in a two-handed grip. The knight charged, shouting his Svata battle cry, closing the distance between them. Leif was surprised how fast the diminutive warrior moved in such heavy armor.

He dodged, narrowly avoiding getting squashed like a bug. The mace slammed into the floor, sending a shower of debris in all directions. Springing forward, Leif attacked. His ax gouged a thin line across his foe's chest plate. The Skala Rycerz grunted out a laugh, and he countered, slamming the metal haft of the mace into his stomach. Leif stumbled back, gasping as he fought to recover his breath. A shadow passed in the torchlight as the Savartalfar pressed his advantage.

Leif dodged a series of wild attacks from the Skala Rycerz, swinging his mace left and right. He knew it would only take one hit to end the fight. The Berserker howled for him to attack, but he held, knowing his enemy's armor was too thick to pierce. He would only get one chance at downing such an opponent. He needed to tire the knight out.

Thankfully, his opportunity came sooner than he had hoped when the warrior overextended himself. Growing frustrated with Leif's constant dodging, the Skala Rycerz brought the mace down in an overhead attack, but he had put too much force behind the strike. The mace crashed down with a boom, creating a massive crater. Seizing on the opportunity, Leif advanced, catching the Skala Rycerz off guard as he smashed the blunt end of his ax head through the T-shaped cut in the knight's helmet. The Dwarven steel smashed into the bridge of the Savartalfar's forehead, causing the warrior's head to snap backward. The Skala Rycerz fell unconscious.

Leif took a step forward, the Berserker pushing him to kill the downed guard quickly. But he stopped himself. Fire raced through his arms, urging him to finish the fight, but he resisted as he considered his foe. The unconscious warrior was no enemy of his. In fact, the knight was just doing his duty. *There is no honor in killing him.* Against the Berserker's howling protest, Leif lowered his raised arm, disengaging from the unconscious Skala Rycerz.

Free from the attack, Leif assessed the situation. From what he could see, the Skala Rycerz had been caught off-guard. They probably didn't suspect an attack on their convoy. The raiders had managed to overwhelm the single guard at four of the prison wagons, freeing their occupants. The newly freed prisoners immediately engaged the Skala Rycerz reinforcements coming from wagons up and down the convoy.

Chaos reigned in the dark confines of the tunnel. The four dancing flame lanterns that hung from the wagons' posts swayed, revealing a pitched battle as more Savartalfar knights joined the fight. The tribe raiders darted from barred wagon to wagon, breaking the heavy metal locks, freeing the prisoners as they searched for their comrades.

Leif spotted a group of prisoners savaging a cornered Skala Rycerz. He watched as a green skinned Orc with a thick brow and one broken tusk pinned the guard to the ground then maliciously crushed the knight's right leg with his stolen mace. The group laughed and jeered in their various languages.

Leif's rage exploded at the casual cruelty. His skin tingled as his rising anger fueled his strength. It was one thing to overwhelm an enemy, killing them in the process. But to torture a defeated foe was something he could not permit. Eyeing the group, Leif knew if he wasn't smart, they could overwhelm him as well, but the Orc raised the mace again, aiming for the knight's left leg.

Snarling, Leif lessened his hold on the Berserker, allowing a savage-tinge to acquire his thoughts. He crossed the distance to the group in the blink of an eye. With their attention on their prisoner, no one saw Leif's approach. He aimed his axe at the outermost member of the cruel group square in the back, snapping the Ljosalfar's spine with a wet CRACK. The Savartalfar standing next to the dying elf looked up at the noise just as Leif's free axe struck his head, killing him instantly.

The two he killed in his opening salvo collapsed to the tunnel floor with a dull thud. Knowing he only had moments to thin the herd. He threw his ax at the chest of another Dokkalfar. The blade buried itself deep into the dark elf's chest, cracking bone as it pierced the stunned dark elf's heart. Leif launched forward, but the Orc he aimed for was quick, side-stepping Leif's axe. Angry shouts rang out from the surviving prisoners as they fanned around him.

Eyeing the jeering crowd, Leif retrieved his axe from the corpse of their comrade. The blade pulled free with a wet sucking sound. He stepped into the center of the assembly, standing protectively over the groaning Skala Rycerz. The mob laughed as Leif slowly turned in a circle, watching for an attack.

A whisper of movement to his right pulled his attention in that direction. Leif turned just in time to see the same quick moving Orc ghost toward him. He had a sharpened metal bar in one hand, like a prison shank, that he hurled at Leif's midsection. Reacting on instinct, his right arm chopped down just as he felt the sharp sting of the shiv punch into his side. The Orc grunted as Leif's axe severed the knife wielding hand at the wrist. He lashed out with his remaining axe, but the Orc sprang backward, narrowly avoiding being decapitated. Trailing blood, the Orc retreated into the crowd.

"Step away from our prey, Midgardian," the mace-wielding Orc said, taking a menacing step forward.

"Not gonna happen," Leif challenged, feeling the Berserker pulse with excitement.

"You are strong and faster than most of your kind," the Orc said, not recognizing what Leif was. "But there is no way you can best us all. We are thankful to you and your people. But that won't stop us from killing you if you get in our way. Step aside. This is your last chance." He growled.

"Piss off, ugly," Leif taunted.

The Orc hefted the heavy mace with a two-handed grip, shouting, "Kill him!"

The crowd cheered as they charged. Leif shouted his defiance, raising his axes in defense. In a flash of metal, Leif spied a knife trailing a silver chain slam into a charging Dokkalfar in front of him. There was a wet thwack when the blade struck the dark elf in the forehead.

Leif heard the shuffle of several booted feet, and someone shouted in Ljosa behind him. The whole mob froze. The crowd slowly stepped back, regrouping around the mace-wielding Orc. Leif saw Bjartr slowly wind her chain weapon, pulling the blade-end free of the dead Dokkalfar with a precise flick of her wrist. From behind the newly freed prisoners, Lagertha and several other tribe members approached. Behind them, Kira spoke with several prisoners, and they were all smiling and slapping each other on their backs in greeting.

"What the hell is going on, Leif?" Lagertha asked, stepping up to him. "We recovered our people. The Skala Rycerz are overwhelming the prisoners. Everyone's fleeing into the side tunnels. If we don't do the same, we may end up getting pinned down." The mob looked left and right.

"These assholes were torturing this guard here. I can't tolerate that shit. We need to shield him long enough for his comrades to get to him," Leif explained.

"Why would we ever do that? We have clashed with the Skala Rycerz numerous times over the long years. They have taken the lives of many of our tribe. Leave it and let fate decide," Lagertha said, growing impatient.

"Killing in battle is one thing, Lagertha. But torturing a defeated foe is something I cannot ignore. Maybe it's my Midgardian upbringing, I don't know. One way or the other, I won't leave without making sure they don't kill him once we are gone."

Lagertha let out an exacerbated sigh as she glared at Leif. Relenting, she said, "Fine, you naïve fool. I will only allow this insolence once. You do not know our customs, and I owe you." She waved her hand in the air, signaling the tribe members to follow as she stepped up to Leif.

"Who leads your people?" she asked the mob.

"I do," the mace-wielding Orc said, stepping forward. "I am Zulk."

"Zulk," Lagertha addressed with a nod. "We can fight here, wasting even more time as the Skala Rycerz cut their way through the rioting prisoners until we are all pinned down. Or you can leave, fleeing down the tunnels towards your freedom. Do you want me to tell you the choice I hope you pick?" Lagertha asked, placing a hand on her ax.

Zulk looked at his companions, then back to Lagertha. The oversized Orc grunted his annoyance as his blood-red eyes scowled at Leif. He placed the mace on his shoulder and turned toward the nearest tunnel. His people followed into a side tunnel.

With the threat temporarily abated, Leif noticed the Savartalfar knights were close to quelling the riot from the freed prisoners. Leif hoisted the injured knight. Throwing him in the empty prison wagon, he slammed the barred door shut. He then pulled the Orc's shiv out of his side and used it to bar the wagon door.

Lagertha shouted, "All right, that's it for us, people." She pointed at the bruised Savartalfar. "Biknre, lead us out of here. We run for the bridge and won't slow until we are sure we aren't being followed."

They ran for hours through the dark tunnels, never lighting a torch lest they reveal their location to any pursuers. Using nothing but the low light of the glowing lichen, they pushed forward. Even berserked, Leif was reaching his limit. Thankfully, Lagertha called the group to a halt just as they entered the intersection where the skalv had attacked them earlier. It was only then, with hands on knees from exhaustion, that Leif noticed two of their group were missing. *They must have died in the attack,* he thought.

"Biknre, check for pursuers. Then mask our movements. I won't have all our hard work be for not if we get attacked by a skalv. Everyone else, hydrate, eat quickly, then we are on the move again. I want to be in the bridge room the moment it opens."

"Aye," everyone called out weakly.

Stumbling to the tunnel wall, Leif leaned heavily against the packed dirt, knowing if he sat down there was a possibility he would fail to get up for the next eight-to-ten hours. He greedily drank from his waterskin. He felt his stomach go in knots, warning him of Lagertha's fast approach.

Wiping his mouth, he pushed off the wall and watched Lagertha stomp her way toward him. Her face was dark with contained rage.

"What the hell was that back there?" Lagertha hissed.

Slow from exhaustion, Leif gasped out, "Huh?"

"Cut the shit, Leif." She snapped. "Your Midgardian sense of honor could have gotten all of us captured or killed. I know you haven't spent much of your time outside of Midgard, but if you want to run with my squad, we don't have time for useless notions such as honor. We do what we need to do to survive."

Anger rose within Leif like a King Cobra readying to strike. "Say what you will, but I won't abandon who I am. You think my being from Midgard makes me weak, but I believe it is the opposite. It is my ideals that make me stronger." Leif shot back. "We were given this power for a reason, Lagertha. To protect those who are weaker than us. To fight side by side with the Aesir in Ragnarok. Not to sulk in the shadows, protecting your own hide. I am haunted by the faces of those I failed. When I started on this journey to ascension, I vowed no one else would die due to my weakness...," he said, letting a hint of emotion into his voice. "... and that was exactly what I did. That guard did not deserve to be tortured to death, so I stepped in. And I would do it again, for friend or foe. To die in battle is one thing, but to torture a defeated foe is another. That leads to Helheim, a place I wish to never see again."

The venom in Leif's retort stunned Lagertha. She pulled her head back quickly and swallowed hard. He could tell she wasn't used to being challenged by subordinates. He was worried she would press him on his slip up of mentioning Helheim, but she let the comment pass.

Lagertha let out a sigh of exacerbation. Her shoulders slumped, and she quietly spoke. "You do not know the Skala Rycerz like I do. I forget that though we are both Berserkers, our upbringing has been drastically different. I will let it pass this one time. If we encounter any trouble on our return trip, I will expect you to stay in line with the rest of our raiders, or I will cut you down." She took a deep breath. "Leif, you need to abandon your foolish notions of honor and the Aesir. It will get you killed. The gods are not the honorable beings you believe them to be."

"What do you mean?" Leif asked, confused by the non sequitur.

"Look at us," she said seriously. "How could the gods be honorable? Our power has pushed us to fight or kill anyone of sufficient skill or strength. Every Berserker in my bloodline has suffered because of our power. I would assume it is the same for your bloodline as well. Thor did that to us. His gift was nothing more than a curse. Don't bank on me answering the Aesir's call. I welcome Ragnarok because the Outsiders can't do a worse job than the Aesir." She turned her back on him.

"Biknre we good?" Lagertha called out.

"Aye, unless they are masking their movement like us, we are in the clear," the Savartalfar shouted back.

"Good! Then we are off. No slowing until we are through the bridge and back on Vanaheimr," she shouted, gesturing for the group to get moving.

LEIF COLLAPSED onto his bedroll with a pained sigh. His back and legs throbbed to their own beat as he thought back over their hurried flight from Myrkheim. This was the first time since awakening to the Berserker that he felt feeling tired and sore. He tried to reach down to massage his calves, but a muscle cramp in his lower back caused him to roll around in agony for a few moments.

*What the hell,* he thought. *I thought the Berserker was supposed to mute this type of pain. Is my body so damaged that it can't shut it all out?* That thought brought him up short as he considered the implications. The soft crunch of grass outside his tent alerted him to Lagertha's approach. He knew it was her because his Berserker flared, sending the weird mix of feelings bouncing around his stomach.

"Come in," he groaned before she could announce herself.

Ducking into his tent, Lagertha smiled as she took a seat on the tree stump next to his bed. She smelled like sweat and was still caked in dirt from their cross-realm sprint. "Outside of our disagreement, you performed well on the raid," she praised. "The others of the party said they wouldn't be opposed to you joining them the next time they are called out for a mission. Naivety aside,

I believe you have proven you are ready to take the final step toward ascension."

"Really!" Leif shouted, shooting up in bed. It was a mistake. His entire back flared in pain, causing him to fall back onto the bed with a groan.

"Rest up tonight. We leave tomorrow at dawn," Lagertha said, rising from the stump.

"Wait," Leif called out. "Did you really mean what you said about Ragnarok?"

"Ask me again some other time. It was a long trip, and I don't particularly feel like going down that road at this time." She slipped out of the tent. "I'll see you in the morning."

# CHAPTER 29

"Can you slow down?" Leif asked with a hint of annoyance leaking into his voice. He hadn't fully recovered from the prison raid and hiking up a black diamond incline in near perfect darkness was not what he had in mind when Lagertha woke him up at dawn. The misty forest was still shrouded in gloomy darkness, so he couldn't have been asleep for more than a few hours. His body felt sluggish from the recent exertion, and that was with the Berserker accelerated healing. Leif had asked why they couldn't perform the ascension ritual there in the camp, but Lagertha had given him a noncommittal answer about safety. Whether that was his safety or that of the tribe, she wouldn't say.

Unlike the past few times he had set out into the misty forest, Lagertha turned sharply to the right once they passed the flickering torches. It wasn't long before their trek led them out of the forest and into a maze of canyons and crevices between building sized boulders that ran along the back side of the tribe campsite. As they walked, Leif had tried to engage Lagertha in friendly conversation, but it seemed this morning she wasn't up for talking.

Not long after entering the canyon, they ran into a dead end. At first, he thought Lagertha had gotten lost, but she confidently continued walking forward. Squinting through the fog, Leif could just make out a small, shadowed alcove barely large enough for someone of his size to squeeze through. He watched Lagertha squeeze into the alcove, and he resigned himself to dive back into the claustrophobic cave system that seemed to run along the mountain range.

Sadly, unlike the tunnels in Myrkheim, this tunnel was tiny, barely leaving him room to maneuver. On more than one occasion, he banged his head on some unseen stalactite that jutted from the ceiling. Head injuries and claustrophobia aside, the real pain of this trip was the steep incline of the tunnel, coupled with the punishing pace his fellow Berserker had set out for them. Leif had trouble keeping up with Lagertha. If it wasn't for the torch she carried, he would have lost sight of her within the first ten minutes of their climb.

Time lost all meaning in the damp tunnel. Leif's world contracted to right foot, left foot as he trudged in Lagertha's wake.

"I have to ask," Leif said, breaking the silence. "How the hell did you guys find this place?"

To his surprise, she answered this time. "Excluding exigent circumstances, when the tribe elders believe it is time to move on from a camp location, we send scouts to hunt for suitable locations. The scouts traverse numerous realms, scouring large swaths of territory. A host of our size consumes a staggering number of local resources, so before a location can be chosen, a comprehensive survey of prospective spots must be done. First by the scout, then by myself and one other tribe elder.

The location we are currently staying at has been on our list of potential sites for centuries, but with the forest perpetually obscured by fog, the counsel feared unknown danger lurking within the mists. With the massacre on Myrkheim, the elders felt we had little choice but to disappear for a while, and what better place to hide than in a hidden forest?"

"What happened on Myrkheim?" Leif asked.

Lagertha let out a weary sigh, saying, "Not here. Once we reach the top, the *seior* will take a few hours to brew. Ask me again later. If I am in a good mood, maybe I will share what tragedies the Berserker's curse had befallen my bloodline."

*Woah*, Leif thought. *That got dark fast.* "Wait!" Leif called out, "What did you mean by top?"

JUST AS HE began to question the sanity of his memories of a time before the endless darkness, Leif heard a soft roar accompanied by a whisper of wind on his face.

Answering his unasked question, Lagertha said, "We are almost there. Hurry up." She increased her already punishing pace.

Leif was left with little choice but to follow. He feared that if he didn't, he would be swallowed by the darkness. Every step sent a stab of pain up his legs. On more than one occasion, he slipped on the slick tunnel incline, banging a knee on the stone floor. Even though he felt pain, his enhanced healing must have still been working, because otherwise his hands and knees would be a bloody mess. Making matters worse, he was pretty sure he was suffering from a severe case of dehydration because he had stopped sweating about an hour ago.

With each step he took, the roar ahead grew louder. As the unknown sound grew, so too did the wind. The soft kiss of a light breeze increased to a freezing wind. Leif had always loved the cold, but in the damp confines of the tunnel, the chilly air cut deep. *At least it blew away the musty smell,* he thought.

The tunnel abruptly leveled out, revealing a dark domed cavern. A relieved Leif took two steps into the room before dropping his pack and sinking to the ground, silently thanking the Aesir it was over. Lagertha, nonplussed by the trek, strolled across the cavern and out a small exit at the opposite end. Despite his exhaustion, he was intrigued. Pushing himself to his feet, he half-stumbled, half-walked after Lagertha, stepping into the chilly Vanaheimr night.

Walking along the open terrace, Leif sidled up next to his fellow Berserker at the very edge of the platform. The howling wind screamed around him. He peered down the mountain into the roiling clouds thousands of feet below. Leif breathed deep, enjoying the feel of the crisp air in his lungs. Exhaling, he took in the view with the wonder of a kid on Christmas. Snowcapped peaks stabbed the sky in the distance. Floating amongst the peaks, a score of floating islands dotted the landscape. The closest, drifted by a stone's throw away.

The source of the roar became evident as Leif examined his surroundings. A small waterfall splashed into a swallow pool next to where they stood. Seeing the water cascade into the clear pool brought Leif's temporarily forgotten thirst to the forefront of his thoughts. He limped to the edge of the pool, taking a knee with a groan.

Cupping his hands together, he dipped his hands into the frigid pool. His hands went momentarily numb, then tingled from the cold. Careful to not lose any water, he brought his hands to his mouth and tilted his head back, feeling the cool liquid soothe his cracked lips.

As he drank, a shrill cry came from above, startling him. A shadow detached itself from the rocks a hundred yards up the mountain. The creature flapped its leathery wings twice before pulling them in close, diving toward Leif, who froze like a deer in headlights. The light from the veil illuminated the creature as it hurtled toward him. Its triangular head was covered in gray scales flecked with red. A howl of defiance from his Berserker echoed through his mind, snapping him out of his stupor. Lagertha, unlike Leif had immediately jumped for cover. With an impatient wave of her hand she shouted, "Hurry!"

The safety of the cave might as well have been a mile away for all the good it would do for him. He was a heartbeat away from being a snack. He dove forward, pressing his body flat against the terrace floor and rolled face up. He got an up-close look at the creature as it flared its leathery wings out wide, slowing its descent. A pair of orange slitted eyes, bore into his, and row upon row of needle-sharp teeth snapped shut with an audible "SNIK" mere inches from his face. There came a heavy whoosh of air as the scaled monster beat its wings hard against the air as it tried to follow the rolling Leif.

With eyes locked on the beast, Leif didn't see the ledge until he had rolled off it. An involuntary yelp escaped his lips as he feared he had just rolled himself off the edge of the cliff to his death. There was a short drop before his cry was cut short. He plunged face first into the icy water. His body immediately went numb from the freezing water. Leif gasped for breath as he broke the water's surface and stiffly waded toward the lip of the pool.

With the creature's focus entirely on Leif, Lagertha darted from the cave, wielding the still lit torch like a club. Her Berserker bellowed a battle cry as she smacked the winged creature on its snout, sending a shower of flaming embers in all directions. The beast yelped and rocked backward, losing several feet of elevation. Recovering, it circled the pair several times before giving up and flying away into the distance, squawking. Free of danger, Lagertha helped Leif out of the pool, and together they walked back into the cave.

The cavern was well stocked with supplies. Leif watched Lagertha grab several logs from the neatly stacked pile in the corner. She set them down and lit them with the dying fire from her damaged torch. The dried wood immediately caught fire, banishing the cold from Leif's aching limbs. In between painful full body shakes, he checked out his surroundings. It was clear from the numerous lit torches hanging on hooks in the stone walls the tribe had used this place for shelter before.

Once his teeth stopped chattering, he stammered out, "Uuuummm, whatttt wasss thatttt?"

"A skaoi ormr," she stated.

"Mmmmmmm?" he mumbled.

Sighing, she asked, "Have you heard of the three great dragons?"

"No, but that sure as hell looked like a dragon that tried to eat me once." he commented, feeling his body aches ease with the growing fire.

"What?" Lagertha exclaimed. Her voice echoed against the cavern walls. Narrowing her eyes, she asked, "Care to explain?"

Taking a deep breath, Leif was pleased that he had stopped shivering. Knowing the truth would lead to too many questions, he once again wove a tale close to the truth.

"Back when I started my cross-realm trek, I crossed a bridge that led to a clouded world with little to no life on it. The bridge spit me out right next to a roiling lake. Intrigued, I set out to investigate. But as soon as I came within a few feet of the shore, a massive gray monster burst from the choppy surface. Even more surprising than facing down a four-story lizard was that it spoke to me."

Awed, Lagertha said, "You met Niohoggr, the corpse eater. Not many survive an encounter with him. How did you do it?"

"Luck," he said with a shrug of the shoulders. "Niohoggr, I guess underestimated me. Using the surrounding terrain, I dodged out of the way as he lunged for me. After that, I bolted for the bridge, never looking back."

"Luck indeed," Lagertha said. "I commend you for your quick action. Many have tried to slay the mighty beast. None have returned."

"Not surprising," Leif said earnestly. "That thing was terrifying. So terrifying, I hope you don't mind a topic change," he not so expertly said. "What happened to your people on Myrkheim?"

"I did promise I would tell you," she said with a resigned sigh. "First, I want to prepare the seior. The potion needs to sit overnight, so I want to get started on it first."

"Go ahead," he said excitedly. He had only seen potions made in movies, and he was excited to see one made firsthand.

He watched with rapt attention as Lagertha opened her pack, pulling out a small metal pot and a cloth-wrapped bundle tied with a leather cord. She set the items down and untied the leather cord, unwrapping the bundle. Within, she pulled out three vials filled with colorful liquids, along with several leaves and herbs. With practiced ease, Lagertha unstopped a purplish tube, quickly pouring the contents into the pot. Next, she grabbed a leafy green herb that smelled faintly like black licorice. She shredded the leaf before dropping it in the pot.

Lagertha repeated the process with the remaining red and green vials. Pouring the contents into the pot, followed by tearing apart one of the herbs and adding them to the mix. With each new addition, the contents emitted an acrid odor. She swirled the liquid several times before setting it back down. Then, without hesitation, she drew her belt knife and in one swift motion cut a long line against her palm. Balling her hand into a fist, she squeezed, muttering an incantation as two thick drops of blood splashed into the potion. Lagertha swirled the seior one last time before setting it next to the fire to boil.

Leif's stomach heaved at the prospect of drinking the strange brew.

Sitting back down next to Leif, Lagertha once again rummaged through her bag, pulling out two strips of dried meat. "Here," she said, offering him a piece. "Might as well get comfortable. I will tell you the tale of my bloodline and the tribe. As with any story with a Berserker involved, it is filled with both tragedy and triumph."

"The first of my line was named Baulder." Lagertha explained. "From the moment Thor departed Midgard, after bestowing the Berserker upon his chosen, the blood began to spill. Without the Jontar or Dokkalfar to battle, the newly risen Berserkers returned to their clan territories, where their power pushed them to fight. The new Berserkers challenged any they believed to be a threat. It wasn't long before the Berserkers had killed their way to the top of their respective clans, each gaining control over their territories with ruthless efficiency. As we know, a Berserker's lust for power is never quenched. After gaining power, the Berserkers then looked outward to other territories. In a short time, the land was in chaos. Total war had broken out. If the power had returned to Thor once a Berserker died, the war most likely would have burned out in a generation. But with each death, came a newly awoken Berserker who would immediately attack the clan that had killed their forbearer. Many years into the war, it was discovered if an entire bloodline was wiped out, the chain of awakenings would be broken, and the Berserker gene returned to Thor. My ancestor, one of the few original Berserkers still alive at the time, decided to leave Midgard. He knew the Berserker war would continue until they were all dead. So, he left Midgard.

"Baulder and his family escaped across the first bridge they could find, swearing his bloodline would never return to Midgard. They first sought out the Ljosalfar, seeking refuge in their forest realm. But in those days, the Ljosalfar were highly reclusive. Much of the realm still smoldered from the Ljosa-Dokka civil war. Mistrust of outsiders was at an all-time high. Doubly so of a Midgardian with mysterious powers. After being rebuffed by the elves, Astrid, Baulder's wife, wrote in her journal that they tried twice more with the Jontar and Savataflar, but they were met with hostility in both realms.

"For many years, Baulder and his clan traversed the realms, staying on the outskirts. Eventually, they took shelter in the Alfheim wilds, relying on the dense forest to take care of their needs. One fateful night, as Astrid was chopping wood, she heard a cry for help from deep within the forest. Calling for Baulder, the pair set out to investigate.

"Not far from their home, they came across a Skogur Borg hunting party. The hunt had captured a pair of Ljosalfar. The Skogur Borg accused their prisoners of treason for harboring a Dokkalfar child. Baulder heard their kafteinn order the execution, right there in the forest rather than drag them back to Karcoa. Seeing the opportunity to gain a powerful ally, Baulder attacked the unsuspecting group. With surprise on his side, he killed two of the black knights. Seeing their chance, the two Ljsoalfar prisoners joined in the fight and together they overwhelmed the remaining warriors.

"The two Ljsoalfar were Galen and his partner Vioarr. Thankful for their freedom, the two joined Baulder's clan. Over the following decades, more and more outcasts joined their wayward group. It was then the tribe was born. They chose a semi-nomadic lifestyle, moving amongst the realms. Not long after, Hesvik joined the growing group. The tribe eventually grew so large that an official leadership was decided upon.

"Galen, being a former clan guard, was elevated to a weapons master. Hesvik was chosen to run the internal workings of the tribe. While the current Berserker was to head up special operations. They believed if the Berserker had an outlet to vent its violent impulses, there would be fewer outbursts at home. With many of the tribe's members high on the realms' most wanted lists, the tribe grew more and more dependent on the realms' underworld. Using our large network of contacts, the tribe became the leading organization for cross-realm smuggling. This is how the tribe has survived for nearly 500 years."

"How have you all been able to keep the tribe hidden for so many years?" Leif asked.

"It hasn't always been easy." Lagertha paused, turning her head to stare out the open cave mouth. Following her gaze, Leif spied an island float silently in the distance.

"It's getting late, but I find it..." Lagertha paused to consider her next words, "comforting to speak with a fellow Berserker. To speak of the shared burden Thor unjustly placed upon our kind. Not all are able to control the power as well as us. Over the centuries, my clan has produced good and bad Berserkers. Some survived to old age, not passing on their gift until even their children were well into their mature years. Unfortunately, many were too weak willed to tame their Berserker, leading to unnecessary bloodshed and strife. The majority died in idiotic duels for power, prestige, or territory. An even smaller number, which a few of my bloodline belong to, were blood thirsty tyrants."

"Tyrants?" Leif asked, confused.

"Oh yes. One attempted a coup against the elder counsel. Another grew drunk on battle, leading our people into unnecessary bloodshed."

"A Berserker tried to seize power? And they still trust your bloodline?" Leif asked, shocked.

"Sadly, yes. My father was a weak-willed Berserker, but he was a master in battle. While we lived on Myrkheim, taking over an abandoned mining cave, our lives grew quite peaceful for a time. Tunnel fungi and game were abundant in the minimally used tunnel system. There was even an outpost town a few miles away that we had a trade compact with. Our warriors rarely saw battle outside of defending ourselves from the deep creatures. This did not satisfy my father.

"At the time of his capture, I was unaware of his exploits within the tunnels. It happened around my 12th year, a time when I absolutely idolized him. When the tribe warriors finally took him prisoner, Galen tried to offer him mercy, but he was too far gone. The Berserker had nearly taken over his entire conscious mind. His pride at being one of Thor's chosen was too strong. Galen tried to calm him down, but he wouldn't listen. He had let the Berserker out and never intended to let it go. So Galen was forced to kill him."

"When I learned of his death…" Lagertha's voice went hoarse with emotion. "I flew into a fury, swearing I would get revenge for my father. But my mother convinced me to stay my hand, bidding me to follow her. We set out through the tunnels to the Savartalfar outpost. Upon our arrival, the town was in chaos. We stayed hidden as we watched the Skala Rycerz interview the survivors of a massacre. Turns out my father had been traveling the tunnels fighting and killing any he came across. Growing arrogant in his strength, he attacked the town, killing many of their warriors for no other reason than they were there. Sadly, a few of the survivors had reported him to the Skala Rycerz. The tribe fled to Vanaheimr shortly after that. Seeing the carnage my father had wrought with my own eyes, I knew he had given in to the darker nature of our kind. I vowed I would never succumb to the Berserker's bloodlust."

"That's horrible," Leif said, knowing all too well the intoxicating feel the Berserker's power can be. The call to battle. The thrill of clashing blades with the strong.

"Sadly, that is not the end of the suffering Thor's gift had in store for me," she said with sarcasm. "Or my family. I was arrogant in my youth, believing because I witnessed the dark path my father had gone down, that I would be strong enough to steer clear of the atrocities he committed."

"You're still here, so whatever you did couldn't have been so bad." Leif commented.

Sadness flashed across Lagertha's face before her emotionless mask hardened again. "Yes, I am still one of the leaders, but that doesn't mean I haven't done horrible things. When I gained my gift, I was young, not even a teenager. It was decided that until I could objectively control my power, Galen would wear two hats on the counsel. Protection of the tribe encampment and he would run the missions.

In those early years of awakening, I was mortified at what my father had done. So, I devoted my body and soul to becoming the tribe's perfect weapon. Unfortunately, the arrogance of youth proved to be my downfall. In my teenage years, the iron will I had worked so hard to gain began to crack. I randomly lashed out at the smallest offenses. I was reprimanded by Galen, of course, but that only seemed to anger me more. Then, during a sparring session, I went too far, nearly killing my partner. It took several warriors to finally restrain me. Their mistake was to treat me like the young girl they had grown up with and not a Berserker.

In hopes of quelling the beast I had become, someone sent for my mother, believing the sight of her would snap me out of my rage. My mother was worried she was about to lose another member of her family to our curse. She ran to embrace me, but I was too far gone at that point. All I saw were enemies to be killed. So, when she sprinted up to me, I mistook it as an attack. With my arms pinned by two warriors, I couldn't break free, but it didn't matter. She came close, and I lashed out, kicking with all my might. My booted foot hit her straight in the chest."

"Oh shit," Leif whispered.

"Oh, shit is right," Lagertha said with a sad smile. "My mother was a mortal Midgardian. She was nowhere near as strong as us. The kick crushed her rib cage, killing her instantly. I was young and arrogant. I hadn't had an outburst in months. I felt I was strong enough to finally train with others of the tribe. but I was wrong, and she paid the price. When I finally suppressed the Berserker, I was bound in chains to a chair."

"I didn't remember much from the outburst, but I knew I had done something horrible. Tears streamed down my face as my insides did somersaults. That was how the elders held my trial. When they recounted the events to me, I screamed so loud I tore my vocal cords. I wished with all my might for the ground to swallow me whole, but that was the coward's way out. The elders waited as I unleashed my shame. Once I felt steady enough to meet their gazes, I held my chin high. Not trying to hide the despair that continued to wrack my body, I wanted them to know I would accept their judgement. If they wished for my death and the end of my Berserker line, I would not shirk from it, but go out as a warrior. Then Galen spoke, informing me of the carnage I had wrought. Shame burned through my gut. I had become just like my father.

"At the end of the hearing, the council spared me, believing my actions were not done out of malice or pride. They believed that living with the consequences of my actions would be punishment enough. I was freed, though I could no longer train with the younger members of the tribe. I would be trained by the tribe's elite, always in twos or threes. After that, I kept the Berserker chained in the recesses of my mind for a long time, too afraid of what I would do if it were to be loosed on the world again. Which, of course, made it that much harder for me to ascend when the time came, but that's a story for another time."

A pregnant silence filled the gap between the two Berserkers.

"I cannot begin to know the pain you must have felt that day," Leif whispered into the silence.

"It is a pain I feel to this day. And it is the reason why I have refused to take a husband, even though I bore a child. I see now the importance of having a Berserker within the tribe. We are fast, strong, and the members of the other races look down upon us. It is an advantage that I have used countless times, but I will not risk killing another one of my family. When I had Bjorn, I still hadn't ascended. Though it hurt him, I kept my distance, passing him off to another family to raise him. He resented me for a while, but after I ascended, gaining full control over my powers, I worked to mend our relationship. I can only hope," Lagertha said with a tinge of emotion seeping into her voice. "When I die, and the Berserker passes on to him that he will understand why I did it. Many of the Berserkers before me did great things, while others committed evils I dare not even mention. Fate has yet to decide where I will fall on that spectrum. But on quiet nights like these, I find myself wondering what life would have been like had Thor not gifted my line with this curse. Would I still know sorrow? Or would we all be living happily somewhere on Midgard?

"Don't get me wrong, I have come to relish the thrill of battle, to take the first life affirming breath after a great victory. I feel rejuvenated from the feel of the sun warming my skin as I stand over my defeated foes. But to be honest, the day I killed my mother, my heart was ripped in two, and it has never healed. If given the choice, I would rid my bloodline of our accursed gift in a heartbeat if it meant Bjorn could be free of this power."

"Not a day goes by where I don't think of those I've lost," Leif said. "I have lost friends and family alike due to the Berserker. I find myself wondering quite a lot about what life would have been like if I had never awakened. But I cannot believe Thor would have so casually bestowed upon our bloodlines this power if it wasn't for a purpose."

"To be a Berserker," Lagertha said wistfully, "is to know glory, but it costs great pain. That is our purpose," she said with venom. "We were created to be weapons for the Aesir, but I say no. Thor's act has caused untold suffering to all those he so cruelly bestowed the Berserker upon. Look into your heart and tell me that's not true, Leif. If it were false, there would be more than just the two of us left. No, I will not raise a finger for that bastard."

Lagertha radiated such rage and sorrow, he felt his Berserker respond, warning him of a potential attack. He bore down. He knew it couldn't be easy for her to always put on a façade. Leif realized he was probably one of the few people in the nine realms who could understand her pain. Though they had only known each other for a short time, he found himself wanting to comfort her. He just didn't know how. No words could ever be enough to fill the gulf of her sorrow. Leif settled for companionable silence. When words fail, just knowing someone is near is enough to lighten a heavy heart.

As time stretched on, the two warriors stared into the crackling fire, both contemplating how becoming a Berserker had changed their lives, for better and worse. Then, with an explosive sigh, Lagertha broke the silence. "Now you know the tragedy of my bloodline and why I have been so strict with you about your training. I could not afford to have another catastrophe on my hands. Now sleep. Tomorrow, you take the final step towards becoming a true Berserker."

CHAPTER 30

Leif heaved as smoke burned his lungs. Opening his eyes, he blinked the involuntary tears away as his body screamed in pain. As consciousness returned to the stunned Berserker, he heard a ringing in his ears. The ringing resolved into an all too familiar sound of combat. He painfully turned his head just in time to see the black blade of a Jontar's sword carve a jagged line through Arias's torso. Blood splattered the cobblestone street as the Jontar continued his assault by slamming his booted foot into Arias's stomach, sending the mortally wounded Ljosalfar flying backward. Leif flinched as his friend's body smashed into the wall next to him.

"Ah!" Leif yelped as his mind tore free of the nightmare. Sitting up, he took several shuttering breaths. Shaking off the dregs of the night terror, he scanned his surroundings. The small fire had burned down to flickering embers. The only light came from the bright beam of Vanaheimr sunlight that shown through the cavern opening, revealing Lagertha's empty bedroll.

Leif stretched, working the kinks out of his sore muscles. He stiffly stepped onto the terrace, finding Lagertha near the edge. Sword in hand, she flowed through a series of attacks, like one of his katas. Sweat creased her brow as she executed a perfect thrust. Pulling the sword back, she shifted into a defensive position with her arm extended in an overhead block.

"Good, you are up," she said, sheathing her sword. "The road to ascension can be a long one. It would be good to start as soon as possible."

"What was that? It looked like the katas I do," Leif asked with a yawn.

"The Ulfberht Vaoa. It's our practice forms. I find it helps clear my mind," she said, leading Leif back into the cave.

Leif sat down as Lagertha added several logs to the dying fire. His stomach roiled with nervous energy as the gravity of the situation set in. "I probably should have asked this a while ago, but what exactly happens next?"

"You drink the seior," Lagertha said, gesturing toward the liquid in the pot.

"And what does it do exactly?" he asked, giving the thick fluid a dubious look.

"As with all power, there are two parts. The body and mind," she said, poking Leif in the temple, then chest. "Through trial and error, my ancestors learned to push past the Berserker's normal boundaries. The Berserkers of the past discovered the strength we wield upon awakening is a fraction of what we can bring to bear. It was only the fragile nature of our Midgardian minds and bodies that kept us from our true potential. Our history teaches us that if a newly risen Berserker, unaccustomed to the burden our power places on us, were to ascend, the power would shatter their mind. With no consciousness to reign in the Berserker, we become nothing more than unthinking monsters, lashing out at anything that crosses our path. Once a Berserker has saddled the rage, keeping our murderous impulses in check, they lessen the risk of their mind being crushed by the sheer weight of our divine power upon its release."

"So, you're saying, if I fail, I pretty much become Majin Vegita?" Leif asked

"Huh?" Lagertha asked.

"Never mind," he said with a wave of the hand.

"What exactly will happen when I drink the potion?" he asked.

"Each Berserker's journey is different. So, I am little help there. But what I can say is the potion is designed to put your body to sleep while leaving your consciousness intact. Due to the Berserker not yet being a full part of your soul, it will draw your mind to it like a moth to the flame. What happens after..." she said with a shrug, "is up to you."

"Hmm," he grunted. "Who would have thought becoming a demi-god would involve an introspective talk with my inner, angrier self? Maybe Freud was on to something."

"What?" Lagertha asked, growing annoyed with his asinine comments.

Waiving a hand, "It's nothing. I ramble when I'm nervous. Let's get the show on the road before I say something stupid again," he said.

Lagertha handed him the pot of magical liquid. For reasons he couldn't explain, he brought the pot up to his nose and sniffed it.

"Ooh, I would not have done that," Lagertha said with a laugh.

"Oh gods!" Leif gagged. It smelled like a bag of black licorice had thrown a party inside the men's locker room, but instead of cleaning up after, they just boarded up the room in hopes no one would come across the atrocity. Leif's eyes watered as he held the pot out at arm's length. "You expect me to drink this?"

"Yes," Lagertha said with a wry smile on her face. "You must drink all of it. If not, you won't travel deep enough, and instead you'll fall into a slumber you won't wake from."

"Awesome," Leif said sarcastically.

"Let's hurry this along. I only brought enough rations to last a few days."

"Fine, fine. Cheers." Leif said as he lifted the pot to the sky briefly, downing the seior in three large gulps. The liquid tasted exactly how it smelled. A fire burst to life within him, running along his tongue, down his throat, and into his stomach. The fire smoldered there for a moment before spreading to the rest of his body. The heat continued for several seconds before dying out, leaving his body numb all over.

Leif's body grew heavy, causing him to fall backwards. He tried to catch himself, but his arms refused to respond. His mind pulsed with confusion as his back hit the stone floor, but he still felt as if he was falling. With his body unmoving on the floor, his conscious mind continued to fall into the dark depths of his subconscious. It felt as if he was falling down a very deep, dark hole. It was so deep that eventually, even the light of the waking world couldn't reach him anymore.

# CHAPTER 31

The lightless void Leif fell through slowly resolved into a bright star filled night. Though terrified, he was in awe of the beautiful snowy forest shimmering in the bright glow of the veil far below him. "Oh, shit!" he screamed into the wind a moment before he crashed through the upper forest canopy. Pain erupted across his body as he slammed through a series of branches. Though it hurt like hell, each branch he crashed through slowed his momentum just a little more. His fall was finally stopped by the snowy ground.

Leif rolled onto his back, wheezing in pain. Thankfully, nothing felt broken, nor did he lose consciousness. *Hmm,* he thought, *can I pass out? I'm already unconscious.* Then another thought slammed into him. *Wait! If I am in my subconsciousness, how can I hear my thoughts? Woah, this is some real Inception shit right here.* Deciding to let the issue drop lest he rip his mind apart, he pushed himself up. His breath misted in the frigid air.

He wondered what a psychologist would think of his subconscious mind being a snow-covered forest.

"AAAHHH!" a scream permeated from deep within the forest. Shooting to his feet, Leif scanned the night air. A flicker of movement to his right caught his attention. That was when he spotted a dark shape fleeing through the trees. It was an older man, fear exuding from his pale face. "Grandpa?" Leif asked, confused. A shadow passed in the moonlight behind Alexander. Peering through the darkness, Leif spotted a cloaked figure hot on his grandfather's heels.

Leif tried to shout a warning, but the wraith was too fast. A black blade flashed in the night, slicing Alexander's back wide open. Blood peppered the white snow as his grandfather died before his eyes. Sprinting to intercept his beloved grandfather, he screamed in anguish. Standing over the body, the hooded figure looked up. Two azure eyes locked onto Leif's as he closed the distance between them.

Leif bellowed his challenge as he dove forward, intending to tackle the cloaked figure. The moment he contacted his target, it exploded into a cloud of smoke. He slammed into the snow with an oof! Coughing, Leif waved his hand to clear the smoke. Once it dissipated, the forest was gone. It was replaced with a brightly lit hallway lined with framed photographs.

Leif hurriedly got to his feet, spinning in a circle, searching for the cloaked figure, but the phantom was gone. As he spun, his eyes landed on one of the photographs. "Hey," Leif said to the empty hallway. "That's me. How the hell did I get to my parents' house?" Suddenly, a crash followed by a muffled scream came from somewhere on the lower floor, interrupting his train of thought. Dashing forward, Leif vaulted the second-floor railing. Landing in a crouch, he saw his parents' front door shattered to pieces. Small pools of blood dotted the destroyed foyer. Following the gory trail into the living room, he found his mother slumped on her couch, blood pouring from a grievous chest wound. The same cloaked figure loomed over her body with a gore slick blade clutched in one hand.

Leif's glassy eyes filled with tears as he screamed. "Why are you doing this? She wouldn't hurt a fly!" The figure's only response was an ominous chuckle. A fire blossomed in Leif's chest, but it lacked the power the Berserker lent him. He charged the wraith, aiming a right hook at its hooded face. But just as before, once his fist made contact, the figure burst into smoke, obscuring his surroundings.

With tears in his eyes, Leif shouted into the mist. "WHY ARE YOU SHOWING ME THIS?"

"Embrace me, body and soul, and you will never have to fear losing a loved one again," a gravelly voice called from the smoke.

"Who's there?" Leif called out, but there was no answer.

A moment later, the smoke dimmed, then disappeared altogether. This time, he knew immediately where he was. For all intents and purposes, it was a beautiful Alfheimian day, except for the burning Savartalfar village, of course. Leif stood on the outskirts of the town he and Arias had visited. Savartalfar bodies littered the area as the symphony of combat could be heard from deep within the village. Leif ran. *This time will be different. I'm stronger now. Arias doesn't have to die,* he thought.

Leif blasted through the narrow streets, homing in on his quarry. It didn't take long to find the street he was looking for. Memories of that fateful day flashed through his mind as he turned a corner, spotting Arias dueling a monstrous Jontar. Leif forgot himself for a moment, seeing his dead friend very much alive again. He stared in awe at the skill Arias displayed while fighting a superior foe. Arias moved like water, effortlessly flowing from attack to defense, but no matter what he tried, the Jontar was his equal. Hope swelled in Leif's heart as Arias's thin blade pierced his foe's side, cutting deep into the giant's flank. But to Leif's horror, the Jontar grabbed onto his friend's blade, locking it in place. Arias was caught completely off guard as the Jontar dropped his own weapon to seize the Ljosalfar by the neck with its free hand. Arias wheezed as the Jontar tightened his grip around his neck. He watched in terror as the Jontar then lifted Arias up, bringing the struggling Ljosalfar to eye level with the giant.

"Leif, please help me. I don't want to die," Arias gasped a

moment before a loud crack resounded off the tight confines of the street.

"NO!" Leif howled as the Jontar dropped the limp body of his friend to the ground. Turning at his outburst the Jontar faced him. Curiously, the Jontar's eyes were an electric blue instead of their typical blood red. With murder in his heart, Leif lunged towards the Jontar, swinging with all his might. But just as before, the moment he contacted the giant, it burst into smoke, obscuring his surroundings.

Leif let out a frustrated growl as his nerves teetered on the verge of collapse. Taking a shuttering breath, he tried to reign in his emotions, but the images of the dead kept flashing through his mind. "No," Leif shouted into the swirling mist. "I don't know what you are trying to prove, but I will not break!"

As if in challenge, the mist thinned, revealing the Icelandic forest once again. Just as before, there was a shout of alarm followed by the fleeing form of his grandfather. Leif reacted instantly, sprinting to intercept the shadow that was pursuing Alexander. As if spurred on by Leif's haste, the shadow cut down his grandfather with one brutal swing of the wraith's obsidian blade. The fleeing Alexander went down in a heap. A cry dying on his lips as he collapsed.

"NO!" Leif screamed, but he was too late.

Changing tactics, Leif went for a submission hold, wrapping his arms around the shadow as it stood over his dead grandfather. But it was no use. The figure disappeared in a column of smoke the moment he made contact. This mist dissipated much quicker than before, bringing him back to the second-floor hallway of his parents' house. Leif wasted no time, immediately breaking into a run. As he reached the railing, he was met with the familiar crashing sound followed by a blood-curdling scream. Vaulting the stairs, Leif landed awkwardly, twisting his ankle in the process. Grunting through the pain, he stumbled into the living room, but it was too late. His mother lay dead at the feet of the phantom.

Overcome with emotion, Leif lashed out at the cloaked figure, but as with each encounter before, it burst into smoke, obscuring his surroundings.

Leif immediately took off, sprinting through the mist with reckless abandon. Running blind, he was unsurprised to find himself back at the Savartalfar village. Within seconds, he was charging down the street toward Arias, shouting a warning to his friend. A wellspring of hope sprung up in Leif's breast as he ran. *I'm going to make it!* he thought.

"He's too strong! I can't hold him on my own!" Arias shouted over his shoulder.

He was within twenty feet of the dueling pair, when Leif watched in dread as the Jontar thrust forward, sending the razor-sharp point of his long sword into Arias's chest. Emotions raw from witnessing so many deaths in such quick succession, Leif screamed, slamming into the Jontar, which, of course, caused it to promptly burst into smoke. A moment later, Leif stood in the snow-covered forest again.

# CHAPTER 32

On and on, the cycle of death repeated itself. Time lost all meaning as Leif watched his loved ones die again and again. He knew he would carry the sight of their empty eyes staring sightlessly back at him for the rest of his days. Through the indefinable days of this torture, Leif had tried everything in his power to save them, but no matter what he did, he was never fast enough.

As the cycle renewed, Leif heard his grandfather's terrified scream again. He staggered but tripped over a snow-covered root, falling to his knees. The cold wet snow stung but failed to numb the pain. With the only energy he had left, Leif blinked to clear the tears from his eyes. He succumbed to the grief and sobbed, "I can't save you. I never could. I must accept this cruel universe. This isn't a movie where the good guy wins in the end. You, Mom, Arias, none of you deserved to die while I lived. But you did die, and I can't change that. I thought I could save you, but I can't. I should have known the past can't be changed. Gods! I wish it could, but what's done is done. I will strive to be better, to protect those who need protecting, to aid those who ask for it. I know I can't change what happened to you all, but I sure as hell will avenge you."

As Leif voiced his vow, the surrounding forest grew hazy and melted away, leaving him in a star filled void. He wasn't sure if it was a trick of the eye or his imagination, but he could have sworn the colorful expanse contained a cluster of stars that formed a multi-colored tree with nine branches stretching into the distance.

The sound of footfalls pulled Leif from his reverie. Dropping his gaze from the abyss, he watched a splotch of shadow darkened, then the nothingness pulled away from its surroundings and walked in his direction. As the figure approached, it formed a humanoid shape. Two glowing orbs erupted from where the thing's head should be. Once it came within ten feet of him, it stopped.

Leif and the black form stared at each other. He watched as color slowly seeped into the apparition. Inch by inch, the shadow became a perfect clone of himself, berserked, glowing eyes and all. His doppelgänger, the creature, turned its head from side to side, looking Leif up and down. The not-Leif flashed a vicious smile, sending a chill down the real Leif's spine.

"So, you finally figured it out?" The not-Leif said. Its voice sounded much gruffer than his own.

"Is that what I sound like berserked?" he asked the specter. The copy merely raised an eyebrow.

"You're right. It's not important right now." Leif said, waving the question away.

A scowl crossed his doppelgänger's face as it continued to inspect him. "You've come seeking power, but I don't think you are worthy. The death of your family and friend are proof of that. Even here, in the depths of your own mind, you couldn't find the strength to save them. What makes you think I would be willing to submit to someone as weak as you?"

"You're the incarnation of the Berserker, aren't you?" Leif straightened himself.

"Aren't you quick?" the Berserker mocked.

"But aren't you a part of me? Why would you reject me?" he asked. "You respond willingly whenever I call."

"You get a drizzle compared to the monsoon. Your line has always been good at keeping control of the trickle, but that's it."

"Then lend it to me!" Leif begged.

The Berserker scoffed.

"When we faced Hel under Asgard, I felt something shift. I was stronger than I had ever been before. I could feel your power merging with mine. Why do you pull away now? Our work isn't done. Hel and Fenrir are still out there."

The Berserker lifted his chin as he remembered the battle. "You speak the truth; you came very close to ascending on that day. Unfortunately, there is still something holding you back. I can feel it even now. There is a weakness within you. It is holding you back from your full potential. Your manifestations are evidence of that. Until you rid yourself of your weakness, you will never claim my power."

"Bullshit," he challenged. "I've killed gods. Gone toe-to-toe with beings older than my entire bloodline, and yet here I stand. You are but a sliver of those beings. My will alone is enough to keep you chained. If you won't give me the power, then I will take it by force." Leif snarled as he charged his evil twin.

Leif half expected the doppelgänger to disappear like the other specters, but the Berserker's right hook slammed into Leif's jaw was very real. The force of the punch rocked him backwards a few steps. Blinking away the pain, Leif glared at the smiling Berserker.

Leif slipped into a bladed stance. "Let's dance, asshole," he growled.

His doppelgänger bounced on the balls of his feet, like when Leif sparred with Arias for the first time. The two circled each other, moving in perfect unison. Feeling that time was of the essence, Leif darted forward with his fists flying.

"You can't best me," the Berserker laughed, deftly evading Leif's attacks.

He was undeterred, redoubled his efforts to beat the Berserker into submission. Two loud THWACK, THWACK sounds echoed through the nothingness as the Berserker caught his punches. Before Leif could react, his doppelgänger clamped onto his fists, locking him in place. Leif growled in frustration as he fought to pull free of the Berserker's iron grip. Leif struggled as his doppelgänger flourished a condescending smile. "My turn. Once I've shattered your mind, I will mold you into a true Berserker. One that is not hindered by emotions or fear."

Something about what the Berserker said resonated with Leif. Before he could focus on it, the Berserker attacked with powerful blows. Leif was frustrated; he instinctively knew where the next attack was coming from, but he was too slow to dodge it.

On the defense, Leif did his best to stay ahead of his opponent, but he failed spectacularly. He fought to stay on his feet. Then his doppelgänger kicked it up a notch.

The not-Leif moved with the speed of the gods. Each punch found its target in a continuous cacophony of agony. Leif tried to fight back, but it was no use. He was outclassed in every aspect. Despair set in as he was pummeled to the ground. Pain became his entire being, consuming his consciousness, which had begun to fade. Inch by inch, the edges of his vision receded into nothing until only blackness remained.

*This is where it ends*, Leif thought weakly. The faces of the friends he made long the way flashed through his mind. Bjorn, Lagertha, Jaeger, and everyone in the Skogur Borg. Heimdall and Thor. At this point, he would welcome the darkness. It was his only way out of this torment.

Suddenly, a spark pierced the haze of pain. "You carry the weight of your lost comrades." Thor's booming voice echoed in his mind. "It is good to consider past battles and lost friends, but you can't let the past govern you. That route breeds fear and indecision, which neither aids the dead nor yourself," Thor chided. "Your friend died protecting you on a quest he believed in. A warrior could not choose a finer death. Do not sully his choice with these fears you carry."

The pain of the Berserker's assault slackened. Leif's mind flashed to the battle against Ares. Smoke clogged the air as the elktre burned in the city's fire. Jaeger's muffled voice rose above the roaring fire. "Leif, focus on the enemy in front of you! Do not trouble yourself with the task of Jol, Selga, and Foste! Worrying does nothing for them and weakens your resolve! Trust them to do their part as they trust you to do yours!"

The pain of his beating lightened more as he relived these past moments. Then, as if struck by lightning, he knew.

"I have to let them go," he whispered.

"What did you say?" the Berserker challenged, with his fist raised for another punch.

"I have to let them go. I weaken them and myself with regrets and by my fear to never lose a friend again," Leif responded. He felt a surge of strength fill his blood.

The Berserker recoiled, like Leif had become lava. He got to his feet, expecting to be in pain, but he felt nothing. He felt good, great even. Leif felt stronger than he had been before.

Pulling himself from the introspection, he glared at the Berserker, who now seemed frail, less corporeal somehow. "That's what's holding my power back, isn't it?" Leif asked. "The guilt of losing Arias broke me. The regrets burrowed into my subconscious and took hold, stealing my strength. The weakness festered, rotting away my power, day by day. But no more." Leif said confidently. "I can see clearly now. The wounds of lost friends will never fade, but I can't let the actions of the past cause me to second guess my actions in the present. Indecision is the killer. I must move on."

While Leif spoke, the Berserker faded and became more and more transparent until nothing but a faint outline of the figure remained. Then it to disappeared.

Blinking, Leif stood alone in an expansive nothing. *Now what?*

Then, as if an answer to his thoughts, a crackling blue ball of energy materialized where the Berserker had stood. Leif slowly approached the floating ball. Small forks of lightning crackled to life around the orb, growing in intensity the closer he got. Leif thought it resembled one of those plasma globes that were all the rage in the 90s.

As he inspected the orb, Leif felt an uncomfortable tugging sensation at the back of his mind, pulling him closer to the electric globe. The pull grew so strong, he nearly fell over. He reached out, intending to grab the glowing ball, but the orb swung itself into Leif's outstretched hand like a magnetic force.

Leif's fingers curled around the object, as a zing of energy coursed up his arm, spreading throughout his body as the orb melted into his palm. The crackle of energy pulsed through his body, shifting to the familiar icy burn of his Berserker transformation, except the sensation didn't die to the simmering fire that he had grown accustomed to. His blood boiled as the power continued to grow and his skin grew colder. The two opposing forces melded into an explosion of steam around his body. His skin was coated in a thin layer of frost. The elemental battle raged on, changing him down to the cellular level.

Once the steam cleared, Leif took in his surroundings. Not only had he changed, but the dark abyss he had been standing in was gone. He now stood on a grassy field. The constellation above had transformed into a massive tree that reached high up into the heavens. Hope swelled in Leif's breast as he lifted his chin to the sky.

# CHAPTER 33

Leif opened his eyes, surprised to find himself back in the waking world. Though happy he had successfully assimilated body and mind with the Berserker, he couldn't help but be a little bummed. He didn't get the chance to explore his inner Yggdrasil.

"Just in the nick of time," Lagertha said as she stood up from the ground next to where he had been lying prone. "I was beginning to think I would have to abandon you up here."

Leif sat up. He immediately regretted it as the blood rushed to his head, making his vision blur. His head grew heavy, and stars twinkled in his vision momentarily.

"You've been out for nearly four days." Lagertha warned. "Take it easy for a couple of seconds."

Leaning back, Leif inhaled the crisp mountain air into his lungs. Once he felt well enough to stand, he got up. His knees popped from laying prone for so long. He thought the world looked crisper, more focused than before. It was as if he just put on a pair of prescription glasses, having never known he needed them. Colors that were once muted jumped out at him. Even the veil appeared brighter, more real, as it snaked its way across the bright Vanaheimr sky.

He was pulled from his newfound awareness by the whisper of bare feet on stone. He turned just in time to see Lagertha launch herself toward him. Her arm was raised for an attack. Leif dodged just as Lagertha's fist sailed past his face. Moving with the ease of a veteran fighter, she continued her assault. Foot lashing out in a roundhouse kick aimed for his face. Taking two quick steps, Leif ducked under Lagertha's foot, then counterattacked with a punch of his own. His fist connected squarely with Lagertha's solar plexus, catching her off guard.

Lagertha ooofed loudly as Leif shifted his feet, preparing to continue his counterattack, but a raised hand from a dry-heaving Lagertha pulled him up short. Dropping his hands to his side as he straightened, Leif smiled as he took in the full breath of his ascension. No longer did he feel the red tinged rage that assaulted his conscious mind. Though he did detect an undercurrent of anger coursing through his veins, but it was muted. It was as if the howling Berserker had died down to a whisper that he had no trouble silencing. Smiling, he let out a joyous laugh. It felt as if the weight he had been carrying over the past year was finally gone, and he could breathe again.

While Lagertha recovered her breath, Leif stepped out of the cave and onto the bright sunlit terrace. He memorized the mountainous horizon. A feeling of determination engraved on his soul. *I can do this,* Leif marveled. *With this new power, I am finally strong enough to hunt down Hel and get vengeance for my mother and grandfather.*

"Looks like it was a successful trip," Lagertha breathlessly commented, stepping next to him.

"It was, but for a second there, I didn't think I was going to make it." Leif said sheepishly.

"What you faced within is for you and you alone. Each Berserker who has ascended into the mental realm is faced with their own personal battles." Lagertha said as she gazed at the expanse.

Moving back into the cave, they both sat down next to their tiny fire. "Now that you've ascended, it seems our time together is approaching its end," Lagertha stated while Leif attempted to shovel four days' worth of food in his mouth. "Interestingly enough, now that you and I are equals, the compulsion to fight has died down considerably. It's still there, but as with all the other urges an awakened Berserker feels, it is nothing but an annoying buzz that can be tuned out."

Leif stopped chewing for a second and he closed his eyes to focus. She was right. The compulsion, just like the ever-present rage was still there, but it had lessened and was more easily ignored. "It appears our kind was never meant to live in peace with one another." Leif mused as he went back to eating.

"True enough. We are warriors. Our lot in life is to seek out those who would challenge our power and eliminate them." Lagertha said, locking eyes with Leif.

Leif felt his pulse quicken as Lagertha matched stares with him. The air crackled with tension as his palms began to itch. The moment stretched, then just as quickly, Lagertha broke the stare with a smile.

"I am glad to know there are still others like me in the realms. Now that you have gained your new power, will you seek out the Jontar chieftain?" Lagertha asked.

"Oh yes," Leif said after a long pause. It took him a few seconds to remember the lies he had spun.

"I wish you the best of luck on your hunt. You are far stronger than you used to be. On par or stronger than many of the other beings of the realms. But I would be remiss if I didn't warn you. You aren't invincible. There are many beings out there who wield magic just as easily as a blade. Do not assume that because you have ascended you are unbeatable. Your quarry is a chieftain, and he won't be a push over. The Jontar live and breathe personal combat. If he has kept his position for this long, he will be a formidable warrior."

"I understand." Leif said, feeling a little bad for misleading her. "Thank you for the warning. And well, for everything you have done for me."

"We are practically family now," Lagertha said with a smile. "I would expect no less from you if I came to you asking for aid. You are welcome to stay with the tribe as you make your preparations. To be honest, I was hoping we could spar once more when we get back. I'm sure those of the tribe would enjoy the spectacle, and I'm curious to see who would win now," she said with a mischievous glint in her eye.

"Deal," he said as he gulped down the last of his rations.

# CHAPTER 34

The trek back to the tribe took considerably less time. Leif hadn't realized it before, but Lagertha had been holding back, picking a pace that was punishing but not unattainable. However, now she moved so swiftly that Leif found himself stumbling after her as he fought to become acquainted with his newly enhanced body. With the power of an ascended Berserker, Leif felt his body exert itself with more force than necessary. The speed of his gait had increased, making the trek an easy stroll. For anyone else, they would probably have to jog to match their pace. He also suspected he would have to adjust his grip strength. A smile came to Leif's lips as the *DragonBall Z* episode with Goku and Gohan as they attempted to adjust to normal life as Super Sayians popped into his head.

For much of the trip back to camp, he was content to walk in silence, letting Lagertha lead the way. It gave him time to assess his upgrades. The gloomy gray forest was considerably louder and brighter than before. The normally silent forest was alive with rustling leaves, chirping insects, and the flutter of unseen wings. Even the mist appeared different to him. He could now make out complex patterns in the fog as it ebbed and flowed around them. It reminded Leif of the subtle eddies on the ocean surface.

After walking for twenty minutes, the sounds of the forest gave way to the bustle of the tribe. It wasn't long before the pair spotted the crackling fires of the torches that marked the camp's perimeter. As they approached the outer boundary, there came a whisper of movement from above. It was so soft that Leif wasn't sure if he imagined it or not. He looked up in time to see a shadowed figure hidden high up on a perch under the forest canopy. A feat that would have been impossible before his ascension. A second later, the shadow called out a challenge. Without missing a beat, Lagertha responded, never slowing nor looking in the direction of the hidden sentry.

News of their return spread like wildfire. So, it shouldn't have come as a surprise when a Savartalfar sprinted out of the mist to approach Lagertha.

"You are needed in the great hall," the dwarf wheezed, out of breath.

"The great hall? I have just returned. Whatever business the counsel wishes to discuss, it can wait until I have had a chance to bathe and a eat whatever Hesvik's people are cooking for tonight." Lagertha said, slapping her hands against her thigh in annoyance.

"I apologize, but Galen has requested for you to report to the council chambers the moment you returned," the Savartalfar said with a slight tremor in her voice.

"Why?" Lagertha challenged.

"Um," she said, shooting Leif the side eye. "A man approached the tribe just this morning. He appeared out of the mists, practically on our doorstep. He requested a meeting with the elder counsel. No one was sure when you would return, so Galen had runners posted around the camp should you return while the stranger was brought to the great hall."

"Galen let an unknown into the tribe?" Lagertha's voice

darkened. "Did he send out scouts to see if the stranger was alone?"

"Uh, I don't know," the Savartalfar responded nervously. "I was only told to bring you to the hall should you return before their meeting ended."

Lagertha let out a frustrated growl before turning to Leif. "You'll have to excuse me. It appears that I am needed. We will meet up at dinner." Lagertha said.

"Sounds good," Leif responded to the perturbed Berserker, who strode off into the swirling mist.

Leif took his time walking through the camp, enjoying the sounds and smells of the tribe. He hadn't realized how much he missed being around civilization. Trekking through the realms is fun and all, but there is something to say about the comfort of society. He eventually made his way back to his tent. Within, he stripped off his dirty clothes. Since he currently only had the one pair of pants, he washed them in the small water basin Bjorn had given him. Hanging the wet clothes along his clothesline, he then lit a small fire to help dry out his laundry and warm the chilly tent. While his clothes dried, Leif decided to take a short nap to help refresh himself.

A FAMILIAR VOICE pulled Leif from his dreamless sleep. It was smooth as honey but carried an unmistakable air of bored superiority. He knew that voice. Ra was here. He was instantly on his feet. His axes raised in defense as he stared out his tent flap. Several heartbeats later, he relaxed when no attack came. He jumped a moment later when Ra's smooth voice came again, but from a distance.

*Ok, Ra is here, in the tribe,* Leif thought furiously. *If he had known I was here, I feel like I would already be dead or captured. What does he want with the tribe? It could be anything. Time to get out of dodge,* he thought.

Leif dropped his axe, threw on his damp clothes, and stuffed his meager belongings into his travel pack.

Ten minutes later, he poked his head outside his tent, surveying his surroundings. He saw a few shadowed people ghosting through the mist, but that was it. Trying to be nonchalant, Leif strode out of his tent, heading towards the nearest exit when he banged foreheads with Lagertha. If Leif wasn't so terrified of being seen, he would have found the encounter comical.

"You're leaving?" Lagertha asked, confused.

"Yeah," Leif said, rubbing the back of his neck. "I have a long journey ahead of me, and I am eager to begin. Now that I am free of the Berserker's more violent urges, I feel as if I can finally get justice for my family.

"I understand," she said, placing a hand on his shoulder. "I still remember the feeling of the weight being lifted from my mind when I ascended. It felt as if I could finally begin to live my life. I am sad to see you go," she said with a squeeze of his shoulder. "We had a rocky start, you and I, but I have enjoyed our time together. Murderous compulsion aside, it has been nice to confide in someone who has suffered as I have. If you have ever need of aid, you know where to find us."

"Thank you, Lagertha," Leif said with a genuine smile. "You have done more than you can ever know. I hope our paths cross again, my friend."

"Aye," she said. "May your ferocity strike fear in all who stand before you."

What followed was an awkward silence, where neither was sure if they should hug or shake hands. Unsure of the protocol and to be on the safe side, Leif held out his hand. A second later, she took it. Giving each other one final nod, Leif left the camp, cloaking himself in the mist.

# CHAPTER 35

Wary of being followed, Leif pushed deep into the shrouded forest. After he felt he had gone far enough to convince any pursuer of his intent to leave, he stepped up to a tree, pretending to pee. Using the pretense, he checked his surroundings. Seeing no one, he turned and headed back toward the tribe, using the marks he had made with his belt knife on the tree trunks he passed as a guide.

With his newly enhanced senses, the once dark forest was alive, allowing him to see and hear with better clarity than ever before. He did his best to move as silently as he could on his way back. Sadly, Leif still seemed to lack the innate skill Arias possessed to move quietly.

He took twice as long on his return trek until the sounds of the forest gave way to the general buzz of the large encampment. Wary of hidden sentries, Leif kept his eyes glued to the branches as he tiptoed closer to the torch lined perimeter.

During his time with the tribe, Leif had learned they rarely posted guards along the side of the camp that abutted the fallen boulders, believing the Vanaheimr mountain range and rocks formed a defensive wall against any potential invader. He planned to use this blind spot to his advantage. He hoped to glean any information about Ra's visit from the tribe members.

Leif scrambled up the immense rocks, as the sun sunk below the mountain peaks, signaling nightfall. The timing was perfect; he knew people below would congregate around the large fire to enjoy their meal with friends. Using the fire as his guiding light, he hopped between towering boulders until he peered down over a surprisingly large crowd. Leif could have sworn the entire tribe was in attendance.

Suddenly, the milling crowd went completely silent. Scanning the area for the cause, Leif watched Lagertha, Galen, and Hesvik enter the area. Every head turned to their tribe leaders as they took up positions at the front of the crowd.

"I am sure many of you are wondering why we asked you all here tonight. It has been many years since we have called for such a gathering." Lagertha said with her arms spread out wide to encompass the gathered tribe members. "If memory serves me, it was when you all chose to elevate me to the position I hold now." Lagertha said with a smile. "I have worked hard every day since to be worthy of your trust in me. For that reason, we called you all here this evening. As many of you know, we were visited by Ra, the leader of the Outsiders, who are currently battling with the Aesir over control of the Nine Realms."

There was a chorus of whispers from the crowd at the mention of Ra's name, but Lagertha pressed on. "He came to us with a proposition. One that, if we accept, would change the course of the tribe forever. We wish to reassure you all that we did not come to our decision lightly."

"What did he want?" a voice called out from the crowd.

Hesvik scowled in the direction of the speaker, but Lagertha and Galen smiled.

"He asked us to join him on their final assault on Asgard."

The crowd went completely still at her pronouncement.

"I understand your reticence. I was of same mind as all of

you," she soothed. "But after Ra divulged their plan and how much they have accomplished, even I became a believer. Especially if he can deliver on his promises."

"What do we get for helping him?" another called from the silent crowd.

"Freedom," Lagertha responded. "If we take part in the assault against the Aesir, we will be given a large swath of territory to call our own. We can finally build a city-state that we govern. We will be free to move among the realms unmolested by the corrupt forces that govern the realms. We will no longer need to slink along the edges of society sniffing for scraps. That, my friends, is what was promised."

"Even with the promise of freedom, we..." Lagertha said, gesturing to Galen and Hesvik, "still weren't fully convinced of the success of his plan. This is the Aesir we are talking about, a regime that has ruled the realms for a millennium. He explained that their forces have made huge advances. Outside of a few isolated hold outs, much of the nine realms are under Hel and Outsider control. Odin and his ilk have retreated to their strong hold on Asgard. They are fighting a defensive battle. Ra promises that with this final push, the Aesir will be no more. We will aid in ushering in a new age in the nine realms, one free of the oppression that has plagued the realms for so long."

"Without proof, those are just honeyed words. Am I right?" Lagertha asked the crowd.

Leif saw several people in the crowd nodding their heads in agreement.

"But Ra was nonplused. Accepting our uncertainty with grace. Not something we would expect from a being so old and powerful. So, he made us a promise. He promised us a boon as a show of good faith. Something that will prove Hel and her forces can truly accomplish what they have set out to do. We only need to travel to Mikill Stoar to see it."

"So, my friends, tonight after this meeting, we are marching to war. If Ra's gift is sufficient to sway us, we will immediately set out with him to attack Asgard. Tribe warriors and those select few the elder counsel believe are ready will be leaving tonight."

This caused a bit of a stir among the crowd.

Lagertha was undeterred and let the crowd murmur for a time before raising her hands over her head, catching everyone's attention again. "I know this is sudden, but this is an opportunity we can't pass up. Under the Aesir's rule, we are merely surviving. Friends, I don't want to just survive. I want us to THRIVE!" she shouted. "And that is what Hel and her Outsider compatriots have promised us. So, tribe warriors, go forth, kiss your loved ones, for tonight we go to war!"

The crowd shouted their approval before rising to gear up.

LEIF FELL asleep while he waited for the troops to move out. Marshaling the tribe's warriors took longer than he had expected, but some hours later, under the cover of darkness, Lagertha and a host of tribe warriors marched into the forest. Luckily, the shouts from Galen's rowdy speech woke him up just in enough time to see the long column of tribesmen and woman set off into the forest. The torch bearing host was so large and slow moving it made following them a piece of cake.

Hours later, as the mist lighten with the sunrise, Leif heard a chorus of shouts run down the length of shuffling warriors. The lead warriors had found the tunnel that led to Mikill Stoar. Knowing the tunnel would provide little protection from prying eyes, Leif was content to let the crowd move deep into the cave before following. He would rely on his newly enhanced senses to help guide him through the dark, mountainous tunnel.

While he waited for the lumbering crowd to ascend into the passageway, Leif mused on the significance of Ra asking to meet in Mikill Stoar. *What is Ra's angle in all of this? I doubt the Rao counsel would take kindly to an armed militia appearing at their gates. Does he intend to lead the tribe in an attack against the Rao, cutting off the mortal governing body of the realms in one fell swoop?* Leif's train of thought did nothing to ease his growing nervousness. He knew whatever plan Hel had for bringing in the tribe at this juncture, it couldn't be good for the Aesir or the realms at large. Unfortunately, there was nothing he could do but wait for his own time to strike.

Close to thirty minutes after the last two members of the tribe entered the passage to Mikill Stoar, Leif sidled up to one corner of the opening. He peered into the ascending tunnel. Within the confines of the circular passageway, he could easily make out the torch bearing warriors as they climbed. For his part, the closest warrior looked to be more than three hundred yards away. Thinking they had more than enough of a lead, Leif climbed, staying as close to either side of the uneven tunnel as he could.

For several hours, Leif relied on the pinpricks of light from the torch bearing warriors to lead the way. When the first dot of sunlight appeared ahead, Leif audibly sighed in relief. *I think I'm done with caves and tunnels for a while,* he thought as he slowed his pace. He really didn't want to spoil all his sneaking around by getting cabin fever and rushing out of the cave too early.

Pausing just below the lip of the cave mouth, Leif strained to hear if Lagertha and her horde had remained near the cave or pushed toward Mikill Stoar. It was during this time that a whiff of smoke blew down into the tunnel, reaching him. His unease increased, and after several seconds of hearing nothing, he peeked.

Unsheathing his axes as he took a few steps, Leif stepped out of the darkness and into the brightly sunlit mountain side. The passageway opened two hundred yards from the lowest tier of Vanaheimr's capital city. Even from his vantage point far below the city, Leif immediately knew something was wrong. Large, noxious plumes of smoke rose from each one of the city's numerous levels. The large guard tower and gate that sat at the foot of the city had been torn in two, leaving the winding road open and unprotected.

Leif watched with a growing sickness in his stomach as the tribe host, led by Lagertha, passed through the broken gates and climbed toward the burning city. Leif needed to figure out Ra's plan and hopefully report his findings to Thor before the raid began. He raced after the invading tribe, hoping their fascination with the burning city in front of them would keep anyone from looking back his way.

Careful to keep a healthy but manageable distance, Leif snuck through the once resplendent city, horrified at the destruction on each tier he passed. Rubble was strewn throughout the terraces as they burned with an unholy purple flame. But that wasn't the worst of it. No matter how hard he looked, he saw no sign of the citizens. The last time he had walked the city, the winding road was full of beings going about their daily lives. But now, the mountain top was a burning ghost town. It sent a chill down his spine.

Leif raced past the upper tiers, hoping to learn what Ra's plan was. Using a burned-out guard post at the entrance to the Rao level of the city, Leif peered out over the grassy courtyard that sat in the shadow of the sprawling columned buildings. It was there that Leif spotted Ra, glittering in bronzed armor, addressing the tribe warriors arrayed below him on the steps.

With all eyes on Ra, Leif capitalized on their distraction, sprinting across the open ground to the fence that ran along the courtyard. Slipping through the destroyed guard gate, Leif ran across the open grass onto the walkway, out of sight of the crowd. Now close enough to eavesdrop, Leif paused to listen.

"I hope you find your gift suitable," Ra's honey smooth voice boomed. "The Rao in their seat of power. Their feeble fortress was so easy to overrun. Oh, how I would love to go into the details of the slaughter, but the final assault on Asgard is underway." Ra shouted to the cheering crowd. "The Aesir were caught off guard, not expecting an attack in their throne realm. Odin's personal guards took heavy losses in the initial strike, but have since retreated to their final stronghold, barricading themselves inside.

With mighty Lagertha and her veteran warriors bolstering our ranks, the Asgardians will quickly fall under our blades. Just beyond these stairs," Ra said, gesturing behind him, "we will use the bridge to infiltrate the palace that they cower inside of. The blood I share with Odin combined with a sufficient mantle of power should be enough to break through the weakened ward net around the castle. With Asgard's troops spread thin, as they battle our forces across the realm, we will be able to slip in unnoticed. Only Odin, Loki, Thor, and their royal guards are left to deal with. Once we overwhelm their guards, we will crush the Aesir under the sheer weight of our numbers."

A familiar voice called out, cutting off Ra's speech. "If you already have them on the ropes, what could you possibly need us for?" Lagertha asked.

"This isn't some raid on a Savartalfar mining camp," Ra mocked. "Odin inherited the lion's share of the strength in our family. Same goes for his bastard of a firstborn. Those two are still alive and fighting wherever the battle is most fierce. I learned eons ago not to underestimate a being on our power level. Just one Aesir is a force of nature. Two fighting together are nearly unstoppable. So, there is no such thing as overkill when the gods go to war. Our joining the fight, leading a surprise attack within the castle's keep, will divide the Aesir's forces, sowing confusion from our sudden appearance. In that confusion, we will pick off the Aesir one at a time, with overwhelming odds," Ra stated.

"Understood. What do you want us to do?" Lagertha asked.

"The moment I open the bridge, enter into the stronghold. We shall split into two groups. One will go with me to the front gate. There, we will attack the defenders from behind. We will let in Hel, Fenrir, and the rest of our assault force. Once the walls have been breached, we will seek out Odin and Thor. Lagertha, you are to lead the second assault force. Stalk the halls, kill any you encounter, but do not engage anyone in a one-on-one fight. If your squad is to be effective, you must attack with overwhelming force. A word of caution. There is a possibility that some of the Vanir still remain alive and are fighting. Avoid them if you can. Your people will be no match against them," Ra commented.

"Ha, we are stronger than you know," Lagertha boasted.

"Suit yourselves," Ra said with an annoyed shrug. "But if you endanger our chances of victory, I will kill you myself."

The calm threat sent a chill down Leif's spine as he thought back to the gods' fight with Thor.

"You are welcome to try," she said, matching Ra's coldness.

The terrace fell silent as the tension between the two parties grew. Then came a booming laugh from Ra. "HAHAHAHAHA! Berserker indeed. It saddens me to know a warrior bloodline like yours has been lurking in the shadows for so long. Curse your obfuscation tattoos for keep you from out of site for so long. But no matter. You are here now. Are you ready to change your fate?" Ra shouted.

The tribe's answer was deafening.

A moment later Leif felt the telltale magical pulse, signifying Ra had opened the bridge. The amount of power the Outsider used in connecting the Vanaheimr bridge to Asgard was staggering. A spike of pain lanced through his skull as the magic pulsed, seeking its destination. It was so strong stars flickered in and out of Leif's vision. Once the connection stabilized, Leif heard Ra shout, "GO!"

The sound of hundreds of warriors flooded through the gate.

## CHAPTER 36

Not wanting to get caught stranded on Vanaheimr, Leif stepped out from his hiding spot on the walkway. The lip of the terrace that led to columned buildings and the bridge within was a level above him. He wasn't familiar with the layout of the area and knew it would take him too long to search the complex for the stairs that led up there. So, he took the quicker route and jumped. Using his demigod like strength, Leif flew nearly ten feet in the air, which was more than sufficient to grab the lip of the balcony.

Landing in a crouch, Leif unhooked both axes as he crept forward, hiding behind a large planter filled with pink and turquoise flowers. Though the host of warriors were gone, he could make out the forms of Ra, Lagertha, and what looked like two tribe warriors talking at the top of the stairs. All four had their backs to Leif, so he took the opportunity to step from cover and run up the stairs.

Moving as quietly as possible, Leif came to a stop just to the right of the open bridge room. With his back pressed against the wall, he snuck a quick peek around the corner. Quickly scanning the wide three-walled room, he was relieved to see the bridge was currently open, showing the gleaming halls of Asgard beyond. On each side of the bridge, marbled statues of Thor and Odin glared at all who passed by.

"Janik and Beltar," Leif heard Lagertha say. "I need you two to guard the bridge. With you two standing on the threshold, it will remain open, providing us with a quick exit should this raid go wrong. None of us mortals can open a bridge while on Asgard, so we need this one to remain open. Got it?"

"Aye," he heard both warriors say in unison.

Risking a second look, Leif was just in time to see Ra and Lagertha disappear through the bridge as the two guards took up their posts.

*Hmmm,* Leif thought. *How do I handle this?* He didn't recognize the two warriors, but that didn't mean they wouldn't know him. With violence imminent, he waited for the telltale signs of the Berserker bubbling to the surface, but no such feeling came. It was strange not to feel the Berserker's fiery rage roiling within. All that remained was a pale echo of the blinding rage. He smiled, then he took a deep breath.

Leif knew he needed to be quick if he was going to make a difference in the battle. He was also looking forward to testing out his new power. Stepping out from around the corner, Leif held his hands out wide as he walked towards the bridge. Both guards reacted immediately. Their hands reached for their swords as they shouted a challenge in Ljosa. The guard on the right opened his mouth to speak again, but Leif blurred forward. He closed the short distance between himself and the guards in a blink of an eye.

Leif flung his right hand forward, slamming it into the pommel of the guard's sword, stopping the blade before he got it halfway out of the sheath. Caught off guard by his speed, the warrior's eyes widened before Leif's fist slammed into his face. The guard was flung sideways, smashing painfully into a statue with an audible crunch.

The sound of the second guard's sword freeing itself from its scabbard alerted him to an eminent attack from behind. Pivoting to face his opponent, he was just in time to see the razor-sharp edge of a straight sword descend toward his face. He dodged two quick slashes before stepping in close to land a punch square to the warrior's mid-section. The warrior doubled over in pain. Taking a firm grip of the warrior's leather armor, Leif flung the Ljosalfar with all his might. He watched the tribesmen soar a good ten feet away, as he marveled at how easily he bested the two warriors.

With both gate guards down, Leif rushed through the bridge into Asgard. Stopping on the other side, he inspected the open bridge, feeling its magical connection. With no one actively feeding or holding the bridge open, the magic holding the two realms together sputtered, then died out, shutting down any chance of escape. *Well, I'm fully committed now,* Leif thought as he stared at the ornate archway that housed the bridge connector.

THE SOUNDS of battle echoed throughout the castle keep, providing Leif with little aid in which direction he should follow. Growing frustrated with his indecision, he picked a direction and ran. He frantically searched for Thor, Odin, or Hel. He would even settle for Loki at this point. But they were nowhere to be seen. In their stead, Leif found the broken bodies of Asgardian guards, citizens, and tribe warriors alike. Stopping at a four-way junction, Leif was appalled to see the number of Asgardians in their once resplendent robes littering the hallway. Interspersed amongst the dead civilians were several tribesmen.

Following the trail of Asgardians and tribe warriors, Leif came across a blood smeared set of large, bronze doors. With fingers crossed that he wasn't too late, Leif pulled open the heavy doors to peer through. He was relieved to see it led to the massive open-air corridor that ended in the throne room. The sounds of heavy combat could be heard just out of sight. Slipping through the door,

Leif crept up to the edge of the alcove and peered around the corner.

Surveying the carnage that lay just beyond, he knew this was where the royal guards made their last stand. Dead guards lay scattered across the floor. Their black and red armor was torn to tatters, as if it was nothing but papier mâché. Only a being of immense power such as Ra or Fenrir could make wounds such as those. Following the carpet of bodies, Leif spotted a mob of warriors encircling a lone figure in shining gold armor.

It was Odin. With his spear in hand, he expertly fended off attacks from all sides. The one-eyed god had sustained several cuts to his face and body, but if they hindered him in any way, he didn't show it. From where he stood, Odin was doing more than hold his own. He was winning. No matter where the attacker came from. In front, to the side, or behind, Odin's golden spear was there, slicing through armor and bone like a hot knife through butter.

Leif watched three figures push their way through the ranks of waiting tribe warriors. He felt his blood boil as he made out the faces of Hel, Fenrir, and Ra fanning out amongst the tribe warriors, pinning Odin in a triangle formation. The three dark gods were momentarily content to remain on the sidelines, watching as Odin effortlessly cut down any who dared get too close. Then, as Odin rammed the head of his spear through the chest plate of a Dokkalfar, Fenrir advanced. The wolf god lashed out, attempting to hamstring the elder god from behind. Odin was ready for him, blocking the impossibly fast sword thrust with the haft of his spear.

Seeing his chance, Ra sprang forward the moment his brother's focus shifted to Fenrir. The god's strange sickle-sword cut a long gouge along Odin's golden chest plate, but that was it. Odin slashed his spear sideways, bisecting the Dokkalfar he had skewed a second earlier at the waist. The sharpened point of the Alfather's spear caught the Outsider in the arm, drawing a bloody line down his tricep as Ra sped by.

"Give up, old man," Hel sneered. "Ra and I killed my pitiful excuse for a father when we broke down the castle gates, and I personally saw Fenrir run his blade through Thor's gut. Uncle is strong, but not even one of the Aesir could survive the wound he received."

This time Fenrir and two tribe warriors leapt at the elder god, but Odin was ready. He twirled his spear in a complex pattern, forming a protective bubble around himself. Fenrir was quick to react, springing out of the way, but the two warriors, a Dokkalfar and Svartalfar, weren't so lucky. The moment they met Odin's spinning spear, their bodies exploded in a shower of blood, guts, and bone. As the Alfather continued to whip his spear around himself, his electric blue eyes fell on Leif. Instantly, something changed in the Alfather as he held Leif's gaze. He gave Leif the smallest of nods before his face became a mask of determination.

In a move so fast Leif would have missed it if he hadn't been watching, Odin lashed out, sending the six-foot length of golden metal flying straight at Ra. The Outsider's blade flicked up pushing the razor-sharp spearhead over his right shoulder. Odin whipped the spear back around, sending it now toward Fenrir, who was sneaking behind him. The spear point cut a gleaming red line across the wolf god's right cheek.

"Enough!" Hel screamed. "We have fucked around long enough. KILL HIM!"

Leif watched in frozen fascination as the throne room exploded in movement. Hel, Fenrir, Ra, and the large crowd of tribe warriors rushed Odin at once. For the first few seconds of the attack, Odin held his own. Whipping his spear back and forth through the crowd, severing hands, arms, legs, and anything else it came in contact with, but then the other gods joined the fray.

The four gods batted aside the tribe warriors, who were now nothing but an afterthought as they tried and failed to keep up. Leif stood in amazement at the epic battle playing out before his eyes. Ra and Fenrir danced in and out of range, constantly searching for a hole in Odin's defense. Hel slowly circled, waiting for her chance to attack.

That moment came as Ra and Fenrir, working together, locked Odin's spear in place between their two blades. Moving as if they had rehearsed the move a thousand times, Hel launched herself forward with a shout as she slammed the point of her sword between two armored plates in Odin's thigh. Leif thought the fight was over at that point, but the Alfather didn't flinch as Hel's blade sunk several inches into the meat of his leg.

Still not able to free his spear from his enemy's grasp, he simply dropped the weapon and lunged forward, slamming a gauntleted fist into Ra's surprised face. The Outsider was flung backward, bowling over several tribesmen who had taken up position behind the god. Leif felt a thrum of hope at seeing Odin take the offensive, but it was quickly snuffed out when Hel kicked out with an armored boot to Odin's injured leg.

This time, the Alfather cried out in pain, as he tried to disengage, hopping to the side. But Fenrir was waiting for him, lashing out with a punch of his own that slammed into the Alfather's chest plates with the force of a falling star. The damaged metal groaned in protest as it buckled inward, forming a perfect dent in the outline of the god's clenched fist. Odin rocked backward but refused to go down. That was, until Hel sprinted across the battlefield to grab the hilt of her sword that was still firmly lodged deep into the elder god's thigh and pulling it out with a savage yank.

Odin went to one knee as his weight caused his injured knee to buckle. The Alfather lunged for his fallen spear, but Ra recovered from the punch he had taken and ran back into the fight, kicking the golden spear with the toe of his boot. The golden shaft flashed across the throne room, embedding itself into a white marble wall with a loud CRACK!

The Alfather tried to stand, but Fenrir lunged forward, slamming his fist into the elder god's face, sending him sprawling.

"Well done, my friends," Ra addressed the spectating tribe as he looked down at his defeated brother. "You all will be remembered through the annals of time for your heroic deeds this day. We three will take it from here. There are still Asgardians within the keep and Thor hasn't been spotted since taking the sword to his stomach. Find Lagertha, take up a hunting party to smoke out the last remnants of the Aesir's resistance. I warn you, though. If you find Thor, injured as he is, do not engage. Keep him pinned down until one of us can arrive."

A chorus of "aye's" sounded from the twenty or so soldiers as they ran out of the throne room and into one of the many corridors that lined the great hall.

"Ah, vengeance is sweet, brother," Ra purred as the four gods were left alone in the throne room. "I warned you we would get our revenge, and here we are." The god boasted, spreading his hands out wide. Odin tried to rise once more, but Fenrir placed a single boot against the struggling god's chest and shoved, sending the Alfather back down to the marbled floor. Odin gave the wolf god a scowl that could scare the sun from the sky.

"You think just because you've defeated me you've won, but you are wrong," Odin challenged, a hint of red spilling from the side of his mouth. "From the ashes of our defeat, our vengeance will rise."

All three dark gods laughed their contempt at Odin's words. "There's no one left to avenge you, old man," Fenrir growled with fangs glinting in the light. "When you and Thor have gone into the void, we will wash over the remaining holdouts, cementing our control of the nine realms in one fell swoop."

"And once our hold of the nine realms is complete," Hel said, stepping closer to the downed elder god. "We will push farther into the void, integrating each realm we come across. A feat you were too scared to attempt yourself."

Odin chuckled to himself. "Oh Hel, always so focused on the future to see what is happening right before your nose. The keys to your defeat were etched into the great cycle centuries ago. It is true

I had hoped this possibility would not come to fruition, but fate saw otherwise, and a contingency was created. The key was to manipulate the players into acting as if it was their own idea. I commend you. You may have won the day, but Ragnarok is far from over."

"Bah, I grow tired of this senile old man's ramblings," Fenrir grunted as he walked over to Odin's lost spear that was still embedded in the wall. With a vicious yank, he pulled the golden shaft free of the wall and stalked back to the group. "No matter what dribble you spout, one thing remains the same. Whatever the future has in store for us, you won't be around to see it," the wolf god said as he slammed the spear down into Odin's chest, pinning him to the floor. A soft gurgle escaped the Alfather's throat a moment before he slumped to the floor.

"Ah!" Hel bemoaned, "I wanted to kill the bastard!"

"You were merely banished. I was imprisoned for eons," Fenrir retorted. "I think my claim was stronger."

"Each of us had a claim," Ra interjected. "But what's done is done. More importantly, we need to find Thor. The crafty bastard may have merely been stalling, but I will not deny his words have given me cause for alarm. We have worked too hard for this day to be foiled now. We cannot allow Thor or anyone else of power to escape this keep alive. Nor can we trust those mortals to accomplish the deed. We must scour the castle ourselves."

Leif watched as the three dark gods left the throne room, disappearing down a side hallway, leaving the impaled Odin where he lay. With the great hall and throne room deserted, Leif hurried across the distance to Odin's still form.

Leaning down on his haunches, Leif looked over the broken form of the Alfather. His golden armor was covered from head to toe in dents and deep gouges. A large, ragged hole the length of his hand ran along the elder god's thigh where Hel had stabbed him. Fenrir had slammed the stolen spear straight through the center of Odin's chest, sinking the metal tip a full foot or more into the marbled floor. The fist size dent Fenrir had put in Odin's armor was right over the god's heart. Blood seeped out of tiny holes from where the wolf god's knuckles had stabbed into Odin.

"AH! Gods, I was worried they would never leave," Odin croaked out, causing Leif to yelp in surprise as he fell back onto his butt.

"What the hell? How are you even alive right now? Let alone speaking!" Leif exclaimed in a hushed voice as he looked around the empty chamber.

"Don't waste what little time I have with foolish questions, Berserker. The void's call grows stronger with each passing second," the Alfather chided. "Heed my words, and all shall not be lost. I foresaw my granddaughter's betrayal centuries ago, but I could do nothing to stop it lest a darker evil take her place. To ensure the continued protection of the nine realms after the fall of the Aesir, I set a plan in motion that would ensure the nine realms would have a champion to rise from our ashes. One who would protect the realms from the evils of my wayward kin. Thor may claim the creation of your kind was his idea, but he would be wrong. It was I who carefully manipulated my son into your creation. It was I who modified your bloodlines to not only be compatible with his power, but to evolve with each new awakening. I enabled you to grow stronger and more capable of harnessing the godly power that thrums through your veins." Odin coughed, sending a spray of bloody mist into the air as the lightning blue of his eyes flickered.

"There is one last task you must complete before you are to rise as the vengeance of the realms. You must find Thor," Odin commanded.

"Find Thor?" Leif asked. "But what about you? You're the Alfather, you can't die here. There must be something I can do to help you."

"What did I say about wasting my time, boy?" The Alfather thundered. "Huginn and Muninn will show you the way. Be ready, young Berserker. You have many trials ahead of you. You must be strong if you are to survive them. The fate of the nine realms now rests on your shoulders." Odin rested his head back down on the cracked floor as the glowing light from his eyes flickered once more, then went out completely.

A CA-CAW pierced the somber silence of the throne room, causing Leif's heart to skip a beat. Getting to his feet, he glared at the pair of ravens sitting on the high-backed throne. The two birds studied Leif for several seconds before leaping from the chair in a flutter of midnight-colored feathers. The two birds flew in a tight circle over Odin's fallen body twice before flying out the open throne room door with Leif hot on their heels.

# CHAPTER 37

Leif followed Huginn and Muninn down a series of
corridors and halls. As he continued to run, he questioned
the sanity of following the two ravens. They could just as
easily be looking for an exit, not wishing to stay around now that
Odin was dead. But in the end, he had little choice but to trust they
would obey the Alfather's final command.

As he ran through corridors, the sounds of combat steadily grew
in volume. Then they went completely silent all at once. Leif had
the sudden fearful thought that he was too late, that Thor had been
discovered and killed. Following the ravens, he rounded a sharp
corner, running into a small chamber that was straight out of his
nightmares.

Within the rectangular chamber, two pairs of black marble
pillars rose from the floor. Golden light spilled from a large lantern
that hung from the ceiling. Below, an ocean of blood covered the
chambered floor, completely coating the stonework. Piles of the
dead, Asgardian and tribe soldiers alike, lay across the crimson sea.
Standing at the center of the carnage, heaving and blood-soaked,
Lagertha stood with a gore encrusted straight sword clutched in
one hand.

"What are you doing here, Leif?" she demanded, confusion plain in her voice.

"No, Lagertha," he challenged. "What the hell are you doing? Hel and her Outsider friends are laying waste to the nine realms! How could you join them? I thought you better than this?"

"My people will rise from the ashes of the old regime. We were promised wide swaths of territory, free of the oppression we lived under with the Aesir. We will hold a seat at the new ruler's table. The Aesir did nothing for the tribe as they were hunted for no better reason than being different or born to a poor clan," she hissed. "No longer will we have to lie, cheat, or steal our way through the realms. We can finally step free from the shadows we so desperately cling to for survival. That is what we were promised. But all of that pales in comparison to what Ra assured he could do for me."

"And what is that?" Leif asked.

"To be free of this godforsaken curse," she exclaimed reverently. "Ra claims he has the power to cleanse my line of the Berserker once and for all."

"Lagertha, that's absurd," Leif shot back. He was astonished at her gullibility.

"Is it? The power our bloodlines were gifted with comes from the gods. Who is to say that Ra, Odin's kin, an elder god far older than Thor, can't undo the curse?"

"You must see Ra is using you. Look around you. The castle is littered with the bodies of your people." Leif challenged. "You were just a means to an end. I watched Odin cut down your people with ease as Hel, Fenrir, and Ra did nothing. They only stepped in when the Alfather was distracted."

"Midgard has made you soft," Lagertha scoffed. "Each one of us understood the dangers of this mission, but we chose to come anyway. All of us are willing to make the ultimate sacrifice if it means our people will not only survive but thrive in the coming days. Someone born to a land of milk and honey can never understand those born to famine and strife. So, spare me your lecture. You don't know pain like me, and my people do. Even if the possibility of Ra burning this curse from my bloodline is small, I would jump at the chance without hesitation, if it means sparing Bjorn the pain of being a Berserker. You've lived with the Berserker for what? A year or two. Ha, try living decades under its oppressive thumb. Seeing the fear in your own child's eyes whenever they are near you. That is a pain no parent should have to bear, and I aim to spare Bjorn from it all."

"Soft?" Leif asked in disbelief. "If I hadn't been so soft, where would Bjorn be right now? Dead. Even with the Berserker's curse, I still strive to save those around me. Just as you should," he shouted. "Don't do this, Lagertha. There has to be another way. Come with me. We will find Thor and ask him to take the Berserker from you."

Leif saw Lagertha rock back as if struck by his words. "I will always be grateful for what you did for Bjorn. But this is much bigger than you, me, and Bjorn. I am responsible for all the tribe, not just my own blood. You want me to beg for help from Thor?" Her voice steadily rose in pitch. "Where was Thor when I killed my mother? He certainly didn't heed my prayers then. I prayed for his help every day for nearly ten years as I struggled to contain the Berserker. I lived in near isolation during my teens, fearing what I might do if I lost control. No, Leif. I learned long ago the Aesir weren't going to save me. It was up to me and me alone. So, no. If he was here with you, I would gladly slit his throat and dance while he slipped into the void with the rest of the useless Aesir. Out of our shared bond as Berserkers and for what you did that day when the trolls attacked, I will give you this one chance. Leave Asgard. Disappear back into the realms. The tribe and I have no quarrel with you. You can leave now, and I guarantee no tribe warrior will ever raise a hand against you. But if you stand against me and my goals, I will crush you."

Leif felt his shoulders slump in defeat, even as he felt the

Berserker stirring to life in response to Lagertha's challenge. It wasn't the all-consuming rage he once felt, but the steady burn of a forest fire. He sighed as his hands went to his axes. "I can't let you do this. You have become the monster your father once was. I will not allow you to risk the fate of billions of lives for the ambition of Hel and the Outsiders." This was not how he wanted this encounter to go, but Hel could not be permitted to see her plans to fruition. If that meant killing Lagertha in the process, he would not balk from this obstacle, no matter how it pained him to do it.

"So be it," Lagertha said, pointing her gory sword at Leif. "Looks like it's time to see who's the stronger Berserker after all."

A small part of Leif regretted the fight, but he couldn't deny the thrill that pulsed through his body at the thought of crossing blades with Lagertha, a formidable Berserker bloodline. Anticipation of the coming fight rose inside him. It was a feeling he knew they both felt. It was now an almost primal force, calling to them to fight for the title of the strongest. The rage filled his blood and drowned out any misgivings. His pulse filled his ears, silencing any second thoughts.

"There can be only one," he whispered as he sloshed into the chamber, coming to a stop ten feet from Lagertha.

The two Berserkers stared each other down as the feeling that this was a fated encounter settled over the room. Leif knew the two had fought before, with Lagertha easily beating him. But that was before he had ascended. He was far stronger than he once was.

Breaking the stare, Leif burst into movement, striking at Lagertha's mid-section. A horizontal sweep from her sword caused Leif to dodge to the side. This time it was Lagertha who went on the offensive, following Leif as he dodged. She lashed out with a booted kick to his stomach. The force of Lagertha's attack sent him sprawling backward, landing with a bloody splash, sliding several feet backwards through the slick crimson pool, only stopping when his back slammed painfully into a marbled column.

Drenched in the viscous fluid, Leif lost his footing as he

attempted to rise, falling back onto his already bruised butt. A shadow fell over him as he struggled to rise the second time. Knowing he was a heartbeat from death, he did the first thing that came to mind. He dropped back to the floor and kicked off the marbled column with all his might. Leif glided across the bloody floor just a second before Lagertha's blade slammed down with an audible CRACK. Lagertha let out a snarl of frustration at missing her target.

*Good,* Leif thought. *The angrier she gets, the more likely she will make a mistake.*

Gliding across the floor, Leif kicked Lagertha in the back of the knee as he went by, sending the Berserker to one knee. While she recovered, Leif got to his feet in one smooth movement, charging at his kneeling opponent. Leif slashed at Lagertha, but quick as a striking serpent, she brought her blade up in an overhead block. Sparks ignited like the Fourth of July as their weapons met.

A savage smile crossed Lagertha's lips as the two Berserkers matched strength. Seconds passed as they strained with all their might, but it was no use. They were too evenly matched. Lagertha was quick to see the stalemate. She dove to the side. Unfortunately, Leif hadn't expected the move and stumbled forward. Quickly regaining his footing, he turned towards Lagertha with his axes raised in defense.

The air was slammed from his lungs as Lagertha's shoulder crashed into his stomach. The two crashed onto the marbled floor with Lagertha on top. Leif's vision flashed black, then red as his head smacked the floor with a thump. Shaking his head to clear his vision, Leif looked up just in time to see Lagertha's fist slam into his jaw. Stars streaked across his vision, only to clear a second before Lagertha's next blow landed. Leif took two more punches to the face before he was able to block.

Undaunted, Lagertha rained hammer blows down on Leif. His head was slammed repeatedly into the bloodied marble floor with such force that the floor splintered, sending a spider web of cracks out from where his head struck. He ground his teeth in pain. His nose broke in a spray of blood, causing his eyes to blur with tears. In a desperate gambit, Leif bucked wildly as he raged.

Though their strength was equal, Leif still outweighed Lagertha. He managed to throw his enemy forward. She lay sprawled partially across his middle. Swinging his legs, he wrapped his knee around her neck. With a twist, Leif smashed the side of Lagertha's head into the shallow pool of blood. Unfazed, Lagertha's fist lashed out, slamming into Leif's flank several times, in hopes he would release his grip on her neck. Grunting through the pain, he felt a sharp crack as a pain that stole the breath from his lungs radiated out from his ribs, but he held strong, managing to grab Lagertha's fist. Leif pulled tight against her arm, thanking Arias for teaching him basic jujitsu.

There was a loud crack as Leif broke Lagertha's trapped arm. Unfortunately, his gore slick grip suddenly slipped, causing him to fall backward as Lagertha twisted away. The two battered Berserkers scrambled to their feet, slipping and sliding in the oily pool. Leif brought a hand to his stomach. The broken ribs sent waves of pain across his chest with each breath he took. Lagertha panted with her arm hanging limply at her side.

Leif's head whipped left to right, searching for his axe, but all he could see was crimson liquid and the dead. Looking back at Lagertha, he saw her eyes were wide with excitement. A bloody smile spread across her face. "FINALLY! A worthy foe," she shouted. "Isn't this amazing!" Running a blood encrusted hand through her war braids. "The berserker's power thrumming through our veins. The primal exaltation of not knowing if you will live or die. THIS!" gesturing with her one good arm. "IS WHY WE WERE CREATED. TO FIGHT AND CONQUER. I understand now why the Berserkers of old incessantly fought with one another. There is no greater adversary save for the gods themselves. It was fated that we were to meet. For you to ascend. The Norns smile down on us this day."

Leif wished to refute her words. To say he is more than a battle hungry maniac, but he couldn't deny the truth to her words, nor could he convince her. Her berserked mind was lost. His own Berserker reveled in the carnage. He felt a savage joy coursing through him. The world has a clarity to it that only one who is a breath away from death can see. Knowing if he were to survive to see his family avenged, he would need to embrace the darker side of his power. Raising his fist, Leif returned her macabre smile with one of his own, growling, "Let's finish this."

There was nothing pretty or fancy about the fight that followed. No flashy tricks or brilliant sword play. It was all fists and elbows. Punches like hammer blows flashed in the golden light. Both Leif and Lagertha had abandoned any strategic defense. They both pounded their fists with as much force as possible into their opponent's face and torso.

As the fight wore on, it became clear to Leif that he was outclassed. Her punches hit with the precision of a seasoned warrior, doing untold damage. He knew his advanced healing would keep him up and fighting for a time, but even he had limits. He needed to change the rhythm of the fight, and fast.

Risking a quick scan of the room, he spied a large battle axe stuck into the body of a dead Asgardian on top of a pile of bodies. Knowing and hating what he had to do next. Leif dropped his guard just a hair. Lagertha jumped on the tiny opening and landed a one-two punch to his chest, followed by the face. The punches caused Leif to stagger, but he went with it, taking several steps backward, tripping as he fell onto the dead.

Pain exploded across his chest and legs as several pieces of jagged and broken armor stabbed into him. Behind him, he heard the soft splash of footfalls. Leif held himself at the ready. Not wanting to waste the opportunity he created. Finally, when he felt she was right behind him, he wrapped his hand around the axe hilt and whipped around, throwing the heavy weapon with all his might. The large double-bladed weapon was badly damaged and unbalanced, throwing his aim off. The weapon flew from his hands, streaking past Lagertha's shoulder, missing her ear by centimeters. Lagertha gave him a cruel smile as she smashed her fist into his already broken ribs. He slammed back into the pile of dead with a groan.

Leif tried to rise once more, but her booted foot struck him painfully across the chin. "And here is where it ends. You fought well for one so young," Lagertha remarked. "Truth be told, I didn't know who would stand victorious at the end of this. But Leif, there can be only one Berserker, and that is me. Go to Valhalla with the knowledge that soon the Berserker curse will be cleared from the realms."

Leif's vision flickered. He blinked several times to clear his eyes, finally able to focus on the nightmarish visage that stood over him. "Yo, you..." Leif tried to say through bleeding lips. Somewhere along the way, he had bitten his tongue, flooding his mouth with the taste of copper.

"Make these words count," Lagertha said, leaning down. "They will be your la–"

Leif lunged forward, pulling on all his rage and pain, using it to push his body past its limits one last time. Leif had pulled a dagger from a body underneath him, and he buried it into Lagertha's neck.

Their eyes locked as her life's blood poured from the grizzly wound. They both knew this was the end for her. Even their accelerated healing could do nothing with a razor-sharp blade jammed through the carotid artery. Her eyes narrowed as she fought to remain on her feet, but it was futile. She wobbled once, going to one knee, then the next. The glowing orbs of her eyes flickered as Odin's did. Then the light sputtered out and her lifeless body toppled to the ground.

# CHAPTER 38

Leif was awash in pain as he stared at Lagertha's lifeless body. He knew he should feel something over her passing, but he was in too much pain to muster anything more than a respectful nod at the fallen Berserker. Back on Vanaheimr, he knew Bjorn would be just now awakening. *The newly awakened power combined with the grief of knowing Lagertha had been killed will be a potent combo for the new Berserker. Galen will have his hands full, that's for sure.*

The sound of heavy footfalls pounding down the corridor pulled Leif from his thoughts. He groaned, knowing he was in no shape to fight. He could feel his accelerated healing working hard, but that was like vacuuming in a sandstorm. Lagertha had nearly beaten him to death. It's going to take days to recover from it, but Odin commanded him to find Thor. So, using the piled dead as a crutch, Leif slowly got to his feet. Pain was becoming his constant companion. His vision flickered as he straightened to his full height, his body protested the entire way. He could feel himself growing light-headed, but he gritted his teeth, holding onto consciousness like a sailor holds onto a life preserver in a storm.

Leif looked down the corridor for the ravens, but they were gone. *Those treacherous bastards Hugin and Muninn disappeared.* Knowing he needed a weapon, he frantically searched for his lost axes. Shuffling forward, he felt a sharp twinge in his right leg. Scowling, he spotted a ragged gash running down his right thigh. His patience was rewarded when he finally spotted two blood-drenched axes near the pillar he had slammed into. He rushed forward, feeling a pop in his ribs as he picked up his gory weapons.

A figure blurred into the room, prompting Leif to raise his axes in defense.

"Peace, Berserker," said Heimdall, coming to a stop before him.

"Heimdall?" Leif exclaimed. Her heart-shaped face was soot covered and bruised. Her eyes were like an electrical storm hung above a nose so sharp she could cut glass with it. Her features were framed by her golden blond hair that was pulled back into two tight war braids. Her six-foot frame slumped from battle fatigue, while her battered chest plate was covered in dents and punctures. An empty scabbard hung at her hip. "Thank the gods you are alive," Leif sighed.

"Aye," the Asgardian said, looking around the chamber. "You have done well for yourself." She said, nodding towards Lagertha.

"How did you find me?" Leif asked.

"Huginn and Muninn," she said.

*They didn't abandon me after all.* "So, you know about Odin then?" he asked.

"Aye, we do."

"We?" Leif asked, hope swelling.

"Thor and me. We must make haste. He is expecting you. Follow me." The Asgardian retreated the way she came.

The two sped down blood-stained hallways, and Leif got his first view of the golden city below. The once resplendent metropolis, with its towering buildings and lush parks, lay in ruins. Fires raged across the city, belching large plumes of black smoke high into the sky, blotting out the sun. Leif hadn't realized he stopped to stare open-mouthed at the travesty until Heimdall placed a comforting hand on his shoulder.

"I never thought I would see the day," Heimdall whispered, emotion clear in her voice. "We reigned supreme for so long that we grew complacent. We never believed our enemies would strike us here, in the seat of the Aesir's power. Now it has cost us everything. Thor is gravely injured, Odin and Loki are dead, and Ragnarok is all but decided."

The mention of Ragnarok snapped Leif from his dour mood. "No," Leif said, trying to sound more confident. "There is still hope. Odin spoke to me. He said there is still a chance for us to turn this around. I may not have liked the old bastard, but I must believe he knew what he was doing." Heimdall's eyes shined with unspent tears and nodded. They left the window and ran down the hall.

Heimdall led the pair around a corner and into an unremarkable hallway that ended in a dead end. In a castle as large as this, one could walk right by without giving the discreet corridor a second look. There were no doors or hallways that led into or out of it and it was marked only by a single hanging cloth with a print of Yggdrasil on it. Leif was about to chide the Asgardian for getting lost, but she confidently strode toward the back wall. He instantly knew there was more to the area than met the eye.

Stopping just shy of the brick wall, Leif watched as Heimdall pressed her hand against three separate bricks, forming a triangle pattern. There was a soft click and the crimson banner fluttered on an unseen breeze. Heimdall pulled the bottom half of the banner to the side, revealing a short tunnel with a brightly lit room beyond. "Secret passageway and a hidden room, very cool," Leif said with a raised eyebrow.

Following Heimdall, Leif spotted Thor's broken form leaning against the back wall. A blood-soaked Mjolnir lay at his side. His gleaming armor was now dented and blood soaked. His chest plate was riddled with puncture holes that leaked blood. But worst of all were three long gouges that ran down one side of his armor. It looked like Fenrir, in wolf form, had mauled him. His chest rose and fell in a stuttering rhythm that made Leif think the god had a punctured lung.

"Thor!" Leif shouted as he ran to the god's side.

Looking up, Thor gave him a faint smile as his glowing eyes flickered with each labored breath. "Good," he wheezed, looking Leif straight in the eyes. "You ascended. I don't know how father knew, but that doesn't matter now." Thor whispered through broken lips.

"He orchestrated the whole thing," Leif exclaimed. "Odin was the mastermind behind the Berserkers. You and I were just his puppets. He told me to find you. He said that there was one last thing I had to do before we take the fight back to Hel and her ilk. So, what do we need to do? We can't stay here long. Hel and the others have taken over the castle. It won't be long till they find us."

"Take my hand," Thor rasped.

"Oh! Can you use the power of the Berserker to heal you? That makes sense. My power does come from you, after all." Leif asked excitedly.

"No, Leif," the injured god said with a shake of his head. "I am not taking power from you. Before I join the Alfather in the void, I will transfer my mantle of power to you."

CHAPTER 39

"W HAT?" Leif shouted.

"Lower your voice, Berserker," Heimdall hissed. "We can't risk being found, not yet."

"Ok, ok, ok." Leif repeated, trying to gain control of his emotions. "Why me? Why not you, Heimdall. Why can't you just harness your own strength to recover?"

"Not possible," Heimdall said, answering for Thor. "Our powers are not compatible. The power may reject me, or I would die in the attempt. Nor can he heal himself. The sly wolf must have coated his blade in some Outsider concocted poison. He's not healing like he should be. We can't risk secreting him away to any of our healers, if they are even still alive."

"Heimdall speaks the truth, Leif," Thor weakly cut in. "Heimdall and I are not compatible. I know this is a lot to take in, but this is the true purpose for the creation of the Berserkers. The Norns and the Alfather foresaw a Berserker being the linchpin in Ragnarok. Your bloodline, through my crafty father, has been slowly evolving to undertake this task. The Berserkers of old were nothing but mindless beasts. As the Berserker was passed down through the generations, each newly awoken warrior gained more control over my power. All the way down to you. The final piece of the puzzle was for you to conquer the power within. How you did it and so fast will be a mystery. Though I suspect Odin had his unseen hands in it."

"But," Leif said, his voice cracking under the strain. "What am I supposed to do after?"

A dark gleam came to Thor's dimming eyes. "You hunt. You will be our vengeance. Hel believes she has won. They will not suspect someone like you within the realms. Hunt them down and kill them. Take back the realms, bring peace back to our people. You grew up mortal. Your mind thinks differently than one born a god. They will not see you coming. And even if they do, they will underestimate you."

"Ok," Leif said, trying to slow his racing heart. His many aches and pains were nearly forgotten as the enormity of the situation settled firmly on his shoulders. "What do I need to do?"

Thor had grown pale during their short conversation, but a look of determination was cemented on his face. "I am proud of you, Leif. I have watched over your kind since your creation and cannot think of a better Berserker to take up my mantle. Good hunting," the god finished speaking as he surged forward, locking one gauntleted hand around Leif's forearm.

A thunderous BOOM sounded from somewhere high above as electricity arched from Thor into Leif. Thick bars of electricity enveloped Leif, causing his muscles to tense. His spine arched backward, and his mouth flew open in a silent scream. For an eternity, all Leif knew was pain, as every atom in his body was reformed by Thor's power.

A bright light flashed and thunder crashed as the last drop of power surged from Thor to Leif. Once the spine arching pain came to a merciful end, he crumpled to the floor as wisps of smoke curled from his still form. Tiny forks of lightning sizzled across his skin, causing him to twitch uncontrollably. After the tiny storm died down, Leif slowly came to his senses. An icy fire burned in his marrow. He squeezed his eyes shut as he waited for the pain to stop. Thankfully, his suffering was short-lived, and the brain melting pain disappeared altogether.

Finally able to breathe again, he was assaulted by the thick smell of ozone. Leif wobbled to his feet as his mind was assaulted with an influx of new sensations. Reaching out to steady himself, Leif's outstretched palm slammed into the brick wall with a THWACK! Confused, Leif looked at his hand, which had pulverized the brick underneath. Large cracks spider-webbed from the impact point.

"What the hell?" he exclaimed in shock. "How did I..." but the questioned died on his lips as he looked down at the shell of Thor's body. A profound sense of loss brought Leif to his knees. Staring at the downed god with new eyes, he instinctually knew his friend was gone. He was unsure how, but he could not only see but feel an emptiness from Thor. True to his enforcer reputation, Leif knew Thor did not go down easily. His body was covered in deep, gruesome wounds.

Heimdall stepped into view, crouching next to Thor. Bowing her head in reverence, Heimdall closed Thor's sightless eyes. Meanwhile, Leif stared dumbfounded at the Asgardian. As a Berserker, Leif instinctively knew Heimdall was dangerous. But as a newly risen god, he could literally feel the power radiating off her. She was ancient and terrifying to behold. He was sure glad as hell she was on his side.

After paying her respects, Heimdall stalked toward one of the three mahogany armoires spaced around the panic room. "We need to make a run for the bridge room," she said as she flung open one of the wardrobes. A variety of bladed weapons, from swords to things Leif didn't have a name for, were arranged within the cabinet. "We can't be sure if our enemies felt your ascension or not. So, prepare yourself the best you can."

Leif was about to mention he was in no condition to fight, but that's when he noticed it no longer hurt to breathe, nor was his leg burning from the deep gash. Leif passed on taking any weapons from the wardrobe. "I'm good. As long as I have my trusted axes, I should be fine," he said, patting the twin weapons at his side. "OH WAIT!" Leif said, looking around Thor's body. "We can't leave Mjolnir! We can't risk such a powerful weapon falling into enemy hands now that Thor is dead. But wait," he said, frantically looking around the room. "Where did it go? I swear it was here just a minute ago."

"Mjolnir's gone," Heimdall said, moving to the next armoire, which contained enough armored pieces to outfit an entire company. "Mjolnir was a physical manifestation of Thor's power. That's why he was the only being who could wield the weapon. Mjolnir acted as a focal point, which allowed him to wield the overwhelming amount of power he and now you must command," Heimdall said offhandedly as she set aside her battered chest plate for a new gleaming silver piece with gold runes etched into it.

"Since I gained Thor's power, shouldn't Mjolnir have merely transferred to me?" Leif asked. His head was spinning.

"No," Heimdall said as she slipped several thin throwing knives into hidden sheaths along the gauntlets she just put on. "The Aesir god of thunder is dead. Though you gained his power, you are not of Aesir blood. You are something wholly new to the nine realms. Thus, you must bond your own weapon," Heimdall said as she moved experimentally with her new armor. She was now encased from neck to toes in gleaming silver armor. She wore a new great sword so long it had to be sheathed over her shoulder instead at her hip.

"Ok," Leif said, growing frustrated. "And how do I do that?"

"How the hell am I supposed to know? I'm merely an Asgardian. This is a journey you will have to take alone, Leif."

"Super," he responded sarcastically.

Leif watched as Heimdall's aura, that's what he decided to call the feeling he perceived from her, flared in anger. But she checked herself, causing the feeling emanating from her to cool. "Leif." The warrior said, turning to face him. "I understand you are overwhelmed. This is a lot to take in, I get it. But quite literally, the fate of billions, if not trillions, now rests on our shoulders and what we do next. This morning you woke up a mortal. A supremely powerful mortal, but mortal no less. All that has changed. You now stand as the secret defense in the fight for Ragnarok. There is no safety blanket or other you can look to for advice and guidance. Thor told you what your mission is: Hunt down and kill Hel and her ilk. You must finish this fight, bring an end to Ragnarok before the final horn is blown. More than you know is at stake. So, will you stand with me to put this rebellion down once and for all?"

Leif felt his resolve harden as the enormity of the situation settled on his shoulders. Before, this fight was nothing but a blood feud between him and Hel. All he cared about was getting revenge for Arias, his mother, and his grandfather. He had assumed the Aesir would take care of the rest, but that was no longer an option. He could no longer act as the child, asking for the adults to help. He was the sole adult in the room, so to speak. Sure, his stomach was doing somersaults as he questioned whether he should even be doing this, but at the end of the day, there was literally no other choice. He had to step up. So, he straightened his back, looked to Heimdall and nodded.

"Good. You are now fully capable of opening bridges to wherever you want, even if that specific connection point doesn't open in your preferred realm. But as you literally just ascended, I think that feat is a little out of your grasp now, so where do you wish to go?"

"Go?" Leif said, confused. "You aren't coming with me."

"No," the armored Asgardian said with a shake of her head. "No, through Huginn and Muninn, Odin gave me one final task."

"Which is?" Leif inquired, comforted that even dead, Odin was still working behind the scenes.

Heimdall let out a long sigh as she placed her gauntleted hand on her hip. Leif didn't need his new power to sense the warrior's annoyance. "I am to go to Valhalla. Odin bid me to prepare the Valkyries for war. Valhalla is the final piece Hel will need to bring Ragnarok to a close. Now that Odin is dead, the entrance to the realm is open."

"VALHALLA'S REAL?" Leif shouted.

"Ssshhh," Heimdall chided him. "There is much you still need to learn, especially now that you have been given the mantle of the Aesir. Aye, the sacred realm is real. It is a place of mystery, even to Asgardians. The Valkyrie is a militant order created by Odin during the early years of his reign. They operate independent of Aesir rule. For reasons known only to Odin and the Valkyrie, only Valkyrie and the honored dead are permitted in Valhalla. Not even Odin would venture there uninvited."

"But what's there that's so important?" Leif asked.

"I do not know. All I was told was how to get to the realm now that it is open, and that I must prepare the Valkyrie," Heimdall said reverently. From the feeling of utter devotion Leif felt from Heimdall's aura, he knew there was no talking her out of going.

"If Valhalla is so important, shouldn't I go with you?" Leif queried.

"No, you have your mission, and I have mine. I am Heimdall, the watchman of the Aesir. If the gates are breached before you complete your mission, I will send for you. Now enough talk, we must go." Emphasizing her point, the Asgardian turned away from Leif and exited the secret room.

Leif followed Heimdall, giving Thor's lifeless body one final glance as she closed the hidden door behind them. Leif vowed once this war was over, he would return and give Odin, Thor, and even Loki the proper burial they deserved. As they slinked from hallway to hallway, a thought occurred to him. In a whisper, he asked, "Why aren't we just using Gjalahorn to move through the realms? We wouldn't risk capture that way."

"You have no idea how much I wish we could." Heimdall whispered back, her aura going dark with sadness. "After Hel's attack and Fenrir's escape, the Alfather was quite liberal with the Gjalahorn. Thor and I, along with a contingent of our Asgardian *Veior*, jumped from realm to realm, putting down Outsider attacks wherever they popped up. But we were quickly spread too thin. That was why Alfheim was left in your care. With forces fighting across the realms, Fenrir snuck through our defenses here on Asgard. Odin quickly called us back to defend the city, but by then, it was too late. Ra briefly joined the fight before disappearing for a time, only to appear within the castle walls. Odin feared what would happen if the Gjalahorn fell to enemy hands. So he destroyed it, nearly breaking me in the process. I had been entrusted with its safe keeping for eons, only to see it destroyed.

"With the Bifrost denied to the Outsiders, we made our last stand, here in the keep. That was when Thor was injured. I begged him to flee, but he wouldn't hear of it. He insisted we needed to hide and wait. Then Hugnn and Muninn brought word of Odin's death and your fight with the other Berserker."

Heimdall slowed their run as she cautiously peered around the corner. Pulling her head back, she whispered, "The bridge room is just down the hall past the double doors. Once inside, we must move quickly. Anyone of power within the castle will feel me opening a bridge. So, where do you want to go?"

"Alfheim," Leif said without hesitation. "If I am to go hunting, I will need the best hunters to aid me."

"Good thinking," she said with an approving nod. "It looks like whoever is calling the shots in Hel's camp isn't a total idiot. They posted two Jontar to guard the bridge room. Probably in hopes of discouraging any survivors from attempting to flee to another realm."

"Two Jontar shouldn't be a problem for us, right? I would think I pack an impressive punch now," Leif boasted.

"Don't get cocky," Heimdall chided. Her aura flared again. "As you have seen today, even gods can die. And take this to heart. Never, ever underestimate the Jontar. They may be mortal, but they are brutal warriors. Thor has been fighting them since before your great-great-grandfather was a babe. But even so, I do not doubt we could best these two. However, you are still new to your powers, and I do not wish to alert the entire keep to our presences should you use them. So, stay behind me. I shall handle this." He felt his face flush red at being chided by Heimdall, but he held his tongue.

Leif watched as the Asgardian pulled two razor sharp throwing knives from the hidden sheaths along her forearm. She quickly examined the two knives, testing their balance before palming them in her right hand. Taking a deep breath, Heimdall stepped out from their hiding spot. Light glinted off the two silver blades as she whip-cracked her arm forward, launching the blades with incredible speed. Heimdall followed a heartbeat later, sprinting down the hall as she unsheathed the broadsword over her shoulder with Leif hot on her heels.

He rushed into the room, watching as the Jontar to his right suddenly jerked backward. Blood poured from the wound in its neck. It wrapped two large, blue hands around the wound to stop the bleeding, but it was futile. Dark viscous fluid seeped out between its fingers. Unfortunately, the Jontar to the left, whether by preternatural skill or luck, knocked the oncoming knife out of the air with a quick flick of his war axe.

Leif locked eyes with the Jontar just as it inhaled a lungful of air, preparing to shout its battle cry. Heimdall would be too late to stop the giant from shouting. Moving far faster than ever before, he snatched an axe from his belt and flung the weapon forward at speeds reserved for cruise-missiles. His axe spun end over end toward its target. Thunder roared overhead as red tongues of lightning crackled to life across the axe.

The bladed weapon slammed into the surprised Jontar's chest. Suddenly there came a blinding red flash followed by a loud sizzling sound as lightning burst from his axe, only to burn itself across the Jontar's body. Once the electrical storm completed its grim work, the Jontar collapsed in a smoking heap, filling the corridor with the smell of cooked meat.

Leif's eyes widened in amazement at the awesome display of his power. He took one more step before his legs turned to jelly. He tried to raise his hands to catch himself, but they too refused to respond, causing him to slam face first into the hard marbled floor. He tried to cry out for help, but his tongue had grown leaden. The only sound that escaped came out as "Hmmhdlf."

Strong hands hoisted him up onto an armored shoulder. "You idiot!" Heimdall roared as Leif felt an odd prickly sensation at the back of his neck. He felt three dark presences focus their attention on him. "I told you to let me handle this! Beings of Aesir blood can sense when powerful beings use their power. You've just sent up a signal flare to Hel, Fenrir, and Ra."

The prickly sensation grew as the three beings inspected Leif, no doubt questing who or what he was. Thankfully, this ability wasn't limited to just his enemies. He had no idea how he performed the feat, but Leif was able to examine the three dark gods just as they did him. He received an overwhelming amount of information from the three. All were old, unimaginably old, and strong. Though he could clearly see each differed in strength. There was a strange tinge to each aura they possessed. Leif believed he could pick out Hel, Fenrir and Ra. Hel was the weakest, cold and calculating. He sensed she was alarmed and confused by his show of strength. The oldest of the group was Ra. He was the second strongest of the trio. Even his aura contained a haughty air to it. The last of the three was by far the strongest. This Leif knew to be Fenrir. True to form, the god's aura conveyed a barely contained animalistic rage.

"Can you shield yourself from them?" Heimdall asked. "Maybe

it isn't too late." In response to Heimdall's question, Leif felt all three auras wink out.

Leif scrunched up his brow as he tried to minimize his presence. Unfortunately, he had no idea what he was doing, so he had no clue if it worked or not. Leif shifted on Heimdall's shoulder, bringing his attention to the present. Heimdall leaned down, "Grab your axe, you damned fool. We need to leave. NOW!"

"Huh?" Leif asked dumbly. His mind was still slow from his excessive use of power.

"Pick up your DAMN axe!" she growled. "You just imbued your axes with your power. Just like Mjolnir was for Thor, only you can wield them. NOW PICK THE AXE UP!"

"Got it," Leif slurred as he pulled the axe free of the smoking corpse.

Once inside the bridge room, Heimdall unceremoniously dumped Leif on the floor before quickly barring the door with a heavy metal latch. With what little strength he had, he tried and failed to push himself up. His body felt heavy, and he worried he was close to passing out.

The sound of heavy footfalls sent a chill down his spine. Leif knew the enemy had found them. "Shit," Heimdall cursed, running to the bridge. "I will drop you off at the Monarch in Alfheim before I head to Valhalla," she said as a loud boom reverberated through the room. Someone slammed their fist into the door. Leif's eyes flicked to Heimdall. He lacked the energy to move his head.

Leif watched as Heimdall concentrated for a moment before she spoke. He felt the magic of each syllable as it rushed into the bridge. There was an odd popping sensation in the back of his mind as a wall of magical force rushed out. The magic kept pushing out, out, out, into the distance before finally anchoring itself light years away on Alfheim.

The moment the bridge connected, Heimdall hoisted Leif into the air and unceremoniously threw him across the bridge. Moments later, he smashed down on the wooden floor of the Monarch. "Happy hunting," Heimdall called out from Asgard.

A crash and the sound of splintering wood came from the other side of the bridge. Without another word, Heimdall cut the connection, leaving Leif alone on Alfheim. With the threat of discovery and capture temporarily over, Leif felt his mind finally relax, letting his exhaustion pull him down into the sweet release of unconsciousness.

*The hunt begins…*

# ACKNOWLEDGMENTS

Thank you to all my readers for continuing to follow Leif's tumultuous journey through the Nine Realms.

I wrote the first draft of *Ascension* during the pandemic in 2020, but I endured a series of devastating events that delayed manuscript's release several times (catching COVID-19 twice, losing over 75 pages of my draft when my program unexpectedly crashed, and the passing of our beloved family dog, Pepper). But I am happy that through those trying times, Leif's story thrived, and it developed into the book you now hold.

There are so many people I would like to thank who have supported me as I wrote *Ascension*. Amy, my rock. Thank you for always being by my side, encouraging and believing in me. Stacey, my steadfast editor, who has been with me since *Awakening*. Brant and Kelsey, thank you for spending the time reading my rough draft and for your valuable feedback. You guys are awesome.

# ABOUT THE AUTHOR

Kevin D. Miller is an attorney in Southern California who spends two hours a day commuting to work while either listening to sci-fi/fantasy books or plotting out the storylines for the books he plans to write. When he isn't working, Kevin can be found spending time with his girlfriend, Amy and their dog, Riley. He enjoys writing, playing video games, hiking and kayaking in Big Bear, and enjoying the ocean air in Newport Beach.

twitter.com/bifrost_books
instagram.com/bifrost_books

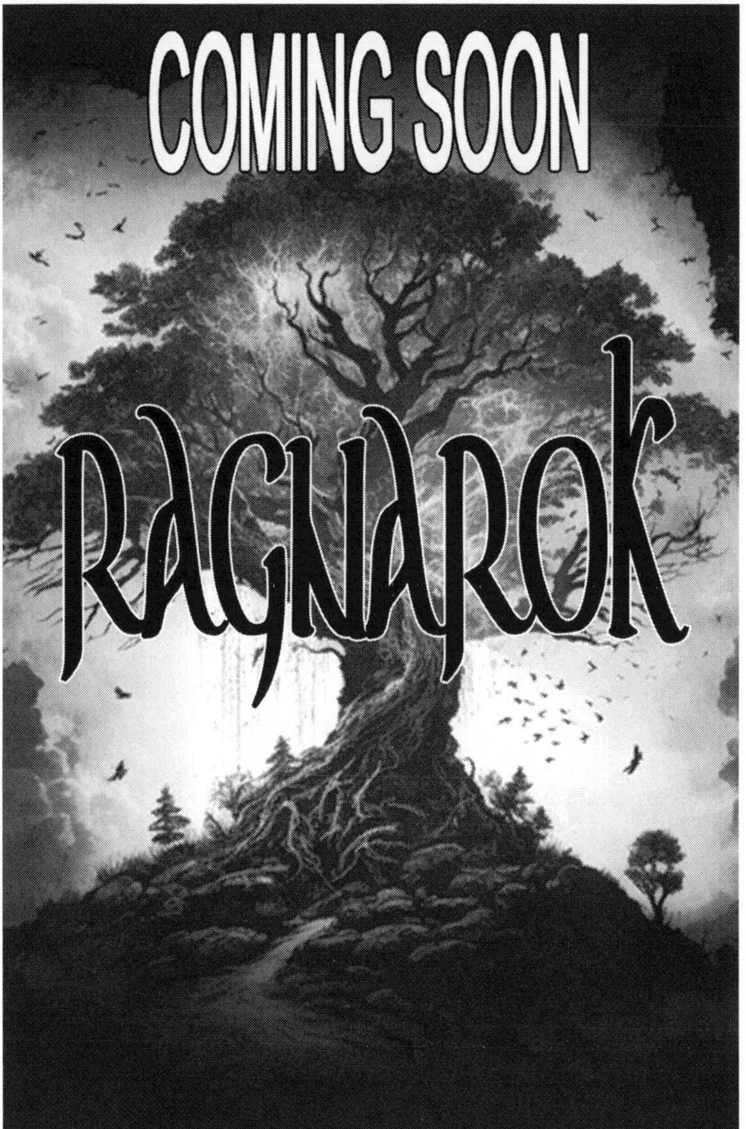
COMING SOON
RAGNAROK

Made in the USA
Las Vegas, NV
16 March 2023

69179692R00180